All that Burns

All that Burns

RYAN GRAUDIN

An imprint of HarperCollinsPublishers

HarperTeen is an imprint of HarperCollins Publishers.

All That Burns
Copyright © 2015 by Ryan Graudin
All rights reserved. Printed in the United States of America.
No part of this book may be used or reproduced in any manner whatsoever
without written permission except in the case of brief quotations embodied in
critical articles and reviews. For information address HarperCollins Children's
Books, a division of HarperCollins Publishers, 195 Broadway, New York, NY
10007.
www.epicreads.com

Library of Congress Cataloging-in-Publication Data
Graudin, Ryan.
  All that burns / Ryan Graudin. — First edition.
    pages cm
  Summary: "As Emrys and Britain's King Richard unite mortal and Faery in
their new kingdom, a dangerous force gains strength, threatening their love
and the world they've built"— Provided by publisher.
  ISBN 978-0-06-218743-7 (pbk.)
  [1. Magic—Fiction. 2. Fairies—Fiction. 3. Bodyguards—Fiction. 4. Kings,
queens, rulers, etc.—Fiction. 5. London (England)—Fiction. 6. England—
Fiction.] I. Title.
PZ7.G7724Alf 2015   2014013836
[Fic]—dc23   CIP
                                                                        AC

Typography by Alison Klapthor
15 16 17 18 19 LP/RRDH   10 9 8 7 6 5 4 3 2 1

First Edition

For Steve, who burned bright even at his weakest.

We are not now that strength which in old days
Moved earth and heaven; that which we are, we are;
One equal temper of heroic hearts,
Made weak by time and fate, but strong in will
To strive, to seek, to find, and not to yield.
    —Alfred, Lord Tennyson, "Ulysses"

All that Burns

Prologue

Once upon a time, there was a king who fell in love with a Faery. He gave her his heart and she gave him her immortality. Together they built a kingdom—of stone and magic and legend—and they lived happily there.

But their happiness did not last forever. Nothing does, after all.

In the shadows I watched and waited.

The Faery's heart slipped away to another.

The king's kingdom burned.

One

"Excellent." The Princess of Wales stands in front of me, tapping a manicured nail to her lips. "Are you nervous?"

"Should I be?" I glance down at the dress Helene has spent the past two hours crafting with adjustment spells under Princess Anabelle's minute instructions. Nude gauze fabric melds perfectly to the tone of my skin, flowing like water down to the floor. The entire length of the dress is embroidered with flowers: twists and blooms of rainbow colors.

Helene, the Fae on Guard duty, is looking at the dress too. She can't help but smile at her handiwork.

"This is your first gala!" Anabelle's eyes roll as she states the obvious. "Your social debut! Your time to shine. Impress the press."

Technically it's not my first gala. It's not even my tenth. The party I'm attending with King Richard tonight is just one out of hundreds I've gone to during my centuries as a Frithemaeg: a Faery Guard sworn to protect members of the royal family.

But the princess is right. This is my debut. The first party I'll go to on Richard's arm. A party where every eye in the room will be focused on me. Where people will look in my direction and finally see. I've been invisible for so long, being hidden and not noticed, that having heads turn my way—even when I'm simply browsing the supermarket—makes my heart pulse like a war drum.

But I've suffered more than a few awkward stares. Much more. Helene knows this. She was there when King Edward was assassinated and Richard was forced to accede his throne at only eighteen. She stood next to me and the other Faery Guard at the walls of Windsor when an army of soul feeders battered us, when we spent all of our magic keeping them at bay.

The princess knows this too. She was there the night Mab—the Faery queen—betrayed us and tried to harvest the royals' dormant blood magic from their veins, powers they inherited from King Arthur himself. The night Richard was gutted with Mab's sword and I thought my heart had died. Anabelle knows what it cost, everything I gave up for the sake of being with her brother.

"The only thing I'm afraid of is twisting my ankle off

in these contraptions." I point at the solid green stilettos on my feet.

"They're called heels," Anabelle laughs. "And they're fashionable."

"More like torture devices." I test my wobbling balance on the four-inch spikes. "How do you walk in these things?"

"It just takes a bit of practice. Here—" Richard's sister takes a few steps back, steadier than a mountain goat in her own towering shoes. "Try walking to me!"

I stick my hands out for balance and walk toward the Music Room's five arched windows. One step. Two. The hem of my dress catches and I stumble forward. Some of my old Fae grace resurges, saving me from falling altogether.

Helene giggles behind me. "You look like a baby duck."

I take a deep breath and resist the urge to snap at the youngling. It's not her fault I gave up my immortality to spend a human life with Britain's king. It's not her fault some of my natural grace leaked out along with the magic Herne the Hunter took from me. The magic I chose to give him in order to become mortal and join my Richard.

I glare at the emerald shoes instead. "I'm not wearing them."

The princess raises a finely tweezed eyebrow. "They make your calves look stunning."

"You can't even *see* my calves," I shoot back. "If this dress was any longer you couldn't even see the shoes."

The princess stares at me. Unfazed. "It's part of the royal package. You're going to have to get used to it, I'm afraid."

I shift my weight from foot to aching foot. Every arch, bone, and muscle feels pinched and stretched. As if it's been run through a medieval torture rack. "I feel like a Green Woman. And they only wore these because they were trying to seduce men and eat them!"

"And you're trying to seduce the press. It's important for you to get off on the right foot. You can eat them later if you want. Try again," Anabelle snaps like a ballet instructor. "And no cheating with magic. Helene, make sure she doesn't cheat."

"As if I'd waste precious magic on this." I feel down deep into my core, where the remains of my old magic slick my insides like oil. Dregs left by Herne the Hunter. A reminder of what I once was.

I take a full, deep breath. The windows at the end of Buckingham Palace's Music Room gape open and I taste autumn on the air: the hint of crumbling leaves and crisp skies. It sparkles inside my lungs, gives me new focus.

One step. Two . . . ten. I make it all the way to where Anabelle stands by the grand piano without so much as a wobble.

Richard's sister claps her hands together. "Brilliant!"

I don't feel brilliant as I collapse on the piano bench. My shoes drop against the marble as I massage my abused feet. It's a small sacrifice, I remind myself. Just one more step in my new life as a mortal.

"You'll be a natural in no time," the princess assures me. "Now your hair. I think you should keep it down. Show off that beautiful red . . ."

"What's all this?" Someone calls from behind us. His voice is velvet and caramel. Every syllable fills me with warmth.

He's standing by the door, smiling at my discarded heels. The grandness of the Music Room rises around him: scarlet drapes, burgundy-gold couches, and powerful onyx pillars. But it's difficult to pay much attention to my surroundings when Richard is before me. His shining, damp-sand hair is ruffled—swept just so out of his sharp eyes and higher-than-art cheekbones. His designer suit jacket is draped over his arm, and the sleeves of his dress shirt are rolled up. Showing off forearms still dark from summer sun.

King Richard. My Richard.

"Emrys and I were just having a bit of girl time." His sister waves at him. "Getting ready for her gala debut tonight."

"What she really means is I'm breaking my toes to be with you." My words echo off of the dome ceiling, make him smile.

"That's rather drastic."

"According to your sister it's all the rage these days."

I gather up my dress and go to him barefoot. His smile grows, becomes a warm, simmering secret between us. It never gets old, the way his lips curve. How happiness lights his eyes—a shine of blue, gold, and green. Bright hazel.

"Hey, Embers." Richard leans in for a short kiss—static and sparks on my lips—and wraps his arms around me. I'm at once wound tight and let loose: at home in his arms.

"You're back early." I bask in the smell of his once-starched shirt and spiced cologne. Remnants of the uniform he wears whenever he addresses Parliament.

He's been wearing it a lot lately, standing before the Houses of Commons and Lords, convincing them of the benefits of integration. Weaving the lifestyles of Fae and mortal together by reducing technology and increasing everyday magic.

Some of these solutions are simple: Faery lights replacing fluorescent bulbs. Freshly planted trees for Dryads to dwell inside. Prototype batteries rewired to run off magic-fusion instead of chemicals.

Others are not so simple: Weaning the mortals from the technology which is so caustic to Fae-kind. Which guts us from the inside with sickness and insanity. Which threatens to end our never-ending lives.

The goal—a Britain powered solely by self-sustaining magic—is a noble one. The reality is harder: the well of power has gone dry. After decades of the mortals' cables and frequencies and electrical singe, there's hardly any magic left to draw from. Not nearly enough to power an entire kingdom.

We have to go backward to go forward. Cut back the use of technology so the land's magic will grow. A painful, slow, uphill transition.

"We did get through the beginning of the Reforestation Bill quickly," Richard says. "Everyone seems to really love trees."

"They were probably all just itching to leave and get ready for the gala," Anabelle says, half-tease.

"I know this might be hard for you to believe"— Richard's voice is low and serious; only his smile betrays him—"but not everyone takes four hours to get ready for a social event."

The princess ignores her brother with the pointed nonpointedness only a sibling can manage. "I've heard Lord and Lady Winfred are throwing it on a yacht this year. A cruise down the Thames." Anabelle's loam-dark eyes shoot straight at me. "You better wear those heels, Emrys. Helene will tell me if you don't."

The youngling leans by an open window, face to the sun, enjoying the taste of autumn in the air. I look down at my raw, pink feet. It's a good thing Helene won't actually be aboard the yacht. She'll be watching from a distance— close enough to tap into the energies the royals' dormant blood magic offers the Fae, and far enough away to be discreet. The way our Faery Guards always do whenever we leave Buckingham Palace's perimeter. There's no way she'll notice if I slip my shoes off under the table.

"You're not going?" The king frowns at his sister.

"I've got an exam to study for."

"Belle, it's Friday!" Richard protests. "You should be out having fun."

"I'll have plenty of fun. Studying," Anabelle says. "Besides, the second Lights-down is this weekend, no?"

Lights-down—the first stage in the mortals' electricity diet—was among Richard's initial bill proposals to Parliament, after the Fae started appearing. It was a simple concept: a few hours without nonessential power every week to slow the sickness the machines caused the Fae—to preserve their strength and allow the land's magic to wake up again.

"You don't need electricity to study," the king says.

"Not that you would know!" his sister quips back. "Besides, it's not just studying. Mum's coming back from her holiday in Greece to give me a hand with coronation plans. Stop fretting over me. Relax. Spend some time with your girlfriend!" She tosses her golden hair back and looks straight at me. "Remember. Hair down. Wear your shoes. And smile! Lots of smiles. You'll be grand tonight."

The princess leaves with steps so graceful that her stilettos make only the slightest noise against the parquet floor.

"I've told her about a million times she needs to leave the coronation planning to the Coronation Commission." Richard sighs. "It would save her so much worry."

"I think she would be worried *more* if someone else was doing it," I point out.

"She does too much," Richard mutters. "Pushes too hard."

"Look who's talking." I stare at the bags beneath his eyes. "It must run in the family."

"Well, I have some time for fun now." Richard squeezes my shoulder. "What should we do with these stolen hours?"

We live in the same palace, but it's not often we get time together—minutes unclaimed by politics and magic. As a liason between Queen Titania's Frithemaeg and the human government, I've barely had enough time for Richard. Half of my weeks I'm not even in London, but traveling up to the Faery queen's Highlands court. When I'm here, Richard's list of meetings and press conferences is enough to keep us apart for days at a time.

Rome wasn't built in a day. London wasn't either. I know that well enough, having watched it rise through the centuries: from mosquito-riddled marshlands into a maze of monuments and high-rises. Our goal of a new

Britain—a country where Fae and mortals exist in harmony just as they did in Camelot—will take just as much sweat and blood.

At least, that's what I remind myself when we're apart. When it's just the jade and silver ring on my finger reminding me why I made this sacrifice. Why I chose this mortal life.

"Something. Anything. As long as we're together." I lean into him, savoring the closeness.

"Belle did a great job. You look amazing." The heat of his body molds smooth into mine—the way a flame dances around a candle's wick.

I smile up at him. It's impossible not to, so close to his dusting of freckles and the laughter lines which crinkle his eyes whenever he sees me. "She's good at what she does. Helene helped too."

I glance over at the window, but the Fae has disappeared. Off to rejoin the perimeter of younglings who constantly guard the palace from Green Women, Banshees, Black Dogs, and all of the other dark spirits who prey on mortals. Soul feeders.

We're alone now.

"It's good to be with you." Richard draws me even closer, buries his face in my neck. I hear him sigh and take in the scent of me all at once. "It's been a long few days."

"A long few weeks," I counter. "Where do you want to go?"

"Let's just sit." He drops his jacket on the floor, moves to the open window where a balcony looks out onto Buckingham's lawns. Richard pushes himself onto its ledge, rests against a Corinthian column. "I haven't just sat and done nothing in ages."

I edge up beside him, and we rest together, looking out over the palace gardens. It's October now. The leaves around us burst into a kaleidoscope of color: ambers, yellows, blushing reds.

"That's better." Richard nests his arm around the curve of my neck. His touch is as thrilling and bright as the leaves. I wish I could keep it, keep him with me always. That these meetings weren't so rare.

"So the Reforestation Bill went over well?" I don't want to remind him of work, but the issue is important. More trees—more forests—mean more magic. Fresh leaves and a fresh start.

"We only got through a small portion of the proposal. But I think there was a general agreement that Windsor is the first district where we should replant the trees."

"That's good. Herne the Hunter will be pleased."

"I hope so. Though right now I don't know what's more terrifying: Herne or six hundred and fifty members of the House of Commons arguing in my ear."

I think of Herne—the jealous spirit who guards the woods around Windsor Castle—towering over his army of Dryads and snow-white hounds. How his eyes smolder bright as coals and his horns twist endlessly into the night. How I never know whether the next word out of his mouth will aid or destroy. "Those must be some pretty intimidating politicians."

"Everyone's a little jumpy about Lights-down. It's made things . . ." He hesitates. "Tense."

"But the first one went so well!" I remind him.

"That was just a few hours. This next one will be a whole twenty-four hours. Not as many people will approve."

"No one likes change at first. But we're making progress. Soon Lights-down will be part of the routine. And once we start introducing magically infused technology, people will forget all about a few days without power."

"I guess . . ."

"We've only been at this for two months and look how

far we've come! Lights-down is already starting. Titania's court is coming up with prototypes and new methods to replace the machines. Our worlds are merging."

"That part started a while ago." Richard shifts. His face is only inches from mine; the warmth of his breath cuts the air between us. The nearness of him washes away all thoughts of high heels and politics.

It's just the king and I. Wrapped in cool autumn leaves.

A soft wind tears across the gardens, into our window, kicking up color and threading every orange strand of my hair together. Richard brushes the tangle from my face, fingertips unbearably light over my cheeks. It reminds me—in a faint, aching way—of magic. The way a spell burned just under my skin. Swelling. Waiting to explode. This is what his touch does to me. Every time.

Our lips meet. I savor his perfect warmth and taste. Cinnamon and cider and apple turnovers. A silent, snowy evening spent by the hearth. Richard is better than all of these.

His fingers knit deeper into my hair, tug me close. My hands roam up his shoulder, his neck. Feel the sculpt of those muscles. The baby-fine silk of his hair.

Before—when I was brimming with magic—I would've been afraid. Terrified of splitting him apart with my spells. But all of that's gone now.

And it's just us.

Together.

The way things should be.

Two

The night is young when I step out of the Rolls-Royce. My heels feel especially perilous on the soft garnet carpet which stretches to the dock. Fortunately, no one is looking at my feet. All eyes are on the dress Helene and Anabelle so painstakingly crafted.

Camera flashes burst like supernovas. Questions storm over, tangled and hurried. Reporters shout them with jousts of their microphones, practically clawing over one another to stretch past the barrier.

A microphone jabs out from my right. "Who was your designer?"

"How are you adjusting to life without magic?" someone shouts.

And another question, biting and unexpected. "What do you think about the people who're saying you put King Richard under a love spell?"

I'm still dazed by the jags of light and shrill questions when Richard appears at my side. This afternoon's disheveled blazer has been replaced with a sharp tuxedo. He's also wearing his paparazzi face: the smile that's just a little too stretched. I try to copy it, give the cameras a show. But this isn't such an easy thing to do when you're navigating a carpet in four-inch heels.

"Need help?" Richard looks over when I start to sway. The press smile quirks into a fleeting real one.

I accept his hooked arm, since the carpet soon gives way to a ramp. It stretches out like the back of a sleeping dragon, connected metallic plates heaving at the will of the Thames.

My balance woes fall away as soon as I step onto the yacht. The boat is built of glamour and money. If I didn't know any better, I'd think it was a house in Chelsea, brimming with furniture and art. There are even chandeliers hanging from the ceilings: fat jewels ready to be plucked.

The string of rooms is already full of tuxedos and designer silks. They laugh, chat, and shake hands. Dresses sparkle and slink. Most of the women look like dolls— painted lips and perfectly coiffed hair, ears and necks dripping with diamonds.

Richard and I step into the room and the chatter dims. The hush, I know, is not for the king. Many of these guests are members of Parliament. No strangers to royalty. But it's not every day people set eyes on a former immortal.

Their eyes are so many colors. Faery-pool blue, long-meadow green, dark like barrows. All of them are on me, searching for a glimpse of magic. Something *other*. Whatever it is, they'll be disappointed. My choice was made. I'm one of them now.

"Your Majesty. Lady Emrys. Welcome!"

"Prime Minister. Thank you for having us," Richard says, and gives Lord Winfred a hearty handshake. The warriors-clasping-wrists-before-they-plunge-into-battle kind.

I think back to the many etiquette lessons Richard's sister drilled into me: *smile wide and graciously, compliment your hosts, wait at least five minutes before you start tucking into the hors d'oeuvres.*

A platter of smoked salmon and chives drifts by. I ignore it and smile at the prime minister. "This is all very lovely."

"Do you like the Faery lights?" Lord Winfred nods at the chandeliers, where dozens of *inlíhte* spells nest in the crystals: silver, aqua, mint, and glow. "Lady Winfred had them installed here and at Downing Street. She thinks they add to the ambience."

The room looks otherworldly cast in the light of the Fae. It looks like *my* other world. My life before. I have to blink before I remember that these gorgeous women in flowing, long dresses are Parliament members' wives. Not courtiers of the Faery queen.

"I, for one, am just astounded at the fact that they'll never die," the prime minister says. "At least, that's what I was told by the Fae who created them. They'll last forever if we want."

I look back at the *inlíhte* spells, pick apart their threads of magic. They've been tied off—looped into themselves to create an endless cycle of energy. The lights will stay lights until someone decides to come unknot them. "It's true. The spell feeds off of itself."

"Remarkable. Self-sustaining energy. Sometimes I still can't believe it's in our reach." Lord Winfred goes on, "I was hoping to find a way to substitute the yacht's engine power as a demonstration this evening, but unfortunately that will take more than a few magic-fusion batteries."

"Emrys tells me Queen Titania's court has been experimenting with larger models," Richard says. "Hopefully we'll have something of note within the month—"

"More like three months," I correct him. Looping

a spell is simple when it comes to small things—Faery lights, hair color, blocking spells to keep mortals from poking around places they shouldn't. The larger the spell, the more complicated the knot. And when there's electricity involved . . .

It's akin to wrestling a giant squid and trying to tie its tentacles in a pretty Christmas bow. While you're covered in ink. Underwater.

The prime minister nods. "Queen Titania—might she be able to come to London soon? I'd love to thank her for all the advancements she's contributed."

"The city is too dangerous for her at the moment," I remind him.

"Ah yes, the sickness."

"Lights-down has been helping," I say. "None of the younglings have felt nauseated for at least a day. But Queen Titania is older. Fae her age are sensitive to metal and gears without electricity. The oldest ones couldn't even stand the Industrial Revolution . . ." I pause, realize I'm rambling. "But Titania is resilient. Perhaps after a few more blackouts she can endure the city for a few hours."

Any more and her sanity would be at stake. She would

end up just like her predecessor, Mab: swept away by the madness of the machines. A dangerous, all-powerful, unhinged spirit.

"I look forward to that day." Lord Winfred smiles like he means it and raises his glass. "To our united kingdoms! A new Camelot!"

"May it be a bit more successful than the last," Richard adds.

Britain's prime minister moves on to greet more guests. The first thing he points out to them is the Faery lights. Their chorus of *oohs* and *aahs* threads through the steady hum of a live string quartet.

My feet are all pain. Tendon and bone ache against the cutting curve of my stilettos. "I'm going to go find our table and sit for a minute. These heels are vicious."

"I don't doubt it." Richard eyes the shoes as if they're poisonous toadstools. "Go and save your toes. There are a few people I've been meaning to talk to. Will you be all right on your own for a bit?"

"I've managed a number of centuries without you. It's possible I'll be able to last a few more minutes." I wink and he smiles—in that amazing way of his.

"Point taken."

"But you should hurry just in case," I add. "I might vanish when midnight hits."

"I thought that was Cinderella, not the fairy god-mother."

I smile as I wobble away.

I find our table close to the open doors of the yacht's bow end, where London's lights sweep by on a current of movement and night. Lord Winfred's boat has been unmoored. It's sliding under the blue cables of the Tower Bridge just as I sit down. The entire structure is lit up like the gates to some ancient god's kingdom.

"Beautiful view, isn't it? I can't get enough of London at night."

The voice comes from across the table. Its speaker is a young man, hardly older than Richard. His skin is pale and smooth—a perfect blend of milk and chalk. His eyes shine almost teal through the dimness: sharp and bright. Clever. The stare of a politician.

"It does have a certain draw." I smile through the bright blossoms of the centerpiece. "Forgive me, I don't believe we've been introduced."

"Julian Forsythe. And this is my wife, Elaine." The man nods to the seat next to him, where a dark-haired woman sits. The whole of her is so slim and pale she looks

like she just stumbled out of a crypt. Her dress is skin-
tight, its fabric shimmering. All of this pulled together by
a pop of red lipstick.

"A pleasure. I'm Emrys."

Elaine's eyebrows rise, like arched raven's wings. The
eyes under them are just as dark, and dewy. They look at
her husband. "I didn't know we'd be sitting at *her* table."

I stare straight at the centerpiece: a whole towering cluster of birdsfoot trefoil. The color is so happy
and yellow it makes my eyes ache. A lump grows in my
throat. For one of the first times this evening, I feel like
I don't belong here. On this boat. At this table. By Richard's side.

I swallow the feeling back. I think of how Anabelle
would handle the situation: she would smile. Say nothing.
That's what I do. Elaine doesn't smile back. Instead she
stares and cocks her head, like I'm some sort of strange
beetle that's been doused in formaldehyde and pinned to
a collector's board.

"Strange choice of flower, don't you think?" Julian
calls across the table. He shows no sign that he heard his
wife. "Where I come from it's almost a weed. We called it
'Eggs and Bacon.'"

"Aren't those poisonous?" The chair next to me slides

25

back, and Richard finally takes a seat.

"They are, actually." Julian Forsythe reaches out, pinches a blossom between neat fingers. The sunny petals crumple—a sad, quick death. "Just don't let it end up in your salad. Seems like some rogue florist means to off half the government!"

"I wouldn't joke about that." Richard frowns and looks over his shoulder. "Jensen! Eric!"

Two officers from the king's Protection Command— his human security—pull out of the crowd. They look like everyone else at this gala: tuxedo-sharp and slick. Only their earpieces and the slight lump of their holsters give them away.

"It seems the flower arrangements are poisonous. Find a way to dispose of them and let the Winfreds know," the king orders them. "Discreetly, please. I'm sure it was an honest mistake."

"You're quite trusting," Julian says, "for a man in your position."

Richard's shoulders grow rigid under his tux. He snaps open the cloth napkin and places it in his lap. "If you call it trusting to believe that people make mistakes. Then yes."

"I find that mistakes are never quite as common as

they seem." The politician drops the bruised blossom onto the tablecloth.

"We're all human."

"Are we?" A smile curls its way across Julian Forsythe's face. His eyes land on me.

I stare back, struggle to keep smiling.

"You're right though," Julian goes on. "The arrangements were probably a mistake. Death by flower is hardly effective. If anything I'd say they were a warning."

Richard still hasn't let go of his napkin. His face is handsome, steady, straight, as he wrings the white fabric under his fingers. I slip my hand under the table, rest it on his.

"I see you've met the Forsythes. Julian is the leader of the M.A.F.," Richard says finally.

"M.A.F.?" I ask.

"The Mortal Alliance Front. It's a new party formed to protect the interests of mortals against monst—" Julian stops short. His eyes still haven't left me. "—other creatures."

Richard's hand twitches under mine but he looks straight at Julian. "I wasn't sure you'd be here. They said you were on your honeymoon."

"It was brief. I'm afraid I can't take too much personal

time, with the state of things."

"Your honeymoon?" I leap at the change of subject, go for its throat. "Where did you go?"

"If Elaine had had her way we would've spent the week in dreary Wales. Reading manuscripts, exploring castles, being cold." Julian looks over at his new wife, his expression softened. "She's getting her doctorate in medieval studies. Those things fascinate her. I practically had to drag her to the Mediterranean kicking and screaming."

"Medieval studies?" Richard's fingers have relaxed, but only barely. "You have a wealth of information sitting right here. Emrys lived through those times."

His words make my toes squirm. As if they needed a reminder of how *other* I am.

Elaine opens her mouth, as if she's about to speak. The boat gives a sharp, unforgiving shake. All across the yacht glasses tumble, dishes rattle, chandeliers sway like wind chimes.

"What the—" Julian Forsythe snaps around in his chair.

I look in the same direction—out over the waters. The Tower Bridge looms well behind us. The wider lights of London have ceased gliding. Instead they hover: jewels of electric, washed-out colors. Oranges, blues, and yellows dancing over dark currents. The yacht sits, stranded in them.

There's a second, startling shudder. A server's scream cuts the night; her tray of cucumber sandwiches scatters all over the bow deck.

"Th-there's something! In the water!"

My chair tumbles behind me, my heels left behind. There's a tug and a rip on my gown, but I keep running—barefoot—all the way to the open deck.

The Thames's dark waters are almost invisible against the night's reflections. But there's one spot where London's lights don't show. A break in the water. A huge mass of *something else*.

It could be anything down there, draped in the river's black currents. A U-boat, a giant sea-beast Kraken, some disgruntled water Sprites. But then a sound rises. Soft and hushed, like a sneeze and a purr and a downpour of gravel all at once. A noise I know well.

The Kelpie is a huge one. In the water it resembles more of a whale than a horse. I can just make out its glistening, seal-like fur and pinned lynx ears as it swims the length of the yacht. Its wake bulges and fans through the Thames.

White fear washes over my face, my knuckles. For years of my former life it was all I did: shepherding Queen

Mab's Kelpies through the Highlands. But I always, *always* made sure to keep them far from the water.

On land they're rideable; some Frithemaeg might even consider them tamed. But once they're in their element—waterborne—Kelpies are deadly. More than a few men have been lured to the great, green deep. Consumed whole at the bottoms of lakes and riverbeds.

Sprites and other water spirits abandoned this river years ago when the sludge of the city made its waters unbearable. There shouldn't even *be* Kelpies in the Thames.

But this giant Kelpie is here. And it wants something. It makes a swift circle; its massive form strikes the yacht. Lord Winfred's boat tilts so far that I have to clutch the rail to keep my balance. A sound like splintered thunder laces the air: fiberglass.

I can't tell if the hull's been breached. That side of the boat is all foam and dark water as the Kelpie wheels around. But I know one thing—the yacht won't be able to withstand another charge. The next hit will sink us. Drag us all into the Kelpie's wild, lusty waters.

I look back over my shoulder. The yacht's world is shattered glass and frantic, glamorous people clutching their chairs. I'm the only soul on the deck until Richard comes rushing to my side.

"What is it?"

"Kelpie," I tell him in a clipped, managed tone. "Whatever you do, don't go near the water. Try to make everyone stay on the boat."

I start gathering the gauze of my skirts, making room for my legs to move up and over the rail. Richard's hand lands on my shoulder. "Emrys, what are you doing?"

"I can get it under control. Lead it away from the boat. Give the captain time to get to shore." I think. I've wrestled Kelpies before, but it was always on land. And I had spells to protect me from the Kelpie's magic.

"Stay on the boat." It's more of a plea than a command, the way Richard says it. "Let the Frithemaeg handle it."

Helene—she should be here. But she's nowhere to be seen. The dark, gliding hump of the Kelpie's hindquarters pulls out and switches back. Charging with even more speed than before.

"The Faery guard isn't here. We can't wait around for them to show up."

"But you're . . ." He bites his lip. "You're mortal now, Emrys. You could die."

"If I don't do something, we'll all die!" I shout back at him. It's getting harder to hear, harder to speak with the roar of the Thames, the screams and sliding tables of Lord Winfred's limping yacht. "This boat is going to sink and that Kelpie will drown each and every one of us. I'm not helpless, Richard. I still have some magic left. I can do this."

There are more people on deck now. Gripping the railing with petrified knuckles. The Forsythes have joined the exodus—faces blanched with righteous terror.

"Emrys." The king's fingers tighten on my shoulder. I hear the fear in him. "Please. This isn't your job anymore. I don't need your magic, I need you. Stay on the boat. Stay with me."

His words cut, but I don't have time to feel them. I don't have time to remember how breakable I am. The Kelpie barrels down; the Thames's water froths white under its speed.

Richard's grip on my shoulder isn't enough to stop me as I climb over the rail and jump. My world becomes nude gauze and the shock of October water on my skin. The gown which was so airy only moments before is now an unbearable weight. The waters pull and lick, hungry for me.

I feel the slick of the Kelpie's fur against my arm. Realize the raw power of the muscle beneath it. Longer hair from its mane or tail threads through my fingers, as slimy and tangled as seaweed. I grab hold.

The beast keeps churning and charging. My arms yank forward, snap tighter than whips. Water rushes into my face. I feel the force of the river clawing at me as if it wants to rip me apart.

My lungs burst with desperate fire. I need air, but I can't let go. Not if I want to draw the Kelpie away from the yacht. I dig deep, scrounge through what little magic Herne left me. Not enough for a binding spell, or a banishment. It isn't even enough to hurt the creature.

I think of Lord Winfred's Faery light chandeliers. The last gasp of air in my lungs is spent in a garbled, underwater yell: *"Inlíhte!"*

It's only enough for an instant: a blinding, blue light. Everything is illuminated, silhouetted like shadow puppets on a watery wall. The deep, underwater pillars of the Tower Bridge. The hulking base of the yacht. The enormous length of Kelpie flesh under me. Even when the light is gone these shapes stay in my vision: neon-lit ghosts.

The Faery light does its job. I feel the Kelpie hesitate. The Thames presses down on my shoulders and lungs. Its water becomes searing. Electric. The Kelpie's spell sings and weaves through the currents, seeking me out.

I'm trying to fight it, trying to break away from the

predator. But my gown is so heavy and the Kelpie's magic is everywhere. In my ears and nose and pores, begging me to unravel. To give it all up to the water's deep.

I don't have the magic to fight back. Some dim, clawing thought bubbles from the back of my mind. *Richard was right. I shouldn't have jumped.*

I'm going to die. Not at the hands of a powerful Old One, or lying next to Richard in a hospital, withered with age. I'm going to drown on the back of a disoriented Kelpie. Trapped in the gauze of my own dress.

I'm not what I was before. I'm not strong enough.

And then, hands and arms wrap around my waist, draw me up into clean air. My lungs claw for it, consume it. I'm being dragged out of the river, away from the boat by the time I can even speak.

"The Kelpie! The yacht!" My words wheeze and splutter. They sound pathetic even to me.

"Stay here! I have to go help Lydia!" The hands let go, rest my body on the shore. I turn just in time to see Ferrin, one of the youngling Fae guard, before she disappears into velveteen waters.

Ferrin. Lydia. What are they doing here? Last I heard they were in the Highlands, doing grunt work at Queen Titania's court.

My body feels weak and crumpled, like the wads of rubbish which string along the Thames. With every breath I feel life flowing back in—how close I was to losing it.

I look back at the rogue Kelpie. Lydia has managed to catch the beast, with some help from Ferrin and another soaked youngling. It must be Helene. After long, thrashing minutes, the trio drags the Kelpie from the muddy currents. Once the creature's hooves hit dry land it stands no chance against their spells.

All three Fae are breathing hard. Helene even has blood streaming down her left cheek.

"Will someone *PLEASE* explain this?" I look around the group. Guilt flashes across Lydia's and Ferrin's heart-shaped faces. Both of them have their fingers wreathed deep into the water-spirit's mane, subduing it with wordless spells.

In the end it's Lydia who speaks first. "It was my fault, Lady Emrys. It's a good thing you shone that light. I don't know if we would've found it otherwise. It shot off as soon as it caught wind of the river."

I stare at the youngling and clench my teeth. She's not the one I'm angry at. Not really. It's the burn in my lungs and the tremble in my limbs. My mortality. My weakness.

But this doesn't stop me from yelling.

"Your fault? It shot off?" My throat catches, chokes on some leftover river. "What do you mean? Did you *bring* the Kelpie here? Into the middle of *LONDON*? BY A RIVER IN A CITY FULL OF MORTALS? You almost got every single soul on that yacht killed!"

"I was acting on Queen Titania's orders," Lydia says.

"Ti-Titania ordered this?" I glance back across the river and see the yacht. I look for Richard, but from this distance all tuxedos look the same. "Why?"

"We were sent to fetch you. Queen Titania ordered us to bring a Kelpie so you could ride back swiftly."

"Ride back?" Normally when I visit Titania's Faery court in the Highlands, I take a train to Inverness and then hike into the wilderness, where I'm met with a Kelpie mount. If the new Faery queen is summoning me with such little warning—and creating even greater risk by sending a ferocious spirit into London—something must be very wrong. "What happened?"

Lydia and Ferrin exchange glances. As if they're uncertain how much they should reveal.

I stare at them, press my thumb hard into my ring. Its swirls of silver filigree dig deep into my finger. A small pain. I try to focus on it instead of what I'm not. It keeps the anger down. Manageable.

Ferrin breaks first under my glare. "One of the Ad-hene sought an audience with Queen Titania today. At her court."

An Ad-hene at the court? I bristle at the thought. The Ad-hene are the Manx spirits—long-hardened natives of the Isle of Man. In the mortals' lore they're spirits too terrible for heaven and too virtuous for hell. In reality they are fierce, brooding creatures who never leave their island. The perfect guards for a Faery queen's prison.

"Why?"

Lydia answers this time. "The Ad-hene . . . he came to tell us there's been a breakout. A prisoner has escaped."

"Escaped." I echo her word. Try to wrap my mind around it. "That's not possible."

A cold fills me. A cold which has nothing to do with my damp skin or the night frost. It's a freeze sprung from memories. Memories of when Queen Mab ordered me to escort prisoners to the Ad-hene's prison: a labyrinth of tunnels snaking from the sea cliffs—wide and deep and never-ending under the Isle of Man.

Anyone the Faery queen deemed dangerous or unlikeable was doomed to at least a time in the endless weave of corridors. Assassins, thieves, would-be usurpers. Spirits more powerful than the entire youngling Guard put together. Cursed to centuries of iron bars and darkness.

Thousands of immortal souls. Hundreds of years. And not one of them has ever escaped.

Until now.

"Queen Titania ordered us to escort you to the Isle of Man," Ferrin finishes. Her fingers tighten into the water-spirit's mane.

The beast glares at us, eyes slit and bloodshot. It whickers, bares its long, yellowing teeth.

My voice is still weak, sapped dry by anger. "Helene, will you tell King Richard I've been called away? I'll be back as soon as I can."

"Of course." Helene nods.

I grip the Kelpie's mane and heave myself onto its back. Beneath me is all muscle, power, and magic. Ferrin climbs onto the creature's back as well, the presence of her own magic a steadying ballast in front of me.

The Kelpie isn't even moving, but already I feel its speed, ready to carry us the entire length of Albion. Faster than any car or train ever could. I look back toward the yacht and wish I could see Richard, tell him good-bye. Tell him I love him.

But the Kelpie is already galloping, leaping across cabs

and buildings and buses—a starless patch of motion and dark on the wind—so fast that for just a moment I can close my eyes and pretend I'm flying. The way I once did. In and on the air, leaving London far behind.

Three

We travel all night. First by Kelpie: through cities, fields, and sleepy townscapes ruled by Gothic belltowers. Then by sailboat, its tarp sails billowing full with Ferrin and Lydia's magic. Their spells cut us swiftly over waves of salt. Double our time.

The sunrise's glow spreads over the sea by the time we reach the island. Castle ruins crown the coast like slumbering giants. The cliffs beneath them stretch into the sea, misted by bridal-veil waves.

Our boat shudders against the rocks. Remnants of night shadow flicker in my eyes—shaping into the form of a person. I crane my neck, stare up into the jutting crags. The Ad-hene crouched against the stones looks more gargoyle than man. His eyes are a strange combination of fierce and dead—fire and slate—as he watches our boat. Even his hair seems woven from shadows, twisting black around his face. A vicious wind licks the coast, but these curls hang still.

"We're here on Queen Titania's orders!" Ferrin calls up to the motionless spirit.

The Ad-hene keeps staring. I begin to wonder if he isn't a statue after all when his eyes shift to my end of the boat.

"What is this?" His words rain down like kicked gravel. "Mortal?"

I want to shut my eyes, block out his words. But my irises stay locked with the Ad-hene's. Green meeting gray.

My thumb digs tight against my ring.

"This is Lady Emrys. The one Queen Titania sent for," the youngling tells him.

The Ad-hene doesn't look at her, doesn't break our stare. He hasn't moved, but something in his eyes has shifted, changed. They glimmer, become more sterling than rock. He's looking more closely—a study which makes every muscle in my body tighten.

"Lady Emrys." My name rolls off his lips like an ocean wave. "The *faagailagh*."

Richard's ring burrows deep into my skin. I keep staring at the Ad-hene, but the spirit is unreadable. Hard as stone.

He stands slowly, looking less like a gargoyle and more like the warrior saints which stand guard in a cathedral's stones.

"*Foshil!*" he commands the rock face in the language of the Ad-hene. I feel the power of his spell from here—all crackle and shiver through the earth. Strong. Hairline cracks appear in the cliff. Stone melts away to reveal the shape of a door. The sheer slope of shale next to our boat becomes crudely carved steps.

The younglings stay in the boat, watching as I gather my ruined evening gown and start to climb.

"Welcome to the Labyrinth of Man, Lady Emrys," the Ad-hene rumbles when I conquer the final step. "I'm Kieran of the Ad-hene. Follow me. Stay close or the island will swallow you."

We step out of the dawn, into the yawning tunnels. They stretch on and on, a maze more complicated than a Gaelic knot, twisting and pure black. Every few lengths the Ad-hene halts and glances at his map—a silver, glowing mark which laces the skin of his left arm. Etchings of the Labyrinth's ever-changing tunnels.

Even in the realm of spirits and magic Ad-hene are strange creatures. Sixteen sullen male spirits who act as one—all sprung into existence from the Isle of Man's dark, earthy magic. All bear silver scars on their arms, strange pieces of magic which allow them to navigate the prison's impossible length and depth. Ad-hene are the only way in or out of the Labyrinth of Man. Even the Faery queen needs a silver-armed guard to lead her into the deep.

I begin to think Kieran is leading me in endless circles, when we're finally spit out into a great cave.

There's light here. It shines high and silver, like moon rays off water. Stalactites dance in its waves. Queen Titania stands in the center of the room. Mercury hair flows down her back and her long lace gown drips to the floor. She's as magnificent as she's always been, but that doesn't erase the worry under her paper-fine skin.

All around her are Ad-hene. If the queen is the beauty of starlight and air, then the Manx spirits are the earth. Raw, brooding strength. Fifteen of them stand before Queen Titania in a filed queue. Chess pieces waiting to be moved.

"Your Majesty." I curtsy. At the same time Kieran bows low. Not even this movement stirs his night-spun curls.

"Thank you, Kieran," the Faery queen says to the bowing spirit before she catches sight of my ruined dress. "Forgive me for summoning you on such short terms, Lady Emrys, but I'm afraid it was necessary."

Her sharp chin turns back to the row of Ad-hene. "Alistair, show Lady Emrys what you showed me."

One of the spirits steps forward. His hair, white as shock, sheathes his brow, nearly covering his beetle-black eyes. His face—like Titania's—is both young and not.

He is the group's leader. I glean this and much more from his aura as he draws closer. Age . . . old, *old* age. This is what Alistair is. Older than sea cliffs and dust. Older than the cavern itself.

He doesn't smile. His words are flat, almost bored. "Shall we?"

We follow Alistair into yet another tunnel. All around our footsteps echo: hollow and empty. The walls change. They're no longer solid stretches of earth, but pocked with cells. The scar on Alistair's arm blazes white into their emptiness.

"Yesterday morning we came to check this wing. The Corridor of the Forgotten," Alistair speaks slowly, as if he's about to nod off to sleep. "We found the empty cell and sent a messenger to Queen Titania immediately."

The Ad-hene's steps fade, come to a stop. He lets out a great heave of weary breath and points. I follow his stare into the vacant cell. Its bars are warped—their iron dripping like spent wax candles. The shallow rock walls behind it are covered in scrawling runic symbols. A language so long out of use I've forgotten how to read it.

Whoever languished in this cell was just as old. And powerful. The aftertaste of their aura buzzes the air: bitter and burning, filled with rage. Unlike any magic I've felt before. Not the black pepper bite of the Ad-henes' surly spells. Or the tingling glow of a Frithemaeg's magic. It's a strange mix: rust and gleam. Old and new. It washes through me, like déjà vu, just out of reach. Leaves me dizzy and grasping.

I try to ignore the pit in my stomach and move close to the bars. The runes stare back: scrabbled, frantic, and white. "Who was kept here?"

"We were hoping you might know," Titania answers. "You're one of the few Mab trusted with prisoner transport."

"That was ages ago . . ." My memory, just like my gracefulness, is one of the things that's fallen victim to my newfound mortality. Ever since I latched hands with Herne, since that power was taken from me, the vastness of my past has been melting. "Most of my transports were minor infractions. Frithemaeg who committed treason. Soul feeders who went on killing sprees big enough for the mortals to notice. Never a prisoner locked away so long. Certainly none with magic like this . . ."

"It is unique," the Faery queen says.

"And the Ad-hene don't know who it was?" I ask this question carefully, dance around my growing panic.

"This is the Corridor of the Forgotten," Alistair sighs out his answer. "Queen Mab's most dangerous prisoners were sent to this wing: nameless, left to rot. She even placed her own warding spells on it, as an extra assurance none would escape. Those spells died with her. Queen Mab preferred to . . ." Alistair's voice coasts, searching for the right word. ". . . have a more direct control over this place."

"Mab was unmade months ago," I say. "That can't be the reason this prisoner escaped."

"I don't claim it was," Alistair says, "but things have been changing in the Labyrinth. Things even we Ad-hene do not completely understand. There are shiftings in the earth. Old powers waking."

Old powers. To hear a spirit as aged as Alistair say this is something indeed. I find myself wondering if there was even an island here when he first took form.

"Yes. I know the old powers are rising. I feel it in my very core. It's the same everywhere. Since last week. The first Lights-down," Titania says. The Faery queen's jaw is grim and jutting as she turns to the Ad-hene. "But you must understand my suspicion, Alistair. The Ad-hene

46

have been the only way out of these tunnels for millennia. I cannot overlook this fact."

"And we have served the Faery queen for just as long." For the first time Alistair looks awake: eyes sharp, lips pinched. The mark on his arm flares extra bright, writhing like a knot of silver snakes. "The Ad-hene are loyal, Your Majesty. Prisoners only leave the island if the Faery queen lets them."

I stare back into the cell's emptiness and try not to be sick. A creature Mab deemed dangerous enough to lock up for eternity, a creature powerful enough to solve the Labyrinth's maze, is now free.

It is free and it is angry.

"What about the other prisoners?" I'm grasping at straws. "Have you asked them?"

"There are no other prisoners in this wing." Alistair hesitates. "Except . . ."

"All secrets sound the same in the dark." The voice that says this is small, fragile. I follow it, find myself staring into another cell. There's no writing on these walls. Just empty, blank space.

And then something moves.

What I thought was a boulder jutting out of the floor is nothing but. Gray rags and hair break apart, revealing a face which looks more like a mask of bone than a human profile. Its eyes are sunken, filmed with eerie, sightless white. The hair on its head is stringy, impossibly scant but long. And the skin . . . it's ruined and spotted, like a plate of raw liver.

Those eyes—the ones I was so sure could not see—snap onto us. More words leave the withered lips, all rasp and shriek.

"Come to gape at the four winds meet? Fools, puppets, knights, kings. All of them sacrificed. No matter. They die with smiles on their faces."

The sentences and syllables make no sense. They're gibberish. But that doesn't stop every molecule in my body from burning. Every atom inside me is alert. Agitated.

"What—who is that?" I tear my eyes from the ruined creature, back to where Alistair and Queen Titania stand in their magnificence.

The voice doesn't stop. Words keep spilling out. "I will show you ruin. Kingdom's fall."

"She's a *faagailagh*." The answer comes from behind me, where Kieran is standing just inches away. "She too sacrificed her powers to be with a king."

The woman rises. The stick remnants of her body are

swallowed by her dress. Bare, gnarled feet shuffle her all the way to the bars.

"Two sides to the coin. Three sides to love. I flipped wrong and the world burned. Cinder and ash. No more. Even sisters fail us in the end."

It's not possible. I find myself shaking my head. Taking a step back from the bars—away from the milk-white eyes. My spine curves into Kieran's chest. The Ad-hene doesn't move.

"This is Lady Guinevere," he says.

Guinevere. The Faery who married King Arthur. Who gave up her immortality to be with the human king. Who broke Arthur's heart and his kingdom when she ran away with Lancelot. Who died a long, long time ago.

Or so I thought.

"She can't be . . ." I step away from the spirit.

The face behind the bars grins. The smile is twisted; the few teeth it holds are rotten, weathered nubs of gravestones. "Wrong. I flipped wrong. Sisters fail us. Poison in our veins."

I try to remember Guinevere. What she was before Arthur. Before Camelot's terrible fall at the hand of the sorcerer Mordred. She was classic in her beauty: hair spun of gold, plaited all the way to her heels. Eyes as blue as the clearest day. A delicate snub nose.

There's no way the skeletal creature before me could be her. Pendragon's bride.

"Is it true?" I look back at Titania. "Did you know?"

"It's her. By the Greater Spirit." The queen's face is paler than a Faery light: shocked and ghost white. "There's some spell keeping her from death. Mab must have kept her alive all these years . . ."

"But why?"

"Mab loved Arthur," Titania reminds me. "The Pendragon chose Guinevere instead, and ended up dead because of her betrayal. Mab never was one to forget things. Nor forgive."

She's right, I realize as I read the magic shimmering around Guinevere. The spell reeks of the old Faery queen. It's looped, which explains why it didn't fall alongside Mab's wards. Guinevere's life is knotted up just like Lord Winfred's Faery lights. Cursed to go on and on.

"The queen had her brought here after King Arthur's passing," Alistair tells us. "We thought it strange that a mortal should be sent to this place. It took us years to realize who she was."

The choke of these walls grows. Crushes. Guinevere

clutches her prison bars with ratted nails.

"The circling sea will swallow us whole. Drowning kingdom! I flipped wrong." Her words howl. They make the sick inside me stretch and swallow.

"The dark has eaten her mind," Kieran says at my back. "She doesn't have magic to protect herself, like the others."

"Magic?!" Guinevere's shriek sounds like a Banshee's. Bone-white fingers choke the bars. "I dream!"

There's no way of knowing where her clouded irises are staring. I feel her gaze nonetheless. It peels at my skin, excavates my bones. "They know not the secrets of sleep, sister. My only escape. Worlds which once were. Are. Will be. These eyes are blind but I still see. Have you found them yet? The dreams?"

My mouth is too dry to answer. The tips of my fingers shake, but my lungs refuse to move. I can't breathe.

"Let me show you!" The creature that was Guinevere lunges toward me. Her body lands against the bars, but her hand keeps reaching. Those ragged nails wrap around my bicep and sink through my skin.

I don't even have time to feel pain, the burn of those nails anchored into my muscle. Kieran's arm hooks around my waist, pulls me back from the cell. Alistair glides to the bars, a spell pulling like caramel from his slow lips. The magic itself is viper fast, tossing Guinevere back. It snaps her against the cell's far wall like a broken doll.

There's red on my arm, weeping from five crimson moons. Guinevere slouches against the stones, wailing. The sound pierces every part of this corridor. Floods its dark with feeling and loss.

"We've seen enough here." Even Queen Titania appears shaken; she has to yell to make herself heard.

Alistair turns and starts to drift back into the tunnels. We follow his scar-light away from the screams of Arthur's queen. Yet no matter how many lengths of carved-out earth we put between us, I can still hear her.

Kieran's arm stays around my waist, guiding me. Every one of my steps shakes. Colors burst into my vision. I shut my eyes but they're still there. Along with the milky white of Guinevere's pupils.

Once the earth surrounding us would have fed me. Made me stronger. Now all I want is to crawl out. Breathe sunlight and sea breeze.

"Air," I gasp. "I need air."

"Kieran." Titania speaks past me. "Take Lady Emrys aboveground. I'll be up to consult with her in a moment. I must talk with Alistair a bit longer."

The Ad-hene pulls me away from the queen and Alistair's murmurings. Step by step we rise. Up the tangled maze.

As soon as my steps grow firm again I stop, let his arm slide from me. It feels strange and unsettling to be touching someone who isn't Richard. Now that I'm so close, I see the markings just under the powder white of Kieran's skin. They swirl like the filigree on my ring—silver currents. The muscles beneath are cut and sloping.

I'm staring at them too close, too long. I realize this and my cheeks start to burn. For the first time I'm grateful for the darkness.

"What's wrong?" he asks.

I look away. My fingers find my ring, turn it over and over on my finger. "I—I can walk myself."

"Can you?"

"Of course." I sidestep him, grateful that my feet are as steady as I claimed they were. "I may be a *faagailagh*, but I'm not helpless."

"I never thought you were." Kieran turns, his coal-black curls still perfectly set as he moves past. Every one of his strides is wide and fast. I struggle to keep up. "I remember you, you know. From the Guard transport. You were very powerful for one so young. Queen Mab's favorite. Her pet. They say you killed her. Before you gave up your magic."

I don't answer. My fingers spin the jade and silver around and around, into a raw circle.

"You intrigue me." Kieran's eyes glitter: dark through dark. "You were a maelstrom. Now you're a fire without flame. I don't understand why you would ever put it out."

"Power isn't everything," I tell him.

"And love is?"

A light springs up ahead. The soft touch of morning. We round a final bend and autumn air curls into the tunnels, cleans out my head. I breathe it in and focus on the day which unfolds before me. Blue sky, bold sea. These keep the terrible pictures of a rotting Guinevere and the empty cell at bay.

I'd been hoping that when we reached the ledge, Kieran would turn and leave me. But he stays. His eyes squint under the daylight. He crouches like before, glares out over the misting waves.

"None of the others understood either," I tell him. "I did not understand."

The etchings of his arm catch the sun. They gleam like chain mail. He almost looks as if he's part machine.

"Do you really think the mortals will let you into their

world? That you can become one of them just by giving up some spells?" He says this and all I can see is the scorn on Elaine Forsythe's face. Tables full of poisonous flowers. Flashing paparazzi lights.

"I'm trying." I stare down at my bare toes, still sore.

"It must be a mighty thing. This love. If you're putting yourself through such misery for it."

Kieran tilts his head to the side as he looks at me. Those eyes cut like the edge of a spearhead. His pale skin catches shadows so easily, highlighting the angles of his muscles and bones. The shine of morning light against his black hair makes him all contrasts. Like a charcoal sketch.

I'm staring too long. Again.

"I'm not miserable," I protest.

Kieran keeps staring back—his gray eyes wash over me.

I clutch my ring so tight I'm afraid my finger might break.

"My mistake," he says. His stare travels down my arm, where the blood is drying in smears. "Would you like me to heal that?"

The punctures still throb and sting. I know that one word from the Ad-hene's mouth could erase the pain. But the idea of his spell seeping into my skin—all smolder and sulfuric power—reminding me of the maelstrom I used to be . . .

I don't need Kieran's magic. I'm mortal now. And mortals' wounds must heal on their own.

Before I can answer Titania emerges from the tunnel, Alistair behind her. The leader of the Ad-hene is almost unbearable to look at in the light; the bright white of his hair and skin is searing. The sterling tracings on his left arm loop and swirl like mixed-up fish scales.

"How long has this prisoner has been gone?" Titania asks.

"We last checked the wings over a fortnight ago. The break could have occurred at any time since then."

"Two weeks . . ." The Faery queen's voice drops off.

A fierce wave dashes against our cliff, spraying frigid mist over our skin. One of Mab's most dangerous prisoners is loose in a world of defenseless mortals. This thought alone is enough to freeze my blood.

Alistair echoes my fears. "The prisoner will be on the mainland by now. My guards searched but found no traces of an aura on the island."

"I'll coordinate scouts," Titania says, more for my sake than Alistair's. "Start a tracking and retrieval process as soon as I find a way to replace the wards. Hopefully we can find the prisoner before any harm is done."

"I offer the service of my Ad-hene." The whitewashed spirit bows. I notice that his hair, like Kieran's, doesn't move against the breeze. As if he's not actually a living thing, but a statue which moves and talks.

"That won't be necessary." Titania's words are as stretched as her lips. "Your place is here. With the rest of the prisoners."

Alistair's all harshness now, face-to-face with the Faery queen. "You'll need the Ad-hene. They're far more familiar with the prisoner's aura. We've lived side by side with these creatures for years. Your kind has forgotten them altogether."

He's right. Titania knows this. But I can tell by the way her lips thin even more that she's thinking of the markings on the Ad-henes' arms. How they're the only way out of the Labyrinth.

Maybe the old ways are shifting, waking while the mortals trim back electricity and plant new trees. Changing things. Maybe the prisoner stumbled upon a crack in the Labyrinth's ancient, tangled spells. Maybe the island's maze truly did swallow the escaped spirit whole.

Or maybe the Ad-hene let it out.

"The Ad-hene's place is here," Titania says again. Her

voice is needle sharp, jabbed straight at Alistair. "Is that understood?"

The weight of the moment between words is heavy. Alistair's great age and Titania's crown crowd the cliff. Each too big for the other.

"The Ad-hene are loyal." Alistair's words are wizened-oak and weary. "We will do as the queen asks."

"What does this mean?" I look to the queen. "What must we do?"

One of Titania's silver eyebrows rises at the word *we*. "This is no longer your battle, Lady Emrys. I brought you here only to see if you recognized the magic, not to strategize. You will go back to London and focus on being a good liaison. The Frithemaeg will handle this."

Her words jar. Remind me of the unspoken rift between us. She has magic and I do not. I'm the one who's powerless here. "And what will *you* do?"

"I'll send an order to the Guard to be put on high alert. Besides that and the scouts, there's nothing I can do."

"What should I tell Richard?"

"Tell him nothing," Titania says firmly. "There's no need to worry the king with this. Not until we know more. It could be that this prisoner just wants to be free. That it will disappear altogether."

Wind licks the cliffside, stealing the last of Titania's words and tossing them into the waters like they're nothing. They are. Nothing. All of us felt the stains of anger on those prison walls. The kind of rage which never fades away. The kind of rage which demands revenge.

The Labyrinth's black shadows have spilled into the world, calling for blood. Both Alistair and Kieran are staring at the vastness of the sea. It's almost as if they can see the doom on the other shore. Pieces of it dance behind their eyes.

Kieran finally tears his gaze away. It lands straight on me. My stomach tightens and my skin prickles. He has the darkness of the Labyrinth behind each and every word when he speaks.

"I wouldn't count on it."

Four

Every muscle in my body is cramped from those hours on the Kelpie. Even without heels on, my feet wobble like dangerously placed dominos. I've been in this mortal form for two months, yet it still amazes me that only forty sleepless hours can weaken me so completely.

I shuffle into the sitting room and Richard is there: curled on a settee, asleep. His cheek is smudged against its embroidered cushion, hands bunched in front of his face. He's still wearing his tuxedo—wrinkled black and stark white. He must have stayed up all night. Waiting for me.

The coffee table supports my theory. Its surface is cluttered with signs of Richard's sleepless night. His laptop is perched there, covered with papers and illegible ink notes. A tray of tea and untouched biscuits sits beside it. And next to that is a newspaper, splayed wide. There are the usual headlines: UNDERGROUND TRAINS MALFUNCTIONING ON THE CIRCLE LINE and THE SECOND LIGHTS-DOWN: ARE YOU READY?

And then there's me.

I'm all over the front page. Pictured mid-leap. Loose hair flares like fire around my shoulders. The flowers and frills of my dress parachute, showing a good deal of leg.

Probably not what Anabelle meant when she told me to impress the press.

Richard's face is on the edge of the photograph, its expression made of agony. His hand grasps at empty space. Reaching for someone already gone.

TURMOIL ON THE THAMES

One of the year's most anticipated social events was crashed by an unwelcome guest on Friday evening. Lord and Lady Winfred's guests were being wined and dined to perfection when a monster appeared in the water.

"It was shiny and black!" said one eyewitness, Doris Hapsley, a waitress at the Winfreds' gala. "It kept ramming into the boat, trying to sink us. I thought for sure I was going to die."

The most notable attendees of the evening—King Richard and his escort, Lady Emrys Léoflic—were predictably in the middle of the fray. Britain's fledgling king and the former Fae were spotted in a heated argument just moments before the redhead threw herself over the side.

"It was very clear they were upset with each other," Elaine

Forsythe, the new wife of rising-star politician Julian Forsythe, told us. "He grabbed her arm and she tore away."

Both Lady Emrys and the creature disappeared moments after. No sign of Lady Emrys has been seen since.

Officer Eric Black of the king's Protection Command also reports that the gala's table centerpieces were composed of the poisonous flower birdsfoot trefoil. One of these deadly bouquets was placed at the center of King Richard's table. Whether an assassination attempt or a bungling florist, Black and the other officers have declined to comment.

Both incidents are ill-timed for the king and his pro-Fae supporters, who will be celebrating their second Lights-down this weekend. They call into question the safety of immortal integration, as well as the general public's support. For some, including M.A.F. leader Julian Forsythe, even the holy grail of self-sustaining energy is not enough to assuage his fear of the magical. "These creatures aren't pixies or Cinderella godmothers. They're monsters. My wife and I might have died tonight. I think it's high time King Richard's motives be called into question. Is he truly doing what's best for the kingdom? Or is he listening to the siren lure of a certain ginger?"

The article goes on, but I've already crumpled the paper between my fingers.

Escort? Heated argument? Monsters? Siren lure?

I toss it aside and collapse into the nearest chair, the muddy remains of my tulle gown puffing out around me. There's a pounding in my head and an ache in my back, jabbing reminders that I'm coming apart at the seams.

Immortals do not sleep. They cannot give themselves to dreams. These are things only mortals know.

The first time I ever fell asleep—after I surrendered my magic to Herne—I was terrified. Nothingness slipped into my mind, as vast and dark as the black around stars. My thoughts became watery, warped. I couldn't grab them. Couldn't hold on.

Then came the dreams. Life which was not life. Conversations, emotions, love and loss, all playing like a movie inside my head. It wasn't until I woke up and took in the crumpled sheets of my bed that I realized it wasn't real.

I know I'm dreaming now because I see Breena— my lifelong friend undone by one of Mab's final spells, months dead now. We're on a solitary hill. All around is cloud. Thick and white—like the inside of a seer's crystal ball. Breena stares into it. Her back is to me, hair an unreal gold against the clouds.

"Bree?"

My friend turns. "Remember, Emrys. You have to remember."

"What? What do I have to remember?"

Breena grips my arm, pulls me back to where she was standing. She points into the mist, her eyes keen, focused on something I'm unable to see.

"Remember." Breena's fingers dig into my skin.

"Bree." I try not to sound exasperated as I look into the fog. "I don't know what you're talking about."

"Remember! Remember!" More voices join: a rough, croaking chant coming from my feet. The ground is black with ravens, their eyes glittering like tiny beetles, their sharp beaks clacking out the same syllables. "Remember! Remember!"

Breena isn't talking anymore. She's just staring. As if she's trying to tell me something, but can't.

And then the mist falls away, crumples like an invisible giant drawing back a curtain. We're standing over a valley, looking down on death. What was once green is mud— churned and mixed with the blood of a thousand men. Full of flailing horses, snapped spears, and knights carving each other to pieces with crude metal. Just below us—on the long low ridge of our hill—a castle burns.

It's been years upon years. So long that the mortals have forgotten it. But I know this fortress even in the thick of sleep. This exact image has lived in my mind for centuries: turrets and stones wreathed high with fire.

Breena and I stand on the hill, watching as Camelot falls apart. Knight by knight. Flame by searing flame.

"Remember," Breena says again.

"I do." I feel King Arthur's fall, tumbling around in my chest: the broken blood magic, the ruined castle, the sink of Mordred's black blade through Arthur's armor.

"No!" Breena's scream is sharp, a needle jammed into my eardrum. "Remember!!"

My neck whips around and I'm ready to yell at her. But Breena is gone. The fingers around my arms belong to Guinevere. Those ratted, yellow nails dig into my skin again. Her eyes are as white as the mists—sucking me in.

I want to tear away from her. But all I can do is stare as her shrieks fall down like rain. "I will show you ruin! Kingdom's fall! I flipped wrong and the world burned."

Heat sears my back, as if the fire from the valley has clawed to where we stand. I try to pull away, but the ancient's grip is tight.

A snaggletoothed smile takes over her face. "You found it. But blind eyes still need to see."

I look away from her, down to the ground. The ravens are gone.

"Puppets. With smiles on their faces. That's how they died." Guinevere cackles and releases my arm. I stumble back. Over the ledge, and into the valley. Onto the coal-hot stones of Camelot.

Five

I'm still reaching for something to hold on to, something to save me from the fall seconds after I jerk awake. My eyes are open, but I still see Guinevere's crazed face. Her laughter rings through my ears.

I'm breathing hard, staring at the golden moldings of the ceiling. I've been asleep for hours.

Richard's laptop and notes are gone, as well as the newspaper. An antique candelabra sits in their place. Its three flames sputter, offering a small globe of light into the vast room.

It seems Lights-down has already started.

I groan and wipe some hair out of my face. My fingers come back slick with sweat. Traces of the dream still rage under my skin. It felt so real. As if I were there again, watching the Pendragon's kingdom go down in flames. A fire so hot and strong it made my arm hairs singe. I can still feel the burn. . . .

"You had a nightmare?"

My heart is already racing, but the suddenness of Richard's voice causes it to explode. He's in a chair just beyond the candles' glow, watching me.

"I—" I stop. Swallow. A nightmare. That's all it was. Just my brain taking fragments of my day. Trying to make sense of the past twenty-four hours.

But terror still clings to the edges of my throat. I look at the trio of flames and all I see is the castle. Twisting arms of fire, eating away an entire kingdom. I lean forward, snuff all three with a single breath. The room swirls into smoky darkness.

I scrape meager magic from my veins, weave it into a whisper: *"Inlíhte."*

The room flickers in my weak, watery light. I don't even have the strength to loop it. The glow is already growing dimmer, shedding brightness every second.

"You didn't have to do that," Richard's voice is hoarse, as if he's been crying. His face looks so sad in my hungry, fading light. "I thought I lost you, Embers. When you jumped and you didn't come up . . . It was awful. A thousand hells."

I think of the newspaper, with Richard's relentless stare begging me not to jump. I think of the way I tore from his grasp, hurtling myself into those dark and vicious waters.

I should have listened. I should have waited for Helene and the other Frithemaeg to show up. I should have stood by Richard's side. But I know I couldn't. If there was another Kelpie, raging and frothing under my feet, I would jump again.

For some reason I thought it would be easy—passing on the baton—letting others handle the fight for me. But the jumping, the fighting—it's in my blood. It's everything I've ever known. Thousands of years can't be let go in a single second. Lifetimes can't be undone so simply.

I don't know how to tell him this.

"I'm all right, Richard." My words are timid, hollowed out like bones. "I'm right here."

"Yes. But—you're not what you were before. And I think that sometimes you forget that." I know he doesn't mean to be cruel. Just the opposite—the love rises up behind his eyes. But his words go deep, remind me of everything I was: Power. Fight. Flight. A maelstrom.

Everything I'm not.

He's wrong. I never forget. Every single time I see

Richard, kiss him, I feel it all: the gain and the loss.

"I love you, Emrys," he goes on. "I can't lose you. Not after everything. Promise me you'll stay safe. Promise me you won't use your magic like that again."

I can't breathe. It's just like being underwater again. Except there's no Kelpie. No Thames. Just words jamming my head.

I should promise him this.

But I can't.

Richard looks at me in that piercing, all-encompassing way of his. Those hazel irises smolder. And I see all of my fear, all of my sadness flung back at me in ghost light.

He knows who I am. He knows I can't promise.

And still he's asking.

"You can't do this to me," Richard fills my silence. "It's not fair. I spent hours waiting, not knowing . . ."

"Not fair?" Everything I've endured for the past twenty-four hours sweeps back over me. The emptiness of the cell. The horror of Guinevere's face. The fear of drowning. The anger that I'm not what I was.

And the nightmare—that's taken all of my feelings, shifted them into the wrong gear.

"Not *fair*?" My words rage in the dying light. "I just

saved your life! I've given you *everything* and you want me to give up more?"

Richard rakes anxious fingers through his hair. His face is crumpled, frowning. "That's not what I meant—"

"Oh really? Then what did you mean?" My insides are snarl and heat.

Before—when I was power and maelstrom—I always had to bite back my anger. The same way I had to hold back my kisses. For fear of harming Richard in my passion. There's nothing in my way now. I can unleash all my fury and the Faery light won't even flicker.

The king doesn't answer. His face is hidden in his hands.

"I gave up everything for a ghost! You're never here, Richard. If you're not at Parliament then you're at some meeting with Lord Winfred or a hundred different people! But never me!

"Every single day I have to watch the Frithemaeg fly in and out. I have to remember that I can't. I can't and you're gone and it just feels like too much!"

Richard lets out a hot, even breath. "I know things have been crazy. This is the way it has to be, Embers. Just for a while, until Lights-down is firmly established and we have more support in Parliament."

"And then what? After Lights-down there's the Refor-estation Bill. And after that there will be something else. There will always be something else!"

"We're creating a new world." He sounds so solid, unshaken by my verbal cuts. Like he's too tired to fight. "I thought that's what you wanted."

"I wanted *us*, Richard. Do you realize we haven't spent an entire day together since I took you to the London Eye? That was over two months ago!"

"Emrys," his voice turns more serious. "This is my job. My duty. I promised Herne. I gave him my word. For *us*. So we could be together."

His words, what he's saying should make sense. I know this in my head, but my emotions are a snake inside me. Coiling tight, crowding out all logic. I want to make him angry. I want him to fight. Yell. Anything. Anything except sitting there with exhausted, glazed eyes.

So I asked the question I know will cut, dig deep. That kernel of a question Kieran planted in the corner of my mind.

"Is this worth it?"

Richard stares. It takes him a moment to find his voice.

It's still steady. Still flat. "You don't mean that."

"Maybe I do! I didn't give up everything for this!" My arm sweeps through the room. "Not Lights-down or Buckingham or any of it. I gave up my magic for us. For *you*."

He closes his eyes. My light is almost out. The Lights-down darkness—so utter and pure—closes in around us.

"You're not even fighting me." I can't tell if I'm yelling or sobbing. Or both. "It's like you don't even care."

"Don't say that." His breath is a knife—sharp, edged with pain. "Don't ever say that."

"Then do something! Fight me!"

"I can't!" His yell explodes hot inside my chest.

The Faery light I thought was dead seizes the room. Angry white—bright as toothaches and sunstruck snow—culls out everything: Richard's knotted jaw and tight, tortured fists, the blood braiding down my arm, the distance between us. We're both frozen, watching with black-hole eyes as the *inlíhte* blazes through its second life. Fading . . .

It seems my anger isn't as safe to express as I thought.

Darkness collapses back over the room.

"Stop," Richard whispers, his words tangled with fear. "Please stop, Emrys."

I don't know if I can. There's too much inside me. Spinning, hissing. Wanting to lunge, to fight like I always do. I have to get out of here, before I say words I don't mean. Before I hurt him.

I walk to the door and leave Richard in the dark.

Six

During my first few weeks as a mortal, when sleep was new and impossible, I walked to soothe my insomnia. At first I looped through Buckingham's halls, but those became rote. Then I started walking the grounds, and later venturing into London's streets.

Tonight the city is especially barren, with the black cloak of Lights-down draped over its blocks. Streetlamps stand—useless pillars of metal and glass—over parked cars and unlit Underground signs. There's no roar of the night train under my feet. No growl of traffic in the distance. It's eerie how silent the city is.

Usually these walks are a way to recharge; my soul thrives on solitude and starlight. But tonight is different. Perhaps it's the quiet. Or the extra layers of dark. Every step I take feels strung and anxious, like a chase. I don't know if I'm running from something or to it.

I thought I could slip into a mortal life. That love was worth it all.

But right now this feels like the farthest thing from the truth. Everything inside me is astir. Storm-cloud emotions rise in bits and pieces, like shattered branches caught in a gale.

Weak.

Powerless.

A fire without flame.

You're not what you were before.

I knew it wouldn't be easy, giving up my magic. I just didn't know it would be this hard.

The windows I pass are lit with lantern glow, like jack-o'-lanterns queued up for All Hallows' Eve. They gleam and grin, offering glimpses inside. A family plays a board game around an oil lamp. A couple drinks red wine at their dining room table, gazing at each other over candlelight.

Normal, happy lives. Never knowing anything else. I envy them. Their flightless, dull, coffee-drinking existence. They don't have to live with the ache of being grounded.

I walk and walk. Feel every step.

The Thames appears. Its waters whisper by. I try to imagine how Richard felt, staring, waiting for me to resurface.

A thousand hells. That's how he described it. I know how it feels. I felt the scorch the moment Mab's blade broke through Richard's belly and he died in my arms. The moment I was far more broken than I am now.

Everything I've lost, I've lost for him.

Richard is enough. He has to be.

Something catches the corner of my eye. A glare too harsh for stars or flame, arching electric across the river. Dozens of lights strung over Westminster Bridge.

It's a parade: people marching with signs and electric torches. The night's quiet is shredded by their voices. There's a rhythm to them, punching like drumbeats.

"Shut down Lights-down! Shut down Lights-down!"

There can't be more than two hundred of them, but their yells are loud, piercing. They rattle the asphalt at my feet. Every scream threads needle sharp through my bones.

I stay still next to the dark lamppost. The crowd slides by like a funeral wake. Their signs stab the air.

GIVE UP POWER, BECOME POWERLESS!

DON'T DRAG US BACK INTO THE DARK AGES.

GO BACK TO HELL, MONSTERS!

Monsters.

Before it had only been a quote in a newspaper. The feeling behind Elaine Forsythe's glance. But here, in front of the Palace of Westminster, it rages. So sharp, so real.

Do you really think the mortals will let you into their world? That you can become one of them just by giving up some spells? Kieran's questions rise up, color the night.

I've hoped. I've believed in the golden age of Camelot—that what happened once can happen again. That human and Fae can exist together. That my past and my future don't have to be at war.

But Guinevere dreamed that same dream.

I'm standing too close. I think this just as a protestor looks over his shoulder. His eyes carve through the dark, land straight on my lamppost.

I will him to pass by, but there are no more veiling spells left in me. The man stops; recognition glints through his eyes. He calls back to the others with a slapping yell, "Hey! That's her! She's the one who spelled the king!"

The air burns with danger. Dozens of stares and lights turn toward me. Root out my hiding place. I've never been afraid of mortals before. But there's something about this crowd which tells me to run.

So I do.

A chunk of the protest breaks away, hounding me with footsteps and yells. I dash down the sidewalk, around the statue of the warrior queen Boudica in her chariot. The mortals' lights blaze up behind me. Just ahead I catch a snag of crimson and blue, the edge of an unmoving escalator. An entrance to the Underground.

I swing around, feet skidding against cool asphalt as I head for the sign. I don't know why I'm running. Why they're chasing me. Or what they'll do when they catch me.

My fingers grip hard onto the edge of the escalator. I take the steps in leaps and bounds. Push faster, harder than I'm afraid this mortal body can take. Just as I reach the final step the first torch swings down, fills my world with harsh, terrible light.

I'm trapped.

The Underground's entrance is shut, laced over with a metal grating. I shake it hard, even though I know it won't open. My insides feel gutted, but I scream the spell anyway: "*Opena! Opena!*"

Nothing. No magic, no power. Just the cold, hard rattle of the grating. The sound of dozens of feet racing down dead escalators.

"She's trying to do magic!" someone screams. "Get her!"

The lights are halfway down the stairs, beams stabbing

my eyes. They sweep closer, closer. I brace myself against the grating. Metal diamonds press hard into my back. The meat-voiced man is almost to the last step. Eyes made of flint as he reaches out.

At the last moment I switch and duck. He falls hard into the grating, but there are more hands behind him. More eyes. They flash from all corners.

Someone grabs my dress. I turn to push them away and another hand grips my hair. Too many. There are too many. More hands shove me back into the grating. There are yells everywhere, crowding my ears with anger and hate. But then another sound rises, cuts through them all. A howl. Pure and powerful.

The metal at my back gives way, crumples against the Black Dog's magic. The creature bursts out of the tunnels, bristling in front of the torches. It's a massive spirit, too large to squeeze into the space of the escalators, where the crowd is now screaming, clawing their way back up to the streets. It snarls, lichen-yellow teeth gnashing.

That aura. I recognize it. There's only one Black Dog which scavenges the tunnels near Westminster Bridge.

"Blæc," I whisper the creature's name. Its ears prick,

head twists around to where I'm sprawled over the broken gate. Those eyes sear like a nightmare. Yellow and so very hungry.

"How do you know my name?" the creature rumbles.

We've met before, Blæc and I. But there's no point in telling the dog this, since I wiped its memory after the fact. "I am . . . was . . . one of the Frithemaeg."

"Frithemaeg?" The beast sniffs at the air. Whatever it smells makes it growl. "No . . . Something different. Something tasty."

Human prey has been scarce in the months of the integration. Most soul feeders have retreated to morgues and funeral homes, living like vultures off the already dead. But some, like Blæc, have stayed in their territories. Slowly starving.

I crawl backward, and the Black Dog edges closer, eyes and teeth fluorescent. Leering like a demon.

A monster.

Maybe the mortals are right.

"Blæc," I say its name again. "Please."

"I'm huuuuungrrrry." The beast's syllables stretch out in a soft howl, crooning.

The escalator is too far away. There's no way I'll make

it without stumbling. Without Blæc's dagger teeth sinking into my calves.

The Black Dog leans in. Its breath curdles up my nose: hot decay. Saliva strings down, drips against my cheek. I shut my eyes and wait for the dive. The teeth.

It never comes.

The gate rattles under my back as Blæc steps away. A long, low growl leaks through the dog's teeth, mixed with hints of words. "Can't . . . not yet . . . won't let me eat . . . sooooo huuuungrrrry . . ."

I open my eyes just in time to see Blæc's tail melt back into the shadows of the Underground. I sit still on top of the mangled metal, afraid to move. Afraid this miracle will not hold.

Yet it does. Blæc is gone. The crowd too. All that's left is a heavy, harsh silence.

It doesn't make sense. Black Dogs are killers—cold and cruel—not known for sparing prey. Especially when they're so hungry. For the second time in twenty-four hours, I should be dead.

Richard's right. I'm not what I was before. My life has become fragile, so easily snuffed. I have to start treating it that way.

My fingers clench hard against my ring.

There's only one reason I chose this life. Only one person who's worth it.

It's time to return to him.

The fire is back. Richard stares straight into the candelabra's shine—three pinpoints of light dancing in his dark eyes. My legs tremble as I run to the settee. To him. Neither of us says a word as we fold into each other's arms. I bury my face into his neck, soak in the warm solid of his embrace.

One of the many things I almost lost.

"Emrys, I'm so sorry." Richard's apology rumbles through me. His arms tighten. "I *do* care. More than anything. The thought of losing you scares me shitless. But that's no excuse. I never should've asked you to promise those things."

"I'm sorry, too," I whisper.

He pulls back, looks at me.

"I d-didn't . . ." Quiver, shake goes my voice—as undone as the rest of me. I'm glad he doesn't ask about it, since I don't think I could bear telling him I almost died. Again. "I didn't mean those things I said."

Richard's hand slides down to mine, weaving our fingers together. "You did."

"I—"

"You meant some of them," he says. "And you're right. You've given up so much for my sake and I—I haven't been there. Not the way you need me to be."

"Richard—" My throat squeezes.

He goes on, "All this king stuff—it's getting to me. I've been so caught up in trying to lead this country. Trying to keep everything in balance. And I've left you behind. Not to mention becoming a first-rate workaholic prat in the process."

"Second-rate. At the most." A smile flickers over my lips.

"That's awfully generous of you." Richard smiles back: all light. His fingers knot tighter in mine. "Do you want me to give up the crown? Because I will, for you. I could abdicate. Pass the throne to Anabelle. We could find a little cottage in the Highlands. No cameras. No press. Just us. For as long as we wanted."

At first I think he's speaking in metaphors: a poet's language. But then Richard looks at me. The burn of those candles still lingers in his eyes.

He's dead serious.

I can't help but imagine it: Waking up late in rumpled sheets. Drinking flasks of Earl Grey on a loch's stony shores. All the time in the world to talk, to kiss, to rest. Together.

But I think of Lights-down and the Reforestation Bill. Magic-fusion batteries and looped Faery lights. I think of all our conversations with Queen Titania, imagining new worlds. Resurrecting Camelot.

I think of the poisonous blossom pinched in Julian Forsythe's fingers. I think of the Labyrinth's empty cell, its escapee loose in the world: impossible, dangerous, and angry. I think of the marching protestors, their hands tearing at my dress. I think of Blæc's teeth, how they too almost tore me to shreds. How wide the gap is between these two worlds.

Richard—with the blood magic sleeping in his veins, with his fiery passion, eloquence, and ideas—is the perfect bridge between magic and mortal. The thread holding the kingdom's future together. No one, not even Anabelle or Titania, could keep things from unraveling if he surrendered the throne.

"The kingdom needs you," I tell him.

"None of this is worth it, Embers." He tucks a stray hair behind my ear. "Not if it means losing you."

My eyes hold Richard's, dig deep past the royal mask—one he's worn ever since his father's death. It fits so well now that even members of Parliament have a hard time remembering he just turned eighteen. But here in the wavering candlelight he looks young. And tired.

I'm not the only one who's made sacrifices.

So I offer up four words, small and whispered: "I'm here to stay."

"I'm glad to hear it," he murmurs. His fingers keep threading through my hair, forging paths and shivers. "We need some time away, together. Let's take a holiday after the coronation."

"Sounds perfect," I tell him. "I'll let Titania know she'll be liaisonless for a few days."

"Make it a few weeks." His fingers pause. "Why did Titania call you away? You were just at her court on Wednesday."

Part of me wants to tell him about the empty cell and Guinevere's tragic insanity, how it's poisoned my dreams. But Titania's order rings clear and true in my head: *Tell him nothing.*

As much as I dislike her orders, the Faery queen is right. I can't unload all these extra worries onto Richard. Not when he's already awake most nights, pacing halls and carving deeper shadows beneath his eyes.

None of this makes me feel better about lying. "There was a problem with some of the second-stage battery prototypes. The shipment of battery shells wasn't gutted out well enough before it was sent to court. Every Fae who tried to get near it was crippled with nausea. They summoned me to dispose of it."

"None of them started going mad, did they?"

I shake my head. "Lights-down is giving them more strength to resist. It won't be as easy for the older ones to unravel. They're strong enough to work with metal now."

"Good." The king sighs. "We don't need another insane immortal running about. Especially now."

Truth lurches high in my gut. I think of the aura staining the walls of the Labyrinth: insane immortal, signed and sealed. I think of how the escapee is running about, probably starting a magical killing spree as we sit here.

Tell him nothing.

I push all of this back down, into the deepest corners of myself. Far from him. "We try to keep our crazy Fae quota to one per year. Preferably less."

Richard laughs: a warm, sunny sound. "Do you know how much I love you, Embers?"

His touch slides along the angles of my cheeks, my

collarbone. The thrill of him—familiar, yet somehow always new—soaks into every pore. Becomes my light and center in this dark room.

His fingers are knuckle-deep in my hair, and he pulls my face so close I can count each summer freckle still lurking on the bridge of his nose. The flames on the table soak into his eyes, smelt them like copper.

His lips are warm like sunlight, soft like cashmere. They melt into me. The places his lips have been shimmer with cold. Richard's breath scarves my neck and his kisses trail down, forging new paths all the way to my collarbone. My breaths quicken and my heart is a smithy hammer. Beating hard. Forging new, brilliant things.

Want rises inside me, like the first surge of an unleashed spell. Swelling, aching, and strong. Sparkling within my chest. I grasp at the settee cushions, pull even closer to him.

I rake my fingers through Richard's hair. A sound rises from his throat: deep, guttural. I start fumbling with the zipper on the back of my shredded dress, just as he goes rigid.

Richard scrambles away from me so fast I nearly tumble onto the floor.

"No." He's breathing hard, as if he's swallowing something back. "Not now."

I'm blinking, trying to make sense of those few, blunt words. "What's wrong?"

He shuts his eyes so he doesn't have to look at me. "I just—can't."

My lungs are breathless. A vacuum sucked dry. The sparkle in my chest has vanished; in its place is a low ache.

And I think of the Faery light, how it exploded back to life during our argument. And I remember all those times we kissed, before I gave my powers to Herne. The times Richard left with a bloody lip or sore ribs because my magic ripped through him.

"Are—are you afraid of me?" The question shudders from my lips. "My power is gone, Richard. What happened to that light earlier . . . that was an anomaly. It won't happen again."

"No." Richard stands. He's turned with his back to me. "It's not you, Embers. I promise."

Not me. His words ring false. Hollow. I hear the fear crammed into every one of his long-strung breaths.

"It's not you," he says again, firmer this time. So I know for certain he's lying. "I'm just—I'm feeling a bit off."

My fingers work over my sad dress. Its ruined tulle and unraveling flowers. I pick at a loose thread and pull. Watch all of its beauty come undone from a single snag.

Not me. Not me. Not me.

I don't believe him.

I gave up my spells and magic. I've tried to become one of them. But the mortals are still scared of me. Even Richard.

I try to ignore the heavy silence that's fallen between us.

"Emrys," Richard murmurs. "You're hurt."

I look to him, so beautiful against the darkness. Candle-glow catches crimson against his fingers. The color is wet, bright. Richard studies it hard in the light before he nods down at my arm. I follow his gaze, realize where the red came from.

Guinevere's mark is still bleeding: a slow, steady ooze. I try to smear the blood away with my fingers, but there's too much. As if the hurt is fresh and not almost a day old.

"It's nothing," I say, even though I know it's not. From what little I've experienced of mortal wounds, I know it shouldn't still be weeping.

"I'll go and find you a bandage," Richard clears his throat. "Mend it up."

It's not the blood that stings. Not the cut that needs a bandage.

But because he's Richard—because he's mine—I let him.

Seven

"Do you think I'm making a mistake?" Anabelle asks as she glides across Windsor Castle's Grand Reception room. So many flowers pour from her arms I can barely see her. Entire bouquets of orchids, carnations, and lilies of the valley.

"Shouldn't the florist be doing that?" I ask as she wrestles the arrangements to a corner table.

Once the princess is sure the vase is secure, she turns, hands on her hips. She's dressed down today: a tailored button-up and indigo jeans, hair pulled back in a French plait. But Anabelle has a way of making these look like the height of elegance. Even if she is wearing flats.

"I was checking the flowers"—Anabelle's voice fades, a cross between a sigh and a hush—"to make sure they're safe. This is the coronation ball, Emrys! We can't afford bad press. They're already abuzz that we're having it here at Windsor instead of in London. One paper called it a 'wretched breach of tradition.' And that was after Mum gave me a two-hour lecture on the subject."

"The flowers are fine. Eric and Jensen have already checked them. Three times," I tell her.

But the princess is on to other subjects. "What if people think Windsor is too far? What if no one decides to come? What if *too many* people come?"

I shut my eyes, try my best to empathize, but the feelings don't surface. Instead I'm rubbing my temples, trying to fight the dull throb of my skull. I know it's because I'm not getting enough sleep. I manage only two or three hours a night before I jerk awake, drenched in sweat, my arm oozing from freshly split scabs.

It's been two whole weeks since the Labyrinth of Man, but the dream keeps coming. Each time it's the same. Breena stands with her back to me, facing the clouds. Ravens crowd at my feet and my ears flood with the same, relentless syllables: *RE-MEM-BER*. Over and over. The mist clears and Arthur's kingdom burns. Guinevere appears, shrieking riddles—insanities into my ear.

And always, the final fall.

It happens every single time I close my eyes, start to drift. So I've stopped closing them. Lived on cups of black coffee and pulled all-nighters helping Anabelle piece together the final coronation details.

The princess is still staring at the flowers, listing off everything that could possibly go wrong. "What if all of this falls apart?"

"You've done an amazing job," I tell her. "We chose Windsor so our magical guests could attend more easily. If the press doesn't understand that then good riddance."

"We need the press on our side, Emrys. They have power. They make quite a nasty enemy."

She's right, but I don't think it matters. The press has made their side quite clear. Every morning, there are new headlines. Choppy, alliterative punches to the gut. Things like: DRAGGING US DOWN TO THE DARK AGES and BRUTAL BLACK DOG BITE BRINGS OUT INTEGRATION PROTESTORS.

"Well, you're not going to get stood up. Half of Parliament is already here for a tour of potential reforestation sites. And Titania plans on arriving this evening." I can't keep the strain out of my voice when I say the Faery queen's name.

The dreams have kept me up at night, yes, but it's Titania's silence that's weighed on me. The utter lack of news. With every messenger sparrow, every youngling Fae fresh from the Faery queen's court, I hold my breath and hope for something which might point to the escaped prisoner. But Queen Titania's notes come to me empty.

Every time I think of asking I hear her words: clean and hard as steel. *This is no longer your battle.*

And then there's Richard. Who pretends that everything is fine, that he didn't pull away. Who pecks me on the cheek between meetings and says he isn't afraid.

But he is. I see it in his eyes when he thinks I'm not looking. I feel it in the way he doesn't kiss me deep. There's so much space between us, even when our bodies are pressed together.

I've given up everything and it's still not enough.

"I just can't help worrying. I can't . . ." The princess shuts her eyes. The circles under them are so dark they could be ink stains.

She's pushing too hard. Just like the rest of us.

"Belle, are you all right?" I step closer to the princess. She's breathing hard, her face pink.

"F-fine." She opens her eyes. There's a smile on her lips, but I still see how they're shaking.

"You're not fine." I reach out for her shoulder. "You're about to have a panic attack. Sit down."

It happens all at once. A whirlwind of sound and shatter. The vase behind us becomes fragments by our feet.

Blossoms spread like leftover confetti, stewing in a pool of water.

Anabelle stares at the mess with wide eyes.

My hand is suspended, still halfway reaching for the princess's shoulder. All the hairs on my arm are alert, humming.

"I—it must have—" The pink in her face deepens to a sunset shade. "I must not have placed it right."

She kneels down in the puddle, starts scooping up shards and petals. I look at the corner table, note that it was far wider than the vase. All the windows in the room are closed, shielding off any wind.

I look at Anabelle, fishing fragments out of the water with panicked fingers.

"Belle . . ."

She looks up when I say her name. Eyes as messy and shiny as the puddle.

"Did *you* do that?" My question hangs, uncertain. Trying to ask without really asking. The tremble in her lip, the shattered vase . . . the barest whisper of a spell.

There are shiftings in the earth. Old powers waking.

Old powers. Like the royals' blood magic.

"I—" Anabelle blinks and stands, jeans dripping. "Of course not. I wasn't standing that close."

Had I really felt something? Or was it all just a mirage? Phantom pains of magic lost? The way an amputee still feels the twitch of his toes.

"It was an accident." The princess wipes her hands over the wet of her jeans. "That's all."

She's so convincing when she says this. So solid and sure. I look down at the puddle under my feet. It's already soaking into my ballet flats. Pieces of my reflection waver off its surface.

I stare at my arm again. The gooseflesh is gone, but the scabs from Guinevere's nails remain. Red and still soft. Barely sealed from last night's dream fall.

Manic dreams and phantom magic. Is this what the seeds of insanity feel like?

Is this how it began for Guinevere?

I try to push these thoughts away as I bend down, use what little magic there is inside me to form a mending spell and make the vase whole again.

For all of Anabelle's fretting, the coronation ball is well attended—by visitors from far and wide. Countless languages drift about the room, tickling the dreamy edges of Faery light chandeliers and nonpoisonous floral arrangements (which Eric and Jensen have checked yet again).

I stand in the corner of the room while the guests arrive. Their coats fall away, revealing tuxedoes and gowns. They grab champagne flutes, gather in herds to talk about politics and prose.

"Is that the king of Tonga?" Richard lingers beside me, studying the newest arrival—a slender man in a suit full of sashes and medals. "It is, isn't it? Oh, drat. What's his name again?"

I watch as Anabelle—who's already trotted nearly a kilometer in her heels, flitting from group to group with a graceful grin—greets the newcomer.

"I'm not even really sure where Tonga is," I tell him.

"Me neither. But don't tell anyone." His warm breath prickles the edges of my ear. Makes me wish he was closer. "Geography was one of those classes I always considered optional. I was supposed to study that massive guest folder Anabelle put together for me, but I haven't had the time."

Richard's sister is glaring at him—*Get over here now or else* spelled out by fierce brown eyes.

"Looks like I'm about to fail a foreign relations test." He sighs and places a hand on the small of my back. Lightly, lightly. These are what his touches have been since that night: careful, never too close. Torturous and aching in the worst of ways. "Care to join me?"

I know I should go with him. Stay by his side and smile until my cheeks go numb. But there's a reason I'm watching the door. Waiting.

I can't do anything about the dreams or Richard's unspoken fears. But Titania's silence—that I can fix. And I plan to, as soon as the Faery queen makes her grand entrance.

"I'm going to stay here," I say.

"I see how it is." His hand falls away. Not that it matters. His touch so barely there I can't even tell the difference.

I think of the pages in the binder I helped Anabelle put together. The one Richard was supposed to study. "His name is King Tupou."

"What would I do without you?" I don't even try to answer as he walks away.

More faces flood through the door. Page after page from Anabelle's binder brought to life. The prime minister of Canada and his wife. Lord and Lady Winfred. The president of France. Richard's mother, Queen Cecilia.

"Expecting something to happen?"

"I'm sorry?" I turn at the voice and there they are. Eyes bluer than blue. Like the aqua wash of a curled neon sign.

"You're looking at the door as if it's going to spontaneously combust." Julian Forsythe smiles, and though his face is handsome, the expression looks all wrong. Painted like a clown's grin. "Though I must say it wouldn't surprise me."

"Fortunately for you I have better things to do than blowing up doors." I look away from the politician, back to the door.

"I see you don't appreciate my humor," he says.

"That's rather difficult to do when one is called a 'monster' and a 'siren ginger.'" I keep my voice as chilled as the champagne in my glass. The one I'm gripping with whitening knuckles.

"Ah yes. The article." I hear the frown in Julian's voice, but I refuse to give him the privilege of a glance. "I was ... upset ... when I said that. After all, we'd just been attacked. Elaine is still having nightmares. She was even too upset to come tonight. Especially considering that the creatures' queen is supposed to make an appearance."

Creatures. Just the way he says it—so silky and snide—boils my insides. "As a politician I'd expect you to be a bit more careful with your words."

"We don't have to be enemies, you know," Julian says. "In fact, I'd rather not. The way I see it, you and I have a common goal."

"I highly doubt that," I manage through gritted teeth.

"We both want King Richard to make wise choices."

I know his words are a trap, but I hardly care. "What part of pushing Britain toward unlimited free energy doesn't fall into that category?"

"Perhaps I should rephrase that. We both want King Richard to make *safe* choices." His *S* uncoils long and slow, snakelike. His chin jerks up to the Faery lights. "You don't give up power to get it. That's not how the world works, Lady Emrys. I know what your queen is up to. Electricity is her only weakness and our only defense. It doesn't take a genius to solve that equation. She's using you and King Richard to strip us bare, before she moves in."

"You're wrong," I say.

The rising-star politician shrugs and takes a sip of his champagne. "I've been told that Faery queens are the cruelest creatures alive."

His comment is better timed than a summoning spell. The room changes as soon as Queen Titania enters. The hum of the mortals' conversations dies and for once the hushed awe isn't directed at me. The Faery queen doesn't even notice the hundreds of stares as she glides—cool and calm—through the door.

It's the Frithemaeg behind her who look shocked. Many of them are nobility—old Fae who haven't interacted with mortals for centuries. They file behind Titania in a V formation, eyes wider than those of a child thrust into the middle of a candy shop.

The world's most powerful men and women part for the Faery queen, keep a safe distance. I can't tell if it's from respect, fear, or both. Her path ends only steps away from Richard.

"Your Majesty." Her voice holds the same cool silver as her aura, but she curtsies nonetheless. All of her attendants do the same.

Richard bows in return. "Welcome, Queen Titania. I'm honored you could make it."

The two aren't speaking loudly, but their every word echoes through the ballroom's stillness. Even the music has stopped: the violinists gawk from their corner, too stunned by the Faes' entrance to keep playing.

Lord Winfred is the first to recover. The prime minister clears his throat and holds out his hand. "Queen Titania. I'm Laurence Winfred. The Prime Minister. It's a pleasure to finally meet you face-to-face."

Titania stares at his hand, eyes narrowed. Handshakes are reserved only for oaths in the Fae's world. I want to curse myself for forgetting to explain this to Britain's prime minister.

The Faery queen's head tilts. Slowly her hand edges out, pale fingers meeting Lord Winfred's sturdy handshake.

As soon as they touch it's as if a spell has been broken. The great silence of the room lifts. People fall back into their conversations. The violins return to their sweet-strung ballads. Waiters start to circulate again, offering silver platters of Anabelle's hand-selected delicacies.

"You'll be at the coronation, yes?" All of Lord Winfred's attentions are wrapped up in the Faery queen. His eyes are lit the same way they were when he pointed out the Faery lights.

Titania's hair glitters and shines as she nods. "I should be able to withstand London for a few hours. Given the proper precautions."

"We've allotted a special Lights-down the night before so Queen Titania can attend the ceremony," Richard reminds the prime minister. "And she'll spend most of the day with Princess Anabelle. My sister's blood magic should energize her. Help stave off the sickness."

"Good, good," Lord Winfred rumbles. "It's an important moment for integration. The press will be watching;

we must put our best foot forward."

I wait until the conversation peters down to pull Titania aside. "May I speak with you in private? Outside?"

The Faery queen nods. Her gown—woven and sparkling like dewdropped cobwebs—dances across the floor, cuts a new path to the door. Out of the Reception Room, past the row of butlers and black-suited security, all the way to the grassy stretch of the Upper Ward.

"Have you found the prisoner?" I ask once we reach the center of the green.

"Is that what this is about?" Titania's voice is as severe as her face. "I told you to forget about what you saw on the Isle of Man."

Forget. She says it so simply. As if I could just erase the terrifying white of Guinevere's eyes. As if what I discovered in the Labyrinth hasn't haunted every moment of this past fortnight.

"Please, Your Majesty."

Maybe it's the bleariness around my eyes which no amount of Anabelle's imposed makeup can hide. Or the stretch and fray of my voice. Whatever it is, Titania answers.

"There's no trace. Nothing. The scouts scoured the whole west coast, but they came up empty. They even went back to the Isle of Man. There were still traces of aura in the cell, but beyond that . . . nothing. I even had some younglings consult the Tower ravens, to see if they'd had any visions. But they were silent." The Faery queen frowns. I watch her closely, studying her profile for signs of sickness. The last time we were both here, Titania nearly died from the closeness of the city's technology.

But Lights-down is doing its job. The air out here is mountain fresh, tinged with hints of winter and the hues of Herne the Hunter's trees.

"Have you had any second thoughts about Alistair's offer?" I ask.

"Involving the Ad-hene?" Titania looks at me sharply. "You think that's a wise choice?"

"No," I answer. "But it might be our only one. Alistair's right. They've existed with the prisoners for years. Perhaps they can find trails your scouts are blind to."

"I'd prefer not to give Alistair any more power in this situation," Titania says, her voice clipped. "The Ad-hene can't be trusted."

I can't argue this point. Not as long as the only key to the Labyrinth's tunnels lies in their silver-etched arms. "You think they let the prisoner free?"

"I don't know. The Ad-hene are difficult to read. Mab

had a much better rein on them. . . . In any case, it's been nearly a fortnight and there's no disturbance we can trace back to the empty cell. I think for now we should consider the possibility that the prisoner is gone for good. Perhaps it simply wanted freedom. Or the island truly did swallow it." There's a rise in her voice which makes me think she actually believes what she's saying.

The old tensions are there, restless between us. From the days when I was a youngling and Titania a duchess. When she scrutinized my each and every move.

"A spirit that powerful doesn't just *forget* centuries in prison—" I begin.

She cuts me off. "Mab was the one who sent them there. And now she's gone. I know you worry about King Richard, but those threats are over. It's a new age. We have new things to tend to."

If I were queen, I would take the risk. Use the Ad-hene to find the fugitive's trail. But I'm not queen. I'm not even a Frithemaeg anymore.

"I'll keep the Guard on high alert." The queen's voice is strained, like that of an adult talking to a petulant child. "But for now I've done everything I can."

Or everything you're willing. "I wouldn't consider the Guard the strongest of defenses if they cannot even keep a single

Kelpie from diving into the Thames."

"The Guard was struggling even before Lady Breena died. With both of you gone, there are only younglings left. If you were truly so concerned about King Richard's safety, then perhaps you should not have abandoned your magic so lightly."

Titania's words burn. Just as she meant them to. We stand in the cinders of silence for a moment before the Faery queen turns back in the direction of the dance.

"You made your choice, Lady Emrys. Now you must live it. Go and dance. Be with your king. Let us speak no more of this. This conversation has wearied me. I think it's best if I go inside, closer to the royals' blood magic."

She glides back the way she came. Silent, silvery grace.

Maybe Titania's right. I hope she is.

But standing here on lawn of the Upper Ward, it's not a hope I have much faith in. Inside, the dancing has started. I see it perfectly through the glow of the window—dresses and tuxedos whirling like toy tops. Princess Anabelle looks like a phoenix in her gold gown—it twists and flares under the light as she dances with Lord Winfred.

And Richard. He's dancing too. His arms are around some woman I don't know, guiding her across the dance floor with bold, steady motions. A touch made of fearless.

I watch them and think of the times we danced together—barefoot in his room, classic rock blaring from Richard's turntable, swaying in the sheer togetherness of it, finding each other through vinyl notes.

Ache, ache goes my heart. Loving him through the hurt.

"It's a good night for dancing. The full moon always is."

I don't have to turn to know that Herne the Hunter stands behind me. I feel his presence the same way I feel that my right hand is attached to my wrist. The night stings with his magic. Against my will I taste some of what was once mine: cloud-strung heights, fire and grace, a palm full of worlds . . .

The ache in my heart stretches.

I turn and see him there, a darker tear of darkness through the night, held together by the smolder of his eyes. His cloak sweeps like tar over the lawn. Two horns stab and twist the air like corkscrews.

It's times like this, standing in front of the woodlord, that I understand the mortals' fear. Why they use the word *monster*.

He's not alone. Hounds gather at his feet, their fur as white and pure as first snowfall. Behind them, his horse looms.

"Herne. How do you fare?"

"As well as one can in a dying season." He growls. Ember-bright eyes blaze over my shoulder, scavenge the silhouettes of the dancers.

"You've come for the ball?" I glance back at the hounds.

"The moon calls. It's a night for the Wild Hunt."

"The princess will be disappointed," I tell him. "She was hoping to see you again."

His eyes narrow. "Four walls and frippery. That is not my world. It would be foolish for me to pretend otherwise."

We both fall quiet. I shut my eyes, try my hardest not to feel the flavors of my old powers. They pulse off the woodlord, calling to me in a way nothing else quite can.

All I'd have to do is ask Herne. Reach out for his gloved hand. One question. One motion. And all of my helplessness would disappear. I could find the prisoner's trail, take matters into my own hands. The way I once did.

I open my eyes. Herne is beside me now, his movements made of silence. He seems even taller than before, his horns twisting all the way to the northernmost star.

"I know what you are about to ask," he rumbles. "The

queen of the Fae is right, Lady Emrys. Your choice has been made. You must live it."

Go and dance. Be with your king.

I keep watching Richard. The way he waltzes. The smile on his face. I haven't seen it in such a long time. Not the way it is now, dancing so carefree in a nameless woman's arms. Wide and laughing, reaching all the way to his eyes.

I haven't seen it since the night he pulled away.

Will he ever *let* me be with him?

My throat is scratchy, dry sandpaper. "What if I did ask?"

"You think you chose wrong?"

"No," I choke out quickly. "No. I don't think that. But if I could get my powers back—just for a time—I could fix things. Make sure Richard stays safe."

"You doubt Queen Titania?"

I let my silence answer.

"I can give you your magic back," he says.

My breath trembles like butterfly wings.

"But—" Herne goes on and the beautiful insect inside dies as soon as it's born. Spins down to the pit of my stomach. "It would not come without a price. Your magic was a payment. Part of a vow. If you were to take it back, the balance of things would shift."

"And what is your price?"

"This choice must be your final one. If you take your magic back, you must never give it up again."

A second chance. A final choice. Richard or magic.

I look back through the window. The thought of giving Richard up, even for magic, is like a knife to my heart.

Richard. The one price I cannot pay. Herne knows this; of course he does. He wants to keep my power.

Cruel, cruel woodlord.

"You cannot live two lives," Herne growls on.

I try to ignore the death throes in my gut, force myself to look straight into Herne's eyes. "You were the one who told me I should never forget what I was. You *left* me some magic."

"I did." He nods.

"Why? All it does is torture me. It pulls me apart." That's not the whole truth. It pulls *us* apart. Makes me jump off boats and out of Richard's grasp. Makes Richard end our kisses with a breath full of fear.

The woodlord's eyes sear orange, too hot. He does not offer any answers, only waits to take them.

"Take the rest of it." I close my eyes, but I can still see his. Twin stars in my black vision. Relentless. "You want it to be all or nothing. Just do me a greater mercy and take it all."

Silence.

I hear the distant strain of the string quartet. Laughter which sounds like Richard's: deep and rich as oak.

The woodlord is gone when I open my eyes. Shadows flicker through the moon's gaze: streaks of black over wide white. The hounds are howling. Herne's Hunt has begun and I'm alone.

Herne the Hunter never was a creature of mercy.

I should go back inside, dance and be with my king. Instead I stand here frozen, staring through the window. Outside looking in. On mortals and Frithemaeg alike.

The night goes on, with dinner and dancing and wine from Windsor's cellars. Even the Frithemaeg start to loosen up after a few hours, blending more freely with the stunned mortals. The crowd is no longer oil and water but an estuary. Two worlds meeting and mingling. Titania even shares a dance with Richard and it seems—to my delight—that Julian Forsythe has left the ball early.

Well past the toasts—during the final dances—Richard whisks me off the floor, whispering, "We can still play hooky," in my ear.

It's almost too cold to stare at the stars, but we do it anyway. Night wind cuts like ice over Windsor Castle's rooftop, burrowing into my hair, under my skin. There's a thick cashmere blanket draped across my shoulders, and Richard's arms wrap tight around me.

We haven't been this close since the night he pulled away.

I bury deeper into his embrace. My cheek slides from his shoulder down to his chest, where I hear the bass line of his heart. Growing quicker just for me.

"Remember the last time we were on a roof? Star-gazing?" Richard asks.

"How could I forget?" I stretch my hand out, look at my ring. The metal on the band is so cold it burns. The night Richard gave me this ring was a rare moment: bright and clear. When everything was perfect.

"I think about that night a lot. Whenever I'm missing you." Richard reaches out and tucks my hand into his. "They're even brighter this time . . . ," he goes on, "the stars."

I tilt my face into the air, brave the chill for a glimpse of what Richard sees. The horizon is a swell of violet, bleeding out into the deepest clearest black. And all across this: pinpricks of pure light. I've stared at them so many times throughout my years; I know every pattern and constellation which spins across Britain's night. But every time I look up there's always something new. Some shimmer of plasma and gas I never noticed before.

Everything changes. Even the night.

Richard's right. They're brighter tonight. There's a crispness in the air which folds back, lets the light cut through and sing.

"They always shine stronger in winter," I tell him.

"When the world is dark and cold," Richard muses. "Perhaps they're trying to cheer us up a bit?"

I'd never thought of it that way. I know it's actually because far fewer stars crowd the sky. That there's more darkness closing in on the ones which remain. Stars calling out for all that the summer lost.

I like Richard's theory better.

"It does help, doesn't it?" I rest my head back against his chest, where I hear his heart keeping time to the pulse of the stars.

"Even a little light goes a long way in the dark," he says.

"Just wait until we get to the Highlands next week. The stars are unbelievable there," I tell him. "I can't wait for it. Two whole weeks of just us. No press, no Julian

Forsythe, no coronation drama."

Richard's pulse skitters like a hunted animal. Fast, fast, fast through his uneven silence.

"You still want to go, don't you?" I ask in a small voice.

"Of course!" he says quickly. "I'd be a lunatic to pass up a holiday with you."

I push away from his chest, look at him. "Then what's wrong?"

"So much is changing, Emrys. And I don't want it to. All I want is to stay on this rooftop, to be in this moment with you. Before all of this goes away."

He stares down at me, like I'm the only thing in the world he sees. My hand slides up his chest and draws him closer to me. His lips are cool, as if he's given all his warmth to me.

And I offer it back, keep kissing him. Hoping hard that he will not pull away.

He doesn't this time. My insides spark and shine. The more our lips touch, the closer our bodies meld together, the less the cold matters.

Those fingers whisper along the edge of my cheek. Slope down to trace the lips he just kissed. "I couldn't do any of this without you, you know. This world, my life . . . it's winter right now." Richard's hands are steady and warm, but his words tremble. "You're the only star I see."

Herne's right. I cannot live two lives.

I will choose Richard. As long as he'll let me.

Eight

"Why aren't you dressed yet?!" Anabelle is an unannounced flourish of blonde hair and perfection tearing through the bedroom doors.

I'm staring in the vanity mirror, frozen in front of my reflection with the remnants of last night's dream.

This dream was different from all the others. Far more terrifying. It seeps through my bones like snake venom. Keeps me from reentering a world of daylight and dresses and coronation preparations.

"Emrys!" The princess pops up beside me. "Are you sleeping?"

The dream woke me at two in the morning. I sat up with its talons latched deep inside my chest. Unable to breathe.

I sat until rose-pink dawn crept in and flushed my face. I studied my reflection. The jade light in my eyes. The tiny creases and lines which are beginning to frame them.

The bandage wound around my arm, and beneath it, five red blooms, scabs split apart while I was sleeping.

Anabelle is shaking my shoulder. "You look wretched! And you have to be in the coronation coach along with Richard in *less than an hour*! Where's the dress Helene and I put together for you?"

I blink, trying to make sense of what she's saying. Sleeplessness is stuffed like cotton in my ears.

She doesn't wait for me to answer, this princess of ever-movement. She's off into the walk-in wardrobe, rummaging through yards of silk and chiffon. Anabelle bursts out of the door almost as quick as she entered it, hands full of my coronation gown. A flowy, aqua-mint piece which falls over my body like cascades of water. Silk chiffon which spreads like the wings of a luna moth.

"Put this on." She stuffs the dress into my arms. "I'll try to do something with your hair."

"Anabelle . . ." I speak for the first time. Breaking through my voice's morning rust.

The princess grabs a silver brush from the vanity. "Do you think it should be up or down? I can't remember what we decided."

"Belle," I try again.

But she keeps talking. "We should hurry. There's no time for breakfast now! The carriage should be here at any moment!"

"ANABELLE!" I stand and the dress tumbles out of my lap, onto the floor. Anabelle stares at it, gripping the brush handle like a dagger.

"Whatever's the matter?" She looks back up at me. Eyes spice brown and wide. Just like they were in the dream.

The dream. I still feel sick about it.

I still feel Guinevere hovering by my side, her curdled breath washing over me as she mutters the same words over and over. I still feel her nails digging deep into my arm, calling up blood and pain. I still feel the heat and ash of the flaming castle billowing up from the valley, carving into my face. I still see all of them standing down in the valley. Far beyond my reach.

They were all staring up at me. Richard and Anabelle. Helene and Ferrin. Lord Winfred and Herne the Hunter. Spirits and mortals alike. All staring as Camelot's flames drew ever closer.

I couldn't reach them. There was no way down. I could only stand and watch as the flames ate everything. Caught against Ferrin's dress and wreathed through Herne's horns. Licked light into Anabelle's hair and fanned sparks across Richard's eyes.

All of them sacrificed.

This is what Guinevere said. Over and over. The phrase crooned and looped through my ears until it was void of meaning. The fire burned until it was void as well. All that remained in the valley was ash and fingers of mist. Desolation.

"I don't think we should do this," I breathe out.

Anabelle's eyes narrow. "What are you talking about?"

"The coronation."

The princess's arms fall slack to her side. "Emrys, you can't be serious!"

"I just . . . I have a feeling that something really bad is going to happen."

"Like what?"

All of them sacrificed. "I don't know. I just have this feeling."

"A feeling?" The princess stares at me like she's studying a cracked vase. Figuring out the best way to fix it. "That's all?"

I feel my heart sinking. "I had a dream."

"You're just anxious." She leans over and retrieves the

gown from the floor. "I have those kinds of dreams all of the time! Like the ones where you show up to class naked and there's an exam you never studied for and all of your teeth start falling out of your mouth. Now turn around!"

I obey, standing mannequin still as the princess undresses and redresses me like her own personal paper doll.

"Besides," Anabelle goes on as she zips the gown into place. "I don't even know if I could stop this if I tried! The press is set up and all the foreign delegates are here and Richard's already suited up. Security's tighter than ever, of course. I've been over everything with a fine-tooth comb."

She tries to tame the snarls of my hair with an actual comb. Turning an amber bird's nest into liquid lava which pools over my shoulders. I could almost believe Anabelle is using magic, the way she creates beauty from sleepless mess. It takes only minutes for her to twist my hair into a stylish bun. To use powders and brushes and paint to wipe the night's terror off my face.

I keep watching in the mirror as she pieces me together. Makes everything right. No—not right. Perfect.

Maybe I'm just going crazy. Maybe my mind is rotting

just like Guinevere's. Creating fears where there are none. Spoiling perfect moments.

"Brilliant!" Anabelle makes the final adjustments to my necklace.

"Do you think things are really going to be okay?"

"Yes." She crosses her arms over her gown: slim, cream silk with an embellished lace backing. "Of course things are going to be okay, Emrys. Why wouldn't they be?"

The empty cell. *All of them sacrificed. REMEMBER, REMEMBER.*

Gibberish. That's all it is. The words of a madwoman trying to infect me.

I won't let them.

"Let's go to the carriage." The princess hooks her arm through mine. "Richard is waiting."

The morning air above Buckingham's courtyard is fresh, capped off with a crisp autumn sky. As soon as I see Richard seated regal as a portrait in the Gold State Coach, all of my night terrors fade away. Today is Richard's day—the start of a new age. The sun is shining and there's no room for dark.

My chest feels light by the time I step into the gilded

carriage, take my seat next to him on the plush velvet cushions.

"You look beautiful, Embers." Richard smiles and slides his hand into mine, filling me with a long, blue calm.

"You look very kingly." I take in the very traditional attire of his coronation outfit: a crimson coat speckled with medals, white trousers, and high boots as black as jet. The cape of ermine and scarlet which covers it all. "And handsome, of course."

He leans in and kisses me—lips as soft as the fur lining on his cape—just as the carriage starts to jerk away. The world moves past our open windows. We canter through Buckingham's black-and-gold gates, into London's streets. A sea of mortals crowds the roped path, jostling one another for a peek into the carriage. Small flags slash the air—streaks of navy, scarlet, and white. Cheers swell through our open window, fill the carriage with the crowd's overwhelming presence. The streets are almost more crowded than they were on the day of King Edward's death.

Richard takes all of this in. His fingers tighten in mine.

"Nervous?" I ask.

"There are so many people watching." Richard gnaws his lip, looks back at me. "I don't want to screw this up."

"Anabelle's had you rehearse this nearly twenty times!"

"It's not the ceremony I'm worried about." He says this so softly I have to strain to hear over the onlookers' constant roar. "It's everything that comes after."

"Richard." My thumb brushes against his. "Think of everything you've already been through. You're a good leader. These people need you."

"Yes, but this is new. . . ."

The Gold State Coach keeps going; rattle, creak, and hoofbeat down the length of the Mall. Coasting under the last lingering leaves of the plane trees. I look out the window and all I see are faces. Old and young. Eager and cheering. Hands outstretched as if they want to seize the carriage.

Richard's people.

But are they?

I catch sight of a young man standing at the edge of the street—a static spot in the crowd—hands tucked into the front pockets of his black hoodie. His mouth is a grim line across his face as he watches us roll past. So emotionless.

Was he there that night? Holding a sign? Shouting for my demise?

My heart rattles in my throat. The crowd keeps stretching on. Smiles and paper crowns propped on children's heads. But suddenly all I can see are the marchers: their stabbing signs and savage shouts.

"Emrys?"

I blink and the crowd becomes normal again. The boy in the hoodie is long past.

"Today *is* new. Think of it as a fresh start. You'll be fine." A smile pries across my face. I wonder if Richard can see how strained it is. "We'll be fine."

He leans down, and our foreheads touch. A pinpoint of skin drawing all my focus into him the way vision tunnels through a telescope. Making him larger than life. Today he smells like spices: the exotic kind which Queen Victoria used to have shipped in from faraway places like India and China.

His lips brush mine—velvet whispering against skin— just the barest of kisses. I want to dig my fingers into his ermine cape and make the kiss last longer. Hold him like this forever.

"You're proving quite a distraction. I should be waving to the crowd," he whispers when we break apart. "Belle's going to murder me."

"Probably not. Because then she'd have to plan a

whole other coronation—"

And then I feel it. Like a stab or a lightning strike. Cutting me off midsentence.

Magic.

Not the soft, flowery freshness of the younglings' spells. Or the rich powerful tint of mahogany, soil, and shadow which flavors Herne's presence. Or even the acrid, metallic sting of the soul feeders' magic.

It's the tension of opposites. Sky and earth. Birth and death. The rust and the gleam . . . It's only a hint. Just a taste, but it's enough for me to remember. To *know* I've felt it before.

In the walls of an empty cell. On the Isle of Man.

My spine grows rigid against Richard's hand.

"What's wrong?" he asks.

"I don't know. . . ." My voice trails off.

There's a stretch of shadow as the carriage pulls through the other side of the Admirality Arch. The horses' hooves clop hollow against the pavement as they tug us past the vast expanse of Trafalgar Square. The crowd is pressed so tight I can't see any of Trafalgar Square's stones. Only its fountains are visible, twin jewels of spewing water.

But I don't stare at them long. I'm scanning faces, honing in on dim echoes of auras. Nothing. The feeling has vanished: come and gone like a wave of nausea.

I don't feel any magic. Any at all.

"Richard," I try to keep my question casual. Just in case I'm wrong. In case the paranoia is ruining even this victorious moment. "Where are the Frithemaeg?"

"Anabelle said they should be all around the convoy!" Richard has to scream for me to hear him. The crowd has gotten louder. Much louder. But they aren't just cheering anymore. There's a new franticness to their energy.

The Gold State Coach jerks to a stop. My heels dig into the floor, but my stomach feels like it's still plummeting. The royal procession is supposed to keep going. Forward. All the way to Westminster Abbey.

I look out the window. Outside is a mass of hair and wool coats and Union Jacks: moving, churning chaos. People are running in the street, up to the carriage and around it.

As hard as I try, I can't see what's making them run. There's too much panic. Too many screams.

"Richard!" I clasp his arm, make sure he's still here, next to me.

The pack and press of the crowd can't dodge our carriage anymore. People are running against it. Shaking and jolting us from our seats. I even see a horse flash by—gray and dappled. The plume on its halter tells me it was one of the beasts pulling our coach. Now loosed.

The door to our carriage bursts open: an explosion of gilt and hands. My fingers punch into Richard's arm the same way Guinevere's clenched mine. The men come anyway.

These are no random spectators—the people who climb into the carriage. They're clothed like night: black jackets and ski masks. They clamber into our compartment, fill it so only four of them feel like an army.

The whole world is shouts and kicks. Richard's mouth is moving, but I can't hear what he says. I can't stop him from being torn away.

Or am I the one being torn? Arms hook around me, pulling with raw strength. I'm twisting, raking out with my nails at anything and everything. Elbows and knees dig against foreign fabric and joints. Someone behind me tries to pin my arms together. I lift my leg up, slam my stiletto straight into the attacker's shin. His howl of pain joins the chorus of riot and noise as he lets go.

Richard is fighting too, but the odds are against him. His arms are tangled in the crimson of his cape. Masked men surround him like vultures, clawing and pecking as if he were already dead.

I throw myself at the nearest one. He shrugs me off with muscle and a grunt.

The man whose shin I mangled grabs me again. By the neck. He twists me down into the velvet seat, pins me with his weight. And I can't move, despite the rage that's blazing through me. These human muscles are weak, powerless.

Out of the corner of my eye I see one of the vulture-men pull a cloth from his pocket, press it into Richard's face. The king's arms and legs fall still. His head rolls back in a way which reminds me too much of death.

I scream his name and the masked weight over me shoves harder.

"Come on!" someone by the carriage door screams. "We're running out of time!"

"What about the ginger?" bellows the man above me.

"Our orders were to leave her!" The same mask who pressed the cloth to Richard's face is bending over me. All I can see is white terrycloth. All I can smell . . . it's sweet: fruit on the verge of rot. It yanks my thoughts back, pulls me into myself.

Fall. Tumble. Plummet.

Black.

Nine

There are no dreams. No thoughts. My mind is empty, crammed full with black, black, black.

And then there's a roar. Like a giant wave pulling fast into the shore. Or the hum of a distant motorway. The noise tugs at my heart. I'm not supposed to be here in this dark. I'm supposed to be doing something else . . . something important.

There's a crack in my eyelids. This isn't my bed. I open my eyes wider, trying to make sense of what I'm seeing. My vision reels like a drunkard kicked out of a pub. At first it's only colors. Wine-soaked burgundy, aching gold, mist and mint. Then shapes. The squares of upturned cushions. The point of my strappy heel.

And the *noise* . . . there's so much of it. Everywhere. Horses keening, the clatter of hooves. Screams and snarls. Pure, utter panic. The sounds swirl around, beat through the windows and open door of the carriage.

The carriage . . . crowds and masks and screams and . . .

Richard. Fighting against so many men. Going limp. And me, trying my hardest to save him.

The memory hits me like ice water. I jolt up, ready for whatever fight I can manage, but I'm alone in the carriage.

Outside is chaos. People running, mouths open to join one long and never-ending scream. I try to scan their faces—searching for black masks and clothes—but this seems to be the only color anyone is wearing. And then—a flash of pure, soul-sucking black.

It takes a moment to process the presence of the Black Dog in the middle of Trafalgar Square, looming under the high shine of the sun. The very air around it looks dimmer, overcast. As if the creature is a black hole swallowing all traces of light.

The beast gnashes through the crowd. Its teeth snap air, shred coats. The edges of its canines are laced with red, but still it wants more. I can feel its hunger from here: the burn in its eyes. So much like . . .

Blæc.

This is the same Black Dog which spared my life that night just weeks before. Frithemaeg fly around the soul feeder, diving like frantic swallows, trying to lash it into submission with roping spells of light. Blæc ignores them, shaking off their magic like water.

"Lady Emrys!"

I turn to see Ferrin crouched in the doorway. Her eyes are impossibly wide as she takes in the gutted carriage.

"Where's King Richard?"

I open my mouth but nothing comes out. I doubt she'd hear it anyway—Blæc has started howling. The air grows heavy with its magic: wet dog, hissing coals, and rain-flecked evenings. It soaks through my shock.

That's when I see it. Placed on the only cushion which hasn't been torn to shreds. It's in the center—where Richard's royal crest is embroidered into the velvet—just between the lion's paws and the unicorn's hooves.

A single, yellow flower.

It's a perfect specimen, petals fresh and unbruised. As if it had just been plucked. The color of sunshine. Beautiful poison.

Not just a warning this time.

Outside Blæc keeps howling. Ferrin keeps shouting questions I can't hear. I stare at the birdsfoot trefoil. Try to understand why it's here and Richard isn't.

"Lady Emrys!!" Ferrin pulls in front of me so that her wide blue eyes are the only thing I see. "The king! Where is he?"

"Gone." One word is all it takes to realize and cement

the truth. Richard is gone. And there was nothing I could do to stop it.

The Black Dog is closer now, just outside the window. The carriage shudders against its howling spells. The flower tumbles off the cushion.

"We have to get out of here. Now." The Fae's fingers tighten around my wrist. Pull.

I stumble forward, crush the birdsfoot trefoil under my heel. The carriage lurches just when we reach the door, leap out.

There's an earth-shattering crash as the carriage keels onto the road. I look over my shoulder and see the Black Dog writhing on top of what used to be the Gold State Coach. The soul feeder twists and flails over the coronation carriage—all magic and weight. Crushing it the same way my heel just demolished the flower.

How easy it is for beautiful things to be destroyed.

We run until my high heels snap and my feet bleed. It doesn't matter how far we go: Blæc's howls still cling to my ears. Visions of black masks and white terrycloth crowd my mind. And through it all, one awful, horrifying thought.

Richard is gone. Gone. Gonegonegone.

Suddenly I'm not running anymore. I'm leaning into Ferrin's sharp shoulder, staring through the wide arch of Westminster Abbey's west doors. Thousands of eyes stare back. Cameras flash and click. The Abbey comes alive with gasps, whispers.

We shouldn't have come here. I want to turn and tell the youngling this, but it's too late. We're here and the cameras are flashing—capturing every detail of my broken heels, this shattered day.

"Your Majesty!" Ferrin's call arcs into the vaulted ceiling, slices through the slants of colored window light.

Titania stands. And Anabelle with her. It's like a dream, the way they turn and walk the wrong way down the aisle. Their steps are measured, silent against the crimson carpet runner. The whole world watches them pass.

Richard's mother follows them both, her lips and steps both tighter than a letterpress. Embedded with deeply written panic. The same anxiety lurks under Anabelle's face—novels of it scrawled under pristine makeup. The princess stares at me with pleading eyes, and it's like I'm back in Herne's wood—with the damp leaves and Breena's shattered body and Anabelle asking me over and over where her brother is. And me: not knowing. Not being able to voice the horrible truth.

Gone.

This time, I have to tell her.

Ever since I unveiled to the mortals, Richard's mother has made it a point not to acknowledge my existence, much less my relationship status with her son. For months I've stood in the same room as Queen Cecilia without so much as a glance. But she's staring now, and her eyes are nuclear.

"What did you do to my son?" The church snatches and radiates her words—a fallout for the whole crowd to hear.

"Mum." Anabelle's voice is low, as solid as the stone pillars which brace the Abbey's roof. "Not here."

"Come, we'll speak in private." Titania turns and starts walking. We follow the wake of her gossamer gown like ducklings. Along the back wall, through a series of corners and doors which swing open at the Faery queen's command. Into the shelter of the Abbey's back rooms.

It's not until the final door swings shut and its lock slides into place that Ferrin speaks.

"There's a Black Dog loose in Trafalgar Square. I don't know how it evaded our perimeter. The mortals caught sight of it and panicked. We left to take care of it." The youngling pauses. I notice her chin is trembling. "When I returned to the coach the king was gone."

Her revelation falls heavy. Crowds the room. Even Titania looks stunned. It's easy to see how just this small time in London has drained her. How even with all the changes brought by Lights-down she'll have to leave the city soon, or else risk Mab's fate.

Queen Cecilia reacts first. Her eyes are still fastened to me, sharp and biting. "This is your fault. I told Richard over and over again you weren't safe but he was too infatuated to listen—"

"Mum, stop being ridiculous. You're not helping anything," Anabelle says. For someone who just had a panic attack over flower arrangements she's eerily calm. "What do they mean, Emrys?"

"They took him . . ." It doesn't feel like I'm the one talking, but it's my voice. Faint and brittle, yet still mine. "Men in masks. I tried to fight them . . ."

But I couldn't.

Weak. Powerless. Fire without flame.

Richard. Gone.

"Men?" Titania's eyebrows dive into a silver V. "Mortals did this?"

Mortals. They were mortals, weren't they? The thought startles me. I hadn't felt any magic in their fight. Their touch. If they'd had any powers, they wouldn't have used chemicals and cloth.

But Blæc. The dreams. The twinge of magic I felt just seconds before the world fell into hell . . . those couldn't have been just a coincidence.

Could they?

The door at Queen Titania's back shudders with the pounding of fists. The handle twists and when that doesn't give way there's a fierce yell. "PROTECTION COMMAND! OPEN THE DOOR!"

"I felt magic"—I stumble over my words—"just before they took him . . . before the Black Dog appeared."

"Ferrin. Stay here." The Faery queen strides across the room, toward the many-paned windows. The glass warps when she draws close, melting around the contours of her body. "I'll go to Trafalgar Square with the rest of the Guard. Do what I can."

The door groans. Titania is all the way through the window when the old lock splinters. The royals' bodyguards pile into the room. There are two I recognize: Jensen and Eric. But even more crowd behind, hands clenched around their weapons. Not guns, but stun guns. The entire room is alight—singeing with bastardly blue light, razing electricity.

Every single, crackling edge of every stun gun is aimed at Ferrin.

"Your Majesties." Jensen sidesteps to Richard's sister and mother. "There's been a security breach. We need you both to come with us."

All of them are dressed in black. The sight catches me. I can't stop looking at the sapphire stun guns, how Eric has his leveled straight between Ferrin's blue eyes, ready to strike. Electricity: the only weapon a mortal has against a Fae.

It's almost as if they planned for this to happen.

The charges aren't touching her, but they're close enough to feed the youngling's sickness. Ferrin doubles over, hands folded over her stomach, where nausea is about to overflow.

Queen Cecilia's arm hooks into her daughter's. "Let's go, dear."

Anabelle stays rooted next to me, swallowing the scene. The buzz of a dozen stun guns dances like fireflies in her eyes. "Officer Jensen, what's going on?"

"Your Highness, your brother has disappeared from the coronation coach. We have reason to believe magical creatures were involved—"

"You think *we* did this?" Ferrin breaks in, panting

through her illness. "We're King Richard's Frithemaeg! We're sworn to protect him!"

"Quiet!" Eric snaps at the Fae and shoves his stun gun closer. Beads of sweat dew her brow as she fights the growing sick.

Jensen keeps speaking as if nothing happened. "Our orders are to take you and your mother to a safe location."

Our orders. His words make the hairs on the back of my neck stand alert. That's what the masked man had said, standing over me in the coronation coach.

I try to feel for magic, any trace of it. But I sense nothing. These men are clean. Then again, so were the men behind the masks. Just because I don't feel it, doesn't mean it isn't there. There's so much I can't sense anymore . . . now that I'm mortal.

But I do feel Ferrin's aura tensing, rallying itself against the stun gun charges, piecing together a spell.

"Ferrin," I say her name, my voice heavy with warning.

"Put the guns away." None of the anxiety I saw beneath Anabelle's makeup comes through her voice as she looks at Eric. "Ferrin is my Frithemaeg. My guard. Same as you are."

"Apologies, Your Highness, but it's not your call," Jensen tells her firmly.

Across the room Ferrin's magic flares, brimming almost over the edge.

"Ferrin, don't! You'll only make it worse," I say before she can release the spell. I turn to Jensen, look straight into his eyes. Try to remember if I've seen them before under a ski mask. They're a plain, unmemorable color. "Ferrin will stay. I go with you."

"Of course you're coming!" Anabelle says. "Why wouldn't you?"

The bodyguard in front of us clears his throat. His stare slides out of mine, refusing to look at me when he says these words, "Princess, Lady Emrys was in the same coach when the king disappeared."

"You think she was a part of this?" Anabelle pauses, takes the whole room in—the buzzing lights and bristling black suits—and steps closer to me, twisting her free hand into mine. "You're wrong. Emrys would *never* do anything to hurt Richard. Never."

"Your Majesty—these creatures—they're not like us." It's Eric who's speaking this time. He's still holding the stun gun high, glaring at Ferrin's flawless snowflake skin through its neon blue sear. "They have powers of persuasion. They can make you believe what they want."

"Emrys wouldn't. She wouldn't." With every steel-coated word she says, the princess grips my hand tighter. Her touch holds all of the room's tension, the clash of electricity and magic, building and warring and ready to explode. "She even tried to get me to stop the coronation this morning!"

"Is that so?" Jensen's eyes flick across the room, skate over Eric and the others. I don't need magic to read the meanings behind their glances. The subtle change in their body movement. Eric's stun gun is still latched toward Ferrin, but his eyes drift toward me. Glint suspicion.

I stare back—eyes green and just as glinting.

"Enough of this, Anabelle." Queen Cecilia is still trying to reel her daughter across the room. "I've lost a husband and a son to these creatures. I'm not going to lose you too. Let's go with these officers."

Anabelle jerks her arm out of her mother's and sidles even closer to me. The edges of our dresses—mint silk and white—pool together on the floor. "I go with Emrys or I don't go at all."

Jensen's unremarkable eyes study me—all questions and calculations. Trying to judge the risk. The reward.

"Fine," he says, and waves both of us forward. "Let's go."

The room unwinds all at once. Stun guns fall to officers' sides; Ferrin sighs with relief and sick. Anabelle's grip loosens in mine, but she keeps holding on as the tide of officers pulls us out the door. I follow, dragged and straggling like seaweed, into the unknown.

Ten

Anabelle doesn't let go of my hand. Her grip is just tight enough to make my fingers tingle. By the time we reach the underground bunker I can't feel anything at all. Yet while my flesh grows numb, my insides become anything but. They're churning and undone. Jolted by each and every pothole the Protection Command officers speed over in their black Jaguar.

My thoughts are on fire, gathering all the pieces of this day, trying to arrange them in a way which makes sense. Yellow flowers. Blood dripping from Blæc's teeth. Masks and men. *Our orders.* That sharp taste of magic in the crowd.

No matter how hard I try, the pieces don't fit. If it was a magical creature which wanted to take the king, then why wouldn't it show itself in full force? Why bother with mortals in masks? And if it was humans—the M.A.F. or some other group—then how was it I felt that magic?

How did they capture and control a creature as fierce as Blæc?

Which leaves me with the same awful questions as before: Who would take Richard? And why was I left behind?

Jensen leads us through the thick steel doors. The bunker is so well pieced together I'd never even suspect it was underground. The room Anabelle, Queen Cecilia, and I end up in has some of the same fineries as the palace: settees and plush rugs. An oak table with a tea tray offering. There's even a television screen half the size of the wall it hangs on.

Ferrin followed us here, as I knew she would. The youngling's outline appears, as wavering as a desert mirage, as she sheds a layer of her veiling spell. Allowing only me to see her, so I know she hasn't abandoned her post.

"Make yourself comfortable, Your Majesties." Jensen gestures to the closest seat. "We're going to be here for a while. I'll have Rita bring all of you a change of clothes."

Richard's mother doesn't sit down. She takes a few steps into the bunker and turns to Jensen, her movements snapping and precise. "What's being done to find my son?"

Jensen's mouth drops open; his eyes dart over to me. In them I see hesitance—some of Eric's fear—as if my presence is the only reason he's staying silent. "Everything we can, Your Majesty. Officer Black will stay here with you. If I hear anything, I'll send him an update."

All three of us watch as Jensen walks out. Eric stares back from his post by the door. His arms are crossed over his chest, so both of his holsters are in easy reach: stun gun and real gun.

I feel him watching, deciding which one he would use on me. If it came to it.

The princess lets go of my hand and moves over to the settee. She falls into the cushion, her fingers pinching the bridge of her delicate nose. Holding everything together.

It's too late for me. The numb is wearing off and I'm in fragments. Like the coronation carriage. Like the vase at Windsor. Splintered, jagged, everywhere and nowhere all at once.

"Is this what you wanted?" Queen Cecilia has no place else to aim her wasteland eyes and words. "Was your little summer fling worth this?"

Anabelle leans forward, hair veiling her face. Her fingers vise her head now, as if she's fighting back a headache. "Mum, *stop*. For the last time, Emrys didn't do this."

But I did. Didn't I? Richard's mother is right. This *is* my fault, in so many ways. If I'd never unveiled myself to

Richard in the first place, never fallen in love, never sacrificed my magic . . .

I could have stopped the men in the carriage with a flick of my palm.

I could have saved him.

"Then who did?" Queen Cecilia asks at me, point-blank.

"I don't know." I make a point to look at Eric as I say this and take a seat beside the princess. "None of this makes any sense. . . ."

Was it magic or mortal that stole Richard?

Or both?

Both is what the signs point to. But that's impossible. How could there be an immortal-human alliance we knew nothing about? And why would they want to kidnap Richard, a leader who's giving his life to champion their success?

There has to be a way this puzzle fits together. There has to be some piece I'm missing.

Anabelle's question is tight and tamped. "Do you think Queen Titania will find something?"

"Of course," I answer. She has to. That magic was too distinct. There's no way I imagined it. No way it wouldn't leave a trail for a Fae as powerful and seasoned as Titania.

"She'll find a trail. She'll get him back."

She has to. Because she's the only one who can.

Time feels like an impossibility down here in this bunker. I don't know if hours or days have passed under these lights. I only know that the pot of tea has long stopped steaming and Anabelle is slouched asleep against my shoulder. Queen Cecilia has drifted off as well. Even Ferrin is quiet and wordless, static in her potted-palm corner.

I'm tired too, but shutting my eyes is impossible. I can't take the dreams. Not now. Instead I stare at the television's dead screen and try not to wonder what's happening to Richard.

"Lady Emrys."

My head snaps up to find Queen Titania standing in the middle of the room. There's less shine than usual radiating from her hair, her skin—the fluorescent bulbs wash her out, reveal just how much London's technology has been eating through her. She's been away from Anabelle's blood magic for too long: swiftly waning. If she doesn't leave for the Highlands soon, the nausea in her stomach will become bloody lungs. And then . . .

Madness.

Hundreds of questions start to climb up my throat.

But then I see Eric watching from his chair, hands lingering close to his holsters.

"I can't stay long, even with Anabelle here," Titania says. "I don't have much energy left and the veiling spell is taking its toll, but I wanted to tell you in person."

Tell me what? I swallow the question back. Now I know how Richard felt all those times I unveiled myself to only him.

The thought of him is agony and lightning in my heart.

"I went to Trafalgar Square. Did a thorough sweep with the rest of the Guard and questioned the Black Dog. The creature was delirious with hunger. The crowd drew it out. It's little wonder this one braved broad daylight; it hasn't fed in weeks."

I frown, remembering the savageness which rolled down Blæc's breath. How the dog turned away, let me live. It seemed like a miracle at the time, but was it something different . . . something more?

If the Black Dog was simply hungry, why break Titania's laws in the most visible place? And why was there only one? How did it get through the parade's intense security measures without detection? The path had been well guarded, by both Fae and mortal.

More puzzle pieces. Refusing to fit.

"I searched for traces of the magic you say you felt . . ." The queen's phrase hangs by a thread. "There's no trail, Lady Emrys. There's . . . nothing. Trafalgar Square is clean."

Nothing. No trail. Gone.

"That's impossible." The whisper pulls out of me before I can catch it.

"What was that?" Eric sits up, scanning the room. They gloss over Titania and Ferrin without a hitch, land on me again. His fingers are too close to both weapons.

"No need to be so jumpy." I try to smile at him and nod down to where Anabelle leans against my shoulder. "Do you think you can get us some fresh tea? Belle will want some when she wakes up."

The officer frowns; his eyes make another lengthy scan of the room. Finally he stands and stretches his legs. The right one seems extra stiff. He stilts on it to the door. "Anything else, *Lady* Emrys?"

I shake my head, wait for him to leave. As soon as I'm certain he's gone I cut back to Titania. "That's impossible. You didn't look hard enough."

"It's entirely possible, if *men* took Richard." Titania's eyes flash and freeze. "There's no magic to trace."

"But I *felt* it. . . ."

"There was nothing, Lady Emrys."

Nothing. Phantom pains. Like the twinge I felt just before the broken vase. Is it possible my mind constructed this one too? That the madness raging in my dreams every night has slipped into my waking?

"You say it was men who took him. Then it was men. Mortals," Titania says firmly.

"So search for mortals then. The Guard knows Richard's aura."

"Whoever executed this worked swiftly. Used the panic of the crowd to cover their tracks. Any trail Richard's aura might have left is lost. . . . It's like searching for a needle in a haystack."

Anabelle groans, tugged from her heavy sleep by our rising voices. Her face is smeared in zebra-stripe makeup and flushed as she takes in the sight of Titania. Queen Cecilia slumbers beside her, unmoved.

"What are you saying?" I bring myself eye level with the Faery queen, so she's no longer looking down her nose at me. This close I can see the awful pale under her skin, jewels of sweat clinging to her hairline. "You're not even going to try?"

"If this truly is the work of mortals, then there's not much the Frithemaeg can do," she says.

"This is your JOB. Your DUTY!"

Spit flies from my mouth, mists over Titania's regal features. But the Faery queen doesn't even blink. Her face is set now, so beautiful and unyielding it might as well have been chipped out of marble by Michelangelo himself. "The Guard's *duty* is to protect the crown from supernatural harm. What the mortals decide to do to each other is their own concern."

I'm staring, slack-jawed. Trying to make sense of her words. "You can't be serious . . ."

"Do you not understand how stretched we are, Lady Emrys? I'm exhausting the Guard enough as it is with their regular duties."

"So you can't find Richard? Or you won't?" My questions scathe the air like acid.

"I am the Queen of the Frithemaeg, Emrys Léoflic. You'd do best not to forget that." Her eyes flash like a blade—dangerous. Something behind them wavers, reminds me of Mab.

There's a crash: china, silver, and too hot tea. I look to find Eric standing in the doorway. A fresh tea tray lies in ruins at his feet. He's holding his stun gun instead.

"Who are you talking to?" He lurches forward, slashing the crackling blue at the air in front of me.

It's a blind-luck hit, straight into Queen Titania's arm. The Faery queen's skin is so paper-thin I can almost see the electricity lancing through her, writhing like veins. Already weakened by so many hours in the city—this charge is enough to throw her to the ground. It peels back layers of her magic and strength like an onion's skin.

Even Eric looks shocked when he finally sees his victim—stripped so completely of her veiling spell. The Queen of the Fae is undone, hair loosed on the floor like a spilled crucible of silver. Every last sign of strength sapped from her willowy limbs.

"I have a code fifteen!" He screams at the doorway. "We've been breached!"

"What the hell did you just do?" I yell.

"Stand back!" Eric waves the charge at me.

I inch closer to Titania anyway.

She's not dead. It takes far more than that to unmake an immortal as old and powerful as the Faery queen. But it's not death I'm worried about. It's the fringes of insanity which could be creeping up, taking over the Faery queen as we speak. Direct contact with so much electricity could be enough to push her over the edge—unbind her into a truly terrible creature of free magic. Loosed from all control or reason. A creature none of us in this bunker would survive.

The stun gun hums blue in Eric's hand. He's looking down at the Faery queen as if she's a cobra, about to strike at any minute.

"Put that away," I tell him.

"What? So you can hex me?" he growls. "You might have been able to fool King Richard, but not all of us mortals are so gullible."

The room is full: doorway choked with security personnel. Anabelle is still frozen. Queen Cecilia is awake and staring, far too stunned to demand an explanation. Ferrin lurks unseen by the brick wall, watching the stun gun, winding her magic tight.

"This is Queen Titania. She's an ally. If you stun her again, you could take away any semblance of humanity she has," I say slowly. "If that happens, we're all dead."

Eric doesn't back away. The stun gun is still raised high, like a peasant's pitchfork. "If she's such an ally, then why is she sneaking around?"

"Would you have let her in otherwise?" I keep my eye locked carefully on the electric current. I can't let it touch

Titania again. "Put the stun gun down. We can talk about this."

"Hold your position, Officer Black!" Jensen calls from the room's entrance, where almost a dozen armed officers have watched the scene unfold.

"Stop fighting!" Anabelle stands next to me. "This is all stupid. The Frithemaeg aren't our enemy. None of this is going to bring Richard back!"

She might as well be chucking a pebble into the ocean. This room—it's like watching a lit fuse, waiting for the moment when the spark hits. Any little motion, any misplaced word could set it off.

What went wrong? Why are we standing here pointing glares and stun guns at each other when Richard is missing?

Because Richard is the thread. The bridge between two vast and unmet worlds. He was the center and without him things fall apart.

Titania's eyes blink. The look in them is on edge, almost feral. Those silver irises slide to where Eric is arched above her. They lock onto the stun gun, glint a wildness which fills me with fear.

Fear for Eric. Fear for all of us.

The Faery queen starts to rise and Eric's stun gun fist starts to fall. My hands are already on the silver tea tray, the one with the pot of cold water. I swing it hard into the frantic guard's head. The stun gun drops like a shocked fly onto the rug, next to a crumpled Eric.

Richard's mother lets out a long, wild scream. Jensen and his team pour into the room. I'm up and over the coffee table, grabbing Queen Titania. The breadth, the magnitude of her power almost bowls me over when my fingers grip her shoulder. Her eyes are wild, confused as I shove her to where Ferrin is crouched, watching the scene unfold.

"Get Queen Titania to the Highlands *NOW!*" I shout.

The youngling doesn't hesitate. She grabs the dazed queen's hand and the pair vanishes. There and gone. Just like Richard.

Hands grip my own shoulders, fingers dig tight into my muscle, spin me around. There are at least three men grabbing me.

"Take her to the interrogation room!" I hear Jensen yell.

"What are you doing?!" Anabelle screams on the other side of the coffee table. "Let her go!"

The men are dragging me, past Eric's unconscious form, through the door.

How did this all go so wrong?

"STOP!"

I never knew a girl as petite as Anabelle could roar so loud. The sound bursts through the bunker with the power of a collapsing star.

And everything stops. Jensen stands in the doorway, his face frozen mid-yell, adrenaline and anger flushing red across his cheeks. The men holding me are suspended—steps hanging just inches above the ground. Even the stun guns are still, their charges like portraits of blue lightning.

The last time I saw a room so still was at Windsor Palace, when Breena shouted *"Stillaþ"* and the mortals got caught up in her magic like mosquitoes in amber. There's magic here too—only it's not mine or Ferrin's or Titania's.

There's only one other person in this room who carries magic in their veins. . . .

"Oh shit. Shit. Shit. Shit." Annabelle's standing on the coffee table, among the ruins of the original tray, looking over the room of mannequin men.

She looks straight at me. "It actually worked."

The current in the air. The tingle on my skin. The princess's white face. There's no mistaking it this time.

The blood magic is awake.

Somehow Princess Anabelle managed to tap into the long-dormant magic in her blood. Her birthright passed all the way down from King Arthur's age. Magic not even the Fae could ever fully understand. Magic she's not even supposed to be able to use.

However she managed to cast it, her spell won't last long. I can already feel it fading. Soon the royals' Protection Command will be thawed and moving, ready to drag me back to the interrogation room.

"I have to go, Belle." I start worming my way out of my captors' grips. "I'm going to get Richard back."

"I know. I'm coming with you." The princess hops off the table, picks her way through immobilized men and teapot shards. She pauses by the cushion where Queen Cecilia is curled up, motionless. "Sorry, Mum. I'll be back."

I want to argue; I want to tell her she's safer here. But the buzz of her magic still edges my teeth, fills my stomach with dread. If I leave her here with the mortals, without *knowing* what the power inside her is capable of . . .

"Besides." Anabelle weaves her way over to a frozen, outraged Jensen. Fishes a pair of silver keys from his pocket. "Someone has to drive."

Eleven

London's streets lash by my window. Pubs, double-decker buses, and old gas lampstands blur into a single streak of color. The edge of my seat belt bites into my palms; I clutch its nylon for dear life. I thought I'd adjusted to cars—but it seems that's only when Anabelle isn't driving.

Her knuckles grip the steering wheel like iron. She hunches forward in her seat, foot pressed all the way down on the gas pedal. My heart stops with every red light we burst through. It's nothing short of a miracle that we haven't been noticed by all the police cars roaming the streets. Though that could be because Anabelle flipped our own blue lights on as soon as she revved the engine.

It reminds me of the day King Edward died, all of these flashing blue lights and neon yellow vests. The throngs of humanity in the streets. Only this crowd isn't sad or shuffling. There are no tears on their faces. The glimpses I do catch are snapshots of raw, animal emotion. Anger. Fear. Rage.

Their eyes widen as the Jaguar wheels onto the side-walk. As they scatter, Anabelle swears and jerks the car back toward the street, narrowly clipping the door of a phone booth.

"If we're going to find Richard, then we have to be in one piece to do it!" My hands twist and strangle the seat belt.

"Sorry!" The princess says, foot still punching hard into the gas pedal. "It's not like I actually drive these things a lot."

"I noticed," I mutter under my breath.

A voice crackles out of the lights and wires of the car's dashboard. "The bunker has been compromised. Two packages are missing and believed to be in a government-issued Jaguar."

"They're looking for us." Anabelle's voice is grim as the radio rattles off our license plate number. "Where do we go?"

I hadn't thought this far ahead. This whole day has been a blur, a horrible dream. It just now feels like I'm waking up, facing the reality of it all. In the space of a few hours my entire world has crumbled. I'd put all bets on Titania, but Julian Forsythe was right: Faery queens are cruel creatures. My lifetimes of service to the Guard,

Richard's sleepless weeks lobbying for her survival—none of these mattered to Titania. She folded when we needed her most.

And now what do I have?

An empty hand.

I lost Richard. I lost it all.

And yet, somehow, I'm not surprised. I knew it was coming. I dreamt it.

I look down at the bandage on my arm. The wound which keeps breaking open every night, no matter how tight I bind the gauze. As if the ragged nails Guinevere sinks into my arm every nightmare are real . . .

"You found it. But blind eyes still need to see," I whisper the *faagailagh's* words back to myself.

It seems Guinevere's mind isn't as far gone as Alistair might have me think. She knows something.

There's only one place I'm going to find answers, and it's not in London. It's in the bowels of the deepest, darkest place I'd hoped never to see again.

It's time to return to the Labyrinth.

Anabelle's driving doesn't improve in the countryside. Our tires shred gravel and dirt, coasting over potholes and stripping leaves off endless rows of hedges.

I felt safer on the Kelpie.

It's dark by the time we reach the coast. The sleepy town we pull into is lit up like a Christmas village: warm-glow windows and sealed doors. It's still long before midnight, but the streets are empty. Long stretches of power lines and lonely storefronts. The feel of the sea rides on the air: life and death and salt and gray.

With a twist of Anabelle's wrist the Jaguar's engine dies. We both sit for a moment, soaking in the heat of the car. For the first time in a day I feel like I can breathe.

I look over at the princess. Lion-mane hair, eyes crusted with day-old makeup. Her fingers are still wrapped tight around the steering wheel. "Belle. What you did back there . . . in the bunker. To those men . . . You did it before. Didn't you? At Windsor. With the flower vase."

"I—" Some color bleeds back into her face. "Yes. But it was an accident. I didn't mean to break it."

"But why did you hide it?" I ask.

Anabelle takes a deep breath. She's staring out the windshield at a pair of seagulls feasting on a pile of fried fish wrapped in newspaper. "Richard made me promise not to tell."

When she says his name my stomach feels gutted.

"It's been happening to him too." She keeps talking. Still staring at the bedraggled, huddled birds. "Ever since the first Lights-down. It's just been little accidents. I had an argument with Mum while we were addressing coronation invitations and the calligraphy ink exploded everywhere. And then the vase . . ."

My throat squeezes tight. I think of all the times we were together. All the times he stayed quiet . . . "Why? Why didn't he tell me?"

"He didn't want to worry you. And he was afraid . . ." Her voice wilts. "He was afraid you would get hurt."

I am hurt. Hurt that something so big, so important was happening to Richard. That the rift of secrets between us was so much larger than I realized.

What else didn't he tell me?

Will I ever have the chance to find out?

"At first I thought it was hiccups: random spurts. But then I realized it happened whenever I got upset. I felt it rising in Westminster Abbey and the bunker. I was holding it back, until Protection Command started taking you away," Anabelle says. "That was the first time I actually *tried* to use it."

"Don't." My eyes bore straight into the princess's. "Don't try it again."

"But—"

"Magic isn't something you play with." I cut her off. "It's wild. Dangerous. If you don't know what you're doing, it can go very, very wrong."

I know what I'm saying is harsh, but I'm not thinking straight. My thoughts are tangled, looping me back through the past. Reminding me how—ages and ages ago—the mortals gleaned the Fae's magic and made it their own. They twisted it into dozens of variations, both brilliant and brutal. Many, many lives were destroyed by such infinite power in such finite hands.

There were very few humans strong enough to bear the burden of magic. In the end, it even ruined King Arthur.

A lone streetlight slants through the tinted windshield, wraps around the princess like a halo. Something about how harsh it is against her face shows me just how young she is.

Just seventeen. How easy it is for me to forget. Despite her brave, steel-hide moments and her almost supernatural ability to have everything perfect, Anabelle is still a fragile thing. A glass ballerina, one fall from cracking.

She doesn't—*can't*—know the power she wields. Not yet.

"I'm sorry," I say slowly. "I didn't mean to yell. It's just . . . it's very important that you keep things under control. If you don't, a lot of people could get hurt.

"I want you to promise me you won't use it. Even if we find ourselves in a bad situation," I add, "try to hold it back, like you did in the bunker. We'll find another way."

Anabelle tears her eyes from mine.

"Promise," I say again, my voice stretched.

The princess's words come out quiet. "I promise."

"We'll get this sorted. We'll find Richard," I tell her.

"What are we doing here?" Anabelle nods out into the ghost village, where the sign for the White Dragon Pub swings back and forth in the breeze.

"We're going to the Isle of Man. There's a sailboat docked on the edge of town. Ferrin and Lydia used it to take me there last time."

"How is this going to help us find Richard?"

"It's—complicated."

"Then uncomplicate it." Anabelle brings her forehead down onto the steering wheel. "I'm going a little bit insane here. My brother has just been kidnapped and I've been spewing magic like a busted fire hydrant. Plus I've just driven a stolen car all the way across the bloody country. I just need something. *Anything.*"

"Look, I know this will sound . . . strange. But that dream I told you about this morning. I think someone *sent* it to me. They were trying to warn me that this was going to happen."

"And this someone is on the Isle of Man?"

"Under it. In a prison for Fae."

"Wait—" The princess sits up straight in her seat. "What? A prison?"

"There's a maze of tunnels under the island. Mab used it to trap her enemies and anyone she disliked." I give her the short version. I'm starting to squirm against the leather seat, watch the road into town for headlights. We shouldn't stay here too much longer.

"And you think one of these prisoners has answers?" Anabelle presses. "You think they know where Richard is?"

I can only hope this trip is something more than grasping at straws and dreams.

"Something like that. We should get going."

"Right then." Anabelle flips down the Jaguar's vanity mirror and rakes her hair out of her face, back into a tight coil. She smudges sparkle and kohl from her eyes. A few flicks and swishes and she's a clean slate again. Repelling chaos like a stainproof tablecloth.

She finishes, turns, and looks at me. Ready. "Let's go sailing."

Twelve

The Ad-hene are waiting.

Sixteen shadows, sixteen flares of silver light winking over the iron-dark waves. Calling us to their jagged coastline. The scar-marks draw closer with the current and Anabelle's secondary-school sailing skills. With every wave which brings us in to shore, I feel a new layer of their uniform magic. Earthy, raw, yearning.

The last feeling must be mine, I realize, as the princess ties the boat off. A yearning for lost things, as empty and cold as the wind licking these stones. The steps have already been sculpted for us. As uneven and toothy as wolf fangs.

"I'm not going to lie," Anabelle whispers as we start our climb toward the Ad-hene's flickering lights. "I'm already a little creeped out."

"Let me do the talking." I push ahead of her.

Alistair stands at the front of the group. Half-lidded and head tilted, as if he's about to nod off into dreams.

But sharp black eyes cut behind those lids: quick and questioning.

"Lady Emrys. We were not expecting you. Titania sent no sparrow."

I stare down the queue of scar-lights. The exact same pattern—tangling and worming, silver and changing—sixteen times. Most of the Ad-hene's faces are too far or dark to see. But a certain pair of eyes snares mine.

Kieran. He's standing just behind Alistair, second in line. Watching me the way he did when we last stood on this cliff. Something about his stare, just behind its gray, winter sky hardness, makes me look away.

I clear my throat, find my voice. "This is quite a welcome for an unexpected visit."

"Your auras called to us, from across the sea. We do not get many visitors." Alistair's dark eyes slide over my shoulder, where Anabelle stands on her tiptoes, trying to watch without being watched. "You—"

Fifteen other gazes shift, lock onto the princess in a single motion. Kieran's eyes narrow—there's a flicker in them I can't fully read. Surprise, familiarity, then nothing.

They stare and stare at her. Anabelle—the princess who handles paparazzi and press with such cool—starts to squirm. "Me?"

"You're not a Frithemaeg." Alistair lets the observation linger on the air.

"Guess that makes two of us," the princess quips back.

"But you're not completely mortal either. Nor a *faagailagh*."

"Of course I'm mortal." Anabelle shivers. "Now if we could please stop talking about *fitzgathers* or whatever, and get on to finding my brother that would be bloody lovely."

"Your brother?" The leader of the Ad-hene blinks. His stare flows back to me: smooth, powerful, dark as a deep sea current. "Why are you here, Lady Emrys?"

"I wish to revisit the Corridor of the Forgotten," I tell him. "To speak with the prisoner there."

Alistair turns to the sheer cliff-face, breaks it apart with a single spell. The stones split open and stale air sighs out of the Labyrinth. It whispers past my cheeks, laced with the strange spice of the Ad-hene's magic. It's bitter and biting, like ground pepper.

"Follow us," the leader of the Ad-hene says before he blends into the dark of the tunnels. The Manx spirits move as one being, swift and rushing. Anabelle and I have to run to keep up with the sixteen scar-lights.

Despite the extra shine of the Ad-hene's marks, the Labyrinth feels even darker now, its tunnels more winding.

As if all this time I've been away, it's been growing, sinking deeper into the earth. We turn and twist together, footsteps echoing. The sound reminds me of the throb under Richard's chest: *bum, bum, beat, beat.*

Richard. I try not to think about him because every time I do it's like a lance to my heart. Sharp and stabbing.

But once the thoughts start, no matter how fleeting (the memory of his voice, the feel of his hair under my fingertips, that smile), they will not stop. They tear through my soul like an avalanche.

Where is he now? Is the blood magic rising, burning in his veins? Is he seeing only darkness too?

"It's a lost cause, talking to Guinevere." It's not until Kieran speaks that I realize he's beside me. Matching me step for step. "Her mind is scrambled. Gone."

"Wait," Anabelle stumbles. "Did you say Guinevere? Guinevere as in the queen who cheated on King Arthur with his best knight Lancelot and single-handedly destroyed Camelot?"

"Not quite single-handedly . . . ," I start to say when Alistair halts. The glow on his arm grows unbearably bright. It strips everything bare, reveals cells, twisted runes, and solid bars. The ruin and rot of this dark place.

Guinevere is waiting for us. Her face is so small—so

birdlike and wasted—it fits easily through the gaps in the bars. That needle-point chin is tilted to the side.

I stop and stare at this woman. The only other creature in the world like me. A *faagailagh*. The only other soul who could possibly understand how I'm suspended, dangling so cruelly between these two races. Who knows what it's like to lose the love of her life.

"Step, step! Pitter, patter!" She mewls like a kitten. One hand lets go of the bars, stretches out toward me. "Up, down. To, fro."

I lick my lips. "Lady Guinevere."

At the sound of her name, the former Fae cackles. "Ladies-in-waiting! There's more than enough. One lady waiting. Waiting a long, long time!"

"Holy . . . That's Guinevere?" Anabelle's face is ghastly under Alistair's worming light. "She's . . . old."

Guinevere's laugh dies. Her next words are a reverent hush. "The sister of a king. Round and round it goes. In circles. Across the sea and back again."

"How does she know who I am? She can't even see me." The princess shudders. At the same time I move closer to the bars, keeping a careful eye on those yellowed nails.

"I found the dreams," I tell her.

The hallway falls eerily quiet. Sixteen scars fight and

flare against the dark—showing me how Guinevere's mouth is shut, lips drawn pencil thin to hide rotting teeth. Her one hand is tight against the bars and the other keeps pointing. Accusing.

"You knew what was going to happen. You tried to warn me. . . ." I watch the *faagailagh*'s face carefully. Those wrinkles and many folds of splotched skin stay still.

"Where is he?" I reach out, grip the same bars as Guinevere. I force myself to look straight into her eyes. Lose myself in their blank, blizzard white. "Where's Richard?"

Her free hand drifts down to my breastbone, two nails tapping lightly against my skin. "There's no map like the heart."

"Where is he?" I ask again, trying my hardest not to flinch away. "Who took him? You *know!* You have to know!"

"*You* know!" Guinevere rasps my own words back at me: a shriveled echo. "Remember! Remember!"

I don't care that Guinevere's nails are still creased against my chest, or that it's my face against the bars now. Just a breath away from hers. I only care that Richard is gone.

"Tell me!" I'm screaming. "Who took him? Where is he?"

The *faagailagh*'s mouth opens, but then her eyes bulge wide. A sound rises from her throat like a dog wheezing against a leash. A tongue lolls over her lips, purple and swollen.

I watch her and feel a strange, distant twinge deep in my chest. Magic.

The same magic I felt in the cell just a few meters away from here. That mingle of old and new. The same magic I felt in Trafalgar Square before the world went to hell . . .

Small bubbles spill from the edges of Guinevere's lips, so much like sea foam. Her voice rasps, managing only a few broken syllables before it cuts off altogether.

"What's happening to her?" Anabelle gasps behind me.

"It's a spell. . . ." My throat feels thick. Guinevere is still thrashing in her cell, like a stranded fish desperate to get back into water. "Someone's keeping her quiet."

I turn to the lights. The Ad-hene are all queued along the back wall: silent watchers. Both handsome and grotesque. Like gargoyles. Unmoved.

Alistair is the stillest, that weary look set on his alabaster face as he watches the cell. "Many times we've tried to ask her about the escape. Every time she chokes up like this."

Guinevere bends double in her cell, like a marionette cut from its strings. Brittle hair sweeps the bare floor, gathering dust. The once-Fae starts to cough—the sound is almost as rough as a Black Dog's howl.

"Can't you help her?" Anabelle asks. "There must be some way to lift the spell."

"For one with so much magic in her veins you do not seem well versed in it." The princess stiffens, but Alistair plods on, unfazed. "This magic isn't of the Fae or the Adhene. I would not know where to begin. And in helping her I would only make it worse."

"Circles. Back again. The sea is circling. Bright, bright water." Guinevere stops coughing. She clutches her neck again. "Like a noose."

"What sea?" I ask.

The *faagailagh* shakes her head. "Riddles are all I have. They couldn't touch the dreams though."

"Who couldn't touch the dreams?" I'm all the way to the bars now, cheeks pressed tight into the metal.

Guinevere's eyes flare wide again, tiny whitewashed planets suspended in the rot of her face. Her head keeps shaking, tufts of hair whip back and forth, back and forth.

Those gnarled roots of hands keep clutching her throat. Nails digging deep. The skin there grows suddenly dark: a thick, oozing burst of red.

"Guinevere!" I shout her name, but Arthur's bride doesn't seem to hear me. She's thrashing, falling over herself.

And I feel that magic again. Taunting my fragile senses through the bars. Ebbing and fading. I'm close to the answer. So close. But the spell's grip is strong, made of impossible knots. Maybe, if I still had my magic, I could find a way around it.

I look over at the cell next to Guinevere's, where I first felt this complicated signature of magic. Where I first *knew* something was very, very wrong. The trail which leads to Richard is right here in front of me. I just don't have the means to follow it.

But the Ad-hene do.

I look back to the queue of stony faces, pick out Alistair.

"Your king is gone then," he says. Dry, factual.

Of course he's not surprised. The Ad-hene knew this was coming. They tried to warn us . . . tried to help.

"He was taken this morning," I say.

"And you think this has something to do with the one who escaped?" The Ad-hene nods at the empty cell, where chalk runes litter the wall like cave drawings.

"I know it does."

Sixteen silver-lattice maps sear into my eyes. Strung out like garden party lights, welding-torch bright. Tears have started to cloy my eyes, trickle down my cheeks, but I don't look away. Those marks: they're the only reason Titania refused the Ad-hene's help. The only reason I'm not sitting on a loch's shore, fingers wrapped inside Richard's.

And now Titania is gone. Richard too. Only the marks remain, bright as winter stars.

The Ad-hene are my only option. My only *hope*.

"The last time I was here, you offered the service of the Ad-hene," I remind Alistair. "The magic that's choking Guinevere. Could one of you track it?"

Silence. Even Guinevere's whimpers have faded. All of us watch the whitewashed leader as he closes his eyes.

"Our offer to track the prisoner still stands," Alistair says finally. "The Ad-hene are nothing if not bound. Kieran will assist you."

If Kieran is surprised, he doesn't show it. He looms by my side— still—as if he were a cast-iron masterpiece planted on a London street corner. His mark flares like Polaris.

Anabelle shivers next to him. A part of her face plays blue against Kieran's mark. The Ad-hene's flint eyes tear from his leader to the princess.

"Aile." A second, softer light springs up from Kieran's hand. Fire licks across the creases of his palm as he offers it to Anabelle. "Take it, Princess."

The orange light ripples over her face as she stares at the fire, uncertain.

"It won't harm you," he tells her. "It only looks dangerous."

Anabelle stares at the bundle of light for a moment longer before she grabs it and tucks it to her chest. Her shivers cease.

"It's not an easy thing you're asking," Kieran tells me. The false fire blooms behind his eyes as he looks back to Guinevere's cell. The *faagailagh* leers against the bars. A patch of blood pools bright at the base of her throat. "This magic . . . It's old. Strong. Angry. If I help you find its wielder . . . I do not think it will end well."

"I've fought old magic before," I tell him.

"Yes. Before. But now . . ." His eyes flicker back to the fire in the princess's palms. She's entranced by the burning sphere in her hands. It dances in her eyes too, revealing all their terror and wonder.

But now I'm a *faagailagh*. A fire without flame. Not dangerous.

"I'm not asking you to fight for me. Just help me find the trail." That's all I need. A trail. As soon as I find proof that the wielder of this magic was in London, I can go to Titania's court and show her I was right: magic was behind Richard's disappearance. Then the Frithemaeg will be forced to keep their oath and save the king.

I'll get Richard back.

Alistair's magic tugs across the corridor, pulling Kieran's attentions back to him. Silent orders hum between them.

"This is a chance to prove our loyalties," Alistair finishes aloud. "Go and make the Ad-hene proud, Brother."

Kieran bows, stiff and perfectly hinged at the waist. He turns to me.

"I'm yours," he says.

"Round and round it goes. A widening gyre. I flipped wrong. Remember." Guinevere's words are a defeated mumble—drained of life and strength and sanity—as she melts into the shadows of her cell. "Please remember. You are not powerless."

Nonsense and gibberish. Too far from the truth to

even be considered a riddle. I feel more powerless than ever as I watch her retreat. Back to her ageless, timeless doom.

"I think I'm going to have nightmares for the rest of my life," Anabelle mutters as soon as we climb back into the sailboat.

If only she knew how true her statement was. My steps sway as I clamber on to the boat and collapse against one of the cushions, reminding me how tired my body is. Soon it will need sleep. I will have to let the nightmares in again.

"How does a place like that even *exist*?" The princess scales the cliffs with her eyes.

"The Isle of Man is one of the great wells of magic." Kieran leaps into the boat, landing on the deck with a litheness I wouldn't have attributed to his kind.

"A well?" Anabelle asks over her shoulder. She's already scuttling across the deck of the sailboat, unlashing knots and winding levers back.

"Yes. Parts of the earth where magic flows more naturally. There are several such places in this kingdom. Stonehenge. Glastonbury. Loch Ness. The Cliffs of

Dover. Back when there was more magic in the land, spirits were born in these places. Every spirit sprung from the Isle of Man is an Ad-hene."

"So what about the tunnels and the cells? Where did those come from?" Anabelle tugs the winch she's adjusting extra tight.

"The very first Ad-hene loved the earth so much they did not wish to leave it. They created an underground kingdom of caves and tunnels. It was a majestic place: walls glittering with mica, lakes so deep you could never reach the bottom, long halls which caught your voice and carried it for miles . . .

"More and more Ad-hene came into existence. The island soon became too small for our numbers, but none of the Ad-hene wished to leave. The oldest Ad-hene found a way to make room for all of us. They cast a spell to make the tunnels endless. Ever-changing and growing." Kieran stretches out his arm, giving us both a clear view of the map on his skin. Impossibly complex, crawling like a living organism. Around and around those severe muscles. "All of us were marked with maps to navigate it."

The Labyrinth of Man is a *spell*. The biggest looped spell I've ever seen. I listen to Kieran's story, watch the light shift restless on his arm—and realize just how much

I don't know about the Manx spirits.

Anabelle looks back at the cliff, where fifteen lights twinkle like Christmas tinsel against the scoured gray dawn. "What happened to the others?"

I think the same question as I count the marks again. Sixteen. Even when I used to come here on prisoner transport duty there weren't many more than that. Certainly not as many as Kieran speaks of.

So what happened to all of them?

The Ad-hene looks up at the marks as well. Obsidian curls cluster his face, frame its blankness. He doesn't answer—I'm not sure he can. His mouth is fused like stone.

The princess stops pulling the winch. "I'm sorry. I didn't mean to upset you."

"There was a war between the Ad-hene. A very long time ago," Kieran says dryly. "We lost many brothers. We nearly destroyed the entire island and fought to the brink of extinction, but Queen Mab intervened. She offered us her help in exchange for the use of our tunnels. That was when it became a prison."

"Oh, *Mab*." Anabelle scrunches her nose and gives the winch a final, vicious yank. "I wasn't really her biggest fan. Considering she tried to kill me and drain my blood like some kind of crazed albino vampire."

"Vampire?" Kieran's face goes from daze to frown. I realize, as I watch his confusion, that Anabelle is probably the first true mortal he's ever spoken with. "What's that?"

"Really?" Anabelle quirks an eyebrow at me. "No vampires?"

I shake my head.

Anabelle looks back at the Ad-hene. "Don't worry about it. So you live in the dark all the time? Don't you ever get sick of it?"

"No. The Labyrinth is part of me." Kieran traces the threading on his arm. "It's my nature."

"Can't argue with that." The princess leans over the side of the boat, unravels the final knot mooring us into place. "Do you think your nature might be able to help this sailboat move faster? Took us long enough getting here and the wind's not in our favor this time."

Kieran's magic billows against the sails and Anabelle mans the wheel, steering us off the coast. I have nothing to do but sit and watch and feel Guinevere's words inside my chest—haunted and clawing. Making no sense, yet meaning everything.

One word rises out from all the rest. Her scream in every dream. Her final plea.

Remember.

Remember what? How Camelot burned and its ashes coated the hillsides like snow? How Guinevere was once bold and beautiful and happy—so in love with King Arthur that you could hear it in every single syllable she spoke? How none of the Fae understood how someone so fierce, so *committed*, could abandon her king for a new lover, destroy everything?

There's something I'm missing. Some key piece to the puzzle, swirling around in those endless lifetimes of memories, just beyond my reach.

I never used to forget things, but ever since Herne siphoned my magic, the past has become fuzzy.

The cushion I'm sitting on dips under a new weight. Kieran. I feel his closeness before I see him. His presence, his magic prickles the back of my neck: a summer evening swelter. Thick and all over.

Kieran is much older than he looks, with those perfect spiral curls and hurricane eyes. His powers are deep, aged strong. If only I had a bit of it. Just a taste—what wouldn't I do?

There it is again. The yearning—stretching as far and wide as this November sea. I shut my eyes but I still *feel* it. So I focus on the bob of the boat on the waves instead.

Kieran speaks with a voice like rum: dark and spicy. "The princess. She's not what I expected. She's *fiery*."

My eyes snap open at this sly, cruel word. I can't help but think the Ad-hene used it on purpose.

But Kieran isn't looking at me. He's staring at the helm, where Anabelle stands by the wheel. Her hair has fallen loose, the wind weaves it in ribbons of gold over her shoulders. The rest of her coronation makeup is gone, washed off by sea mist, but I think she's prettier without it. Beautiful. The Ad-hene does too, I think.

Or perhaps he just stares this intensely at everyone.

I shut my eyes again, focus on the sudden quease of my stomach. So much like the sickness I once fled from. The sickness I lost when I chose Richard, turned my back on power and eternity.

"She's driven," I say. "Just like her brother."

My eyes are still shut, still pinned on dark and nausea. I can't tell if Kieran is shifting closer or farther. "You were there? When he was taken?"

The shelter of my closed eyes is suddenly compromised, flooded with pictures. Richard swarmed by those masked men, being torn from my arms. Me pinned into the cushions. Powerless.

So weak and failing. This fire without flame.

I draw a sharp breath, open my eyes.

"Yes. Men came into the carriage and took him. They tore him straight out of my arms." I try to recite this like pure fact. As if I were reading off a recipe. But my voice betrays me, comes out half-sob.

"Men?" Kieran tilts his head.

I don't have the energy to explain it. So I don't.

"You told me before that your love did not make you miserable. It seems a cruel twist . . ." He doesn't go on, but I know where his words would go if they did. I know because I've been thinking it myself over and over.

If I still had my magic, I could have saved him.

I gave up power for love. And lost love because I gave up power.

A cruel twist indeed.

"I'd rather not talk about it," I manage to choke out.

Kieran watches me. His stare is careful and intent. His words are the same. "Forgive me. It was not my intention to cause you suffering. I'm still trying to understand how love is worth all this. . . . It's haunted me, you know. Our conversation. You have such a conviction, a will. Seeing it left me wanting . . . wondering if there's something more.

"This is the first time I've left the island," the Ad-hene goes on. His eyes break away from where I sit, back in the

185

direction of the cliffs. The lights of his brothers are gone, swallowed by distance and daylight.

The boat sways on the waves, up and down through silence.

"I never knew about the war between the Ad-hene," I say.

"It was many ages ago. We are united now and we try our best to forget." Memories chip and spark through his eyes. "We try our best to forget, but sometimes I think the island remembers. It stopped creating us. There have been no new Ad-hene since those days. My brothers and I are all that are left."

Bones of a once great kingdom. There's a longing in Kieran's voice I know all too well.

"I'm sorry," I whisper into the waves.

"It is behind us now. We can only look forward." Kieran looks away from the boat's wake, up to the helm, where Anabelle's hair licks gold. Where the sea stretches out like a story waiting to be read. "Hope for better things."

The dip and rise of the Irish Sea is too much for my heavy lids. I try my best to fight it, but weariness wins out. I fall with the boat into black, into sleep and chaos.

The mountainside is above me now, towering like a

dragon. A lone figure stands on the edge of the hill, look-ing down at all that's unfolding around me. I can't see the face. It's too shrouded by fog and distance.

The hell of battle stretches around me: blood, splin-tered bones, and death. Planted in the mud a few meters away is Arthur Pendragon's banner: a scarlet standard with a white dragon. Its staff is snapped like a twig, the flag's edges dragging in the mud. Across the grim field the castle's fire is already beginning to spread. Soon it will ravage everything.

I know it's a dream, yet my heart is all terror inside my chest: punching, beating, trying to flee. It feels too real. The braided scents of sweat and blood. The nail-curling shrieks of gutted horses. Men.

Then I see him and my heart stops.

Richard stands in the center of the field. All around him is scarred earth and the insides of men turned out, but he's untouched. His ermine cape flows flawless over the mud and his boots are unscuffed. His eyes are wide as they take in Camelot's doom. They comb through the field and land, finally, on me.

"Embers?" His voice breaks through screams, the rag-ing song of war. Reaches to where I am.

I start running for him, ankles sinking deep in the

mud. Moving forward is a struggle, but I do it anyway, dodging bodies and fallen swords. Blades and knights blur around me, but all I see is Richard. Standing alone. Vulnerable. I'm pushing, pushing, as fast as my feet will allow.

Movement just behind Richard's ermine cape catches my eye. Black armor. Black blade. There's only one man in the entire world who wore such armor. Only one blade which had such a black-adder bite.

He was the leader of the northern armies. The man who invaded Camelot and planted his blade in King Arthur's chest.

Mordred. Killer of kings.

I know this is a dream. I know this man has been dead for more than a thousand years, but still my blood becomes ice.

"Run, Richard!" I scream at the top of my lungs, but he doesn't seem to hear. He's still staring in my direction, reaching for someone who isn't there.

I lunge through the mud, but Mordred is faster. He grabs the end of Richard's cape. Starts to pull. The king is just tumbling back when I reach him. Our fingers touch.

Real. It feels so real. These are his fingers. The ones which traced every intimate curve of my face. Which threaded through my hair every time we kissed.

These are his fingers. The ones which are being torn away. Yanked in the direction of Mordred's blade.

And—again—there's nothing I can do to stop it.

Thirteen

We return to a restless city. A London pulled tight. It's not a dead silence in the air, as it was the night of Lights-down, but a hush. Trains still run. Cars clog the streets as they always do. People hail cabs and stride down sidewalks.

But just under everything is a strain. Sleepless eyes are lined with fear. Walks clip faster. Women grip their handbags tighter. Everyone avoids alleyways, darkened corners.

Kieran is all eyes, drinking in the city's steel and stone. He fidgets and twists in the wool peacoat Anabelle designed for him. All of us are in new clothes, fashioned by the princess's instructions and Kieran's bewildered magic. The clothes he produced are mostly scratchy gray wool. A far cry from Helene's colored silks.

"It's better for blending in," Anabelle said once I pointed it out.

The new outfits seem to be working. So far no one has recognized us.

"Your city is impressive, Princess." Kieran's neck is permanently craned, taking in the vastness of buildings and open sky. "I've seen the towns of my island grow, but nothing like this."

"It's not *my* city," Anabelle says, "but thank you."

"You don't feel ill?" I haven't taken my eyes off of Kieran since we first entered London's outskirts. Even dressed in modern clothes he can't completely hide his *other*ness. At first glance he's an advertisement campaign: a well-knotted scarf, wool peacoat, cabbie hat highlighted by a clean-cut face. But if you look too closely you'll see the hardness of that jaw, the eyes too clear and cutting for any human.

"The sickness," he pauses. "Now that you mention it there are hints. Waves. It's not so terrible. But I'm an Adhene; I carry the earth in my bones."

"Right." I tug at the edge of the cap Anabelle fashioned to hide my hair. "Well, if you feel yourself getting too worn down you can go to the Underground."

"Underground? There's a Labyrinth here too?"

"Kind of." Plus a few rats and malfunctioning trains. Minus tattooed guards and ranting, emaciated prisoners.

"Stop fidgeting with that!" Anabelle smacks my hand off my cap. The night's sleep has centered her, revived some of her old type A self. "The last thing we need is for your hair to come loose. It's a dead giveaway. People are already staring as it is."

She's right. Though it's Kieran most people's eyes snag to. Women especially. I've even seen Anabelle stealing a glance or two when she thought no one was looking.

Even though I know I'm supposed to be discreet, I can't help staring back into the passing crowd. As if Richard just disappeared around the corner for a cup of coffee, bound to return to me at any moment. Every time I see high cheekbones or desert-sand hair my heart lurches.

The Ad-hene seems oblivious to all this. "I could change your hair," he offers. "It wouldn't take much, just a small alteration spell."

I know it wouldn't take much, because I've changed my hair before as well. But the long, flowing red . . . it's the hair I love. The only hair Richard has ever seen me in. I wouldn't be Embers without it.

"No," I say quickly. "The hat's fine."

We keep walking, but the closer we get to Trafalgar Square the more the sidewalks thin. *Closed* signs dangle from shop doors; some storefronts are boarded up altogether, covering jags of broken glass. All roads to the square are empty and full at the same time: littered with miniature flags, lost gloves, signs cheering Richard's coronation. Things bent and trampled under a panicked crowd's feet.

The street ends at a police cordon: large metallic walls cutting across asphalt and sidewalk. A lone patrol car sits, its lights throbbing. As if the barrier itself wasn't enough.

Trafalgar Square has become a fortress.

"Cameras!" Anabelle spits out the word like a curse and swivels around, her trainers scuffing the concrete. She jerks the hood of her sweatshirt even farther over her eyes. There are only a few, stragglers lingering by the edge of the cordon. Newscasters reciting their lines for cameramen. Photographers capturing pictures of the barrier from all angles, hoping for some fantastic breakthrough.

"Stupid!" the princess mutters. "Of course the police and paparazzi would be crawling all over this."

I grab her arm. "We have to go to the square!"

"Agreed. But that's not going to happen as long as it's crawling with investigators. In case you've forgotten, we happen to be at the top of the list of London's Most Wanted."

"Belle, we've wasted enough time already." It took us the better part of a day to travel back and forth from the Labyrinth. Valuable hours for the magic's trail to fade.

For Richard to be pulled even farther from my grasp.

I turn to Kieran. "Does your kind have the equivalent of a veiling spell?"

"Veiling spell? Hiding from the mortals' sight?" It's almost catlike, the way the Ad-hene's stare travels, both aloof and piercing, to the caravan of press and police. "Yes."

"Could you get all three of us into the square without detection?"

He shrugs. "I've never tried before. There's not much need for invisibility in the Labyrinth. Much less hiding others."

"Will you try?" It's Anabelle asking this time. "Please?"

Her plea—so hopeful and desperate from the shelter of her hoodie—seems to soften the Ad-hene's face. The edge of his lip twitches. "I'll try my best, Princess."

Anabelle slides her hand into mine. I hold it tight, brace myself for his spell.

"Follee-shiu."

Kieran's magic breaks over my head, drips down like an egg yolk, covering every inch of my skin, my clothes. The spell isn't physically heavy, but I feel a weight to it. And even though it feels like armor, there's a strange warmth to the magic. It prickles like pinecones, flushes my cheeks.

I grit my teeth, trying my best not to show how unnerving it is to have the Ad-hene's magic soaking over me. Anabelle squeezes my hand. The tremor in her fingers tells me she feels this too.

"You're hidden now." Kieran doesn't have to tell me. The knowledge weighs my limbs. It feels as if bricks have been bound to my feet as I walk past the flashing patrol car, through the police barrier.

It's as awful as I first thought it would be, that morning when Kieran knelt on the cliffside and offered to heal my wound. *Magic.* The feel of it dances across my skin: sparks and longing. I can't help but remember the rush of my own spells, golden and unyielding through my veins. How the world and everything in it—the sky, the sea, the earth—was at my fingertips.

"Watch it!" Anabelle yanks me directly out of the path of a harried-looking detective.

"Sorry." We're almost in the square. My steps sway a bit, as if I've had too many gin and tonics. I guess I am drunk in a way, reeling under so much magic after so many months without.

I catch Kieran staring.

But I don't have time to think about any of this.

Trafalgar Square is at our feet. So empty. The sea of humanity is no more. Instead there are only clusters, islands of investigators and authorized press. Lanes of yellow tape. Hints of the Black Dog's carnage outlined in chalk and bloodstains. The remnants of the Gold State Coach: splinters and gold in the middle of the road.

When Anabelle sees the carriage she stops. Her eyes flicker, unable to hide the ruin she sees. My muscles tense as I wait for another reaction, some flare in her blood magic, but the princess keeps her promise. She swallows it all back, makes her face hard, stays in control.

Getting close to the carriage takes skill. Human investigators swarm all around its carcass. It's not so difficult for me to slip through their maze of suits, but I've had centuries of practice. As I navigate the obstacle course of cameras and blue-gloved hands I can't help but catch snippets of the conversation.

"Still no confirmed sightings of His Majesty or his sister." A detective in a bright yellow vest says as he blows on his coffee.

"What about the Faery?" the man next to him asks.

"Nothing. There's a warrant out for her." The detective's face twists. "They found the Jaguar on the west coast. Abandoned. No telling what she did with the princess."

They're talking about *me*.

"This is a bloody mess. Looks like Forsythe was right."

"You're not on about that M.A.F. crap again? Mark my words. Julian Forsythe's up for a power grab."

"Maybe that's not such a bad thing." The other man shrugs. "Someone's got to stand up to these creatures."

Kieran and Anabelle follow slowly, carefully. Backpackers picking their way through a china shop. The princess only has eyes for the coach. Several times Kieran has to hold her back, guide her through the buzz of mortals.

"Feel anything?" I ask when they reach the edge of the carriage.

Kieran runs his hand over the wheel's twisted remains. "Titania's been here, hasn't she?"

"Yes." I touch the same wheel. Try to feel what he feels. Just grains of wood and paint brush under my fingertips. The only magic is his. Power and pepper-spice against my skin.

Always reminding.

I pull my hand away.

"There's hints of Black Dog too." He removes his hand as well, wiping it on the wool of his peacoat. "Where exactly were you when you felt the prisoner's aura?"

"In the carriage. We were just pulling under Admirality

Arch over there." I point to the grand building and its trio of arches. "Shall we go look?"

"Hold on." Kieran frowns and reaches for the wood again. "There's something . . ."

"What?"

"The Black Dog . . ." His frown grows. "Something about its aura is off."

I bite back my questions, watch as his hand moves over the wood. He shuts his eyes, lids fluttering in concentration. Reading all the things I can't.

Anabelle presses close, smashing hard into my shoulder to avoid another quick-walking detective. "Is it really safe to be standing here? I've had about twelve close calls already."

She's right. Even in the short time we've been standing by the carriage the crowd of mortals has grown. It's only a matter of time before one of them jostles into one of us.

"Kieran." I grab the edge of his coat. "Let's go to the Admirality Arch."

"Just a moment." His eyes are still closed. His hand is now fully gripped around the rim of the wheel. "Some of the prisoner's magic is here. Very faint. Buried in the Black Dog's aura."

I think of my own encounter with the Black Dog—how,

instead of tearing my flesh from bone, it retreated into Westminster's Underground. How Blæc's breath hissed as it vanished into the shadows: *Can't . . . not yet . . . won't let me eat . . .*

Not a miracle.

A curse.

Blæc didn't spare me out of mercy or restraint. He was being *starved*. So he could wreak havoc in Trafalgar Square on the day of the coronation. Draw all defense and attentions away from the carriage. Create the perfect window for the masked men to come . . .

"We find the dog, we find the trail," Kieran says.

"Last I heard it was in Queen Titania's custody."

"With the Frithemaeg? That should be easy enough."

I can't hide my doubt; it's all over my face. "Titania isn't well. And she's not exactly supportive of this investigation."

"You're at odds?" Kieran steps away from the wheel.

At odds. What a civil way to describe how the Faery queen withdrew her help when we needed her most. *Abandoned* or *betrayed* feels far more fitting.

"I'll send a message asking about the dog." I look back over to the Admirality Arch: three gaps which open up to the Mall, lead the way to Buckingham. I can even see a few of the plane trees beyond. Leaves brown and shriveled. Dying without color.

"We should go over there." I point to the arches. "Where I felt—"

All of a sudden I feel like those trees, shedding and peeling off dead layers. Kieran's eyes shine bright with horror as he watches his veiling spell unravel. The power which was not mine slips away—gone again.

All three of us are stripped bare. Exposed for every eye and camera lens in Trafalgar Square to see. The scene around us freezes, detectives stunned and us caught like deer in a car's headlamps.

Then the moment shatters. I grab the hem of Anabelle's sweatshirt, tug her with me as I lunge from the ruined carriage. The princess doesn't hesitate. Neither do the investigators. Cups of coffee splatter on the ground. Stun guns—blue and bright fragments of lightning—jag into the corner of my vision.

We run. Dodging streetlamps and parked police vans. Sprinting around statues and fountains. My feet jar against asphalt and stone, over those horrible chalk outlines of the souls Blæc took. Anabelle runs beside me, keeping perfect pace. Kieran is nowhere in sight. I don't have time to stop and look for him. If these men catch me, so much more time will be wasted. Time Richard can't afford.

But all ways out of Trafalgar Square are blocked. Choked with metal barriers and eavesdropping reporters. We're like rats in a trap, running in circles, trying to find a way out.

There's none.

Someone claws my shoulder, jerking me back so hard my cap tumbles off. Another detective grabs Anabelle. The princess twists in his arms—movement made of fury and panic. I feel her strength swelling. Magic ready to spill over at any second.

"Don't, Belle! You promised!" I spit the words at her. "We'll find another way!"

For a moment I fear the princess won't be able to stop the surge. But Anabelle manages to push it down. She screams instead, jousting a sharp elbow into her captor's stomach. He doubles over, releases her onto the stones. I dig my feet into the asphalt, pull hard against the fingers looped into my jumper. There's a fraying of yarn and I'm free.

Then I see Kieran. He's looming over the street, perched next to a statue of Charles the First. Looking very much the way he did when I first saw him: fierce and dead, fire and slate. Something to be feared. He glowers over our pursuers. His arm stretches out and through the thick of his peacoat I see the glow of his scar. Blazing.

His magic thunders through the square, lances through the ground like silver lightning. The asphalt which was so sure and solid under our feet becomes quicksand, tugging first at toes. Then ankles. Trapping those standing on it like flies in a pool of tar. Some of the detectives are knee-deep in the softened street.

The Ad-hene is the only one who does not sink. Kieran walks toward us with firm steps and tugs Anabelle up from the viscous street-gunk. He offers his arm out to me, the one where the scar's light still throbs through his clothing. A slight singeing smell drifts from the sleeve's wool: magic burning through.

I stare at his outstretched hand another moment. It's steady, strong, unflinching. Just like the magic warping the asphalt at my feet, it lures me in: deeper and deeper.

Kieran doesn't wait for me to reach. He grabs my arm and I feel the heat of his mark—searing against my skin. All it takes is one pull and I'm free. Back on solid ground.

Fourteen

"This is a terrible idea," Anabelle whispers as we walk into the pub. The hood of her sweatshirt is tugged halfway down her face, so I have to guide her around the dimly lit tables.

I've already commandeered Kieran's cap. His scarf too. I take in the early evening crowd, mostly paunchy, middle-aged men leaning over pints, watching reruns of a football match. The man closest to the end of the bar gives us a side glance as we walk in. The rest stay glued to the screen.

The princess is right. This isn't the best of ideas, but our need to get off London's streets has escalated to crucial levels. Just like my hunger. It's been over a day since I've had anything more than the expired, crumbling granola bar I foraged from the Jaguar's glove box.

"We need to eat and regroup," I tell her. "If someone recognizes us, Kieran can wipe their memory."

"Right. Because his spell worked so well last time." Anabelle flops into a booth. "That was a Grade A, bloody circus of a disaster. I think every news venue in Britain caught that on tape."

Most of the pub's screens are switched to the football match, but the closest one is all news. In the brief time we've been sitting here Richard's image has flashed twice. The first photograph shows him in his polo gear, arm slung around Edmund, one of his Eton buddies. The second is from the red carpet at the Winfreds' gala. It has to be, because I can see the embroidered sleeve of my dress.

My face is cut out completely.

Kieran shrugs off his peacoat and moves into the booth next to Anabelle. "I underestimated the power of this city. I'm sorry, I didn't feel the spell slipping until it was too late."

I look at the coat still draped over his arm, burn marks wormed into its sleeve. The ring of ruined fabric hugs his thermal shirt too, in the exact pattern of his scar—the one Titania was so certain meant betrayal.

The Ad-hene can't be trusted.

Was Titania right? I think of how solid and sure Kieran's magic felt in the square. How little the sickness of the machines seemed to affect him, despite his age. Was it possible Kieran *let* the veiling spell fall? That he meant for us to be exposed?

Kieran's slate-gray eyes catch mine. "I won't be able to hide all of us again. Perhaps just one. If the situation is dire."

"At least we found something." Anabelle picks up a menu. Lets it fall back down to the table without so much as a glance. "Queen Titania will send us the dog and we can find out who spelled it."

A woman comes up to the table, takes our order. Anabelle slouches far into her end of the booth, and I can't help but tug down my cap. But the waitress has eyes only for Kieran. She doesn't even seem to notice the burn on his sleeve.

I can't help but look at the screen. The reporter's voice buzzes through the speakers. Eternally loud.

"What was supposed to be a national celebration turned tragic yesterday when King Richard's coronation carriage was attacked by a spirit known as a Black Dog."

The screen flashes to shots of that morning. Eight plumed horses pulling the Gold State Coach through a sea of cheers and flags. Richard peering out the window. Then, a sudden jerk of the camera, to the huge hulk of shadow which barrels through the crowd. The Black Dog.

I wait for the camera to pan back to the carriage. To show the masked men and my fight, but the scene stays glued to Blæc. The swirling chaos of people and Fae around it.

A distraction. That's all the Black Dog was. A savage, deadly distraction. I wonder if *any* of the hundreds of cameras managed to capture Richard's kidnapping.

It's like the stage magicians from the Victorian age. The ones veiled in smoke and capes, who yanked rabbits from top hats in the name of magic. Who used beautiful women and shining lights to lure the audience's attention from the truth. The simplicities of hidden compartments and trapdoors. The art of sleight of hand.

So what were the mechanics of this trick? How did all those men and Richard simply disappear under so many watchful eyes and lenses? In such a space as Trafalgar Square?

Another piece of the puzzle. Missing.

"The monster left a wake of bodies and missing persons. The most notable being King Richard himself. Rumors are circulating that Princess Anabelle has gone missing as well. Like King Richard, she was last seen in the company of Emrys Léoflic. The alleged former Fae has also dropped off the radar."

A portrait of Anabelle seated at a grand piano flashes across the screen. Another picture fades in over it: me leaping off Lord Winfred's yacht. Braced for battle with the Kelpie.

"Many are speculating that Emrys's involvement in the royals' disappearance is more than just coincidence. Meryl Munson uncovers more in an exclusive interview with one of King Richard's closest friends."

The screen flashes over to Edmund. He's suited in his polo gear, smiling at the pretty brunette reporter beside him. *"I never did like Emrys. Richard never was the same after she started showing up. Almost like he was possessed, like he'd been put under some sort of sick love spell."*

"Do you think this is the case?" Meryl Munson leans in close.

"Definitely." Edmund nods. *"The Richard I knew was never into gingers."*

I sigh at the steaming plate of food the waitress shoved in front of me. Anabelle mumbles something about first-rate arses and stabs her fork into her jacket potato. Kieran stares doubtfully at the fish and chips he ordered for show.

"Ever had chips before?" The princess nods at the basket. Its newspaper lining is nearly translucent with grease spots.

"I don't eat."

"They're best with vinegar on them." Anabelle grabs a

bottle from the condiments stand, douses the greasy pile. Once the chips are thoroughly soaked, she shoves the basket closer to the Ad-hene. "Try it."

To my surprise Kieran fishes out one of the larger pieces, gripping it between his fingers like a cigarette. His nose wrinkles as he shoves it between his lips.

"Delicious, right?" The princess grabs a couple of chips for herself.

The Ad-hene's eyes turn to slits, his cheeks puff out like an angry fish's. He nods anyway.

I can't help but smile at the squeeze of distaste on his face. Anabelle doesn't seem to notice. She's too busy shoving past Kieran, out of the booth. Excusing herself for the water closet.

As soon as the princess is out of sight the Ad-hene grabs a napkin and spits out the chip. His handsome face is still crinkled as he downs half a glass of water, trying his best to drown out the taste.

"You didn't have to try it," I tell him.

"It's a small thing." Kieran shrugs, looks over his shoulder to where Anabelle's hooded silhouette coasts past the bar. "If I hadn't tried it, I would not have known how terrible it was."

I snatch a chip of my own. Salt and vinegar swim

like cold fire across my tongue, through my nose. "Some things are an acquired taste."

"Like mortality?" The Ad-hene pushes the entire basket across the table. Scar-silver glints through the elaborate burn of his shirt. Some of it has already changed, shifting to the color of flesh with the pattern of the Labyrinth's tunnels.

Kieran glances down at the singe-mark. "You don't trust me."

"I never said that."

"You don't have to. It's in your eyes." His eyes meet mine—so steely, so beautiful—and for a moment I believe the mortals' stories about the Ad-hene. Too evil for heaven. Too pure for hell. Forever in limbo, suspended on the earth. "You don't trust me, but you need me."

I don't know what to say to that.

"Let's say the Ad-hene are tricking you. Let's say we did free the prisoner. Why would they send me to help you? What would I have to gain from you finding your king?"

I bite my lip, stare at the basket of soaking chips.

The Ad-hene pulls his arms off the table. "Stories of you traveled through the Labyrinth. How gifted you were in the art of your magic. You and I both know you could follow this trail yourself. If you truly did not trust me."

"My magic is gone." I say this with force. As much for myself as for Kieran.

"Is it? Beyond recall?"

I think of the day Herne's gloved hand grasped mine. How my powers twisted out, leaving me grounded. I think of the night when I stood on Windsor Castle's green and watched mortals and Frithemaeg dancing together. Laughing, happy. How I turned to Herne and asked without words. Bared the weakness of my soul under the Wild Hunt moon.

Not beyond recall. Not completely.

I could return to Windsor and accept Herne the Hunter's offer. I could have power again: singing through me like a hurricane, some fearsome force of nature. The want I felt at the first touch of Kieran's veiling spell returns. Swells through my insides with fearsome strength.

No more weakness. No more being pinned down like an insect while my heart is torn away.

But the cost . . .

As if on cue, another clip of Richard flashes on the screen. It's from the same night as the red carpet. I know because this time I'm still in the frame. His eyes are on me: smiling, full of light. Our arms are hooked together as we walk to the boat. I'm smiling too.

Another emptiness rears inside, the pain of him gone. It's a wonder I can sit here at this table. Swallow vinegar and chips, talk like a normal person.

"I can't." Take my magic back. Give Richard up. Go back to living the way I was before.

"I saw the look on your face in Trafalgar Square. You want it," Kieran presses. He's speaking in that sly voice of his—sowing words and ideas into the folds of my brain. To seed and sprout and grow. "You were never meant to live this way."

"There are some things I want more. I made my choice," I say again. "Some love is worth death."

"Is it worth him dying?" Kieran nods at the television, where Richard is still guiding me to the yacht ramp. The words TAINTED LOVE: KING RICHARD'S FATAL MIS-TAKE? scroll across the bottom of the screen.

I want to tell him his question is ridiculous. Pointless. But it's not. And we both know it.

Anabelle returns, pushing Kieran to the far end of the booth. Worry is all across her pretty face. She nods at the screen. "We might want to eat quick."

The television blares, extra loud: *"This just in. There's been a fresh attack in Trafalgar Square. Emrys Léoflic and an unidentified male were sighted, just before a brutal spell was unleashed on authorities.*

Princess Anabelle was also seen with them, apparently as a hostage."

A shaky camera shot shows my hair, streaming so very red behind me like a banner as I drag Anabelle across the square.

My hand drifts up to my new cap. A dead giveaway.

I steal a glance over to the bar. The football match is gone, the bartender's remote flicking all the screens to the news report. The man who gave us that first side glance is looking over his shoulder. His pint is half-empty and his cheeks are ruddy, but his eyes stay keen. Straight on me.

"A *hostage?*" Anabelle straightens, the worry on her face twists into indignation. "That's ridiculous!"

How did the truth get so warped? So out of focus?

The man at the end of the bar stands, drains the rest of the beer from his glass. His eyes don't leave our table.

I might not know where I'm going, but I know it's time to leave.

Fifteen

I half expect to wait out the night huddled in an alley-way. But Anabelle walks us straight to a house in Chelsea, asks Kieran to magic the locks open, and punches the correct string of glowing numbers into the security system pad.

"What is this place?" I gape when she flips the crystal chandelier on. We're standing in the foyer of a grand house. With polished hardwood floors, marble busts, and gold-framed oil paintings, this place could almost be Buckingham Palace itself.

"My friend Bridget lives here." The princess walks around the room, loosing all the voluminous curtains from their ties. "Her family's in Thailand on a rather lengthy holiday. I used to come here and hide out after nasty fights with Mum."

The place does look closed up for the winter: every piece of furniture is covered in white sheets to ward off dust. I glance out the last uncovered window. Dusk is gathering. A flock of starlings coasts through the firelight sky.

I need to find a sparrow to send Titania, before the birds go to roost for the night.

Almost as if they read my thought, the murmuration of birds washes over the rooftops, disappears altogether.

I'm running out of time.

The sparrow isn't hard to find. I grab a canister of gourmet Italian breadcrumbs from the pantry and climb all the way to the rooftop. Like the rest of the house it's packed away for the winter. The shrubbery is covered in thick plastic sheets and the lounge chairs have been stowed in a frost-covered corner.

I kneel down in the center of the roof patio, spread the crumbs out like a blanket of wares, and wait. They come—feathered and fearless—skipping just by my boots, chirping between bites. I choose one of the smaller ones.

The parchment is short, cramped with my blunt, handwritten sentences. Their letters angled tight with abandonment:

Found trail with Ad-hene. Black Dog's aura is tainted. Question it further. —Emrys

I wind the paper around the sparrow's leg, weave the sending spell through its wing feathers. Even this small magic leaves me winded, but it seems to be enough. The bird hops out of my palms with purpose, launches over the moon-slanted rooftops into its long flight across Albion.

The horizon is a collection of cookie-cutter silhouettes: houses, trees, bats, and the last stubborn cling of leaves. I stare at it until my eyes start to burn with tears.

The sparrows are gone. It's just me here on the rooftop. Alone.

Gone. That's what the bird cries sound like as they weave through the stark naked tangle of the trees. *Gone. Gone. Gone.*

I grip the rooftop's ledge. The sun's final light catches against my ring. Reminds me of Richard's promise. The life we wanted to lead . . .

I thought we could have a fairy-tale ending. A happily ever after. But perhaps that's not how our story was supposed to end. Perhaps I was better off as Richard's guard. Perhaps I was never meant to be in his arms, in his heart. Perhaps I really was his fatal mistake.

Maybe we're Guinevere and Arthur all over again—a Faery and a mortal king: a doomed love—tragedy on the brink of legend. Our Camelot going up in flames.

I thought I knew myself. I thought I knew the path I'd chosen.

When I lost my magic Richard was my north. Without him I'm a compass sans magnet. Drifting through questions without direction.

You were never meant to live this way.

Then how was I meant to live?

You are not powerless.

Then what is my power?

And through it all, Richard. The ache of missing him—a hurt deeper than marrow, more violent than blood—soaks through me, creeps into old wounds. I can't help but think of the secrets. The gap we both knew was there. How there was so much distance even when our lips touched, when our skin grazed like velvet. There are still worlds between us. A life I haven't fully been able to surrender, even when it was no longer in my grasp.

Magic. I never really let it go. Not in my deepest of hearts. And I still want it, still yearn.

Richard or magic.

I can't keep holding on to both.

Something has to give.

The emerald flare of my ring recedes with the glow of the sky. The dark is swallowing everything, but there are no stars yet. I'm beginning to think they'll never shine again.

Just as this thought crosses my mind, a new light appears at my side. Kieran's arm stretches out just a breath from mine, his mark showing through his thermal. I don't move or speak. He doesn't either. Moments pass: still and cold.

"You sent the message?" he asks finally.

I look over, where Kieran's face is painted in two lights. Dying sun and silver dream.

"The sparrow should reach Titania's court in a few hours." Whether or not the Faery queen responds is a different question altogether. A fear I don't have the strength to entertain right now.

"So now we wait?" the Ad-hene asks.

"It's probably best to stay low for a while. After that little news cameo we had today." I can't help but look back down at Kieran's mark. Every second the twilight plunges darker, it pulses brighter.

"This city is so strange. I thought I would be able to withstand it, but it seems I am only my old strength in the Labyrinth." His eyes are a mixture of hard and sorrow as he watches the west. Where, far off and away, his island home is still languishing in the last remnants of daylight. "How do you bear it? Being away from everything you know?"

"Sometimes I don't." My truth slips out into the cold air. Saying it aloud feels like sin or blasphemy, yet I don't stop. "It's easier when Richard is here. But even then . . ."

The sun is completely gone. Kieran's light flickers, star soft. My words settle and I realize how much lighter my chest is for saying them. So I say more. *Slip, slip* goes the truth.

"The mortals think I'm a monster and the Fae think I'm weak. The only other soul like me in the world is insane and locked away in a prison cell. And Richard is gone and Queen Titania is gone, and . . ."

I can't go on anymore. My fingers feel frozen to the ledge. Gripping as if I'm holding on to life or Richard or something else I can't bear to part with.

"You're not alone, Emrys. You have the princess. You have me." Kieran shifts and his arm presses into mine. My skin prickles: a warmth too solid to be just magic.

I pull away, but the Ad-hene doesn't seem to notice. That he touched me. That I felt something.

I pretend not to notice either.

"We'll find your king." Kieran pushes off the ledge and starts to drift back to the doorway.

"Kieran?" I call out, and the Ad-hene pauses. He looks

218

like the statue of some garden god, stowed away between the blanketed plants.

"Thank you for leaving your home. For helping us. It—it means a lot." I'm lying. Him being here doesn't just mean a lot.

It means everything.

The Manx spirit plays his statue role well—as if my gratitude has wintered his very bones. Finally he gives a stiff nod and disappears back into the house. I rub my arm and watch the space he left.

In the harsh black patch of sky beyond, the north star begins to bloom.

We wait.

I spend hours on the rooftop, scanning blue skies for the sparrow. There are scores of them, but none wing my way. None of them carry the news we so badly need.

Anabelle treats the house like a medieval fortress, or a blitz bomb shelter. The window shades stay drawn, even in the height of day. Every thirty minutes she peers through the front door's mail slot—scanning the street for suspicious vehicles. At least one of the six television screens is always on: an endless barrage of Coronation Day replays, riot reports, and exclusive interviews.

The princess's second distraction is a slightly more useful one. Cooking. She plunged into the vast walk-in pantry, armed with spatulas and whisks and Kieran's magic to help substitute all the missing ingredients. By the end of the next day, the dining table is crammed full of Anabelle's culinary pursuits: soufflés, cucumber sandwiches, petits fours, a whole lamb drizzled in mint sauce.

More food than we could eat in a month. And I certainly don't plan on being here that long.

I didn't even plan on being here *this* long. Titania's answer should've been here by now. A thought which makes my stomach turn. Makes the platters of food in front of me useless.

"I can't believe you lied about liking the fish and chips!" Anabelle's pretty face is twisted into a mock scowl—more smile than smirk—as she looks over at Kieran.

Kieran looks only half-petrified as he watches the princess sort through all the dishes she fixed between newscasts and mail-slot spying. He stumbles for an answer. "It—it was not my favorite. I didn't want you to feel poorly."

"We're going to find *something* you like." She grabs a spoon and a soufflé and sets them both in front of the stiff spirit. "Try this. It's chocolate. Everyone likes choco-late."

He grasps the stem of the spoon full-fisted and shoves it into the airy cake. Chocolate—molten, sweet, and crumbly—drips from the spoon's edge into his mouth. Kieran swallows the spoonful and sets the utensil down. I can see he's trying his hardest to keep his face straight.

"Really? But it's *chocolate!*" The princess rescues the soufflé and takes a spoonful of her own. "Delicious, gooey, fattening chocolate!"

"It's—not my favorite," he says again.

"Right, then. We'll strike all things sinful and deli-cious off the list." Anabelle reaches for another dish. "What about black pudding?"

"Sounds ominous." Kieran looks from the dish of blood sausage to where I sit. "Still no sparrow?"

I shake my head, and Anabelle then prods the Ad-hene on, "You're not getting out of this that easily. Try it."

He obeys, using his chocolate-coated soufflé spoon. This time he doesn't bother hiding his distaste.

"Let me guess. It's not your favorite." Anabelle isn't even pretending to scowl now. Her smile is the kind which holds back a laugh. An infectious thing which spreads to Kieran's features: The lines of his face rearrange into something soft, almost human.

The Ad-hene shakes his head. She reaches for another dish.

I'm not sure if I can keep sitting here. With so much food and almost-laughter I have no appetite for. Neither of them seems to notice when I make my exit up to the roof, where the skies grow dark and no birds fly. I pull out a lounge chair anyway, watching and waiting for something that never comes.

By the time I go back downstairs the kitchen is clean and the food put away. Most of the lights are off, and with all the curtains drawn I have to fumble my way around islands of antique furniture. There's a single slice of light, drawn down the very end of the long hall.

I stop just at the end of the jarred door, peer into the master bedroom.

The television is on, flashing the same awful footage of the Black Dog taking apart the crowd. Anabelle sits in front of it, cross-legged, her hair damp and dripping from the shower. But she isn't looking at the screen. She's focused on the fire in her palms—the same false heat and harmless flames Kieran offered her in the Labyrinth. She's bolder with it this time, molding it like artist's clay with her fingers.

The twist of heat fills Kieran's eyes as he watches Anabelle. In his hands are a fork and a canning jar full of beetroot. He chews the vegetable slowly as he focuses on the flames, the princess manipulating them.

I see he's found something he likes.

"Impressive," the Ad-hene says as she lassoes the fire into a knot.

Pink begins to creep into Anabelle's cheeks. "I was just muddling around."

"No one's taught you how to wield your magic, have they?" The Ad-hene edges closer to her. Her flame.

"Who said anything about magic?" Anabelle's voice goes sharp. "I just wanted this for my hair. Next best thing to a blow dryer."

"You're manipulating my spell." Kieran nods at the fire in her palms. "Changing its very structure. That's something not even the Fae can do."

Anabelle's eyes widen. She takes both palms and crumples the flame, traps it like a moth in the cage of her fingers. "I—I didn't know."

The Ad-hene stays still for a moment. Embers flicker in the gaps of the princess's fingers, flecking light into both of their faces. The screen behind them slides into a shot of the Palace of Westminster. Protestors and signs swarm around it, boiling with anger.

"In the square you were building a spell, but you did not unleash it. You're afraid," Kieran says, as sure and solid as if he's read her soul. "Why?"

"I don't—I'm not—" The red of Anabelle's cheeks grows deeper. I've never seen her so flustered before.

"You shouldn't be afraid of power," Kieran tells her. "It's a gift."

"I'm not afraid of power," the princess says, her hands still clasped over the flame. "I'm afraid of hurting people. Of losing control."

"So you think that it's better to hide your nature? Ignore it?" Kieran sets down his half-finished beetroot jar and grabs her hand, folding her palms open. The fire rears up again, sears the air between them. "You can't escape who you are, Princess. Perhaps for a while. But your true self will always rise in the end. It will always shine through."

The princess looks down at the flame in her hands. At the Ad-hene's fingers wrapped around hers. "Emrys told me it's dangerous. She made me promise not to use it."

"How can Lady Emrys tell you what to do with your power when she's too afraid to embrace her own?"

My breath goes sharp, taking in the stab of his words. I'm leaning so hard against the hallway wall that my shoulder's gone numb.

"She's not afraid." Anabelle is playing with the fire again, letting it dance up her arm, wrap around Kieran's fingers. "She's in love."

"I'm not sure I would know how to tell the difference." The Ad-hene watches the tendrils of flame creep up his sleeve. His eyes grow brighter. "Have you ever been in love?"

"There were a few boys I fancied in school, but not like that. Not yet." Anabelle looks at him through the fire. "You?"

He doesn't answer. Their fire burns in silence: shimmer, flicker, shake. Beautiful heat. The whole room radiates with it.

"Do you think I could learn? How to do spells without . . . without hurting people?" Anabelle asks. "Could you teach me?"

I nudge the door with my foot. It falls open with a creak. Anabelle jerks away from the Ad-hene's touch. The fire in her palm flares, as if it's been fed a shot of petrol. Kieran doesn't move.

My heart beats hollow in my throat—all the emptiness

of the sky and the hollowed space inside my chest threatening to spill out. I point to the fire in Anabelle's hands. "Put it out."

"I was just drying my hair. Bridget took her blow dryer with her," she says. "I'm not doing anything wrong."

"Belle, you don't know what you're messing with. . . ." I'm not sure if I'm talking about the Ad-hene or the flame. Probably both.

"What?" Anabelle stands, so we're eye-to-eye. "Because it's dangerous?"

"Yes." My throat strains from trying not to yell.

"Dangerous how?" There's an edge of challenge in the princess's voice. Her steel-self rising, clad in all of Kieran's clever, silver words.

"The Fae's magic is fueled by nature. Mortals' magic is fueled by emotion. It's less stable," I tell her.

"What's so bad about that?" Anabelle asks. "I'm sick of sitting in this house and baking soufflés! I want to *do* something, Emrys! And now I *can*."

I think of the last age when mortals wielded magic so freely. How its reign ended with King Arthur's death—in an awful field of blood and fire.

I cannot let our new Camelot burn.

"You're not ready," I tell her.

The flame in Anabelle's hand jumps brighter, becomes a flickering veil between us. I feel its heat, her anger, from all the way across the room. "You just want to keep me from doing magic because you can't!"

Her words wrap around my heart like a bullwhip. I can't stop the anger it wakes.

"I chose it. To be with your brother."

"Then let me have my choice!" she yells back.

The fire soars now. Behind that raging screen of flames the princess looks . . . wild. Her hair is everywhere, streams of gold touched by Midas. The fire's light hollows out her cheeks, burnishes the anger in her eyes.

I walk over to where she stands and grab the flames. My palms smart, sting with the heat, but I don't let go.

At first it's like plunging my hand into a bucket of eels, grasping writhe and slip. But then I dredge up the remainder of my magic. It's enough to reap the flames, pluck them from the princess's trembling fingers.

"You don't know what you're dealing with, Belle." I press the fire down in my raw palms, squash it like an insect. The room flickers with its death throes. "This isn't a game. This is life and death."

For a long moment we stand, opposite each other. Anabelle's hands have curled into fists.

"I don't know because you won't tell me! Stop treating me like a child!"

I open my mouth to speak, but it doesn't matter. She's already left the room. The door slams shut behind her, so hard the window frames shudder.

"I think, perhaps, the princess is right." Kieran stands. One side of the Ad-hene's face is lit bright by the screen. It's showing the mob by the Parliament building again. Patches of fire rise up from the vastness of the crowd. I blink, wonder if I'm seeing things.

I tuck my throbbing palms into my sleeves. "I thought your fire was harmless."

"Only to those who can handle it," he says. "The princess has power. It will keep rising whether you show her how to harness it or not."

"You don't know what you're talking about." I grit my teeth, angry. He wasn't there, standing in the mud-churned field, surrounded by so much blood and death. He doesn't know, can't know, the destruction human magic has wrought.

"Perhaps not. But I know you are afraid." Kieran places a hand on my shoulder. It's a deliberate touch this time, the furthest thing from an accident. The prickly feeling blooms in my stomach this time, winds up my spine.

Magic and want and the something else I tried so hard to ignore on the rooftop.

I feel the same way I did in Trafalgar Square—frozen, exposed. Too stunned, too aware to pull away.

"You're afraid." He stares straight into my eyes as he says this. The gray of sorrow and storm, vicious and vulnerable all at once. "But you don't have to be. You feel alone, but you aren't."

Another moment passes. The Ad-hene's hand falls away. He bends down and picks up his unfinished jar of beetroots. "The princess is scared too. You shouldn't punish her for your own choice. Your own fears. She deserves to know who she is."

His words smudge inside me, leave marks like charcoal alongside the prickles his touch left. I hate them, wish I could erase them all.

"Go and make things right." Kieran holds his fork like a knife hilt—all fist and awkward stab. The beetroot looks dark and bleeding as he plucks it from the jar, holds it to his stone lips. "Before someone gets hurt."

Sixteen

A quick search tells me that Anabelle isn't in the house. The front door's dead bolt is unlocked, and her hoodie is gone from the coatrack. I don't have enough magic left to follow her aura, but I brave the streets anyway.

My stride is angry. Smarting hands turned fists are shoved into my jacket pockets. Streetlamps pool like halos on the sidewalk. I skirt their light altogether, keep to the shadows.

I leave Kieran behind in the house, but the Ad-hene's silver-dart words haunt my every step. Knifing my insides with perfect slice and accuracy.

You're a fire without flame.

You shouldn't punish the princess for your own choice.

Is it worth his death?

Afraid. Alone. You don't have to be.

Cut, cut, bleed. Every word hits its mark. Why does the truth hurt so much? What is it about Kieran that makes me question everything?

As much as I hate to admit it, the Ad-hene is right. I can't shield the princess from the force growing inside her. I can't bind her with promises she can't keep.

It's time to tell her why I'm afraid.

Tree limbs reach like skeleton hands into the night sky. Bony twigs grasping at where the stars should be. They still aren't out, even in the utter darkness. There are too many lights tonight, too much haze for even the winter constellations to pierce through.

Once I round the corner I find out why.

The fires on the screen, springing up from the crowds. An oil barrel sits in the middle of the street, stuffed full of snapped branches and wads of newspaper. People huddle around it, cheering as a limp, crude effigy is staked into the middle of the barrel.

I've seen this tradition before. Every year on the fifth of November the mortals gather around fires with beer and song. Every year they watch the likeness of Guy Fawkes crumble to ash in front of them.

But never in those four hundred years have I seen an effigy with such long, red hair.

I keep to the dark, watch as the first match is struck, tossed into the barrel. People cheer as the paper catches, roars with orange and light. The flames fan and the song starts. A hum which rises and roars. Just like the fire eating away my likeness.

Remember, remember the fifth of November
The Gunpowder Treason and plot
I know of no reason why Gunpowder Treason
Should ever be forgot

Someone grabs my arm. I try to yank away, try to fight, but it's not some random bystander from the crowd.

It's Anabelle.

"The fires are everywhere," she says.

We stand in silence and shadows. Watching the bonfire's fury stab through the smoke. Up, up. Close to the claw of the trees.

"I haven't been completely open with you, Belle." I stare hard at the barrel's glowing coals. "Kieran's right. I'm scared, but not because you'll have magic and I won't. It's bigger than that."

Anabelle pulls me farther from the streetlamps and flames. Where we can watch without being watched. "So what happened? Why are you afraid of mortals' magic?"

"Emotions are a powerful source. The magic which springs from them is just as strong. Most Fae are indifferent. Emotions don't come naturally to us—them," I correct myself. "It wasn't until I met your brother that I really understood the power of emotions. They're strong, but they're also shaky. Unpredictable. When you base magic on something like that . . ."

"It can go wrong," the princess finishes my sentence for me.

"It's like fire." I nod at the oil drum. "You think you have it under control, but one flare, one slip, and suddenly you're the one who's trapped.

"In my early days, magic wasn't a foreign thing to mortals. They'd lived among Fae for many years. The more ambitious ones watched and learned. But they could only perform magic with the help of channeling instruments. Potions, staffs, amulets, sacrifices. The spells they performed were small things: healings, divination, luck work. Too small for anyone to notice the consequences of emotion.

"But a few mortals delved deeper into the art. Arthur and Merlin were among these. They discovered a way to bind magic inside a mortal's veins, so they could cast spells without a channeling device. It's one of the reasons Arthur's kingdom became so great."

"Of course," Anabelle says. "Everyone knows Camelot."

I go on. "The mortals held the king in awe because he worked magic like a Fae. The Fae held him in awe because his magic was so *different* from ours. Different yet just as strong. When Arthur asked us to become his allies— to protect him and his people from immortal threats in exchange for access to the blood magic's energy—we agreed. The Frithemaeg fought many battles at his side. Camelot grew and the Pendragon's name became known in many lands.

"But we started to notice how his magic wavered. The strength of Arthur's magic fed off the strength of his heart. Spells he cast when he was happy were vastly different from the same spells he cast in anger or fear. For the most part he learned how to control it. He kept his emotions in check, didn't work magic when he was too upset. But some emotions are too strong, too overwhelming to avoid. They consume you."

I take another breath. Smoke chokes the air, snakes down in my lungs.

"The very first time Arthur Pendragon visited Queen Mab's court he met a Fae. They fell in love and she gave up her magic and immortality to be with him."

"Guinevere," Anabelle breathes out the name like a secret. The spook of the Labyrinth still glimmers through her eyes. Makes her shoulders hunch. "She was like you."

Like me. The only soul in the world like me. The thought leaves a rotten taste on my tongue—white eyes and ashes, black blades and iron bars.

I swallow past it. "Guinevere became Arthur's queen. It was easy to see the love between them, even for Fae. We could feel how the emotion fed Arthur's magic, made him stronger. You could see it in Guinevere too. When she was around Arthur she almost seemed to glow. . . ."

Like me. I can't get the taste out of my mouth because these ashes are real. Flame and ruin flake the sidewalk.

"But then she ran away with Lancelot?" Anabelle prods me on. "Just like in the stories?"

I nod. "It never quite made sense. One day she was laughing and happy in Arthur's arms, the next she rode away with his best knight. When Arthur found out about Guinevere's affair, he broke. His heart was shattered and his magic started spiraling out of control. There were earthquakes, fires, floods. Camelot started coming apart at the seams. It wasn't even a day before Mordred—a great sorcerer from the north—invaded with his armies." I shudder, can't help but think of the dream. "It all happened so fast. We didn't even have time to summon Mab and the other Fae. Mordred and his men swarmed the valley and burned everything. Arthur fought, but he was too defeated at heart. His magic failed him, and the Frithe-maeg were too few to face the sorcerer's armies, so the Pendragon fell.

"For years there was no king. No crown. Sorcerers and magicians divided the land. Fought like wolves. It was pure anarchy. Mab commanded the Fae into hiding, so mortals would forget about magic.

"Time did its work. Generations passed. Mortals died and the art of their magic with them. New kings and queens sat on Albion's throne, carried the inheritance of Arthur's blood magic in their veins without knowing it. We guarded them as we promised Arthur we would and drew energy from the blood magic. All the way to you and Richard."

"And now we're back where it all started. Fae and mortals together." Anabelle looks down at her palms. They're pale and shaking in the November cold. "My magic . . . it's just like Arthur's. Whenever I get stressed or angry or happy, that's when I feel it the most. That's when it's strongest."

"Do you understand now?" I ask. "Why I asked you not to use it?"

"You're scared I'll get too strong, that I'll lose control

like Arthur." Anabelle frowns at me. Her eyes are twin pools of dark in the shelter of her hoodie. "But I don't think it matters. Sometimes the magic just spills out, like with the ink and the vase. I can't not use it. I've been trying, but it's hard. And after everything you just told me . . . what if the little accidents get worse? It was just a vase at Windsor, but what if next time it's a window? Or a building?"

It will keep rising, whether you show her how to harness it or not.

"Wouldn't it be better if someone would teach me? So I at least have some chance of control from the start? Kieran—"

The Ad-hene's name is like a needle's point, sharp, provoking an instant reaction. "Kieran has spent his entire existence in the Labyrinth. He has no idea how mortals' magic works."

Anabelle's lips press together, turn almost as white as her hands.

"Well, even if he doesn't, you do," she says after a moment. "Emrys. You used magic. And you're a mortal now. You could teach me."

She's not wrong. I could teach her. But it's bad enough having Kieran's spells to taunt me with the old ways. Luring me back to an impossible choice I'm trying my hardest to avoid. I'm not completely sure I could resist the force of the princess's spells too.

"Besides," she says, "if I learn some spells, I can help you and Kieran find Richard."

"You've done plenty, Belle."

Her glare creeps ghoul-like out of her hoodie. Ominous and unnerving.

"Honest. We wouldn't have come this far without you. Where would we be without your sailing? Your awful driving? Your chocolate soufflés?"

She laughs, but then her face returns instantly to seriousness. "But that's not really *doing* something. All this time I've been dragged along like some kind of accessory. I hate feeling helpless."

I swallow, keep staring at the coals. They burn like her words.

How much of my fear stems from Camelot? How much of it is my own weakness returning to haunt me?

"Emrys, I know you'd do anything for my brother. And I will too. If this magic inside me can help us find Richard, then I have to try. I'm good at controlling things. I've done it my whole life. Controlling my image, my grades, every word I say in public. I know I was angry back at the house, but I can manage it. Now that I know. I'll just pretend like I'm at an eternal press conference."

Anabelle is right. For as long as I've known her, she's been the model of togetherness. Controlled even in the worst situations.

Kieran is right too. Anabelle's magic will grow whether she's taught to use it or not. It won't go away just because I tried to ignore it.

My silence stretches out, pushes the princess into more words. "Remember Trafalgar Square? I held my magic back when you asked me to. I controlled it. I can do this, Emrys. I have to."

All of a sudden my thoughts flash back to the edge of Lord Winfred's yacht. When the Kelpie roiled the waters below and Richard's fingers sank into my shoulder, begging me to stay. Trying to stop the inevitable.

Anabelle knows the danger. She still wants to jump. . . . Who am I to stop her?

"Fine," I exhale. "We'll try. But just for little things. Like veiling spells. If you even show a teensy sign of losing control, we stop. If you get anywhere close to being as angry as you were just now . . ."

The princess bites her lip. "Emrys . . . do you remember, back in the prison? How Kieran described that magic?"

Her question catches me by surprise. Unexpected. All I remember are Guinevere's howls. How she choked and frothed and stabbed her own nails into her throat. How her riddles were layered with riddles.

"He said it was *angry*." Her eyes widen, drink in more of the distant firelight. "*Angry.* What if this prisoner who escaped isn't a Fae at all? What if they're mortal?"

Her words spin and scatter like marbles in my head. I try to make sense of them, try to gather them all back into a perfect formation. "That's not possible."

"Why not? Guinevere's still alive."

I argue that it's not the same, but I realize the princess is on to something. Guinevere should have died. Every other *faagailagh* did. If a looped spell has kept her alive this long, then why not some other mortal?

"It makes sense, doesn't it?" Anabelle asks. "That's why Titania thinks it was just mortals who took Richard. And why Protection Command is accusing the Fae."

Not magic or mortal. Magic *and* mortal. A dangerous, brilliant hybrid.

That's why the magic felt so different. So strange. That's how magic and mortal mixed, worked together to make Richard disappear in the middle of a crowd.

It makes sense. But pieces of the puzzle are still missing. Who was this mortal, locked away in a prison for the Fae? Why would they, just weeks after escaping the Labyrinth, want to kidnap a king they know nothing about?

"It's someone Guinevere knows." The princess seems to be talking to herself now. Mumbling. "Someone *you* know. She said it herself!"

The flames in the oil barrel are dying now. My effigy didn't feed them for very long. The crowd doesn't seem to notice. They're still passing around bottles. Still singing: *Remember, remember . . .*

Someone I know. A mortal who worked magic in the age of Camelot.

"Magic was more common in those days," I say. "It could be anyone. Lancelot. Arthur's sister. Merlin. Mordred. Arthur's knights. Arthur himself."

"You think King Arthur is still alive?" Anabelle's eyebrows rise.

"No." I remember how Mordred's blade slid through the cracks of Arthur's armor, so dark I couldn't even see the king's blood on its edge. It was the last time I ever laid eyes on the Pendragon, before I flew back to Mab's court, delivered her the ill news. When I returned, Camelot was razed. A field of bodies gutted and gone.

"So the legend about the Lady of the Lake taking him away to Avalon so he can rise again when Britain needs him isn't true?"

The mortals' stories of Camelot have changed so much over the years, taken on hundreds of forms. Anabelle's is a hopeful twist. Something for desperate mortals to cling to in final hours. But I think of how many final hours this kingdom has been through: wars and plagues and famines. So many countless times where people were beyond hope.

"He would have returned by now, don't you think?"

The song carries on around us, notes growing sloppier with each beer glass shattered on the ground. Voices grow rowdy with alcohol. *God save the King! God save the King!* This chorus becomes a chant, edged riot-hot. It makes every hair on my arm bristle.

"We should go back," Anabelle says with a shiver.

They're bringing out another effigy as we walk away. Her hair is fire itself under the slants of the streetlight. Even before they set the match to it.

Seventeen

I stand in front of the mirror. Stare at the lava locks which have been a part of me for so long. Swirling all the way down my shoulders. I twist my fingers around the ends, the way Richard used to whenever we sat close.

A dead giveaway. I knew this even before Anabelle said it. Before my cap tumbled off in Trafalgar Square and the color poured out for the world to see. Before the citizens of London taped it to stick dolls and doused it in petrol.

Yet I still held on.

I can't keep it. Not when every eye in London is searching for it. Waiting for a veiling spell to slip. A cap to slide off.

"It's just hair," I say into the mirror. But the girl there doesn't look convinced. Her knuckles clench tight around the strands. As if I have to fight her for it.

Kieran offered his transformation spell again, but I couldn't stand the thought of his magic sliding in.

Touching. Making me want. Changing things already on the brink of collapse.

Anabelle offered to cut it. She even hunted down a box of dye in one of Bridget's cabinets. But this is something I have to do myself.

The girl in the mirror lets go, the hair unwinds, falling from her fingers. I grab the scissors from the washroom counter, start to cut. Chunk by chunk it comes away. Pieces of me fall to the floor like red, red snow.

I try not to look at this pile, try not to think of what else—who else—I might have to give up, before the end of all this.

I cut, cut, cut. Until there's more hair covering the floor tiles than my head. It ends sharply, just below my jawline. With a fringe which hangs all the way down to my eyes.

It's not enough.

I set the scissors down, pick up the box of dye.

In the end, black is everywhere. Black like raven's wings. Black like shadows in the corners no one notices. It drips down the edges of the sink, stains the towel around my neck.

A stranger stares out through the glass. A different Emrys.

Everything changes.

I tear off my gloves, toss them in the rubbish bin. One of the glove's fingers had a nick in it, so the dye bled through, glossed over the jade of my ring. My heart is heavy and fast as I thrust my hand under the running faucet, scrub against the ink stains with a vengeance.

Water and silver blur together and suddenly my finger is weightless. It takes me a moment to realize why, to see the ring Richard gave me sliding down the marble basin. Glimmering green just before it's swallowed down the drain.

"No!" I turn off the faucet, claw at the stopper, gut it.

But my ring—that memory of starlit moments and Richard's promise—doesn't shine out of the black. I hover still for a moment over the sink; my heart tries its best not to stop.

It's not gone. Just lost. I can ask Kieran to find it with his magic.

But these thoughts don't stop my heart from thudding inside my chest. They don't help me stop thinking about what else I might have to let go.

The news is blaring when I step into the master bedroom—reporting about the riots which grew out of last night's bonfires. Crowds like the one which hunted me down that night on Westminster Bridge started roaming the streets, shattering store windows, cornering redheads and anyone who looks immortal. Suddenly I'm glad Anabelle made us leave the bonfire when she did.

The princess sits on the floor, opposite Kieran. She's staring at him so intently I wonder if she even hears the television at all.

I feel magic searing off both of them. Kieran whispers and the flame sparks to life in his hand. Anabelle returns the word and fire flutters up in her palms. She squeals, delighted. The flames lick as high as her voice.

"Excellent!" Kieran smiles, a grin so wide and true it's startling. The fire in his own hands dies. He only has eyes for the princess.

I step farther into the room and his smile vanishes. He shifts away from where Anabelle is crouched, eyes snapping straight to me. The princess looks over her shoulder, flame forgotten.

"Emrys? Your hair looks so . . . different. It's pretty!" she adds quickly, as if she's afraid she's offended me. "It's just going to take some getting used to."

"Black suits you," Kieran says.

"It was my only choice," I tell him and nod at the spell-fire still wavering in Anabelle's hand. "I thought we agreed I would teach you magic."

Her palm curls shut, squeezes the fire out. She brushes sparks off against the sleeve of her hoodie. "Kieran was just showing me a few tricks. That's all. Nothing big. There's no harm in it."

I grit my teeth. We don't need another fight. Not with all the magic charging the air.

"She's a quick learner," Kieran offers. "I simply wanted to show her the basics. The foundation of the spell. I didn't expect she'd actually work it."

I'm surprised she was able to imitate the Ad-hene's spells at all. "Just . . . be careful. Humans' magic is different."

"So you say." The Ad-hene crosses his arms. "The princess tells me you think it's a mortal who orchestrated this attack on the king. One who wields magic."

I bite my lip. Glance back at Anabelle. She's shoved her hands in her pockets. I hadn't exactly planned on sharing the theory with Kieran. Not until I'd thought it through. "It's a suspicion."

"Perhaps you're right."

My eyebrows fly up. *"Perhaps?* Are you telling me there's a possibility a mortal was kept in the Labyrinth for centuries and none of the Ad-hene noticed?"

Kieran shrugs. "As Alistair said, it was Queen Mab's wish that we ignore the prisoners in that corridor. Let them be forgotten."

"That's *awful!*" Anabelle gasps. "Trapping people for eternity? With no parole?"

The Ad-hene gazes at her with eyes like the sea—vast yet swallowing. Beautiful danger. "Parole?"

"It's . . ." Anabelle's nose wrinkles as she searches for the perfect word. "A second chance. A fresh start."

"No." The Ad-hene's voice cracks. "Queen Mab offered no paroles. No mercy."

I don't take my eyes off Kieran. "You knew who Guinevere was. You knew *she* was different."

"The only reason we singled out Guinevere was because she possessed no magic at all. An oddity none of the other Labyrinth's inhabitants shared. If the prisoner was a mortal, they hid it well."

A sudden flash of the television catches my attention. Ice-core eyes meet mine. They're so real, so sharp, it takes me a moment to register that they aren't actually in the room. Julian Forsythe stands in front of a bouquet of microphones, his face growing a shade paler with every camera flash.

The news channel's somber narrator speaks over the

scene. *"Despite promises of a self-sustaining energy utopia, the immortal integration movement is quickly losing support in the wake of King Richard's disappearance. Fringe parties such as the M.A.F. have swelled dramatically in just a matter of days—attracting the endorsements of public figures such as Queen Cecilia herself."*

"Oh, Mum," Anabelle murmurs.

The narrator goes on. *"Julian Forsythe's November fifth press conference drew in thousands, despite many Londoners' newfound fear of venturing into the streets."*

The camera pans out to the crowd. A tight pack of bodies and signs. Some of the cardboard protests are the exact same I saw that night on Westminster Bridge. GO BACK TO HELL, MONSTERS! and DON'T DRAG US BACK TO THE DARK AGES, and so many others. I scan the shot for black ski masks, but there are none.

Julian Forsythe's face fills the screen again. Handsome and grim as he addresses the crowd: *"The facts are plain and simple: as long as these monsters lie among us, we are not safe. Men and women should not have to be terrified every time they step out their doors. It's time for mortals to band together and take a stand. We must show these beasts that we are not weak. We are not fodder."*

Julian Forsythe raises his fist and the crowd lets out a thunderous roar.

So much for common goals.

The newscaster talks over the spectators' cheers. *"Julian Forsythe is among the many calling for a motion of no confidence against the current government. If this motion were to pass, Lord Winfred's Parliament would dissolve and emergency elections would take place. The current prime minister has yet to hold any press conference or comment on the king's disappearance."*

"Funny." Anabelle walks up to the screen, points at the politician's bared wrist. "I never knew he had a tattoo."

I catch a glimpse of ink tails poking out of his sleeve before the shot focuses in on the young politician's brilliant eyes. He's looking out over the crowd the same way he studied the yellow flower on the yacht. With sharp, unmistakable intent.

That unreal blue pierces through the screen, through me. I would remember those eyes . . . wouldn't I? Even from as long ago as the Camelot days. But appearances can be deceiving. Appearances can change.

My fingers comb absently through my damp hair.

"Belle, how long has Julian Forsythe been around?"

The princess stares at the screen, entranced by the same eyes. "On the political scene? I'm not sure. People really didn't start noticing him until the integration started."

I swallow. Think of the birdsfoot trefoil on the embroidered coach cushion. The masked men who left it there. I look at the crowd in front of Julian. How they roar with each pump of his fist. They would do anything he asked. Some of them might even kidnap a king. . . .

"He's young," Anabelle goes on, "only graduated from Oxford a few years ago."

"He went to Oxford?" I feel my hopes falling. All those fragile suspicions caving in on themselves.

"Yes. Rumor has it he was quite the ladies' man in his time." The princess raises her eyebrows.

The crowd keeps screaming. The reporter keeps talking about riots and potential elections and Julian Forsythe keeps staring. That sick twist of a smile on his face.

I reach out for the power button. The television screen collapses with the same speed as my heart.

Somewhere downstairs a timer goes off. A high, electric hum which pulls Anabelle to the door. "Oh! That'll be the flan! I hope you're both hungry. It's beetroot!"

But my insides are hollowed with an emptiness food can't fill. I look at the blank screen, the open doorway, my too-light ring finger. The Ad-hene watches the doorway too. His eyes are the only full thing in this room.

"Kieran?" When I say his name his gaze snaps to me, called from a trance. "I need your help. My ring fell down the sink."

He follows me to the washroom, where dye still streaks like tears down the marble basin. Where the floor is covered in pieces of my old self. Kieran steps through them gingerly, over to the black-hole sink.

I hold my breath as he peers into the abyss. His lips go tight with concentration, form summoning spells aimed into the drain's U-bend. Nothing good returns. The sink only fills with gunk: pieces of molding hair and ruin.

Kieran steps away from the rot, tells me what I already know. "It's gone."

I look down at my bare finger. Start to wither under the weight of this terrible truth: I waited too long, wasted too much time. The ring is so far gone not even magic can retrieve it.

I'm on the floor. Curled like a baby mouse in a nest of my own hair. The Ad-hene kneels next to me.

"It's just a ring," he says. "It can be replaced."

This truth does not reach deep enough, doesn't even begin to tap the fears, the loss inside.

"It's been three days since Richard was taken. Three days . . . What if we're too late? What if I lose him because I didn't know when to let go?"

These truths, these questions, tremble through me. Shudder with tears.

I expect Kieran to add another cutting truth to my arsenal of doubt—and be done with it. But the Ad-hene says nothing. His arm slides around my shoulder. His magic fills me like a ballast stone, evening out the swells of fear.

I'm not frozen this time, but I'm not fighting either. I'm so tired of fighting. Tired of trying to be someone I'm not.

So I stay and lean into this rock of a soul, resting my head against the granite of his muscles. It's nice, having someone here beside me, someone who isn't afraid or pulling away.

He's closer than he should be. His voice is warm in my ear, low and close, like secrets. "If we don't hear from Queen Titania by tomorrow, we'll go out and keep searching. I don't think—"

"Hello? The flan is going cold!" Anabelle calls from the bedroom in a clear bell voice. The Ad-hene stands just as the princess halts in the doorway, takes in the scene: black sink, hair everywhere, me on the floor, Kieran looming. "What's going on in here?"

I don't know, and even if I did I'm not sure I could bear to tell her.

I'm all off center again.

"The flan is ready?" Kieran asks instead.

Anabelle nods at him. "Beetroot with fennel and goat cheese. I might have already tried some. And it might be amazingly delicious."

"I can't wait." Something like hunger flints through Kieran's face as he joins the princess in the doorway. He looks back at me. "Are you coming, Lady Emrys?"

"You two eat," I tell them. "I just—I need a moment."

"Are you sure?" Anabelle's eyes trail the room again. Try to see where I fit in to all of it. "We'll save you some flan."

"Not if it's as tasty as you say it is," Kieran adds.

"Don't be greedy!" The princess turns, so I can barely see the smile invading her pursed lips. "You don't even need food."

"Right, but I want it. And it's all your fault." Kieran trails her through the bedroom, following the promise of beetroots and flowing gold hair. Their banter fades down stairs.

"I'll be fine," I lie to the empty doorway. To the dark-haired stranger in the mirror above.

Eighteen

This time I'm running as soon as the dream starts. Away from the watcher on the hill, churning through a sea of mud. My steps are heavy, but my will is stronger. I lunge and dive, tear all the way to Richard.

He looks mostly the same: black boots, ermine cape, crimson jacket full of medals. But there are little differences. His jawline is blunted by scruff and his hair is tousled, slanted at all angles.

He looks just as dazed when I reach him, grab his sleeve. Again it strikes me how real he is. The feel of the jacket's fabric under my fingers—the muscled arm beneath it. Even the *smell* of him—cinnamon and cloves—is the same. It pulls at my heart.

I want those arms around me. To pull me close and hold me there.

But I know what's coming. This dream always ends the same.

"Come on, Richard!" I'm tugging him away from where

I know the black knight is marching. Just past Richard's shoulder I see Mordred: blade held high, coming for us. "We have to run!"

Richard doesn't move. He's staring at me with a dazed, confused look.

"Embers?" He blinks, like a man underground who's suddenly thrust back into sunlight. "What happened to your hair?"

"We have to—" I stop midsentence. His question hits me, leaves me breathless. "What did you say?"

"Your hair. It's different."

His fingers brush my new hair from my eyes, so I can see him more clearly. His freckles are almost gone now, a fleck or two over the bridge of his nose where there was once a salting. His almond eyes—flashing and swirling like all the precious metals and stones in the world were twisted together.

Details far too intricate for mere memory to stitch together. Even in dreams.

Is it possible?

Is he actually here?

I reach up, frame his face in my hands. His skin smolders under my fingertips.

So real.

It's just a dream. Just my heart wanting and longing for all it's lost. But his touch skates so softly over my skin. Summons shivers. I bring his lips to mine. The meeting is a thrill of light, glowing all the way down to my toes. Richard pulls in closer. His kiss is yearning, tinged with the perfect chemistry of give and take. His hands slide down to the small of my back, fill my insides with a hot, blooming feeling.

The kiss ends and he's still here: cheeks flushed. Eyes clear and full of spark. My fingers trace the still-tingle of him on my lips. And I know.

But it's too late. Mordred's mailed fingers sink like dragon talons into Richard's shoulder. Tear him back. Away from me. Into the cruel steel of Mordred's blade.

When I wake, my lips still tingle and burn. My heart lurches into my throat, high and thrumming from the feel of him—the swell that's so much like magic. I'm gripping my pillow so hard that the fabric has torn.

I lie still. The bedroom is wrapped in night. A blackness only equaled by the feeling in my chest. Richard's touch, his kiss, was all light. His absence is just as powerful. A deep ache, streaking down my soul like the dye in the sink. Accenting the chill of the room, the emptiness of the sheets beside me.

Richard was real. He was there. It's an impossible thought, but it floods me with a certainty which leaves no room for doubt.

I shut my eyes, try to will myself back to sleep. Back to him. But all my insides are awake.

Richard is alive. And he's out there, waiting for me to find him.

I sit up. The sheets are tangled at my feet, as if I was actually running through them. The nail marks Guinevere left on my arm a few weeks ago have burst again. Weeping red down to my elbow.

"Oh good. You're awake." It's only when Kieran speaks that I see him, sitting in the darkest corner of the room. He melts almost completely into the shadows, only his marking glows. A phosphorescent whisper of ever-changing swirls.

Though I'm clothed, I seize my sheets up anyway, hug them against my chest. "What are you doing in here?"

His scar flares brighter. It's not until I see the confusion scrambling his handsome features that I realize how angry my question sounded.

"It's just . . ." I fumble for an explanation, my mind still fogged over with dream. "The mortals consider it strange to watch someone while they're sleeping."

I think of all those nights I sat by Richard's window, watching him sail through dreams. How a smile lit up his face as soon as he woke, saw me. Always that smile. How I miss it.

"I was waiting for you to wake up. This came just an hour ago." The Ad-hene holds out a tight roll of parchment: Queen Titania's response. My heart drums war songs inside my chest when I take it from him, tear the seal.

Dog escaped. Still in London. Do not trust the Ad-hene.

I stare at the script for a long moment, to make sure I read it right. It's Titania's writing, a shaky earthquake version, yet still hers.

Three sentences. After lifetimes of loyal service as a Frithemaeg, after days of waiting, that's all the Faery queen has to offer me. Three wobbling fragments of thought. No help from the Guard, who should be at Anabelle's side regardless. Not even a hint of whether or not they intend to return.

Do not trust the Ad-hene. Bitterness rises up my throat as I reread the final sentence. It was Titania's pride—her willful, stubborn ignorance—which allowed Richard to be taken in the first place. And now she's telling me to do nothing. Just like her.

Has she broken her oath to the crown and abandoned mortalkind altogether? Is that even possible?

I think of the stun gun's savage stab. The anger which thinned her voice even before that. Suddenly the possibility doesn't seem all that remote.

The parchment crumples easily in my fingers. Without a fight.

"News?" the Ad-hene asks. "Should I wake the princess?"

The clock on the bedstand glows an early, sunless hour. All I want to do is fall back asleep, kiss Richard again. But Kieran is sitting on the edge of my bed and Blæc is roaming London's foggy streets, the answers to my many questions buried beneath all that shadowy fur and razor teeth.

"No. Let Belle sleep while she can. She won't be much help where we're going."

His eyebrows rise: dark arches sweeping with questions.

I take a breath, let go of the sheets. "We have a dog to hunt."

The air around Westminster tastes of morning: heavy with fog, drear, and damp. A steady drizzle falls, turning gutters into rivers. The Thames roils through the city, a swollen beast.

Kieran walks with me over the bridge, watching currents of rubbish rush under our feet. Remnants of bonfires bob past: burnt pieces of wood, hollow beer bottles, even the half-charred face of an effigy, trailed by sopping strings of orange yarn.

There aren't many souls out at this hour, but a few have already started their morning commute. Cars, double-decker buses, and people trickle past us, their attentions deterred by Kieran's veiling spell.

My attention, however, is completely gripped by the Ad-hene's magic. He seems to have no trouble holding the invisibility spell. It's stronger, more potent than last time, dripping over me more wholly than the rain. My new hair is already sopping wet. Even my bones are chilled.

"You really think the Black Dog is still around here?" Kieran asks.

"This is his territory," I say over my shoulder. "There's no reason he shouldn't return to it."

We cross to the east shore, where the London Eye spins round and round. I loop all the way down to where a tunnel stretches under the Westminster Bridge. Blæc's lair.

"Wait!" Kieran's hand falls on my shoulder, a startling,

261

physical weight. He holds me back just steps from the tunnel's entrance. "I should go first."

I'm not sure what's worse now. The feel of his magic or his touch. They're almost one and the same. Both root into me, raw, feeding power and possibilities. What might have been. What could be . . .

No! Richard is my future. My center.

Isn't he?

Kieran steps forward; his eyes bore into the tunnel entrance. His hand reaches out, pauses in the air. "This is *your* magic!"

He's right. One of my old enchantments is still in place. A blocking spell, meant to keep mortals from entering the Black Dog's main tunnel.

"It was a good spell." He goes on, his fingers dancing through the air, plucking at webs of magic I can't see.

"Was?" I say stiffly, tasting what's no longer mine.

"It's broken. Someone tore through." The Ad-hene's fingers become a fist, pull the remnants of my magic away like a bothersome cobweb. Pieces float past like dandelion seeds. I hold my breath until the traces of my old spell fade altogether.

This tunnel is blacker than midnight. Kieran strides in—arms up and ready—prepared for the Black Dog's teeth. The mark of his arm is all-dark, his steps full of hunter's stealth. I follow, bracing myself for the sudden snarls, the flash of demon eyes.

But they never come. Kieran halts in the middle of the tunnel. We both wait, still and tight in the silence. One minute. Two. Three.

We are alone.

Kieran's scar flares through the dark. The walkway burns to life: stark black and white, like a film negative.

My throat catches.

Runes. Everywhere runes. Written out in black marker, covering the tunnel's white tiles like a madman's scrawl. Harsh, angled lines strung together like a physicist's equation. Too clustered and tight and ancient to be graffiti.

I stare for a long time, trying to understand the sheer number of these symbols. Many of them look familiar, but I know this only because I saw them chalked inside a cell on the Isle of Man.

Kieran's staring too, stunned. His mouth is cracked open, lungs swelling.

The marks are on the floors too, running like ants along the concrete all the way to the center of the tunnel.

My muscles seize tight when I see the Black Dog on the

floor. Blæc's legs are curled up, almost as if it's sleeping. But Black Dogs don't sleep.

This place isn't a tunnel. It's a grave.

There are no markings on Blæc's body. No blood. The beast's fur has lost its gloss. Those burning acid eyes are closed. Never to open again.

Kieran crouches down by the Black Dog's body, threads his fingers through its bristly black fur. The tendons of the Ad-hene's hand cord tight.

"A fresh death. Very fresh." Kieran looks around. As if the killer might still be lurking behind us.

I feel it, suddenly rising and swelling around us. The prisoner's magic rushes through the tunnel like a wave. I spin around, but the space behind me is empty. My eyes snap back to Kieran. He's still hovering over Blæc's body, watching its carcass crumble to pieces. Reduced to a pile of ash in seconds.

"How . . ." I look back over my shoulder. The burst of magic is already fading. Gone. Just like Blaec's body.

"The runes." Kieran points to the ground, where the Black Dog's outline is crowned by symbols. "I think the magic is *inside* them."

"Belle was right," I whisper.

The Ad-hene looks up at me. His fingers trail through the ash.

"A mortal did this. That's why they tore through my spell at the door. They had to. They couldn't enter otherwise." I kneel down, placing a hand over the symbols on the floor. There's nothing but the chill of concrete under my palm. "The runes are *spells.*"

Kieran's hands sift through the ash, edge closer to mine. Our fingers are almost touching. Only a few symbols apart.

"All mortals needed something to conduct their magic." Except Arthur. I make a mental note to strike him off of the list of possibilities. "The runes—this writing is that channel!"

"A mortal," he repeats softly. "A mortal with magic. Like the princess."

"Someone from the Camelot days." I let my voice rise, hopeful. "Perhaps you remember . . . it would be a prisoner brought in around the same time as Guinevere."

"I have no memory of those days. I was in the Labyrinth's darkness then. It clouds many things. Erases them."

"You remembered me," I tell him.

"That's different." His finger slides forward, touches

mine. "You're different, Emrys. You intrigued me from the first. You have a way of shining."

My heart stutters. My palm presses hard onto the dead runes. Kieran's touch is the only warmth there is in this damp riverside tunnel. His magic is still everywhere, hiding me from all eyes but his. Even though I'm draped in a veiling spell, I feel more exposed than ever.

"You don't know how deep your darkness is until there's a light." His eyes flicker to the tunnel entrance, back the way we came. Then forward again, to me. "I think I'm beginning to understand."

I don't think I can understand anything anymore. Why the mortals I fought so hard to protect are torching effigies of me. Why Titania has left us to fend for ourselves. Why Richard pulled away. Why he was taken. Why my dreams relive heartbreak, night after night. Why my fingers are still touching the Ad-hene's. Why my eyes burn into his. Why his face is suddenly so close to mine. Why I stay still, my breath quivering in the air. Waiting.

Somewhere above us a horn blares. The sound sweeps across the river, rattles the tiles.

The moment breaks. Shatters like an undone spell.

I pull my hand away. There's ash on my fingertips.

"He's not your only choice." Kieran's words are as soft

as the feathers in my pillow. Complete with prickling quill ends. "Remember that."

"We found the trail." My voice is ice, but my insides are flaring. I have to get away from him and his pulsing magic. I have to get away from whatever has taken root inside me. "The Ad-hene's oath has been fulfilled. You're free to go. Queen Titania and her Frithemaeg can track it from here."

Kieran stays crouched over the pile of ash. All danger, power, and curiosity.

"This is no trail," he says, nodding at the marked walls. "It's a taunt. If this magic works as you say it does . . . then we have no way of tracing it. If it doesn't flow in its worker's veins, it's not a part of their aura."

I edge away from Blæc's remains until my spine curves against the wall's arch.

"Where is the Faery queen? Where are the Frithe-maeg?" His questions echo through the tunnel, come back to haunt me. "They've left the princess completely unguarded. It does not seem to me that Titania is your strongest ally. You still need me. Unless you wish to reclaim your magic."

And lose Richard forever.

He's right. The Frithemaeg aren't coming back to

London. They've abandoned us. I'll need more than a pile of ash and some scrawls on a wall to convince Titania to return.

Dead ends everywhere. Trails which tangle up inside themselves. Endless looping circles, just like the silver lines on the Ad-hene's arm. And, just like inside the Labyrinth, Kieran is my only way out.

Nineteen

The sky is the same color as Kieran's eyes: brimming with silver storm glow when we arrive back at the house in Chelsea. It's not until the door yawns open and heat blasts around my body that I realize just how cold I was. Every inch of my skin is glazed with rainchill. My fingertips have a lavender tinge; the rain slapping against the window sounds heavy with ice.

Kieran rubs his hands together, whispers that infamous fire to life between his knuckles. He offers some to me with open palms. I shake my head, stick my own hands into my pockets. They still sting from the last open flame I handled.

"Where the hell were you?" Anabelle's greeting is quick and brutal. "Get out of the doorway before someone sees you!"

Kieran looks startled. His flame vanishes, smoke braids through the air. Gray as Blaec's ashes.

"I've been worried sick for the past hour. I was half

expecting your mug shots to flash up on the news! You could have at least left a note!"

Looking at the princess I doubt she's even been up for an hour. Her appearance has the irksome fresh of morning. Rose-powder pink tingles her cheeks. Her hair is pulled back in a long ponytail, but a few angel wisps have escaped, gold playing against the tilt of her cheekbones. The almond of her eyes. The same features she shares with Richard.

Kieran studies her too, his head tilted like some curious, cautious panther. "You're angry?"

"Ye—" Anabelle catches my stare, sees how I'm tensed and waiting for an outburst. Another broken vase. "No. Just worried. I thought you'd left."

"Only for a short time," the Ad-hene says. "I would not leave you without saying good-bye."

Silence falls over the foyer, but it still feels like they're speaking. Pouring through entire conversations with their eyes. The quiet stretches on and on: wasting more seconds and minutes.

"We found a clue," I say when I can't stand it any longer.

Anabelle looks away from Kieran, her brown eyes sparkling with hope.

"It's not much. . . ." I try to counter her excitement. "We found the Black Dog which attacked the carriage, but it was dead. The prisoner found it first. You were right, Belle, a mortal's doing this. They're using magic through runes."

Anabelle's breath is sacred and quivering. "Runes?"

"Yes. There was writing all over the tunnel. . . ." I trail off when the princess turns. Her bare feet pad on the wood floor as she runs to the grand piano, snatches up some decorative sheet music. "What are you doing?"

But the princess is all mumbles, searching through every shelf and drawer in sight. "Pen. Pen. I need a pen."

We follow her into the study. A room of leatherbound books and mahogany. The air smells distinctly of pipe smoke—sweet cloves and tweed.

"Belle, what's going on?"

The princess doesn't seem to hear my question. A plump black fountain pen has captured her attention. She leans over the desk she found it in, glides its elegant arch tip over the back side of the sheet music. Skitters and scratches crowd the page like claws.

Finally Anabelle steps back, wipes that crown of angel hairs from her face. "The runes. Did they look like this?"

My heart snags at the sight of black ink on paper. The

princess's rendering is softer than the tunnel symbols, filled with more bend and curl. Even so the etching is undeniably similar, a fragment from the long nightmarish web Kieran and I were just caught in.

I snatch the ruined sheet music from Anabelle's fingers. Its edges warp in my trembling hands. "Where did you see this?"

"Last night," she answers. Her voice is nearly as shaky as my hands. "On the television. It's Julian Forsythe's tattoo."

"Are you sure?"

The princess nods. "The cameras didn't stay on it for long. I just remember thinking it was odd. That's why it stuck with me."

"But—but you said he went to Oxford. . . ." I trail off as the complete oversight of my statement rings through my head, showing just how much my mind has settled into the mortals' thought patterns.

This is a land of magic now. Full of shape-shifters and spells which can alter your appearance in an instant. The man standing on the podium looks like the Julian Forsythe who walked the halls of Oxford, but that hardly means he actually is. A sorcerer could have easily killed the young politician and slipped into his skin, his life.

I think of that night in Windsor Castle's ballroom. That eerie smile on Julian Forsythe's face. The scathing, surgical precision of his eyes. The cool lilt of his words: *We don't have to be enemies. The way I see it, you and I have a common goal.*

Who'd really been speaking that whole time? Mordred? Lancelot? Merlin? A soul I've forgotten entirely?

"It's him, Emrys. It has to be." The gleam is back in Anabelle's eyes. Lighting up her words.

My insides are all dread—thinking of those blue, blue eyes and that dark, dark cell and the rage which lurks inside each. Now that the prisoner has a face, I'm even less certain I can challenge him as I am.

"So what now?" The princess asks after a pool of silence.

"We should tread softly," Kieran says. "It's an adder's nest. This magic is too potent and untested for my strength alone. Even without magic, this man wields a good deal of power. The mortals drink his words like mead."

Anabelle's face scrunches with frown and thought. "What about Queen Titania? The Frithemaeg? They can help us!"

I shake my head. "She won't come. Not without solid proof."

"So we get it." The princess takes back the paper, stares hard at the letters. "If Forsythe is the one behind all of this, there will be more than just a tattoo. More runes. Or evidence that he orchestrated Richard's kidnapping."

"What are you suggesting?" My words dance on eggshells.

"I know where his office is. I sent a coronation invitation there." Anabelle's eyes go sharp. She's looking at Kieran. "We'll go at night, when he's gone. Use veiling spells. Be quick. Find some evidence and present it to Titania. He'll be back in the Labyrinth before he knows what hit him."

My stomach plunges at the thought of what she's suggesting. Whoever is staring out from behind Julian's sapphire eyes has spent countless years plotting. They stole a king out from under the eyes of an entire kingdom. Pitted mortal and Fae against each other with clever speeches and damning evidence. Took thinly veiled prejudices and worked them in their favor, blinding Faery queens and human governments alike.

It seems almost *too* simple, walking into this soul's office. Finding what we need and leaving. Just like that. I can't help but think that maybe, just maybe, this is a trap.

"I don't know," I begin. "It will be dangerous."

Anabelle puts her hands on her hips. "Do you have a better plan?"

Not without reclaiming my magic. I look back at Kieran. He leans in the doorway, lithe and brawny, so I can't help but notice the muscles gathered under the cling of his thermal shirt. His power fills the office, pedals my weary heart. Chains it through the moment under the bridge: our fingertips touching, words he said, things I felt . . .

"Emrys?" The princess snaps with fingers and voice and I'm back in the office, trying my best to think of a better plan.

"Kieran can only veil one of us without risking exposure," I think aloud.

"So teach me," Anabelle says. "You said you would."

"I think maybe Lady Emrys is right, Princess." Kieran pushes off of the doorway. Night curls spill and spool against his regal brow. "Searching through this soul's office will be dangerous. It might be best if you stayed here."

Hurt flashes through Anabelle's face. "You're the one who told me I shouldn't be afraid. I'm not getting left behind this time!"

Kieran frowns. His shale eyes cut over to where I stand.

We'll be alone again, if he has his way. He'll call me Emrys instead of Lady Emrys. His voice will dip low and I'll have trouble remembering what Richard's touch feels like. I'll start to think more and more about the futures Kieran pried open with five small words: *He's not your only choice.*

I can't let that happen.

"All right." I nod at the flustered princess. "I'll teach you."

I take her to the rooftop, where we have the least chance of her spells deflecting and collapsing a wall. The rain is lighter now. Clouds hang low over the city, drape over rooftops and weather vanes. I can barely see past the next house as I face the princess.

"First you have to focus. Center yourself."

Anabelle nods. "Kieran says it's like staring at a pinpoint of light. Or concentrating on a candle."

"Well, Kieran isn't here right now." A fact I'm more than thankful for. I'm not sure if I could concentrate under his gray stare. "But yes. That pull, that energy you feel inside you is what you must concentrate on."

Anabelle shuts her eyes. Draws several deep breaths of frost-laced air.

"Veiling spells are tricky," I explain. "They have a lot of different layers and details, depending on who you want to see you. We'll start with a very general one. It will hide you from everyone."

It feels strange, trying to put into words something that's always been so reflexive. Like teaching someone to walk. Or speak a language you've known all your life. So much of it is innate, beyond explanation.

I try my best anyway. "Keep concentrating. Now I want you to take that energy inside you and twist it into this word while you speak it: *behyd*."

Her eyebrows furrow together. The word rises up and out of her. As naturally as a breath. *"Behyd."*

She vanishes—a shimmer and gone—like summer heat rising. I blink, but the air in front of me is only swirling mist.

Kieran's right. She is a quick learner.

"Good job," I say, even though I don't really mean it. Not in my deepest of hearts.

She reappears like a wraith through the fog—bright face and open mouth. Her joy wilts fast into a frown. "It didn't stick."

"I didn't even expect you to disappear that time," I tell her, trying to ignore the jealous pang under my chest.

Anabelle's magic fills the air, burning thicker than the cold. My skin sings with it. "Holding the spell for a long time is where your emotions come in. Whatever feeds your magic will maintain the spell. Try to think of a strong emotion. A positive one. Something which makes you happy. I know that might be hard with everything that's happened, but—"

"Got it." Anabelle shuts her eyes again. Nibbles the edge of her lip in concentration. Her whole face is pink with near-winter cold. *"Behyd."*

She's gone again. I'm alone and stunned in this island of mist. Waiting for Anabelle's emotion to waver. For her spell to fail.

Mist spits through my hair, plasters it to my cheeks. A few sparrows land by my feet. Heads cocked, ready for crumbs I don't have. The minutes stretch out; the birds realize I'm empty-handed and head back off into the almost-storm.

And still I wait.

The princess is a natural. Of course, I don't know why I expected anything different. Everything she does is perfect. The emotion Anabelle is tapping into is strong, wealthy. Made of stolen glances, beetroot flans, and magic sessions.

I think of all the smiles I've seen on her face the last few days, so at odds with everything crumbling around us. I think of the reason why he almost kissed me. How I almost let him.

We're in very dangerous territory.

"Am I ready?" Anabelle's voice springs up behind me. Grenading all sorts of emotions through my body: shock, guilt, green, green envy.

I spin around and she's there, standing by a stack of folded lounge chairs. Where just a few nights ago Kieran stood, and I told him how much his presence meant.

"Let's practice it a few more times," I tell her. "Just to make sure."

She nods and we do. But there's no need. Her spell is dead-on. An arrow into a bull's-eye. Every time. In the mist and out of it again.

My thoughts feel just as cloudy. Swirling with the feel of Anabelle's magic all around. And the memory of Richard's kiss, echoing so far into my waking hours. And the dark, brimming smolder of Kieran's touch.

He's not your only choice.

I came up here to the rooftop to escape Kieran and his words. But it's too late. They're already lodged inside, creeping like feeler roots. Finding all the cracks in my mortal soul, prying open a Pandora's box of thoughts.

What would it be like? If I'd never met Richard. If I hadn't retreated from Kieran's lips. If magic and love could both be mine . . .

No.

I don't love Kieran.

But . . . there's something there—a glimmer—which makes me think I could.

He's not Richard. He never will be. But he is a choice: a never-ending life of power and magic. A life where I can keep Richard safe from every threat. A life where Richard isn't forced to be fighting, always fighting for a cause which isn't even truly his.

Maybe Queen Mab was right. Maybe mortals and Fae can never be together. Maybe Richard and I were never truly meant for each other. No matter how much we thought otherwise, no matter how much we wanted it. We were just a fling—fleeting as summer—and now the autumn has come.

Maybe all this time I've only been choosing what *I* want the most. What's best for *me*. Maybe my choice to be with Richard was just as foolish and destructive as Guinevere's. Maybe it's time to undo it before the kingdom burns. Before there are only ashes left.

No. No. No.

All I want to do is go back to sleep. To be with just Richard. Only Richard. In a place where all of these other forces and wants and choices don't exist.

But all dreams must end. Both the real and the waking.

"Emrys, are you listening?" We've been up here so long that Anabelle is almost soaked through with the storm's breath. She's a mess. Hair plastered to her face and skin mottled with cold. Yet I've never seen her look more alive. She's kindled from the inside, her spells flashing like a lighthouse on the rocks. I can hardly stand to look at her for it.

"I was asking you what spell we should work on next."

Next? I wrap my arms around my chest and shiver. I'm just as wet and dripping as the princess, but there's no light inside me to ward off the dreary November chill. I don't think I can stand on this rooftop much longer, watching Richard's sister gain back everything I've lost.

"We're done for now." My breath rises like dragon's smoke between us. "Belle?"

Anabelle looks at me. Bright, life, innocence. And I hate what I'm about to say. Why I'm about to say it.

"Be careful, with Kieran. I know—" I swallow a lungful of mist, wonder if I'm saying too much. "I know he's attractive. But—"

"Really, Emrys?" She laughs, but the sound is too loud. Pounding decibels trying to drown out the truth of things. "Don't get me wrong, he's cute and all, but I'm focused on finding Richard. Not getting a new boyfriend. Besides, can you imagine what Mum would think if I brought home an Ad-hene? Two immortals at family dinners. She'd have a conniption."

Too loud. Too many words. Crowding, crowding, crowding. I even it out with a silence.

"You've got nothing to worry about, sister." The princess smiles, flashing pearly edged teeth. "Thanks for helping me today."

Every one of her words is a bitter pill. But I can't let her see how they're choking me. I turn and start to head for the stairs.

"Let's get out of the cold," I say.

Twenty

The world is all rain, darkness, and streetlamps as Anabelle leads the way up the sidewalk. Across the street Big Ben chimes the hour, the glow of the clock's face hidden by fog. Twelve low, mournful notes shiver over the tops of the puddles, under my skin. They call out the start of a new day. Another twenty-four hours of Richard gone.

I tried to sleep more, once my lessons with Anabelle were finished. Tried to find my way back into the dreams. Back into Richard's arms. But every time I shut my eyes all I could see was Blæc's body, crumbling to ash in a sea of symbols. And Kieran's hand inching toward mine. His eyes snagging all those stray pieces of my soul. And Anabelle's spells weaving together perfectly, filling her face with joy.

I saw these things and I could not dream.

"This way." Anabelle waves us around the corner of a Victorian Gothic building. It towers above us, banded bricks and Portland stone. A few of the dollhouse windows still have lights shining: members of Parliament pulling late nights in their offices. "His office is on the top floor."

I don't know why she's whispering. All of us are under veiling spells, invisible to the few souls we pass: a smoking man waiting on a bus bench, a security guard planted in the office lobby, flipping lazily through a copy of *The Sun*, frowning at pictures of the latest riots. Neither of them bats an eyelid when the princess walks past. She's held her spell amazingly well, even putting into practice a layering trick which allows Kieran and me to see her. The Ad-hene must have taught her when I retreated to my room, tried to see Richard again.

I walk ahead of Kieran. Between him and the princess. I can feel his stare boring into my back. Feel his magic wrapped around me like a Kelpie's seaweed mane. All the way up the stairs. All the way down the hall of oak-paneled doors and gold nameplates. To the very end where the script reads: JULIAN FORSYTHE—M.A.F.

Anabelle speaks the lock open, another skill Kieran must've taught her while I tried to sleep. I feel my heart high in my throat as the door swings wide, gives us our first glimpse into the lion's den.

Julian Forsythe's office is tiny, cramped against the slant of the roof above. Its limited wall space is covered in shelves, filled with titles like *The Prince, Behemoth,* and *Discourses on the First Ten Books of Titus Livy.* There's a desk with a few gilded picture frames and a Newton's cradle. A corner piled high with boxes.

"Looks like he's getting ready to move." Anabelle nods at the buckling tower of cardboard. The edges of files and embossed leather books jut out of the lip. "He must really be counting on those emergency elections. I heard on the news that the motion of no confidence passed. The elections are actually happening. Tomorrow."

The thought of Julian Forsythe inscribing PRIME MINISTER on his nameplate scrapes like fingernails inside my stomach.

Anabelle grabs a silver-framed photo from one of the top boxes. It's a picture of Julian and his wife on a beach. Mediterranean waters fan behind them, vast stretches of aqua and near-green. The couple is smiling, fingers interlocked. Julian's crescent of white teeth still reminds me of a joker's grin.

"I wouldn't be caught dead in that." Anabelle's finger smudges over the long, flowing fabric of Elaine Forsythe's long sleeves and yoga bottoms. "Especially on a beach."

"Says the girl who's spent the last four days wearing a hoodie," I can't help but point out.

The princess rolls her eyes and tosses the picture back in the box. "I'm a fugitive. I have an excuse."

"She probably sunburns easily. Her skin is so pale." I sigh. "Contrary to your long-standing beliefs, Belle, wearing ugly clothes isn't a crime."

"It is when you're a politician's wife! People *see* you. They *expect* a certain standard of fashion! I feel bad for her."

I think of the woman who sat across from me at the Winfreds' gala. Those dark doe eyes wide with horror, hate. "I wouldn't feel too bad for her. She did marry Julian."

"Yes, but that was before some crazy Camelot magician swooped in and stole his body," Anabelle shoots back.

I look back at the picture, notice how white Julian Forsythe's knuckles are around his wife's. Tight. Probably not sunburn then. I wonder how many bruises and secrets she's hiding under that fabric.

"Speaking of crazy Camelot magicians, where do we start?" Kieran brushes past my shoulder—iron strength and wretched tenderness—and joins Anabelle in the middle of the office. "And what are we looking for?"

"Everything. Runes. Contracts for hit men." The princess's hands fall from her hips as she approaches the mountain of boxes. "Something's here. I know it."

The pair tackles the first box while I watch from the doorway, trying to feel for rune magic. The office air is tangled tight with the richness of blood magic. The razor edge of Kieran's spell. If there are rune spells here, they aren't strong enough for me to feel out.

I go behind the desk, have a seat in the leather chair. Its drawers are mostly packed away, populated by a few stray pens and a thick wad of papers entitled *A Treatise on the Evils of Immortal Integration.* I scan the shelves, flip through hundreds of dry-leaf book pages. Find nothing.

Big Ben strikes again. A clear, single call through the night. Anabelle and Kieran are through the fourth box, rifling through sheaves of paper.

"Nothing. Just traffic law proposals from ages ago." Anabelle stands, throws the beige folder back into the growing pile. "My eyes are going cross-eyed."

I pick up a copy of *Behemoth* for the third time. Its words streak together as I flip through it. End in a page of empty, blank white.

There's nothing here.

The trail is dead.

Julian Forsythe's tattoo is just ink spread under flesh. Not magic.

I shut the book, slide it back onto the shelf with all the other useless volumes. "There's nothing here. We would've found something by now. Felt it."

The last box sits between Anabelle and Kieran, a lonely thing. Both of them look at it with drawn-lipped grimaces. As if they know it too holds nothing. The princess doesn't say anything as she reaches out to open it.

All I want to do is sleep. There's such weariness inside, my soul stretched thin. Like a woman's nylon sock, ripping. Full of gaps and holes.

I lay my head down on the desk. Shut my eyes.

But instead of black all I see is a pure and blinding white. The spell is like the first stab of a headache, forking through my head. It stings across my scalp, bristling every hair. I jerk back in my seat, away from the desk.

"What's wrong?" Anabelle asks, a clump of files forgotten in her hand.

"I—" The charge is gone but my head is swimming. Made of spin.

Kieran is like a wolf on a scent, rigid and alert. He approaches the desk with measured steps. Eyes keen and focused on its wood. "Lady Emrys found something."

I frown and rub my temple, where magic buzzes like a hangover.

Kieran kneels down so his eyes are level with the wood. He wipes a palm across the desk's surface, pulls it back as if he just pressed his flesh onto a searing iron.

"In the center," he says, his hand still hovering above the desk.

The wood is varnished—all gloss—not even a hint of a scratch. Julian Forsythe must not use his desk very much. I pull out the center drawer again. It's just as barren as it was the last four times I scanned it. Hollow space. Everything in plain sight.

But there are still some hidden places. I slide my hand into the drawer, feel out the wood of the desk's underside. It's as glossy as the top, sleek like fish scales.

Until it isn't. I barely have time to register the harsh carve under my fingers before the magic strikes. It cramps pain through my fingers, burns under my arm, reaches all the way to my shoulder before I pull away.

I yank the drawer out with my good hand. Kieran shines his mark into the new gap.

And there they are, ugly scars in the wood, carved out by something sharp and determined. Runes cramped into a long, deliberate string. Eating into the desk like termites.

My fingers are tingling now. Numb with the spell's aftermath.

"I'd say this proof is solid enough." Anabelle leans into Kieran's shoulder. His light flares with the motion. "Queen Titania won't be able to explain this away."

I frown at the marred wood. This proof might be solid, yet I expected to uncover something a bit more transportable. "She'll have to see it first. She won't be returning to London any time in the near future. And it's not as if we can send this along with a sparrow."

"We could cut it out of the desk," the princess offers.

"He'll notice it's gone, know we're on to him. That would put Richard in danger." My throat feels thick even saying this.

Anabelle frowns, looks up at Kieran. She's still nudged against his shoulder, her hair haloed bright by his scar light. "What is the spell anyway? It didn't seem to do anything."

"This magic is still strange to me," the Ad-hene tells her. "It could be the spell did nothing."

I squint at the runes again. There was something familiar about the spell's feel and form. It tugs at my thoughts like the first few notes of a song I can't place.

My frown grows.

"I still think we should send Queen Titania a message," Anabelle goes on. "She can't ignore us forever."

I'm quite certain she can. No matter how many parchments I tie to a sparrow's leg. No matter how many messages I scroll and seal.

My thoughts halt.

And I know what the desk's rune magic reminds me of. Something about it is stunningly similar to the sealing spells Fae place on their most secret correspondence. Spells which notify the caster exactly who opened it.

And when.

My eyes go wide—taking in the chiseled symbols with a growing sense of horror.

They aren't a sealing spell. They're an alarm system.

"We have to go!" I leap from the chair, send its leather bulk crashing into the shelves. Books shudder and fall like dominoes. "It's a trap! He knows we're here!"

"Emrys, what are you talking about?" Anabelle stumbles after me, skipping over the discarded drawer, the snowfall of Julian's treatise papers on the floor.

Kieran reaches the door first, in bold, fluid ink movements. He rises, broad-chested, in front of it, blocking the way. His mark is all glare, filling the room with more shadows than it needs.

"What are you doing?" I brace myself, ready to push past if I must.

He holds up a lone finger, calls for silence. His gaze is trained on the door's solid wood. The whole of the Ad-hene's face is still so wolflike, alert, ready for a fight.

And then I hear the footsteps. *Thud, thud, thud* down the hall. Getting louder, closer with each second. Like the pound of an enemy's drum rippling over hills. Announcing doom.

My eyes stray to the lone window, where fog presses into the glass, hiding the five stories of fall between us and freedom.

"We can't," Kieran says softly. He's looking at the window too. "Ad-hene are of the earth. Not the air."

And I'm still grounded.

Thud, thud, thud. Doom, doom, doom.

My heart is a sledgehammer, threatening to smash out of my throat.

"Veiling spells won't work. He knows someone's here." I swallow. The floor shakes under the approaching steps. It can't be much more now. "We have to fight him."

"No!" Anabelle's eyes flash fierce at both of us. She reaches out, wraps a hand around the moonsong of Kieran's mark. The room's light shifts, falls dim. "Stay hidden. I'll take care of this."

"Princess." The Ad-hene's words waver like his light. "What are you doing?"

"You said yourself you aren't strong enough to face him. I can't let you get hurt." Her fingers tighten around his arm. There's a tightness in her voice too.

Thud. Doom. Closer.

Kieran's jaw tenses with danger and dark. "Don't do this, Belle!"

"Belle—" We say her name at the same time.

She looks at both of us. First me, then Kieran. "Trust me."

I feel her veiling spell lift.

The door opens.

For such a creature of the earth, Kieran moves like wind. Swinging away from the door, pulling me to his side with steady, boulder grace. The magic of his veiling spell feels heavier than ever, cloaked wide over both of us.

Julian Forsythe stands in the doorway, sour-faced. I can only wonder how he arrived so swiftly and dressed as well. Despite the hour he's wearing a fine-cut suit, silver cufflinks glinting from the hall's light. They glow almost as bright as his eyes—teal ice picks which chip through every bit of his ransacked office: the avalanche of books, the dismantled box tower, the wide-eyed princess standing in the middle of all these things.

"Your Majesty!" The ice of Julian's stare breaks at the sight of the shivering blonde girl. "I wasn't expecting to find you here. . . ."

The princess's face has shifted too. Instead of fierce and steely she looks close to tears. Her lower lip trembles along with her shoulders. "Thank goodness you came! They heard your footsteps and ran. They didn't have time to take me with them!"

"Who?" Julian Forsythe takes another step into his office. His eyes do another long sweep, investigating every nook and cranny.

"The Faery, of course. The one my brother was so smitten with." Anabelle breaks apart her syllables with just the right amount of breathless fear. "She and her friend have kept me hostage for days. They thought they could use me as leverage if they ever got caught."

Blue eyes—jagged and electric. So sharp that for a moment I believe they're slicing straight through Kieran's veiling spell.

Does he know we're here? Despite Anabelle's lies? Despite Kieran's magic?

I edge closer to the Ad-hene—as if that will actually

make a difference in his veiling spell. I feel Kieran's breath pulsing against his ribs, the flutter of his once stony heart.

The princess grasps Julian's arm. An actual tear gleams down her cheek. "I tried to escape. But they kept using magic. They took me everywhere with them. . . ."

Slowly, slowly Julian looks away, back to the girl in front of him. "Why were they here? What were they looking for?"

"They wouldn't tell me." Anabelle sniffs. "Look I—I know you and Richard haven't exactly been allies since the integration, but you have to help me get my brother back! Rescue him from these *monsters*."

The princess says the final word with such venom that my stomach clenches. Even Kieran goes stiff beside me, every muscle in his body winches.

Julian Forsythe just smiles.

"Don't worry, Princess. You're safe now." He guides her to the door. "I'll get you back to the palace."

Anabelle leaves with false tears still streaming down her cheeks. Julian Forsythe follows. His eyes cut once more through the room, focus on our corner like a sniper's rifle.

He shuts the door.

Twenty-One

We follow them at a distance. Kieran moves like silk and night down the hall, eyes never leaving Anabelle. The politician's arm stays braced around the princess's shoulder, guiding her through the building.

I keep waiting for the strike. For Julian's blue eyes to go feral with a surge of rune magic. For him to grip the princess's arm, use her as bait to lure us out of hiding.

But it never comes.

One phone call from Julian summons a small army of shiny black Jaguars. Red-eyed Protection Command officers swarm the lobby. Prodding charged stun guns into every available corner, hoping to root out hidden foes. Some of them even have the weapon wrapped around their knuckles like brass rings. A new design. Meant for a quick punch and jab. A serious fight.

Jensen is here. Eric too. Julian Forsythe ushers Anabelle into their arms like a parcel. Kieran watches the exchange with sharkskin eyes, letting nothing go. All of his powers are gathered, ready to break apart the lobby's marble floor.

"We need to stay hidden." I place my hand over his mark. He doesn't even notice. All of his focus is poured on to the herd of men, Anabelle ringed inside them like a baby calf.

"Take the princess back to Kensington Palace," I hear the politician saying. "Have men search my office. See if they left anything else behind. And make sure the press is given access. I want to be certain they cover this incident properly."

Eric nods—head bobbing like a circus seal offered a bucket of fresh fish. Jensen looks less enthused, but this doesn't stop him from sending several stun gun-wielding men upstairs.

Since when did Protection Command take orders from a member of Parliament?

But he isn't just a mere Parliament member, is he? My eyes flicker to Julian Forsythe's wrist. The tattoo is still there, barely visible against the stark white of his shirt cuffs. I haven't felt any magic rolling from the mark yet, but Julian doesn't need spells to control these men. Kieran's right. The mortals drink his words like mead.

He's their Beowulf. Their savior. Their monster slayer. And he's ready to lead them straight into battle.

My heart is not ready for Kensington. A palace of firsts.
The bedroom with its frescoed ceiling of angels, where I
first laid eyes on Richard, when the magic of our soul-
tie first anchored itself in my chest. The garden of gravel
and marigolds where my veiling spell first slipped and I
couldn't make myself bring it back. The moment Richard
first became mine.

The marigolds are gone now, withered by frost and rooted
out by dutiful gardeners. But the angels are still here, painted
in a slant of forever-gold light. Their smiles unchanged. I
stare up at them, curled tight in the elegant chair I once sat
in every night and watched over Richard as he slept.

We're locked in Richard's old room, which Anabelle
promptly took over when her brother made the move to
Buckingham ("more walk-in wardrobe space" was her reason at the time). Kieran and I are still coated thick in his
follee-shiu. We speak in whispers regardless, all too aware
of the human security standing guard on the other side of
the bedroom door.

"What now?" I keep staring at the angels, implor-
ing the heavens. "I thought getting caught by Protection
Command was what we were trying to avoid."

"We're exactly where we want to be," Anabelle assures

me. She's pacing: back and forth, back and forth. Over the Persian rug I used to study during the hours Richard slept. "Now that we know Julian is . . . someone else . . . the only way we're going to find Richard and expose Julian is if we take him by surprise. He believed my story. He doesn't see me as a threat."

"That's because you aren't." My spine goes rigid in the chair as I sit up to look at her. "That was an awfully big gamble you took in the office! If he'd discovered you were lying, he could have killed you!"

"If I hadn't thrown him off the trail, we would all be just as dead," Anabelle answers, "or locked up in a dungeon somewhere. Or wherever it is ex-Camelot sorcerers stuff their prisoners."

"Julian's just as good as made you a prisoner. Have you seen the guards outside your door?" I nod to the white-paneled wood. "I don't think they're going to be letting you out of Kensington by yourself any time soon."

"Then it's a good thing I plan on staying." The princess is going in circles. Stamping over and over on the same visages of woven horseback warriors in her anxious track. "Julian may be a sorcerer, but he's a politician too. There aren't many politicians who would turn down a personal invitation to dine at a royal residence. Especially if it's a banquet held in their honor for rescuing the princess from the hands of some villainous Fae. It's good press for him."

"You want to invite Julian Forsythe to a dinner party? This evening?" I can barely believe what I'm saying. "Are you mad? What are you planning on doing? Feeding him some bad eggs? This is a *sorcerer*, Belle! Not some schoolgirl frenemy."

Anabelle pauses and taps her fingers together. "Eggs isn't a terrible idea. Though I was thinking more along the lines of spiking his drink."

"You don't want to use magic at all. You mean to trick him." Kieran shifts. He's crouched in the window ledge like a cat, an equal distance between the princess, myself and the night outside.

I'm trying my best not to notice him—here in this room where Richard and I shared so many intimate moments. But Kieran's veiling spell is a stiff cocktail—oozing into my every pore, blurring even those memories.

"You want to drug him?" I ask. "To what end? As soon as he wakes up we'll be outmatched again."

"We won't be there when he wakes up. You said Titania won't aid us without proof. What better proof than the sorcerer himself? I'll give him a heavy dose; you and Kieran can take him to Titania before he even knows what hit him. Once the Faery queen realizes we're right, she'll question him. Find Richard."

It's not a terrible plan, but it's not foolproof either. I run it through my head like a marathon show, with dozens of alternate scenarios. Most of them don't end well.

"How are you going to explain his disappearance? To the staff? His wife?"

"You can teach me memory alteration," she says, as if stealing someone's memories and replacing them is the simplest thing in the world. For her, it probably will be. "I'll make them think he was called away to an emergency meeting. That the abduction happened outside the palace grounds."

"And what about the press? They'll make it look like a silencing attempt. Paint Forsythe as a martyr."

"He won't go missing for long. As soon as you rescue Richard we can set the record straight. Expose Julian for what he truly is. We'll use the power of the press to turn things around."

"What if the drug doesn't work? It's likely he's warded against such things. Poison was as common as daylight in Arthur's day." I think of the birdsfoot trefoil on the table at the banquet. How Julian stared at it with such intent. How had I missed so many signs?

"This is the way it must be done, Emrys," Anabelle says firmly. "If we can't face Julian head-on, then we come at him from the side. Take him blind. It's this or groveling at Titania's feet. And I don't think we can wait for her much longer."

I stare across the room at Richard's sister. She's standing so straight, so sure. Just like that iron statue of the warrior queen Boudica on the Thames's shore.

Gone is the party planner who smashed a vase in her panic attack over the coronation ball. Gone is the girl who strangled my arm like a lifeline in the black Jaguar.

She's her own version of warrior royalty. The stress of Richard's disappearance has only compressed her into a tighter, tougher version of herself. While I've been falling apart, she's been pulling together. It's as if all the seams ripped out of me have been rewoven into her.

I have no doubt she can do this.

The bottle-green velvet of the chair and the lulling sounds of Anabelle's last-minute party planning are the perfect recipe for sleep. It doesn't take me long to reach Richard. I feel his presence along the edges of the dream. Guiding me through layers of sleep, like a boat to safe harbor.

The world is chaos around us. Still. Always. But my

eyes find his and refuse to let go.

Richard's boots and cape twist deep into the mud. His hair is matted, eyes edged with weary red. His jaw bristles with shaveless days. I've never seen him so raw, so worn. Yet just knowing he's *here* and *real* fills me to the point of bursting.

I reach him, slide straight into his outstretched arms. He pulls me tight into himself. Arms strong and steady: my anchor in these treacherous waters. I bury my face into his chest, fill myself with his nearness. His touch which sparkles and swells like a spell in my chest. And for a moment, even in the folds and depths of a dream, I feel whole.

But I can't feel this way forever. I can't always be sleeping.

I look up, straight into his fire-gold eyes. "Richard, this dream, it's real. We're actually here."

"I know." His whisper is hoarse, as if his throat is lined with dust and he's just now brushing it off. "I've been waiting for you all night. Hoping."

My heart is a thousand shards inside my chest: grinding, wanting, and so close to having. I want to kiss him again, but our time is short. Mordred is coming for us. Just as he has in every other dream. His footsteps are thunder through the earth. He leaps and lunges across the battlefield like a tiger. Honing in on the king, his prey.

"Where are you?" I gasp out the words. "In the real world?"

His arms stay tight around me. Unyielding. "I don't know. The last thing I remember was the carriage, and then I woke up here. They've brought me food, but I never see any of them. It's all dark."

I hear the creaks and groans of Mordred's armor. So close. Soon the dream will end and I'll have nothing. Nothing but more pieces of Richard lodged everywhere, stinging, reminding me of how I still haven't found him.

Time. I need more time.

The fierce of Richard's kiss still burns on my lips, within my chest. I hold on to this as I step out and around Richard, plant my feet in the mud. Wait for Mordred's always-fatal blow.

He lunges toward us, the same way he does in every dream. But this time something catches my attention. It's not the sword which makes me pause, but his armor. The steel is black as Kelpie skin, glaring against Camelot's distant firelight. Fine writing wraps around the knight's limbs and face, so small and neat it could just be random scratchings in the metal.

But these scratchings are far from random. They're small, precise, and complex. Rune magic at its finest.

The jagged letters are everywhere, swarming across Mordred's armor, protecting him with all manner of spells. Armor over armor. Shield over shield.

It's little wonder Arthur couldn't defeat Mordred in the state he was in. So ravaged and hamstrung by grief.

Runes. Everywhere runes. Just like the signature of Blæc's death. Only this time the symbols are a sick silver white—bursting my vision like ill-strung stars. Constellations writing down doom and maligned fortunes. Spelling out the ever-exact ending of this dream.

Blades and burning. Always.

I can still see the letters, swarming and confused behind my lids—like lamp-lit moths. But I'm awake. I know this because the armchair brushes soft velvet against my cheek. Because the voices murmuring like soft streams beside me belong to Anabelle and Kieran. Because my arm aches with fresh blood the way it does after every dream. Because the glow and song of Richard just under my breastbone has vanished.

Mordred.

That's who's been watching from behind those eyes

of blue. The brutish invader from the north who found the weakness in Arthur's armor. Who plunged his sword straight down and watched the Pendragon's blood mix deep with mud.

All these years I thought he was dead—reduced to ash and vulture feast by Mab's enraged magic. (Once I gave Mab the news, she returned to fallen Camelot faster than I could fly, even then. By the time I reached the battlefield again, the Pendragon and the sorcerer were gone.) But the Faery queen never unmade Mordred, like I'd thought. She had different plans for him: long years of agony in the earth's deepest shadows. She must have looped his life like Guinevere's. Cursed him to lifetimes of darkness. A fate worse than death.

He told me himself, that night at Windsor: *Faery queens are the cruelest creatures alive.*

And now Julian-Mordred has returned. To undo another king. To take back the kingdom Mab wrenched so brutally from his grasp. To get revenge on the Fae and the crown in one fell swoop.

A crack in my eyelid shows me Anabelle cross-legged on Richard's old bed. Her party planning tools fan out in front of her: a series of notes, a laptop, a half-empty cup of tea. The whole setup—the shimmering light of electronics on her face, the focused scrunch of her nose, how she types a few words and then chews her lip—reminds me of the way her brother used to work.

Kieran has moved from the window to the edge of the bed. The computer's presence doesn't seem to bother him the way it would sicken a Frithemaeg. Instead its glow shifts and melds with his scar. This too lights up the princess's face. Her laptop keys *tap, tap, tap* away: making lists and menus and specifications for flower arrangements. The Ad-hene watches the flight of her fingers with open awe.

Anabelle pauses, looks up at him. "What do you feed your prisoners? I want to make sure it's not on the menu I'm putting together. Don't want to let him catch on that I suspect anything."

"We never fed our prisoners," Kieran tells her. "Most immortals never acquire a taste for food."

"But—what about Guinevere? And fake-Julian? You never gave them anything to eat? That whole time they were there?" Anabelle's eyes get wider with every question—glimmering horror and Word documents. "They must have been so hungry. . . ."

Kieran tilts his head, all of his curls spilling to one side. "What does hunger feel like?"

"It's like wanting something, except worse." Anabelle studies those curls—spiraling in and out of the electric light. Her hand is tight by her leg, as if she's pushing back the urge to reach out and touch them. "If you ignore it, it starts to hurt. And if you keep ignoring it, it becomes all you can think about. Until you get what you need. Or you die."

"Like love," Kieran suggests.

The princess's breath goes sharp. I wonder if Kieran notices: how she's watching him, how his words must be spearing her heart like a hunted whale.

"I—I wouldn't know." This time her denial is quiet, a whispered thing. She shifts gears, driving their conversation into a whole new direction with a louder voice. "I can't imagine being hungry and vitamin D–deprived for so long. . . . No wonder fake-Julian is so angry. That literally sounds like hell."

The Ad-hene says nothing. His face goes back to its hard, stony stare. The one which was once so constant—the one that's been crumbling under jars of beetroot and sunlight as gold as the princess's hair.

"Sorry," Anabelle says quickly. "I know it's your home. I don't mean to criticize it so much."

"It's where I came from, yes. But it hasn't felt like home

in a long, long time." Kieran's words are slow and careful. Handpicked. "It's not a nice place. Not anymore. Especially compared to all of this." He nods up to the sky-born angels, their white feathers splaying over us like a canopy.

Anabelle's mouth pulls to one side, wry. She snaps her laptop shut. "I know it might be hard to believe, but there were times when these palaces felt like a prison."

Kieran keeps watching the angels. Taking in every intimate detail of the artist's brushstrokes.

"I mean—it's not at all like the maze you live in. But there were so many times growing up when all I wanted was a normal life. I spent hours looking out windows watching children play in St. James's Park. Scraping their knees. Getting dirty. I wanted more than anything to be out there with them. Chasing ducks and fighting with stick swords and not caring about manners or harp lessons or whether or not my stockings had runs in them."

Even from here, with one ear smudged against velvet, I hear the thickness in her voice. Kieran hears it too. His stare has fallen from the angels, drifted to Anabelle. The princess looks down into the teacup, as if she's really telling all of this to the leftover sips of Earl Grey.

"People see this life and they want it. They think it's

something out of a fairy tale: castles, pretty dresses, magazine covers, and all the rest. But they don't realize how much it weighs. My life—it's never really been mine. I've always had people telling me how to act. Where to study. Who to be friends with. I have to be flawless all of the time or else I get pounced on by the press and my mother.

"Richard always hated the pressure. He ran away from it. But I've tried to please everyone. To be Britain's perfect princess. And it's just bloody exhausting." Her last few words are edged with anger. She places the teacup back on its tray with such vigor that it rains amber drops across her wrist.

Kieran shifts; the bed creaks under his weight.

"These past few days . . . they've been awful, but they've also been illuminating. For the first time in my life I've felt free," she drifts off.

"I know what you mean." His hand rubs up the ridged muscles of his bare arm. Over his mark. "Not all prisons have bars or walls. To be someone you're not is a prison in itself."

He says this and those eyes cut over to my chair. I wonder if he knows I'm awake, if he hears the extra-heavy patter of my heart. How it flutters and stings under his words.

"But I can't just stop being a princess."

"I suppose not." Kieran frowns. His fingers are still on his mark, tracing it round and round. Following the silver lines without even looking at them. His eyes are still latched on to my chair.

It's no use pretending anymore. I'm awake and he knows it.

"What if who I want to be and who I'm meant to be aren't the same?" Anabelle goes on. "What if they never fit together?"

"That's the question, isn't it?" Kieran asks my chair, my barely closed lids.

I sit up, as if I'm just twisting awake: all limb and yawn. "What are we talking about?"

Anabelle flinches, puts on a face. The softness from just moments before hides behind curtains of tense brow and a cocktail-hour voice.

"Dramatic, philosophical things." Her voice goes deep. Like a play narrator. "Fate versus free will. What if the person you were born to be isn't who you want to be?"

I give her the only answer I can think of. "Then I suppose you must decide which life you want more. Make your choice."

Kieran slides off the bed, leaves the princess alone in

the downy waves of comforter. He moves back to his window perch, where the first hints of dawn smudge against the glass.

"Easy words," he says softly. The icy light blooms and spreads across his face, making him look like some sort of winter god. "Not all of us are strong enough to fight fate. To wage war against the nature of things."

Fate. The nature of things. Is that what I'm battling against? Is that what's dragging Richard away? Wrenching us apart?

No.

"It's Mordred," I say suddenly, replaying the final moments of my dream over and over again. Silver-scratched runes branding my eyes as the black knight plunged his sword into Richard's chest. Plunged me into waking.

How many more times will I have to watch him die?

"What?" Anabelle chirps from the bed.

"Mordred," I force the name out again. "He's the one pretending to be Julian Forsythe. The same sorcerer who killed King Arthur."

Kieran looks over at me, painted in frosty surprise and morning sun. "How do you know?"

I'm about to tell him. About to let the truth slip out, when I catch myself. The dreams, they're the last corner of my life that belong to just me and Richard. The last hint of mortality I can cling to when I'm around the Ad-hene, listening to the siren call of other choices.

"I—I just remembered," I say. "He used rune magic. The symbols were etched into his armor the day he invaded Camelot."

Anabelle looks too pale, almost sick as she asks, "Do you think he's going to kill Richard?"

The question—same but different—circles in Kieran's eyes like a wolf around prey. *Is it worth his death?*

"I don't know." I look down at my ringless finger, lined up with all the others in a tight fist. Ready for a fight.

But if it truly is fate I'm up against . . .

Am I willing to accept the cost?

Twenty-Two

Anabelle keeps plowing through the day. Before breakfast her invitation to Julian Forsythe is sent and she's perfected basic memory modification spells under Kieran's careful tutelage. By lunch she's already agreed to an exclusive interview with the nation's largest news network to tell her version of the kidnapping and cement her innocence in Mordred-Julian's mind. Kensington Gardens become overrun. Extension cords wind alongside leafless vines. The hustle of the camera crew sprays gravel off the neatly raked paths.

Kieran and I stand on the edge of the garden. Watching as camera techs set up their equipment and a makeup artist erases the sleepless night from the princess's eyes. Eric stands watch from the opposite side of the garden, looming like a dark omen in the middle of bare rose brambles. His eyes rove the gravel paths; his hands stay rigid by his stun gun.

"Are you really going to let the princess go through

with this plan?" The Ad-hene's eyes are anchored on Anabelle's back, as attentive and alert as Eric.

I take a deep breath, look down at the flowerbed by my feet. I can't be certain, but I think this is where the marigolds once were. Before the frost settled in, turned everything to black and wither.

"You think I shouldn't?" I ask him.

"You know the risk as well as I. Mordred is a powerful sorcerer. Cunning. If he catches the princess in her deception . . ." Kieran's jaw tightens, an intricate weave of muscles. "Are you really willing to let the princess risk everything?"

"Anabelle's right. We have to try." The Ad-hene looks down at me as I say this. His silvery attentions pouring like a storm over my shoulders, into my awareness.

We're not alone, but with the veiling spell wrapped tight and the princess's back to us we might as well be.

Futures are branching out before me. Forking with every breath. Every fresh pulse of Kieran's *follee-shiu*.

"We're running out of options," I keep talking, as if more words could keep what's coming at bay. "The Frithemaeg are gone. The princess is too new in her magic. And you yourself said you weren't strong enough."

"Not alone." Kieran's words hang like ripe fruit, begging

to be plucked. "We could face Mordred. *Together.*"

There's no mistaking his meaning. Not with the gleam in his eyes which reminds me so very much of the tunnel. The words still echoing off of those rune-struck tiles: *He's not your only choice.* The empty space that's slowly collapsing between us.

"I—I can't." Why do these words feel like molasses stuck on my tongue, the back of my throat? So hard to get out?

"You've trapped yourself, become what you're not." He reaches out, fingers ghosting along the ends of my black, black hair. "I still see the fire in you. You're only hurting yourself by trying to put it out."

It's as if the world has melted around us, fallen away. It's just Kieran and me, standing in the hot cocoon of his veiling spell. I'm so very aware of his fingertips. How they hover just a moment from my skin.

The pine-needle prickles in my gut have grown, swallowed everything. The whole of me is a forest aflame.

"You gave up magic for love. But what if you don't have to?" His whisper slides around my neck. Possessive, gripping, desperate. "I know you feel it too. There's something here. Between us."

I can't tell him there isn't.

"Take back your magic." He leans in. Closer, ever closer. "Set yourself free."

Sweet, sickly poison: the taste of these words. It crawls sluggish through my veins, makes me still. Unable to move or even breathe. I'm simply standing in front of the Ad-hene, drunk off of his magic, his words, my mind spinning.

Richard. I love Richard.

But that doesn't stop Kieran from pressing his lips to mine.

He kisses me. Hard.

Kieran is all storm and sea. His lips draw me in like a whirlpool, spin me. Deeper into the rawness of his spirit—the pieces of him no body could convey. The true, wild danger of the Ad-hene.

It's like catching the crest of a wave, plummeting through the water's foamy fury. Fast and fierce and uncontrollable. I feel Kieran's magic tugging my soul, riptide strong, wanting to consume. Carry me away to the other shore.

Back to where I started.

Kieran's hands glide like water down my neck, my shoulders, my arms. His palm passes over the five crusty nail marks. They call out—sharp pain—howling Guinevere's words back at me:

The circling sea will swallow us whole. I flipped wrong.

All of me goes stiff. The Ad-hene's kiss becomes fraught. Beyond hungry.

The only other soul in the world like me screams, screams, screams in my memories: *I flipped wrong and the world burned.*

Like me.

I tear away. My hair is a tangled mess over my eyes— webbing black through the sight of Kieran. His face belongs to someone who just lost something important—jigsawed with emotions. Furrowed brow for confusion. Hard jaw for anger. Shining eyes for pleading. Chin wrinkled for hurt. And something else I can't seem to place—swimming in the tension of those lips which just touched mine.

"No. No. This is all wrong." I shake my head, as if that will clear it. All it does is set me spinning. Everything inside me is so far from north.

I look away from the Ad-hene, try to get my bearings. Down at the churned soil where the marigolds used to root: an empty bed full of holes. Over to Eric's stern, knight-like vigil.

And then I see Anabelle.

318

The princess stands alone in a crowd of people, staring at me with eyes that could pierce stone. They hit me like twin javelins, sink deep into my gut.

She saw everything.

Kieran's breath goes silver-edged, as if Anabelle's eyes have gutted him too. "Emrys . . ."

But whatever the Ad-hene has to say, I don't want to hear it. I step away from him, into the dirt of the flower-bed. The loose, broken soil swallows my feet, just like the mud from the dream. Only instead of running to someone, I'm fleeing.

Soil clings to my steps, leaving trails of filth where I walk. Veiled dirt only Anabelle can see.

But she isn't looking anymore. She's sitting on the garden bench, getting her microphone fitted to the collar of her designer dress. Her hands are folded into her lap like a neat valentine. Her long hair is wound up tight, showcasing the beautiful sculpt of her face.

There's nothing in her expression, not a flicker or flinch to indicate what she just saw.

I halt only a meter away from the bench, where I'm drowning in a sea of gravel, grips, and gaffers. So close I could speak to her. But she's not alone. On the other end of the bench is the same brunette reporter who interviewed Edmund: Meryl Munson.

Even if I could speak to Anabelle, I have no idea what I might say. No apology, no excuse can wash the stain of Kieran from my lips.

With one shout from the crew Meryl Munson looks straight into the camera, all smile, telling her viewers the story they already know. How, the very same day King Richard disappeared, Britain's princess was snatched straight out of a high-security bunker, a victim of the very magic her brother swore to protect.

Anabelle's smile grows tighter and tighter—a rope on the verge of snap. It's winched as taut as possible by the time Meryl turns and finally asks her a question.

"You've had quite a past few days, Your Highness. Can you tell me a bit about your ordeal?"

The princess takes a deep, steady breath. "After Richard vanished, my protection team took my mother and me to a secure location. I insisted Emrys accompany us. Once we arrived at the bunker she overpowered the guards and kidnapped me."

Meryl Munson leans forward, yet somehow manages to keep her face angled always at the camera. "What was going through your mind when you realized Emrys had betrayed you?"

"I couldn't believe it at first. Didn't want to." Anabelle swallows. The short golden charm on her necklace dips into the base of her throat. "She seemed to love Richard so much. . . . She was already a part of our family. I thought of her as a sister. To see her true nature come out so viciously—it was a shock."

I know this is the story she meant to tell when she agreed to the interview. The words she planned on saying. Yet every one of them tears into me, until I'm riddled through with holes. All of me feels uprooted.

"Not everyone seemed so shocked." Meryl says this like an admonishment. "Julian Forsythe has been preaching the dangers of immortals ever since Emrys first appeared. Wasn't he the one who rescued you?"

"I was very fortunate he came into his office when he did. Without him I'd still be out there, a prisoner." The princess's brown eyes don't move from the reporter's face. She doesn't look at the camera. Or at me.

"He's certainly become the hero of the hour." Meryl's smile is saccharine—sugar cubes dunked in syrup. "The emergency elections are scheduled to take place tomorrow and according to polls, the tides have turned in the M.A.F.'s favor. Julian Forsythe will become prime minister, which should make it much easier for all the mortal defense and anti-integration bills to pass through the houses of Parliament. Do you have any thoughts on this?"

"Richard believed we could live in harmony with the Fae. That their presence would enrich our lives and launch us into a new age of progress. But my brother believed many things which have turned out not to be true. It seems he was being deceived." There's a slight tremor in Anabelle's voice. She's an excellent actress. If she's acting. Her eyes don't find me again. Not even once. "I think we should do what we must to keep this kingdom safe. If that means appointing a new prime minister, then so be it. The Fae are dangerous. They can't be trusted."

Kieran is still standing in the ruin of marigolds. Staring. Even from here I can see the rawness of his face.

Meryl stumbles into the long stretch of Anabelle's silence with a squeaking question. "So you would say this experience has swayed your stance in favor of segregation?"

Anabelle's face tilts farther toward the camera, but her stare lodges straight into me.

"We're better off without them," she says.

I follow the princess around like a desperate puppy all afternoon. She's pacing the way Richard used to when he was upset. Round and round the maze of Kensington. Past the ghosts of old men looming in oil portraits. Past all the many windows which look out on the world's bleakness: London passing, trees stripped and crippled by autumn.

Eric follows the princess too, copying her wordless march around the palace. And Kieran—I haven't seen him since we left the gardens. He can't have gone far; his veiling spell is still choked tight around me. The only thing between me and an army of stun guns. I keep waiting for her to return to the bedroom, where Eric's eyes and stun gun cannot reach.

But Anabelle does anything she can to avoid the bedroom. She has tea with her mother, who spends half of the hour talking about all the dead ends Protection Command has hit in their search for Richard and the other half talking about me. After that Anabelle speaks with the kitchen staff, going over the dinner menu for the tenth time. She confirms the florist and edits the guest list as responses trickle in.

It's not until she ticks a neat check beside *Mr. and Mrs. Julian Forsythe* that I finally speak. I don't care that any odd movement or word of hers could give me away to Eric's falcon eyes. I have to get this out.

"Belle, please."

Nothing. Her face is motionless as she guides her pen over the paper.

"What you saw," I go on, push past the thickness in my throat. "It was a mistake."

The line she's striking through a couple's name wavers; her hand is shaking. The princess puts down the pen and folds the list away.

"I think I'm going to retire for a bit," she tells Eric. "Last night didn't bring me much rest and I want to make sure I have plenty of energy for the party tonight."

I follow her wake to Richard's old bedroom, Anabelle shuts the door and marches across the carpet, her heels digging deep—punching through fruit and warriors' faces. The staccato of her step, the cold, clear blaze in her eyes reminds me so very much of her mother.

She stares and stares. Without a word.

"What you saw in the garden. It was a mistake." Did I say that already? My words feel scrabbling and useless, like a tortoise on its back. "He kissed me and—"

"I saw it all," she says.

"I love your brother. Very much." I offer this up like a sacrifice. Wait for her knife.

The princess shuts her eyes. Her fingers press like spindles against her temples, the way they did in the bunker.

"If I could undo it I would," I go on. "I've just been so confused and Kieran has been saying all these things—"

"Stop." Her eyes fly open. Flash out a kaleidoscope of emotions. The ones which are worming out of her grasp as we speak. "Just stop."

But I keep going anyway. "Kieran was the one who kissed me. I didn't—"

"You think this is all about *you*. That everything's about *you*!" Her voice finally breaks, I hear the sharpness in it. Know it exactly for what it is.

The jagged edges of a heart broken.

She's right. This isn't about me at all.

It's about beetroot flans and twisting *Aile* flames and nights whispering about hunger and the people they wanted to be. It's about the too-loud of the princess's laugh and the too-quiet of her denial. It's about how the princess's heart was slipping in tandem with mine—called into orbit by the Ad-hene's gravity.

"Oh, Belle . . ."

I feel the princess's blood magic stirring, creeping over the bedroom like frost. It settles into my skin, wraps around the many veins and passages of my heart.

We've stepped out of dangerous territory and into a minefield.

There are creaks and groans, like frozen water breaking. Suddenly I'm seeing snow. It falls around us, dusting our hair, smothering the rug. Coating the green, velvet chair like ash.

I hold out my palm, catch a flake.

Not snow. Paint.

There are cracks in the ceiling. Snaking off of each other, writhing through the heavenly scene. Splitting apart the angels' sweet faces, prying their smiles wider. Pieces of them fall, chip by chip, down to the earth they've watched for so long.

It's just paint now. But soon it will be plaster. The cracks will go deeper if Anabelle lets them, bring the roof down.

"Breathe, Belle. You need to center yourself."

"I need you to leave." Her voice is glacial. Frozen so thick not even a fire could touch it.

"But what about the dinner? Our plan . . ."

The flakes keep falling, thicker and thicker. The angels are almost gone, their feathers plucked bare.

"After the banquet tonight I never want to see you again. Or *him*." Her words are like Black Dogs on a lead. Tugging and snapping. Ready to rip.

The room is so cold it feels like a furnace. Her magic

keeps falling, an avalanche threatening to bury us alive. She looks the way she did when she clenched Kieran's fire in her palms: wild. Unhinged.

And this time, I can't extinguish it.

"Belle, you *have to control* it. You can't let it consume you." But even as I say this I sense it's too late. I feel her grief: the shards of her heart spinning across the floor. Beyond repair.

"Get out," she says with a voice like death. "I won't ask you again."

I can't move. I can only stand in this room. See the ruin of everything. Feel the weight of chaos inside and out.

Anabelle takes a lungful of air and howls, "ERIC!! Help!"

The door bursts open with the fury of a dozen horsemen, but it's just Eric behind the wood. Sapphire lightning rings his knuckles, ready for anything. Ready for me.

I slip past him, leave the princess and her shredded angels behind.

Twenty-Three

I cannot stay in the palace. I go where I once did when I needed to escape from it all. Underground.

High Street Kensington Station is unchanged. Full of shiny silver turnstiles and grimy tiles. Yet like everything else in this city it feels dimmer, lesser in the shadow of Richard's absence. The life which once swarmed its shops and corridors seems muted. People walk with their heads down, eyes scraping the floor. Checking watches or phones, never looking up.

Which is fortunate, since just after I slipped around the turnstile I felt Kieran's veiling spell lift. It came as a sudden lightness—like clouds rolling away and letting the sun in again.

I'm visible, but no one seems to see me. And for now, that's just the way I want it.

I find a seat in the last car on the train. The one most commuters avoid. There's no one in front of me to block my view out the window. The streak of the tunnel as it rips by. Someone has left a pane propped open; cold air ribbons and shrieks through the car.

With the Ad-hene's magic gone, my head feels like winter. Cruelly clear. My thoughts crystal sharp.

Anabelle let her heart slip to Kieran, only to have it shattered. Her magic is a dam, barely holding back chaos. I think of all the cracks in the ceiling, the coldness of her voice, angels tumbling down like snow. I can only hope Kensington Palace is still standing when I return.

If I return.

This thought—this doubt—catches me. I have to go back. This is my one and only chance to find Richard's trail without losing him forever. Without considering Kieran's offer . . .

My lips still burn—branded—no matter how many times I wipe my sleeve against them. I think of how close I was to giving in to the swirl of the Ad-hene's dark mysteries. Kissing him back.

I catch the girl sitting across from me glaring. Her eyes are like blades—thin, unforgiving. It takes me a moment to realize she's only a ghost of myself: an echo on the glass.

I still don't know the girl in the mirror.

I'm beginning to think I never will.

The train starts to slow. White streaks across the midnight glass. At first it's just a blur, but when the brakes howl louder I catch glimpses of its true form. Serrated letters streaming along the far wall.

I blink and they're gone. The platform for Westminster station settles next to the train: sleek metallic walls and digital displays flashing arrival times. The train doors hiss open.

Runes. Is that what they were? Or was it simply one of the many strands of graffiti which cake the Underground walls?

There's only one way to find out.

I slip out of the doors just as they *shnick* shut, careful to keep my head turned away from the platform cameras.

This station is busier than the others. The crowd is hot and excited. Words like *ballots* and *emergency elections* buzz out of mouths, echo off the walls. A lot of travelers are clustered into groups, carrying signs with Julian Forsythe's not-quite-smile splitting across the paper. There must be another M.A.F. protest happening in the world above. Another step in Mordred's grasp for power.

I keep my head down and weave through the crowd, all the way to the closest service door. A quick breath of a spell sends me through the locks, down into the tunnels.

The station's glow reveals the length of the tracks, littered in trash and swimming with the shadows of rodents. Signal lights wink like predators' eyes from the edges of the tunnel. I feel as if I'm back in the Labyrinth, with the strangeness of the earth crowding in.

I think of the digital number which blinked on the platform: *12*. Twelve minutes until the next train.

Sounds swirl like bats through the tunnels: My steps crunch, crunch along the gravel by the tracks. Distant trains thrum and twang. Rats chitter. I scan the walls, trying my best to interpret through the poor light. They're covered in many things: lichen, the crisscrossing paths of roaches, old maintenance signs, a long-forgotten, peeling advertisement.

But no runes.

I keep walking down the tracks. Farther and farther from the light. Until the dark coating the walls is thicker than I can pierce. Even if the runes are here, I can't see them. I have no light of my own—most of my magic spent on breaking through the locks on the doors.

I have to turn back.

A light springs up ahead. My heart stutters with thoughts of a train, a quick death sliced across the tracks. But then I realize it's far too silvery to be a headlamp.

"Emrys?" The tunnel warps Kieran's call, stretches it into something like a question. His scar flares mercury. "What are you doing down here?"

He draws closer, his silver glisten drenching everything. His face is so still and immovable it looks like a mask in this haunted light.

"I should ask you the same thing." I stand rigid by the tracks, still feeling the edged spice of his kiss. It turns my stomach. Reminds me of how much like Guinevere I really am—kissing another's lips while my king suffers.

Kieran stops—three long wooden ties away. "I was looking for you. I got worried when my spell slipped. I followed your aura."

"Did you know? About Anabelle?"

There's a flicker, a movement behind that wall of a face. His voice is brittle and ice. "I did not know she would see. I'm sorry if I caused any discomfort."

Discomfort. Such a prim, proper word. So distant from the realities of angels torn from ceilings and a soul scalped raw. So delicate for the collapse I just witnessed.

"She lost control of her magic," I say. "She almost brought the palace down on our heads."

The Ad-hene stares at his feet. "I had not suspected she would be so angry."

The tracks shudder. Somewhere in the tunnel's far deep a train begins to howl.

"Angry?" I echo his final word. "Kieran, you broke her heart."

He looks up, his eyes wide, swallowing the light. For a glimpse of a moment they appear like silvered glass: transparent, oh-so-breakable. His jaw shuts and his lips go thin.

The train is drawing closer. It feels like the earth itself is shifting under my feet.

"We should go," he says finally.

Maybe it's the tightness of the tunnels. Or the heavy growl of the tracks. Or maybe it's because Kieran has stepped closer, filling all my senses with his brooding face, but my head is buzzing again.

I think of the runes which cut through my reflection. They should only be a few more steps away. And now there's more than enough light to see by. I've let myself get distracted again.

I look back at the walls. The Ad-hene's light stretches on, shows how the tunnel curves round, like some ancient coiling serpent.

"I think I saw some runes from the train," I tell him. "They should be just around this bend."

Kieran blinks, his lips draw even tighter.

I turn and start walking again. Follow the iron slant of the tracks which quake under my feet.

"Do you have a death wish?" His words echo. Loud and hard. "There's a train coming. You're walking straight toward it."

Crunch, crunch, crunch. I keep walking. Away.

All of a sudden Kieran jumps in front of me, landing with the grace of the supernatural. As if all those steps I just took brought me nowhere at all.

"Get out of my way," I say.

"Emrys, you have to turn around." Those gray eyes flash at me. I see the clench of his jaw growing, all rigid sculpt under his powder skin. "It's not safe."

"I've faced worse than a train." I keep walking forward. But he doesn't move.

I stop, just a breath away from his skin. His arms are crossed, his scar dimming under the cover of his unmarked flesh.

"Don't be foolish," he says. "Don't throw your life away."

And suddenly I realize this conversation isn't about finding the runes anymore. Maybe it never was.

"You said you understood, but you don't know a thing

about love." I'm screaming now, trying to make myself heard over the train's growing roar. "Because if you did you'd know why I have to do this. You would know why I could never be with you. . . ."

Kieran's face twists, almost as if he's in pain. There's a tempest behind his eyes. His arm streaks out—as fast and bright as a fork of lightning—grabs me by the wrist.

I don't feel the prickles anymore. It's anger which swells hot through my veins.

"Don't touch me!" My words are all hiss, but that doesn't stop Kieran's fingers from wrapping tight.

The roar is overwhelming now. Pebbles and debris start raining down, so much like Anabelle's angel dust. The tunnel walls behind the Ad-hene edge with a glow that's not his. The headlamp of the train is tearing through the earth, straight toward us.

And—in the moment between moments—I see the runes. Only a few steps ahead: chalked white over the sign of a second service door.

The Ad-hene flings me across his back like a sack of flour, flashes down the tracks. Away from the runes and the train. Even with all his swiftness we reach the first service door with only seconds to spare.

We barrel in just as the train sings by: a whiplash

of windows, dull steel, and commuters. Kieran's face is flushed; the gust of the passing cars whips through his curls. I stand with my back tight against the wall. The train is here and gone in the space of seven heartbeats, leaving the tunnel just as hollowed and dark as before.

It's not until the rush of its wheels is past that I realize how much I'm shaking. From fear, anger, or both. Adrenaline is thick in my veins, but even with that I know I never could've run as fast as Kieran just did. Not in this mortal form.

"Thank you," I manage.

Kieran doesn't say anything. His eyes are as hard and blank as the tiles he's staring down.

"Maybe there is—was—something between us. But it doesn't matter. It never mattered." I will not be Guinevere. I will not flip wrong. I will not watch this kingdom burn.

"I understand." There's pain—so base, so primal—in his voice. It catches me off guard, betrays all the stone of his features.

"Maybe I was never meant to meet Richard. But I did. Maybe I was never meant to be a *faagailagh*. But I am." I keep looking past him, into the pitch-black rectangle of the open service door. "Loving Richard has changed me.

I'm not who I was before. I'll never be that Emrys again, even if I did get my magic back. Maybe it's not who I was made to be, but it's who I chose to be. And I can't give that up. I can't let him go. I won't."

My words are loud, steady, strong. They fly out of the door, into the tunnels and echo back to me. I know they are the truth.

The life I want more is Richard.

"Not all of us can be as strong as you," he says slowly. "Even when it comes to loving someone."

After tasting the desperation in Kieran's kiss I expected more fight out of him, more—anything. But the Ad-hene just stares at the tiles, eyes and face vacant, as if he's a wax figure on display in Madame Tussauds.

I try to change the subject. "There were runes back there. Etched straight across a service door, almost like a blocking spell. We should go back and look before the next train."

This information seems to bring Kieran to life, at least a bit. He shifts, blocks the way to the door. "No. It's too dangerous. The runes could be another trap, like the desk. Besides, we know who wrote them."

The man who's somewhere above us. The man who

will soon be sitting at Kensington Palace's banquet table across from Anabelle, hands wrapped around a glass, raising it to his lips.

"Anabelle still means to go through with the banquet," I tell him.

Kieran shuts his eyes. His head pushes against the wall, black curls smoke up and out on the tiles; it looks as though his own dark soul is trying to pull out of his body. "You're going to let Belle put herself in that danger? Risk her life?"

"I'm not *letting* her do anything. I might have been able to talk her out of it before . . ." I let the rest go understood. "But Anabelle wants to do this. And I have to help her."

"So you're not going to reclaim your magic? Even if this plan could get Richard killed?" The guilt—the paper-cut nicks Kieran's words are so good at—weaves around me. Choke and doubt.

Is it worth his death? My insides start to gasp.

And a response, spoken in Richard's brass bell voice: *I don't need your magic, I need you.* It's what he said to me on the Winfreds' yacht. Just before I jumped onto the Kelpie. How had I forgotten?

I will not be Guinevere. I will not abandon my king when he needs me most. If there's a chance, even a *chance*

I can find Richard without magic . . . I have to take it. "I have to go back to the palace."

"If there's ever a soul I've met who can fight fate and win, it's you, Emrys Léoflic." The Ad-hene says this with his eyes still closed, his face wrenched tight. If I really wanted to, I could dash past him, back into the tunnels. But Kieran's right: it could be a trap, and I can't risk things going badly. Not when we're only a few hours away from seizing the largest piece to this puzzle.

I've found my course. And now I must stay it.

Twenty-Four

Despite my fears, Kensington Palace still stands.

Yet even if the palace had crumbled to dust, Anabelle's banquet would go on. The dinner is set up in the Orangery, a slender building off the edge of the garden, where Queen Anne once held many teas and dinners of her own. Its walls are all windows—swallowing the evening light and bathing the room in a hot amber shine, preserving the delicate balance of this moment. Before we slip the drink into Julian Forsythe's hands.

Kieran and I are sheathed in his veiling spell, tucked in opposite corners of the room, away from the path of the serving staff. I know Anabelle can see us, but she does everything in her power not to look our way. She watches out the window instead, waiting for guests. As the light outside dims, I can see her face more clearly in the glass. Composed and perfect. In the space of hours Anabelle has pulled together two impossible things: a dinner party this lavish and herself.

We watch her, waiting for the ice of her expression to slip. For one of the many panes of glass to crack and shatter. But things stay whole. At least on the outside.

The princess was right: she's good at controlling things.

Guests start filing in—names from Anabelle's small, select list. The only one I recognize is Queen Cecilia, who walks almost hand in hand with Jensen, as if terrified to leave his side.

And then, the guest of honor.

The sun is gone by the time Julian Forsythe strides down the gravel path. The only light left comes from the torches which line the way, and the glow of the Orangery's windows. These catch his eyes, make them electric.

Elaine is with him this time, her frail frame swallowed in a coat of blinding white fur. Her skin is almost as pale, set off only by the sleek dark of her hair and eyes. The only spot of color on her is the bright scarlet swathe of her lipstick.

The doorman offers to take her coat, but Elaine shakes her head, shrugging the fur even farther over her bony shoulders.

"My wife has a chill," Julian says, guiding his wife into the Orangery with a wide sweep of his arm. "She'll keep it on, as long as Her Highness approves."

I frown, thinking of the tightness of his knuckles in that photo, the bruises I imagined. I wonder how deep they go under those layers of fur. Elaine's dewy eyes are wide, almost skittish as they take in the room. Something like fear passes behind them, quivering under her thin red smile as she greets the princess.

It will all be over soon, I want to tell her. *You'll never have to see this monster again.*

"This is *your* dinner," Anabelle says in her sweetest voice. "Can I get you anything to drink? A Pimm's Cup perhaps? I heard it was your favorite during your Oxford days."

"Did you?" Julian's eyebrows fly up. "That was ages ago. . . . The stories of your past have a way of catching up with you, don't they?"

"He doesn't drink anymore." The prim and prick of Elaine's voice suddenly reminds me of why I disliked her so much on the yacht. "He needs a clear head for his job."

"Prudent." Anabelle's face stays ice. "I suppose if there's anything these past few months have taught us it's that our government's leaders must be ready for anything."

Elaine Forsythe nods. "It's a dangerous world. I'm just glad men like Julian are taking a stand."

"Someone must," Richard's mother joins the conversation. "Lord Winfred is just as blinded by these creatures as Richard and Anabelle once were. Thank goodness your motion of no confidence passed, Mr. Forsythe. With you as prime minister we can finally do something."

"I'm not prime minister yet, Your Majesty," Julian reminds her.

"But you will be. After the election tomorrow," Queen Cecilia says without a doubt. "And once you are we'll take more extreme actions to protect our city and find my son."

Anabelle clears her throat. "The first course should be arriving shortly. I think you should enjoy it, Mr. Forsythe. Oysters fresh from Whitstable, where you grew up."

"Ah! How thoughtful." Julian Forsythe's smile is stunted as he leads Elaine to the table. Her coat blends in with the white of the back wall, the crisp blank of the tablecloth. If it weren't for the color in her hair and lips, she'd disappear altogether.

Dinner begins. Attendants bring out silver platters, trailing mouthwatering scents as they make their way around the table. I stand in my corner, still as death, watching Julian Forsythe. That wilted grin stays on his face while he wields his utensils as delicately as a calligrapher's pen. A silver goblet of water gleams by his right hand—shimmering full of the drugs we need him to take. Every muscle in my body keeps winding tight as I wait for him to take a sip.

He doesn't drink.

Anabelle watches the glass too. By the second course her smile is shorter, fading.

When the third course arrives Anabelle's smile vanishes altogether. From where I stand I see her hands wringing under the table. Knuckles knotting into knuckles.

I move to Kieran's corner, dodging trays of stuffed wild mushrooms and glazed Cornish game hens. The Ad-hene's expression is brooding, his signature stone stare taking everything in: the queue of diners, the muted flower arrangements, the china plates full of extravagant food.

I'm so close to him our arms are nearly touching. The prickle hasn't returned. Not since I shouted it away in those tunnels. Banished it like a demon.

"What do we do now?" I ask.

"Wait until the moment is right," he says this without looking away. I follow his stare.

Anabelle sits close. Even from such a short distance away I have trouble picking out any flaws. Her perfect summer-gold hair, her skin soft under the light of the table's candelabras. The dress she's wearing tonight is silvery; it glows under the candlelight like the Ad-hene's scars.

I look back at Kieran, see the princess's form in miniature, shining through the iron of his eyes.

"Do you think she really loved me?" His question is quiet, but it hangs heavy. I try to make sense of it. Why he's asking. Why it matters. Why he speaks in past tense, as if the end has already been written.

I look at the princess again. From this angle I cannot see her twisting hands. Just as I can't see any sign of the agony which swept over her this afternoon. The heel-crushed heart which colored her words, fed her magic.

"I know you really hurt her," I answer, thinking of the paint flake storm.

"I'm sorry." Kieran's voice is as cracked as Kensington's ceilings. He's still looking at Anabelle as if she's the only soul in the room. "Know that I'm sorry."

The chandeliers' light cuts out. The Orangery becomes an archipelago of candlelit faces. Garden torches glare against the window panes, so the whole wall looks as if it's on fire. Gasps rise from the table, swelling louder with every second the dark stays.

"It's them! They've come back for you, Your Highness!"

Julian Forsythe rises from his chair, a jerking motion which sends his goblet tumbling. A harsh light blooms from his hand. The sight of it fills me with sick.

"We have to do something!" I reach out for Kieran's arm. But where I expect his solid, steady build, I find only empty space.

Kieran is gone. And so is his veiling spell.

Queen Titania—in all her stubborn pride—was right.

I never should have trusted the Ad-hene.

This revelation burns through me along with stares and darkness. Every burnished face at the table is tilted in my direction—their expressions slowly melting into horror. Elaine Forsythe lets out a terrible whimper.

Her husband moves in a flash. Julian Forsythe's hand rises, a fist. I see his tattoo clearly: a ring of runes inked around the veins of his wrist. Lit blue by the glow between his knuckles. Not a spell like I thought, but a stun gun.

He's coming for me, with the same tiger lunge Mordred performed in dream after dream.

The force which rushes through me as soon as Julian's fist meets my skin feels almost like magic. It's the stab of a hundred wasp stings all across my body, freezing my muscles, binding me with electricity. All of me collapses on the marble floor, deadweight.

The stun gun charge is gone, but I still cannot move. All I can do is stare, helpless, watching everything unfold like a dream before me. Julian Forsythe stepping away. Queen Cecilia's beetroot-flushed cheeks: all shock. Anabelle's expression as frozen as my muscles. And then Eric's face: furious and twisted like some cornered wildcat as he bends over me. Hauls me to my feet.

On the other side of the room Julian barks orders. "Check for others. She's not working alone."

I want to speak, I want to scream out the truth to all of those wax-figure diners. How the real threat is standing in front of them, cloaked in all the handsome manners of an Oxford graduate. But my words are trapped inside, caught in the jellyfish stun of Julian's knuckles.

My eyes catch Anabelle's, but the ice of her magic I felt this afternoon has only grown. The princess is sheathed in it now. Controlled, yet impenetrable.

She watches Eric drag me away without a word.

The garden path is all flicker and fire, shadows dancing over hedges and gravel. Everything feels unsteady in the blackout's fresh dark, as if the whole world has tilted on its side. My muscles begin to throb as Eric pulls me down the Orangery's front steps. I stay deadweight anyway, hoping he won't notice and stun me again. I let my feet drag: two long, sliding protests in the path's gravel. My mind churns frantically through plans of escape.

Jensen and other Protection Command officers join Eric's side, talking into radios and shining electric lights into the dark between the hedges. A wind rushes through the garden: winter's breath tearing at the evergreens. So strong, so cold, that it snuffs many of the pathway's torches. Eric stops at the sudden dark. I wait for him to drop me and rearm his stun gun, but he keeps still.

After several seconds I realize the other officers are just as motionless. The wind is gone and the remaining torches don't flicker. Eric gapes over me like an opera singer mid-note, his eyes glazed. The world is caught in a single moment—bound by some strangely wrought spell.

This magic hasn't just frozen people. There are no sounds. No motion. Nothing. Time has been suspended. There's only this moment, reaming through itself over and over with no signs of stopping.

The Orangery doors swing open. Julian Forsythe appears in its gap, his wife on his arm. They walk together—their steps deafening through the gravel. Elaine's stilettos stamp through the mark my heels left. I hang from Eric's frozen arms like a criminal caught in the stocks, awaiting my final sentence.

Julian stops only a few steps away. His arm stays tight around his wife's coat, digging into that white fur.

"I know who you are, Mordred." I shout his name like a challenge. "So let's drop the subtleties and—"

"Mordred?" Elaine Forsythe's eyes startle, go wide. She looks her husband up and down. "Now that's a name I haven't heard in a long, long time."

A smile curls up onto those crimson lips, coy as a cat's tail. She goes on, "Do you know I'd nearly forgotten about him? It's hard to remember faces when you spend so many years in the dark."

Her smile keeps rising and I feel my stomach falling. Swirling into itself like water down a drain.

I was wrong.

Elaine's arm slides out of Julian's grip. Her fingers start drawing back her coat, exposing the snowy skin of her breastbone. Mink fur falls away, slides down her arms. Her dress is all black, melting like silk into the night, covering her arms in long lace sleeves.

No. I squint closer through frozen firelight. Not lace. Not even sleeves. The entirety of her arms is covered in ink: thousands upon thousands of tiny rune tattoos, so close and cramped together that her skin is more dark than white. Novels of spells and power etched into her very flesh.

The markings of a sorceress.

She turns and I see how the dress dips down her back in a luxurious V. The runes are there too, so small and complicated even the pure skin between them looks like a foreign language.

"Be a dear and hold my coat for me?" She looks at Julian Forsythe, her voice all bright. "And would you go inside the Orangery and make sure everything is in order? The *faagailagh* and I need to have a little chat."

Julian doesn't hesitate. He takes the armfuls of fur and walks back the way he came, into the Orangery. He leaves the door open and I see Anabelle seated at the table, her gaze suspended on the garden path, seeing nothing as this sorceress from another age faces me in the dark.

"The runes on his wrist . . . ," I think aloud. "You put those there. You're using spells to control him."

"Catching on, are we?" She twists her white swan neck until the joints pop—a sound like die being cast. Her face turns in the preserved light and I see lines spidering onto the skin around her eyes. Growing in front of me.

I hang limp in Eric's arms, mind spinning. "Who *are* you?"

The sorceress doesn't answer; she's noticed the web of wrinkles too. Her hand dips into the folds of her dress, produces a sharp, ebony quill. She places the fanged tip at the end of her wrist—where the skin is still sheet white—and starts to carve. Blood and pigment swirl down her palm, together black as she incants old, old words. With every syllable, every deeper dig of the quill the age which appeared so quickly on her skin vanishes.

"Feeling your years?" I ask when she puts back the loaded quill.

"Routine maintenance. Not all immortality can be sustained as effortlessly as the Fae's. Runecraft, unfortunately, cannot be looped. Spells fade and must be rewritten. It's kept me busy all these years." She looks down at the hundreds of tiny symbols on her arms. "It seems I'm finally running out of room. I'll have to find myself a new skin. A shame. This body has seen so much."

But who is this body? What did I miss?

I try my question again, in a different form. "Runecraft was never common in Camelot. Where did you learn it?"

The sorceress doesn't ignore me this time. The dew vanishes from her dark eyes—become a stare which twists into me like a maelstrom. "You should know, Lady Emrys. You were one of those who sent me across the sea."

Her words hiss and spit. A memory settles in, drifts into the cracks of my mind like stray ashfall. It was one of my first shifts as a Frithemaeg Guard. The day I followed King Arthur and a train of his knights down to the sea—where the boat waited. His sister rode close to me: a sallow-faced girl with limbs like twigs. Never saying a word while Arthur greeted her betrothed with a handshake and a formal treatise. It was the sister's shoulders which gave her away. They were rigid as grave markers as she watched the sails of the longboat hoist high, prepare to steal her to the shores of Normandy. To the castle of a lord more than twice her age.

I remember, even then, feeling sorry for her. This slip of a girl, being sacrificed to keep the peace. Married off to a foreign warlord. Never to be seen again. I'd always thought ill of Arthur for it.

"You're Arthur's sister. Morgaine le Fay." The whisper hardly leaves me before I remember Guinevere's words, the ones which made the princess shudder and shrink behind my back: *Sister of a king. Across the sea and back again. Even sisters fail us in the end.*

Guinevere hadn't been talking about Anabelle at all. She was fighting the silencing spell, trying to tell us about Morgaine.

The sorceress's lips curl back at the sound of the Pendragon's name. Red as fresh hurt. "Half sister technically. But no one ever seems to remember that. I was the oldest of King Uther's children. My blood was the purest, the most royal. Arthur was the bastard son of a scullery maid, and still he was favored for the throne.

"We grew up together in my father's palace. We shared everything and we were close in age, yet we were as different as the sun and moon. Everyone saw it. Even Merlin, our magic tutor. He taught us together at first. Small things like hemming gowns without a stitch and mixing healing poultices. Then he taught us how to channel our emotions and work larger spells. I was the stronger one, I always was. But as our lessons progressed Merlin started favoring Arthur. The sorcerer told me I was not ready—even though I was better at magic than my half brother. I was too angry, he said. I had too much darkness in me." Morgaine's eyes harden like the torches' enchanted light. "But my half brother—a weakling boy who slept by ten lanterns because he was scared of the dark—Merlin found a way to thread magic into his very blood. Arthur became powerful enough to move mountains and I was stuck with tricks any hedge-witch could muster for a few copper pieces.

"Merlin refused to continue my magical education, so I taught myself. My father died and Arthur, the bastard prince, was crowned king. He sat on the throne which was rightfully mine and I hated him for it. My hate grew stronger and my magic did too. Strong enough to fight my half brother and become queen. But Merlin discovered my research before I could take the throne and warned my brother of what was to come. Arthur would not believe it at first, but when he came to my chambers to confront me, I fought him. I'd always thought my brother a weakling, but whatever powers Merlin gave him were stronger. Arthur snapped my staff, burned my grimoires, and banished me from the kingdom in secret. He was too kindhearted even to subject me to public shame. He pretended to marry me off, for my dignity. I was shipped to a land of tattooed savages, exiled from the kingdom I should have ruled.

"But that hardly stopped me." Morgaine looks down the length of her bare arms—storied and spelled. "In the land of savages I became a savage. I learned their magic, carved their runes into my skin. Each symbol means something different: life, power, strength, control. There are hundreds, thousands of spells which can be written out, in skin or on walls, unleashed at just the moment I choose.

"When I had learned all I could, I returned to Camelot. But Arthur's blood magic was too strong for me to face outright, even with my runecraft. So I watched from the shadows. I watched as Arthur fell in love with a Fae. I watched knights and peasants alike praise his name. I watched him sit on my throne, wear my crown. I watched all this and I waited for the perfect moment to take back the kingdom."

"And then you destroyed everything," I say, trying to keep up with all the puzzle pieces which are now *click, click, clicking* into place. Too many to count. "It wasn't Mordred at all. You were controlling him with the runes, the same way you've been controlling Julian."

"Is that who they credit for Pendragon's doom?" One of the sorceress's raven eyebrows lifts high. "Mordred was a pawn. I needed his armies to assure my victory."

"And Guinevere?"

"Ah yes. The other *faagailagh*. Key to my brother's golden heart." Disgust curdles her words. "Merlin taught us that emotions were the key to our magic's strength. Arthur always did draw from love. A vulnerable, feeble emotion—one which breaks. It didn't take long for me to realize that Arthur's magic and heart were tied up in Guinevere. She was the crack in his armor. His weakness. And she herself was weak, undone by a handsome knight and one of my love spells. As soon as Arthur learned that his dear bride had ridden off with Lancelot, his magic faltered, and I struck.

"I stood on the hill and watched it all turn to ruin. But it wasn't enough. I wanted Arthur to see my face before he died. I wanted him to know I was taking back my kingdom."

"So you killed him? After Mordred stabbed him?" After I'd left, flown back to Mab's court in a flurry of anger and fear.

"I wanted to watch him suffer, but I waited too long. The Faery queen came like Judgment Day." A sigh leaves her. Almost dream-like. "All white and fury. So much *power*. I'd studied Arthur's magic. I knew his weakness. But I had not prepared for a Faery of Queen Mab's caliber. My runecraft was no match. The Faery queen threw me into the Labyrinth's darkness, thought she had taken care of the problem. Much the same way my half brother did. Again I found myself robbed of a crown, stripped of freedom.

"Again I endured. I knew my prison wouldn't last forever. Nothing does, after all. I kept myself alive with runecraft and rage. I knew that once I found a way out, I would have my vengeance on the Fae. I'd get my kingdom back."

I think of the cell—its furious runes. Years of agony and revenge chiseled into the very walls of the earth. That same feeling—that same black sick which roiled through the bars, haunted my dreams—stands here in the garden. Morgaine's voice still gleams as bright as a collector's prized coin and her face remains a strange beauty.

But the inside of her . . . her aura. It's every hurt, every long stretching second of the Labyrinth's dark, every drop of Arthur's blood, every needle which ever marked her skin. If Anabelle was all whirlwind and blizzard, then this . . . It's all blackness. A powerful, soulless void. Swirling and pulling and tugging and wanting to consume. Like those forces in the far reaches of the heavens which have the power to eat the stars whole.

Morgaine keeps speaking, all calm. "It didn't take long to persuade the Ad-hene to my side. Not after the Faery queen tricked them in their most desperate moment: turning their home into a prison, binding them into her service. They wanted freedom and vengeance on the Fae as badly as I; they were only too eager to help. But they couldn't undo the wards Mab placed on my cell.

"But then Mab was unmade and her wards vanished. I found I could bend my bars. The Ad-hene guided me back into the light and I found a world where the Frithemaeg's power is crippled by technology. A place where mortals know little of magic. A land ripe for the taking.

"But the more I studied this new world, the more I realized I could not claim the crown openly," she goes on, "not without calling an army of Frithemaeg and a horde of angry mortals on my head. But there was quite a crack in this kingdom's armor: the gap between mortals and Fae. I knew I could pry it wider, fill it with chaos. So I used Julian's speeches to stir up mortals' fears; I organized King Richard's kidnapping to springboard the emergency elections. Tomorrow Julian will become prime minister, and I will have the power to spread technology so far that Fae will be wiped off this island forever." Her smile flashes teeth and I think of the runes on Mordred's ebony armor, the tattoo circling Julian Forsythe's wrist.

Circles. Back again.

A new Camelot means a new fall.

"You won't get away with this," I hiss at her. "As soon as Queen Titania realizes what you're doing—"

"But that's the beauty of it," Morgaine is still all teeth and smile. "She won't. The Frithemaeg are gone, and even when they were here they did not see me working in the shadows. All they see are the puppets—the show in front of the curtain. And that, Lady Emrys, will go on. Whether you decide to join me or not."

"Join you? Never!" I try my best to spit the word, but my mouth is so dry. Parched in fear of this void woman before me.

"I wouldn't be so quick to refuse if I were you," the sorceress says. "You haven't heard my offer yet."

"I'm not so desperate for power." My throat croaks and rasps, weakness.

Morgaine's laughter is like knife blades: iron and clanging through the cold. Her breath curls high, melts into the vast void of night above us. "You say it as if it's such a terrible thing. To want power. Yet that's all anyone ever really wants, isn't it? These men in fancy suits might talk of justice and peace. The women hanging from their arms might speak of love and drink tea from fancy china, but behind it all, they're just animals struggling to reach the top of the heap. Savages who will do anything to get what they want.

"Take Eric Black here—an officer who swore a solemn

oath to protect the king. All it took was a few of Julian's speeches, a personal invitation to M.A.F. leadership, and he kidnapped His Majesty straight out of the carriage. To him, a little power was worth a great deal of treason.

"Or take the Ad-hene. All I had to do was offer them a new set of tunnels they could rule all their own, and they were willing to set me free and lie to the Faery queen.

"Even you want it." Morgaine's smile curls like a velvet Christmas ribbon. "Ever since my escape I've been watching you, Emrys Léoflic. At first I did not believe the rumors that you'd become a *faagailagh*. That a spirit as strong as you would throw all your power away for a man's sake. But then I saw you on the Winfreds' yacht. I saw the way you looked at Richard—how you clutched his arm—and I knew the rumors were true. Like Guinevere, you'd given up, become *weak*.

"But then I saw you jump. I saw the look in your eyes when you dove after that Kelpie and I knew you still had strength inside. Potential for greatness. A power I could use. So I decided to test you."

My mind is racing, webbing through stories of Camelot and shadows and what lies beneath. If Julian is playing the role of Mordred and I am so like Guinevere . . . then the parallels must keep stretching. "You tested me with Kieran. You were using him, just like you used Lancelot." I think of all those silver words, all those moments the Ad-hene touched me and my insides prickled with magic and mysterious want. Smaller at first, up, up, up until that desperate, last-ditch kiss. When I broke away and it all vanished. "He was dosing me with a love spell, trying to seduce me. . . ."

"When Alistair informed me that he'd sent one of his own to aid you, the opportunity was too good to resist. But seduction was only a part of it." Her scarlet smile wreathes into a smirk. "The Ad-hene are excellent guides and I needed him to guide you to the edge. Force you to choose, so I could see where your true desires lie."

"And where is that?" I grit my teeth.

"In the realm of the impossible. You want a life you cannot have, Emrys Léoflic. It wasn't Kieran who was tempting you. Not really. What tortures you, what tears your heart, is the magic you lost. That need Richard can never fill, no matter how much you *love* him. Richard or power. That's always the question in the back of your mind, isn't it?"

I feel like her eyes have sliced me open, peeled back

layers of muscle and bone, rooted out all the ugly truths.

"I made my choice," I tell her, remind myself. Richard. The life I want more.

"What if you don't have to choose?" Morgaine walks closer, heels grinding down the garden path. The scent off her pale skin is honey and coal dust: the bitterest of sweet. It fills my nostrils as she steps close, leans in. "I can give you both."

Her nearness is dizzying. My eyes swim, and it looks almost as if the runes—all the spells she etched into her arms over the years—are flowing as they reach for me. Her fingers wrap around my wrist, cold as bands of iron as she pries me free from Eric's grip. She stretches my arm out, yanks up my sleeve.

"Serve me. Take my runes into your flesh and I'll allow your king to live. I'll teach you runecraft, return all the power your heart has ached for." Her words glide through the night air, smooth as a serpent's belly. I stare down at my arm, try to imagine what Morgaine's marks would look like, snaking up its pure peach skin.

She must need my permission to slide the ink into my veins. She wouldn't be asking otherwise.

"I wouldn't ask much," she says softly. "You'll keep an eye on your king, of course. Make sure he does not interfere with my plans. I'll only call upon your powers when I need you."

"You want me to control Richard. . . . You want us to be your puppets." Like Mordred and Julian. Like Blæc and the Ad-hene. I wonder what she offered them. What lives they couldn't refuse.

"You'd be taking a great burden off his shoulders. Without the pressures of leading, Richard would have all the time in the world for you. It's what you both want. Isn't it?"

I think of the cabin on the shores of the loch. Its empty rooms waiting to be filled: with blankets and laughter and Richard's fingers dancing through my hair, over my skin. Over my inked, mottled skin . . .

Morgaine's fingers grip tighter. Pain creeps up my wrist, shatters the thought of Richard's face.

"And if I don't?" I ask, though I already know the answer.

She drops my arm. Her lips purse. "I'm afraid you're too much of a threat. If you refuse my offer, then tonight when midnight strikes the Palace of Westminster will collapse into flames. King Richard's body will be found underneath the rubble and yours with it. But not to worry, your deaths would be quite productive. The Fae will be blamed for his assassination and the M.A.F. will sweep tomorrow's elections, making my dear husband the new prime minister. I'll find another royal puppet to fill the throne and the show will go on. Either way I win. Either way I gain control of my kingdom."

I look down at my arm. It's covered in goose bumps, white as marble. The skin where Morgaine's fingers were is red. Stinging.

If I take her ink into my skin, I'll never be mine. No matter how much power I gain. I'll never be Richard's. No matter how many precious hours I spend wrapped up in his arms.

I'll be hers.

Sucked so entirely into the black of her soul. Swallowed with the stars.

I would become that. Emptiness collapsing into emptiness. Hate crumbling into hate. *Round and round it goes. A widening gyre.*

Down.

Down.

Down.

Down.

A down which never ends.

This time I cannot jump to save Richard's life. I cannot

do what it takes to protect him. But it's not because I'm weak.

I think of her aura again . . . so empty, so hungry. Never filled. I knew that feeling once. I brushed the edge of it that summer night when I was sprawled across the stones of fortress ruins. When I knew that meeting Richard had changed everything. That the edges of my soul were jagged with a hole only he could fill.

I think of this and look back at Morgaine. "Have you ever loved anyone?"

The beauty of the sorceress's face spoils as if her rune of youth has already expired. But it's only disgust wrinkling her brow, twisting her lips into a snarl.

Such a hard, impenetrable soul. Spun into so much darkness. Crystallized into a cocoon of death. A coffin nailed tight. I can only feel sorry for her.

"If you had, you'd know your offer is useless," I say.

If she hears the pity in my voice, she doesn't show it. "And so you choose to throw your life away. Again. How disappointing."

Morgaine snaps her fingers and the garden's dark shifts. The gaps between the hedges fill with faces. The sharp, fault-line features of sixteen Ad-hene loom in the torchlight.

Alistair steps in front of the rest. He doesn't look at me at all. His lazy lids are focused solely on the sorceress. "Yes?"

"The Ad-hene's bargain has been fulfilled," she says. "The tunnels I've marked are yours to loop as soon as you escort Emrys underground."

"Thank you, Lady le Fay."

"Now go. I have some memories to modify." Morgaine reaches out for Eric's frozen face. Her nails sink deep into his cheek, carve out skin like a carrot peeler. She stares at me, smiling as her nails run all the way down to his jaw. "Though after the tray incident I don't think it will take much to convince him you did this, in your desperate attempt to escape."

The scratches must be deep because Eric's blood washes down Morgaine's fingers. Staining that white skin, mixing into the rune ink.

I look away, down the row of stoic faces and see Kieran, lurking in the far fringe of the hedges. Finally, finally, his stare is not on me. It's not on anything. It's adrift, floating through the night in front of him, glossing over the Orangery's windows.

I want him to look at me. I want to gut him through, the way Anabelle did.

But he doesn't care. He never truly understood. There was never a word out of his mouth which wasn't a twisting lie, a means to an end, a key to his prison.

He's stone, like all the others.

Twenty-Five

I expect the earth to yawn open under the Ad-hene's feet, to swallow us whole as they haul me up from the gravel and start walking.

Alistair leads the way out of the garden in that slow, swaying way of his. The world is still frozen with Morgaine's spell as the Ad-hene file along the asphalt of the pitch-dark streets. All of the electric streetlamps are dead, glass bulging and dull like a bovine's eye. It seems the power outage has reached far past Kensington's walls. The city is all darkness except for the stunned headlamps of cars, the Ad-hene's scarred arms.

"Foshil!" Alistair calls out from the middle of the street. There's a grating sound and a manhole cover slides across the road, spinning like an Olympian's discarded disc. Along its metallic edges I spy a scratch of runes—the very same combination I glimpsed on the service door.

"Get her under, swiftly." He points to the gape in the earth. With the extra shine of his arms I can see the hints of a ladder. "The spell is due to lift at any moment."

One by one the Ad-hene leap into the service hole. They toss me down like a bushel of fruit. The air down here is warm, heavy with awful smells. Scents which make my tongue curl and my throat close. London's filth.

"This is to be your new labyrinth?" I look around at the cramped concrete walls, the murky sludge swallowing my captors' ankles. "You betrayed your oath to the Faery queen for sewers?"

"Our oath?" Alistair lands in front of me, a burst of fallen light and brown droplets. His eyes meet mine for the first time: black and vicious and old, old, old under those paper-thin lids. "There was never an oath, *faagailagh*. Oaths are made out of good faith and fealty. What Mab did was pillage. She found the Ad-hene torn apart, ruined by years and years of war. She promised to rebuild our home, make us whole again, if we bound ourselves to her. But she desecrated the Labyrinth—made it a place of pain and despairing dark. We became her prisoners, trapped in the tunnels which were once ours. But Mab is dead. Her wards have fallen and we are now free. We are betraying nothing."

"*Dooin!*" He barks his spell and somewhere far above us the manhole cover slides back into place. *Schnick.*

The sound jars me more than it should. It seems far more real—far more final—than anything else about this night. I hear it and wonder if I'll feel the sun's rays on my face again. If anyone will ever know the truth about how the earth swallowed me like a magician's trapdoor . . .

Click.

The final piece of the puzzle falls into place.

Richard never left the city. Trafalgar Square swallowed him and his kidnappers like quicksand. That's why no one saw him being taken. There was nothing to see. Just the spin of a manhole—lost in all the chaos of Blæc's bloodbath.

Richard is here, underground.

For the first time in a long time my chest jars with a feeling which isn't doom or burning or loss. I'm slung like a spring lamb over this Ad-hene's broad shoulders, probably being taken to my slaughter. I have no reason to hope, but that doesn't make my heart thrill any less.

I'm going to see Richard again.

The Ad-hene move as one. They flow—cobra swift— through tunnels, through hatches, through halls, down stairs, down holes, over pipes, over tracks. Through layers and centuries of cramped humanity. The one who carries me runs without jarring. A stale wind rakes my hair, plasters its black strands into my face. I only glimpse flashes of London's vast underbelly through it, images skating along the silver rays of the Ad-hene's scars. Tiled walls, a Roman-era well, a tribe of brown rats, a brick archway from Victorian times, train tracks so long out of use they're coated with moss.

And runes. Everywhere runes.

They're scrawled in odd places: on the rungs of ladders, the backsides of iron hatches, above arches like mistletoe. Always the same string of symbols. The same spell from the manhole cover and the service door.

After what seems an eternity, the river of Ad-hene slows, becomes a trickle. I'm slung to the ground, facing Alistair again, and behind him, a steel door. The paint on it is peeling, old and neglected.

"She's using you," I say over Alistair's shoulder as he opens the door. "Look at what you're doing. Opening cell doors, guiding prisoners. Just like before. Morgaine has made this place a prison! Just like Mab."

More dark yawns past the open door. Alistair turns. "This is no prison, *fuagailagh*. It is your tomb."

"Do you think Morgaine is just going to hand you these tunnels?" I think of the vastness of London's underground network, how it reaches up into every building, delves deep into every secret. How many things move unnoticed by the world above.

"She already has. Now that Kieran has fulfilled our bargain, I can loop this labyrinth with my own magic," Alistair informs me. "Even Lady le Fay will not be able navigate these tunnels without us."

"But her runes are everywhere," I say.

"Morgaine marked out our tunnels before we arrived. They're blocking spells to cleanse our territory of common mortals. Just as you thought." Kieran speaks from behind me. And I remember how eager he was to keep me from going back to study the runes on the service door. I'd been so close to the truth.

"Now go." Alistair—the oldest Ad-hene of all, father of labyrinths—sweeps his arm into the dark. "Die the death you chose."

I look over the chorus of faces, lit and somber like mourners at a candle vigil. My eyes catch Kieran's. Finally. Finally! His face doesn't flinch. His eyes don't shine. I stare and stare. I want to haunt him. But his expression remains like all the others. Blank. He is only one of sixteen pale bodies, surrounding me like a half-moon, pressing in, leaving no room to run. I have no way to go but forward.

I walk on, stay my course. All the way into the dark.

* * *

The door clangs shut. Sealing off every glimmer of the Ad-hene's scars. Leaving me wrapped in underground darkness: an absolute black, all claw and dazzle.

A lock grinds into place behind me, though I don't know why they bothered. I'm not sure I could find the door again. The darkness is too thick, too stifling. Everything has closed in on me—pulled tight. Yet the room I'm standing in must be large. There are noises from great distances. Drips. Clicks. Breathing . . .

My heart stops. I stand perfectly still. Listen.

Nothing. Was it just my own breath circling back to me? The darkness taking on a soul of its own?

And then—a footstep. A scuff of sole against a concrete floor.

"Richard?" My call trails off, gets tangled up in the dark. "Is that you?"

The steps stop. They're close. So close.

"Embers?" His whisper is barely there, wrapped up in shrouds of disbelief. "You're here. . . ."

"Where are you?" I reach out through the black.

"By the wall . . ." He pauses, as if just now realizing the darkness we're in. "Follow my voice."

He keeps calling to me, in that warm, summertime

way of his: *Embers, Embers, Embers.* With every new syllable I take a step forward. Draw closer to the rich toffee smooth of his voice. Closer, closer, closer.

Here.

My fingers find something even warmer and softer than Richard's voice. His hand. Our skin meets, almost electric. I pull completely into his touch. His arms fold over my shoulders. We stay like this for a long time, clutching each other like lifelines.

"You're here," he whispers again.

I want to say something, but there's so much feeling in my throat. Swelling, choking out any explanations. All I can do is breathe in, press my face into his neck.

I found him. I lost him, but I found him again.

"Richard . . . ," I finally manage.

His hand hushes back around my shoulder, dances like feathers through my hair. "You really cut it. The dreams were real. . . ."

"I don't know how—" I start to say.

"Can you make a light? I want to see you."

A light. Of course. I had one this whole time.

"Inlíhte." At my whisper our world flares to life. With Richard at its center. Suddenly I'm glad I didn't try to fight Morgaine or the Ad-hene, that I didn't steal any of

the light now wrapping around Richard's face. There's so little of it: a flash and a long, agonizing dimming.

We gaze at each other through the watery rays of my Faery light. Trying to capture and preserve these new images of ourselves. As we are. Richard looks much as he did in the dream: hair tousled, face thinning and covered in scruff, eyes red-rimmed: tired without the bleariness. Their stare is all focus, drinking me in. The hand which hovered by my jaw brushes back into my hair.

"I didn't want to change it." My voice wavers, just like my spell. "I had to. I loved the red. And I know you did too. I had to do it—"

I'm sobbing now. I know it's not about the hair. It's about every impossible choice I've been faced with since he was torn from my arms. It's about the death I've brought down upon our heads.

We're standing in a tomb. I can see that now as I try to wipe the tears from my face, finally look away from Richard. The walls around us are grimy white tile, the room itself filled with ladders and machines. Runecraft winds tight around bricks and pipes. Far too cramped and complicated to erase, even if I did have my old magic.

It's not hard to guess what spell they will unleash. And when.

Tonight when midnight strikes the Palace of Westminster will collapse into flames. King Richard's body will be found underneath the rubble and yours with it.

We must be somewhere in the Palace of Westminster's basement. I look around frantically for an exit, but all I can see is the steel door Alistair locked. Slowly my light fades. And my magic with it. I don't have the strength to open the door. All because I wanted a glimpse of Richard's face. My last glimpse.

We're going to die. In a few short hours Morgaine's runes will eat their way through these walls with flare and fire. The stones will collapse and swallow us whole. Because I chose it.

I've buried us alive.

"I don't care what color your hair is," Richard says softly.

The tears come harder, after the smile which breaks across his face. I can barely see it. My Faery light is just a shimmer now, the size of a firefly. Darkness collapses back on us.

My fingers dig into him, holding on.

"She's going to kill us," I hear myself saying. "Elaine Forsythe. She's really Morgaine le Fay—a sorceress from Camelot—and she's going to kill us to rig the elections and take control of Britain."

"What are you talking about?" Richard asks.

"I thought it was Mordred," I go on, unable to stop the avalanche of words and tears, "because of the dreams Guinevere was sending. The ones you were in. But I wasn't paying enough attention. I wasn't listening."

"Dreams? Guinevere?" Richard's arms stay wrapped around my shoulders. The only thing left holding me together. "Emrys, slow down. Start from the beginning."

My story pours out. I start with that night on the yacht and tell him everything: about the Labyrinth of Man, Guinevere's curse, Herne's offer, Titania's abandonment, his sister's courage, the effigies the bonfires ate, Blæc's ashes, the circle of runes cuffing Julian Forsythe's wrist, Kieran's lips crushed against mine, the magic Anabelle used to tear Kensington's angels from their heights.

I'm hoarse by the time I tell him what happened in the garden. The path I chose for both of us.

And after this: a long silence. I wish I could still see Richard's face. At least his arms haven't pulled away.

"I'm sorry," I say, when the quiet becomes too much.

"Why?"

"All of this is my fault. Guinevere tried to warn me, and I could have stopped it. I could have taken back my magic and protected you . . . but I didn't. I didn't have the courage to let you go." I hold him tighter as I say this, my arms looped firm around his waist. "I failed you. I chose this."

"Is that what you think?" he asks slowly. "That you've failed me?"

Richard's heartbeat is steady. A constant *bum, bum, beat, beat* metronome.

"Do you know why I fell in love with you?" he asks. "It wasn't because you protected me, or because you could use magic. It wasn't because of your red hair. It's because you saw every part of me—the good and the bad, the rotten and the ripe. You saw me and you didn't give up. You decided to stay.

"You didn't choose this," he says. "You chose me, *us*. Again. And I'm so, so glad for it.

"Also, I think it goes without saying that I'd rather not be a witch's puppet," he adds.

"The lochside retreat was tempting. But the collapse of the Palace of Westminster seemed like too much to miss. Plus I'm not much of a tattoo girl."

"I don't know. With that new hair?" I can practically hear the grin on his face. "I definitely think you could pull off some ink."

"Right," I say. "Well, as soon as we get out of here it's straight to the tattoo parlor. I'll get a heart with *H.R.H. King Richard* stamped on my arse."

He laughs, as clean and clear as church bells. How long has it been since I've heard that sound? Such lightness in his voice which hasn't been there since before the integration . . .

Here we are, about to get crushed flat, and he's laughing. We're shivering and wrapped in dark, but we're finally together with time for just us. These might be our last moments, but they're ours.

We must make the most of them.

He pulls me even closer. His heart is beating harder now, tapping like some edgy drum solo. It reminds me of the music we danced to, so long ago.

His lips find mine. Or mine find his. There's no telling how they meet, but they do. It's a gentle kiss at first: the softness of heather blooms, the barest glow of dawn's east edge. It takes me back to the night we walked together in Hyde Park, when the nightingales' song threaded through the colors of the sunset and Richard kissed me. The night it all began.

Sunrises. Sunsets. Beginnings and ends. Who knew they could be so much alike?

This kiss is so different from Kieran's. There's no thrash and rage. No heaving, raw hunger. It's steady and true and fearless—like the beat of Richard's heart. Like his love for me.

There's no wild spin, but there is a depth to the way he kisses me. A sweet swim through hair and skin as we reach for each other. And I'm diving—down, down, down— into his touch. Pulling into his warmth.

But there's something else. Not a pull, but a blooming. A rising . . .

Every hair on my body stands on end. An unmistakable feeling rushes through my veins, bursts forth.

The room is all light. Bright, bright white, burning with a power which returns the tears to my eyes. I blink them back. See Richard. He's blinking too, his face made of color and life. His eyes shine like a spell, full of stun as he looks at me. Then above us.

I follow his gaze. To the Faery light which hovers over our heads. My *inlíhte*—the spell I thought was dead and gone—is suspended above us like a miniature sun. Stronger than it ever was before.

Its blaze rushes through every fiber of my being— magic. But it feels nothing like my old Faery powers. What dances inside me now feels more like the veiling spells Anabelle wove so well on the rooftop.

Blood magic.

And I remember the last time I cast a Faery light—during Lights-down. The night we fought and my *inlíhte* exploded with anger. It hadn't been *my* anger the Faery light flared against. It was Richard's emotions . . . his blood magic pulsing, somehow feeding my spell.

Richard lets out a breath that's been held a long, long time. It weighs of weeks and worries. "It didn't hurt you."

"Hurt me?" I think of the fear which shone so feral behind his eyes, that night he pulled away and said *it wasn't me* and I knew for certain he was lying.

Except he wasn't.

"It's been getting stronger ever since Lights-down started." He looks back down at me. "Every time we were together, every time we kissed, I felt it rising. I was afraid it would hurt you, the way your spells used to hurt me when we kissed. I was afraid that after everything you gave up, we still couldn't be together. The thought of losing you—I just couldn't bear it. So I fell back into old habits, tried to run away from the problem. Ignore it."

"That's why you were afraid? That's why you pulled away? Because you thought the blood magic would hurt me?" A laugh bubbles up in my throat, so full of relief and love for him. "Richard, I was made to carry magic. Meant for it."

The Faery light spins above us, brighter and brighter. *Our* magic. My spell, fed by his strength. I am the fire and Richard is the flame. My flame. Together we are whole. Powerful.

"I've been trying to use it," he says, staring at the light. "I thought I could get that door unlocked, but it's a bit tricky to figure out blind. I think I've only managed to break a pipe or two."

The door. Richard might not be able to use his magic to open it, but I can. I weave my hand into his, feel for the power sleeping in his veins. The connection is easy to make, now that I know it's there. I don't even really need to use physical touch, but I grip his fingers anyway, start pulling the blood magic into myself.

The door is close, nested beneath ladders and pipes, swimming under the glow of the Faery light. I breathe deep, reach out for the corroded latch. My fingertips tremble with magic and hope. *"Opena."*

The spell I weave is almost as rusty as the latch, but still it flows, pries through the steel bolts. The door pulls back with a groan, reveals a dim passageway beyond.

"If we are actually in Westminster's basement, this

should be the main pipe vault," Richard says as we start walking. Our footsteps sound empty against the hall's concrete. "The stairs ought to be just down this way."

Long walls of pipes crowd around us. The flicker of my light makes them look like snakes, weaving in and out of shadow. There was no other way beyond the door. Just this hall and its long stretch of wires which run along the ceiling like nerve bundles.

Yet I don't remember being carried past all these pipes. Or walking so straight for so long. The Ad-hene were all twist and speed when they brought me here. . . .

We keep walking. Until every step we take feels like another drill into the pit of my stomach. Something's wrong. The pipes shouldn't be stretching this far. There should be a turn, a dead-end, stairs . . . something.

"How do you suppose no one at all has been down here since coronation day?" Richard's voice echoes off the dark. "These are maintenance rooms. Workers should be in and out all the time."

Dread swirls like hunger in my stomach. Chasing Richard's question with an answer: "Morgaine has written blocking spells all over London's underground—to keep mortals from going where they shouldn't." I scan the hall for runes. Sure enough there's a band of them, thick and white against the shiny silver piping. A few centimeters from that is a dent in the pipe. "The workers couldn't come down here without remembering some other urgent job."

We keep walking and I try not to think of what else the runes could mean.

But I know the truth. It's hounding me with every step. With every next minute we don't reach the stairs.

"We should be in the Central Lobby basement by now. If I remember right." Richard stops and looks back at the darkness behind us. There's a frown on his face. "Maybe we're going the wrong direction."

I look back at the pipes. There, glimmering a few inches away, is another band of runes. Identical to the ones we passed a few dozen meters back. No—I look closer, see the dent in the pipe—not another band. The same. Any hope I might have had dies inside my chest.

"We're not going in the wrong direction," I say. "We're going in circles."

"What?" Richard stares at me, his face sharp in the light. "How is that possible?"

Alistair has already looped the tunnels—woven them into endlessness with his older-than-dust magic. This hallway has become part of the new Labyrinth, another stretch of silver on the Ad-hene's arms.

Alistair didn't need to lock the door at all. We're trapped down here by a force far greater than iron or lock. Swallowed whole by the earth.

"There's an enchantment on the tunnels," I tell him. "Only an Ad-hene can break it. It doesn't matter what direction we go . . . we're still trapped here."

Suddenly I'm so, so tired. I wilt to the floor like a thirsty rose.

Richard kneels next to me. He wreathes his hand into mine and holds tight. "Guess you won't be getting that tattoo after all."

In spite of everything I smile at him.

His thumb runs over my ringless finger. He looks down, noticing its absence for the first time.

"I lost it," I whisper. "It fell down a sink and I couldn't get it back."

Richard's hand tightens over mine. "I had another ring, you know."

I can't hide the shake of my lips anymore. "Even though you thought your kisses might kill me?"

"I was still hoping I was wrong. And even if I wasn't, I wanted you to know . . ." Richard's voice fades off and he swallows. "I was going to do it right. I was going to take you to the Highlands after the coronation. I had it all planned out—we'd hike to some castle ruins where a picnic would be waiting. My vintage records would be playing on a turntable. We'd dance until the stars climbed high. I would pull you close and ask you to be my wife."

I shut my eyes and see the scene. Old weathered stones lined with candles. The table set with finest china—beef Wellington and strawberries. I hear the music playing: stanzas of classic rock sounding across snow-dusted peaks. Stars scattered like mercury tears overhead. And us—together—spinning beneath them.

"I would hold my breath until you answered." Richard's voice is all softness, calling me back through the dark.

I open my eyes, find him. The glow of the Faery light sculpts out Richard's face. He's holding his breath as he watches me. Waits.

I tighten my hand in his. "I would say yes."

Richard's really smiling now too. And there's a tremble to it, just like mine. "And I'd be the happiest man in the world."

I feel the tears again, swelling to the top of my throat. A pure blend of fresh and salt, sorrow and joy. These emotions swim through my eyes; what little light there is haloes Richard's face. Swallows it.

I start to stand, because I know if we keep sitting here—if we keep talking about *would be*s and *what ifs*—my heart won't be able to bear the weight.

"We're not dead yet." I pull Richard up next to me. "So let's do it. Let's dance."

Richard rises, his arms slide down my waist. "Without music?"

"Brec." I whisper to the Faery light and it blows like a spent dandelion—spreading pieces to all corners. Less light, more shine. Like the winter sky has folded and burrowed into this small canopy over us.

"To stillness and starlight," I tell him. "To the end."

Twenty-Six

We dance and dance. I keep waiting for midnight to strike. For fire to rip through the tunnels, peeling our souls from our bodies even as we cling to each other. For the passageway and everything in it to collapse into dust.

But the darkness around us holds fast and our steps start to slow. We sit back, together, against the wall. Whispering words, weaving fingers. Waiting through unsaid agonies. The end is still out there, lurking like a wolf in the dark, waiting to devour us whole.

I don't remember falling asleep, but suddenly the shadows melt—give way to green and air and stone and sky. The grass at my feet is thick—lush and woven through with flowers. A whole sea of yellow petals stretches out across the valley floor.

A castle sits on the edge of this golden shore. Turrets and unbroken stones. A Camelot not yet sieged. Banners bright as poppy petals lash images of a white dragon into the sky. A string of knights gallops along the valley's edge, their armor winking bright in the noonday sun.

"Where are we?" Richard is by my side, shielding the bright sunlight off his face with a hand to his brow. Wind gusts back at us—cold and clean. A few sunny petals lift and strip from their stems, swirl up past our faces.

"A dream," I start to say, but another voice speaks. As chill as the wind.

"The paradise before the fall."

We turn. A woman stands behind us, her gown of ivory and gold embroidery fanning out into the grass. At first glance I see Anabelle, with that long yellow hair flowing over her shoulders. But then I see the color of her eyes: a soft cornflower blue.

"Lady Guinevere," I whisper.

"You remembered," she says. Her hands are clasped in front of her, like a prayer. "I was not certain you would solve my riddles."

"You're not speaking riddles now," I say, my words as pointed as the ends of the pennant staffs.

"Morg—" A look of pain lances through Guinevere's eyes. She clears her throat, chooses her next words carefully. "The . . . sister's attentions are elsewhere. Runecraft is like a garden. It must be tended or it will wither and die. The runes she wrote on the walls of her cell to bind me into silence are fading. Slowly," she adds with a rub to her throat. "I could not tell you—not with the silencing spells and the Ad-hene always watching—so I tried to show you. I brought you here."

"So you *were* sending the dreams." I look down at the five crescent-moon scabs which will split open as soon as I wake. "When you cut me with your nails you spelled me . . . but how?"

"The Ad-hene call us *faagailagh*. To many the word means quitting. Surrender. Weakness." Guinevere's eyes are so *clear*, blue as plunging skies. Such vast worlds apart from the whitewashed orbs which haunted me in the Labyrinth. "But it also means changeling. You and I. We are changed. There's a power in love that people like Arthur's sister cannot understand. All they see is the weakness, the cost. To share your soul with someone, to become one with another takes sacrifice. But what you get in return . . ."

Guinevere falters for a moment. There is a pain—high, high, high—in her stratosphere eyes. Cloudy with guilt. "When I gave up my Faery powers to be with Arthur, he found a way to give me his blood magic. We shared it through our soul-tie."

"Just like what happened with your Faery light," Richard murmurs, low enough for only me to hear.

We're sharing the power through our soul-tie. Just like Arthur and Guinevere.

"One of the things Arthur learned from Merlin was the mortals' art of dreams: second sight. He taught me how to walk in them, a long time ago. I knew it was a way I could warn you without the sister noticing. She has forgotten what it means to be mortal; her sleep is dreamless."

"Morgaine . . ." The sorceress's name rings loud from my lips, over canary fields. "She tricked you. She used a love spell to make you fall for Lancelot."

"I should have been stronger, but I flipped wrong. Every minute, every hour, every day, I remember this." The pain of Guinevere's eyes spreads. Wrings her face with a thousand years of regret, fresh as new blood. "I rode off with Lancelot and now I bear the cross of a burning kingdom. I carry the weight of Pendragon's doom on my heart. But you . . . I see my warning was not in vain. You chose well."

"It's too late," I tell her. "Morgaine has won. The kingdom will burn anyway."

"There are more powers waking than just yours and Richard's," she says softly. Her eyes stray over my shoulder. "Our stories are not over. Our ends have yet to be written."

I follow her gaze. One of the knights has broken off

from the long train riding up the road. His horse leaps through the waves of yellow petals, toward us. His armor forged of flash and silver, blinding against the sun.

"You must wake up now. It's time for you to go." Guinevere reaches out, her fingers wrap warm over my five scabs. "I do hope we meet again, sister. In a better light."

"No! Wait!" I want to ask her so many things—all the questions bunch on the tip of my tongue, get tangled there.

She lets go.

I don't fall this time. My arm still hums with Guinevere's ghost grip when I wake. I look down, expecting to see five weeping trails of blood, but the red is gone. There aren't even scabs. The wounds Guinevere's nails left have closed—five pearly scars are all that's left.

Guinevere's spell has been severed. Her dreams are gone.

My stars are still all glimmer and glint above us. Clinging to the pipes and concrete like living jewels. One is brighter than the rest, pulling closer into my dazed vision. I sit up straight, rub the dreams from my eyes.

And the light keeps growing, as bright as Polaris.

This is no star. No fragment of Faery light.

This is the scar of an Ad-hene.

"Richard!" I grip his shoulder and he sits up, hazel eyes trained on the same point of light.

All of me is awake now. Magic hums from Richard's shoulder; I gather it to myself, start weaving. As I do, the fragments of Faery light above us flare brighter, flush out all the secrets of this hall.

Kieran stops in his tracks, taking in the sudden light with those concrete eyes. His body is angled half-forward—like a jungle predator suddenly stripped of all foliage. Caught mid-lurch.

"Emrys?" he calls out with caution.

"Come any closer and you'll wish you never rose up out of that miserable island of yours." My fingers tingle, burning to let go of the curse they're holding. The only reason he isn't a pile of ash already is because of those godforsaken scars.

There are two, I realize now. One for each Labyrinth. The old and the new. Flashing betrayal and hope.

Our only way out of here.

"I've come to help. We don't have much time." Kieran takes a step forward, as if he knows I'm bluffing.

Unfortunately for him, I'm not.

"Cyspe!" The blood magic is so different from my old

powers—it feels slippery and clumsy as I wield it. The spell works well enough. It wraps, all light, around Kieran's torso, binds his legs together. The Ad-hene falls to the ground, like a monument of some dethroned king tugged down by an angry mob.

I take care to make sure the binding spell is tight, tight, tight around Kieran before I go any closer. He doesn't fight it. He just lies there, like a rabbit in a snare.

I stare at him. My eyes and heart are stone.

"I see you found a way to fight fate," he says, nodding to the light which ropes around him like a python.

"I trusted you! Anabelle trusted you!" The anger in my words rattles even me. They brim with heat. "This whole time you were *using* us. Leading us straight into Morgaine's jaws!"

Kieran's own jaw bulges. I'm not sure if it's because of my words or the binding spell I'm winching as tight as I can without slicing him through like a sushi roll. "You found your king, didn't you?"

"You were dosing me with love spells for that witch's amusement!" The magic inside me flares hot. "You KISSED me!"

"Ah." Richard steps up behind me, he looks down at the Ad-hene with the coolness of a scientist observing a microbe. "You must be Kieran."

"Your Majesty," the Ad-hene grunts. Beads of sweat sprout on his brow, catching the Faery light like morning dew.

"What are you doing here?" I ask through locked teeth. "Did *she* send you?"

"I left my brothers to come guide you out of here before the building is destroyed." He looks up at me through those night-spill curls, pleading. "Emrys, you have to unbind me."

My teeth grind harder when he says my name. As if he knows me. As if I know him. As if we kissed and meant it. All I want to do is pull the spell tighter, make him hurt. "You had *plenty* of chances to change your mind! So many chances to tell the truth . . ."

"You're right." He swallows; sweat shines in the hollow of his throat. "I did. I have no excuse."

I want him to fight. I want *something*, anything to lash against. But Kieran stays still.

"I told you about the Labyrinth. How it was a great kingdom once. How there was a war among us and we destroyed ourselves. How Mab intervened. All of that was true. But everything Alistair told you is true as well. The Faery queen tricked us. We've spent lifetimes trapped in our own ruin. Confined to a cliff ledge, doomed to watch the world sail by. To wonder if there was anything more."

I think of the sixteen lights winking and calling when Anabelle and I sailed up to that wolf-fang shore. How a yearning for lost things sang sharp through the air. Calling out for home, freedom, hope.

Kieran goes on. "Mab's curse on the Ad-hene broke when you killed her, yet we were not willing to risk the same fate at Titania's hands. Morgaine promised that if we aided her, she would rid us of the Fae and find us a new home across the sea."

"But you can't live in London . . . the sickness . . ." I stop, think of how many ages Alistair bears on his shoulders. Exponentially more than Titania. "Alistair shouldn't even be able to come near this city. He should be going mad."

"We carry the earth in our bones and stone in our hearts," he says. "The sickness does not touch Ad-hene the way it withers Fae."

I think aloud. "So when your veiling spell failed in Trafalgar Square, it wasn't because of the sickness. You dropped it on purpose."

"You were too close to discovering the truth. I was ordered to keep you at arm's length—to lead you in circles and make you doubt—until Morgaine could decide how to weave you into her plan."

"What a good little monkey you are," I hiss. "Dancing for peanuts."

Kieran's voice is no longer steady and stone. There's a sadness to it. "I was earning a new home for my brothers and me."

The want to pull tighter stretches like a shadow in my heart—shows me how easy it would be to take Morgaine's road. To let the darkness grow, tow me into endless circles of revenge.

I swallow it back. "Why are you helping us now? What made you change your mind?"

"The Labyrinth is my nature," he explains. "It's carved into my very skin and soul. I'm meant to live beneath the ground, follow my brothers, and build a new kingdom in these tunnels. I was ready to do anything for it.

"When I first met you, I truly did not understand why you would leave your own people and give up your essence for a mortal. Your choice made no sense to me. But then I met her. She crept under my skin—found all the cracks in my soul. I felt myself changing from the inside, and there was nothing I could do to stop it."

"She?"

You don't know how deep your darkness is until there's a light. I think I'm beginning to understand. Those words in Blæc's tunnel—they were never meant for me. I think of the rare smiles which broke through his face. The softness in his voice whenever the princess stepped into the room . . .

Anabelle. Those smiles were always for Anabelle.

"This whole time you had feelings for Belle? But—you broke her heart!" Suddenly the Faery lights above us look very much like those paint chips Anabelle tore from the ceiling. Fragments of angels' wings, plucked free and falling.

"I don't deserve her. I have no qualms about that." The pain of my binding spell is starting to shred through Kieran's voice, mixed with so many other emotions a heart of stone should not feel. "But I can save her. If you both die in here, Morgaine will secure her grasp on this kingdom. She will find a way to either kill Anabelle or control her."

I'll find another royal puppet.

Kieran's right.

My ropes of light loosen, start to fall away from the Ad-hene's body. "But why didn't you tell us before? Warn us?"

"After the war among ourselves, Alistair decided that the Ad-hene should be as one, so we would not fight again. We are webbed together in a psychic link. My brothers were watching through this connection." Kieran sits up. I can see deep red lashes on his arm where my bonds sank tight. "If I had strayed from the plan, they would have intervened. That's why I had to kiss you in the garden . . . why I had to let Anabelle see . . ."

"Are they watching now?" I look up at the stardust ceiling, down the dark hall.

"I've broken my bonds with them, but we must hurry. Midnight is coming soon." Kieran stands. His scars are brighter than ever, carving the halls out with silver rays. He starts walking back in the direction we were going.

We follow. I take a sharp breath and fold my hand into Richard's. He stares hard at the Ad-hene's back. As if he can't decide whether he'd like to knight him or cut off his head.

"Belle sure knows how to pick them," he mumbles finally. "At least you'll no longer be Mum's worst nightmare."

So Kieran is a knight. Our knight in shining armor.

I think of the dream and laugh. Kieran plows forward, and our path curves, spits us out into a wide cavern of a room: a mess of pipes and more concrete, electrical boxes hunkered in metal cages, warning signs about voltage. And in the very middle of the room: the way out. A wrought-iron staircase swirls up like a vine tendril inside a ring of eight columns, crowned with a green exit sign.

Our escape. I squeeze Richard's hand tight. My heart throttles in my throat.

The shadows in front of us flicker and bend, so it seems as if the columns themselves are moving. Ad-hene step from behind them. Fifteen sets of scars blaze silver. Queued up like some warped constellation.

Kieran stops short. His face does not change, but his hands clench, curling into themselves.

Alistair steps into the center of the columns, blocks the staircase with his back. He stands: all power, ghost skin, alabaster hair, and age upon age.

"Brother Kieran." His words are slow and dangerous. The way a wolf stalks before it lunges: all teeth. "What are you doing? Why have you severed ways with us?"

Kieran doesn't answer, his fists grow tighter. I count the Ad-hene again. Fifteen. Too many. I hold Richard's hand tighter. Start to gather all of the magic I can.

Alistair gestures to Richard and me, fingers wispy slow and elegant, like seaweed. "If they go free, Lady le Fay's plan will fail."

"We have our new home," Kieran says. "What does it matter?"

A snarl lurks on the edge of Alistair's lips. I scan the *V* of Ad-hene behind him. All fourteen faces echo the same expression. Snarl stacked on snarl.

"Have a few days of daylight addled your brain?" their leader asks. "Have you forgotten how the Fae used our island like a rubbish bin? Made us slaves? This is our chance to see them destroyed."

Alistair's black beads of eyes are completely set on Kieran and so are the rest of the Ad-hene's gazes. None of them has noticed the spell I'm frantically piecing together. I feel like a maid at a spinning wheel—tugging the blood magic out like yarn, collecting it in a mess of knots and loops, trying to create a masterpiece in moments. My hand is on Richard's like a vise. His palm is open and flat, offering me all he has to give.

If Kieran senses what I'm doing, he doesn't show it. He speaks, his eyes locked straight into Alistair's. "The mortals do not need to die."

"What do you care of their lives? You are an Ad-hene," Alistair says this like a nanny scolding a mud-encrusted toddler. "You do not belong with these creatures. Their fight is not yours."

Pull. Spin. Weave. I grip Richard's hand tighter.

"I am what I choose," Kieran says.

Spin. Spin. Spin.

Almost there.

I feel Richard sway beside me, his hand almost limp in mine. I keep pulling power from his veins, keep weaving, hoping against all hope that it is enough.

"We have made our decision as one, Brother Kieran. They cannot leave." Alistair's voice is honeyed and slow, but his magic is bracing. "If you do not step aside, then you leave us no choice."

Kieran doesn't answer. Only his scar flares, melds with the light of Alistair's. Their spells unleash at the exact same time. Thunder meeting thunder. At first I think the runes have finally unleashed—that the roar around us is collapse, flame, and death. The Central Lobby basement becomes a supernova—searing light and shake—as the Ad-henes' dueling spells clash like dragons. The concrete floor gallops.

"*Coad-shiu!*" Kieran's protection spell wraps around us and the earth at our feet falls still, a portrait of cracks and ruin.

Dust settles and all of us remain standing. The other fourteen Ad-hene haven't even moved. Alistair's handsome face is spoiled as he snarls at us: more demon than angel.

"Don't waste your magic. Your life. Step away."

Kieran stands firm.

Spin. Spin. Spin.

Richard's hand crumples beneath mine. His face is pale and sweat.

The spell is done.

I speak before Alistair does—catch just a glimpse of his stunned face before our magic rushes forward. The *stillaþ* surrounds the fifteen Ad-hene like an iron web, freezing them against their columns. Before it even settles I can feel them fighting it. Their spirits beating against their frozen bodies like fists on glass.

The blood magic is still strange and fresh; the spell is not woven as skillfully as it should be. Soon, very soon, something will shatter. And we can't be here to see it.

I start running, pulling Richard over crumpled pavement. His steps are weakened, not as fast as I'd like as we start to climb the stairs. Kieran falls in step behind us, shoving Richard up the corkscrew turns of the staircase.

Through the lattice in the staircase I can see the Ad-hene starting to move again. Thawing like March fields. Alistair has recovered the swiftest. He's already moving toward the first step—scars flashing bright. We aren't even halfway up the spiral staircase when it shudders with Alistair's added weight. I look down in horror, watch as the father of labyrinths starts to rise, closer and closer to us.

I shift to the side, push Richard ahead of me. Brace myself for what's coming up the steps. Kieran's face is grim—his eyes hold the same weight they did that day I first met him. The day he stood at the edge of the cliff and looked out over the sea.

Except this time, the doom isn't on the other shore.

"Go!" He looks straight at me. "Keep Belle safe!"

Before I can argue—before I can even begin to realize what he means—Kieran's scars flare. His magic slices through the iron of the staircase between us. The whole bottom half collapses, crumples to the broken ground. A mess of wire and half-thawed, flightless Ad-hene.

The rattle and crash of the stairs' carcass spooks new life into Richard's step. Whatever energy I gathered from him has been returned as he clutches the railing like a lifeline. We stumble to the top.

Below us Kieran is fighting. The Ad-henes' spells flash like lightning, tangle like behemoths of another age. It feels as if an earthquake is under our feet as we emerge on the ground level.

"This way!" It's Richard pulling me now—through the Palace of Westminster's long, empty halls. The building is shaking at its very roots, crumbling from the bottom up. Its vaulted ceilings tremble. Stained glass falls like rain—dashing against stone. Ornate tiles shiver beneath us, their patterns of lions, thistles, roses of Sharon, and Latin script rearranging into nonsense. Statues of kings, queens, lords, and saints tumble from their pedestals, smear like pillars of salt across the floor.

The roof over our heads is fragile and doomed, but it holds until we reach a door, and after it, the terrace. It's impossible to tell if the Ad-hene are still battling beneath us, or if the groans are simply the bones of a weary, old building on the verge of collapse.

We run to the terrace edge—where the Thames creeps along the river wall. Richard climbs onto the stone ledge, one arm hooked around a lamp. The other reaches for me. He pulls me up beside him.

Big Ben strikes midnight. Beginning and end.

The bell tolls, wide and deep. There are no thousand hells this time. Only the one we're running from: the underworld which bursts to life with Morgaine's runes.

Flames bloom. Heat licks and shimmers, punches through what's left of the jagged windows.

Richard's hand is firm in mine. There's no tearing apart or pulling away. This time we jump together.

Twenty-Seven

By the time we resurface there's nothing left. Cinder and cloud, ashes peppering the Thames like snow. I can't even shiver as I tread icy water in front of the tower of smoke. It's as if the Palace of Westminster was no more than a sand castle—a beautiful lump of dirt erased by the tide. Swallowed whole—along with Kieran and all the other Ad-hene. Not even an immortal could survive such destruction.

"It's gone." Richard gasps next to me, watching the roiling smoke. Dark billowing into dark. It swallows the city lights. Blots out the stars. "J-just gone."

His words are stiff with shock. The water rushing around our limbs is mere degrees away from ice. Already I can feel my strength sapping—that rush of adrenaline and magic which swept us out of our tomb bowing to the cold.

"She hasn't won," I say, as much for him as for myself. "We're still here."

Though we won't be much longer if we don't find a way out of this river. The Thames's currents have seized us with freezing strength. We float with clumps of ash and glass dust—under the bridge where Blæc's tunnel rests. Past the London Eye's ring of light. The shore tears along: a blur of stones and docks and moored boats.

I can't feel much, but I grab out and snag the edge of Richard's sleeve, so we don't drift apart. His eyes have a mist in them, still taking in those fragments of flame.

"Come on, Richard! Swim!" I scream at him, try to break through the cold's grip. His face seems almost blue. "We can't let her win!"

The freeze sneaks up my fingers, loops through my bones and joints, starts to drag my whole body down. The deep is calling again—luring me down with a cold, crooning song.

I feel the mist crawling over my eyes too, spreading across my vision. Is this what Guinevere sees? A wraith world? Fire. Ice. Death.

And then: the water in front of us parts like a miraculous sea. Two slicked ears, hellish eyes, and flaring nostrils rise of out the froth. I stare at the Kelpie, so shocked I start to sink. Down to a silt-bottom death.

The water spirit vanishes, weaves under me and rises.

I'm lying limp on its back, and Richard next to me. I wait for it to dive again. For the final wall of water to come crashing down on our heads.

"Drygap!" Instead there's a voice. A spell. A warmth.

The Kelpie's hooves churn through the rough currents as it pulls its way out of the Thames, onto dry land. The beast stops, its massive hooves still on the city concrete. I look up and face our savior.

Titania's face is a clean canvas: no surprise, no signs of chill or fear. Her crown glints bright under the lamps of the river walk. We're on the same shore as the ruined building—plumes of smoking chaos rise behind the Faery queen's head like a peacock's fan.

"Your Majesty." I gulp in clean, cold air. It slices my newly warmed insides like a razor.

"Lady Emrys," she addresses me with her mouth pulled tight. The wild edge I saw in her eyes before is gone. At bay for now.

I slide down to the ground and look around. We're not alone. The night is alive with the gleam and power of Kelpie flesh. There's well over a score of them, crowding the street's shadows. All bear Fae on their backs. The younglings ride two or three per Kelpie, their faces strained with the effort of keeping the spirits out of the water.

The Guard has returned.

Richard lands next to me, his eyes wide and clear as he takes in the sight of this army.

"You came back," I manage.

"I was afraid we were too late. Ferrin told us you'd been imprisoned beneath Westminster." Titania looks over her shoulder. "We saw the fire on the horizon and feared you were still inside."

"But—you left us." I can't keep the blame out of my voice. I look around at the restless herd of Kelpies, the beautiful Fae on their backs. Where were they all those cold nights I sat on the rooftop, waiting for an answer? Where were they when Morgaine froze time itself in the garden?

"I did what was necessary," Titania replies in true Faery queen fashion. "The mortal's strange weapon drove me to the edge. It was not safe to stay."

"Yes, but the Frithemaeg never returned. Princess Ana-belle was left unguarded!"

"You really believed we abandoned you altogether?"

I blink. "What was I supposed to think?"

"It's true, we left the princess unattended for a moment. The younglings dropped everything to take me back to the Highlands—including the Black Dog. The entire Guard stayed with me at court—prepared to destroy me if the machines' madness set in. It didn't, thank the Greater Spirit. By the time I stabilized we'd received your letter that you'd sought the Ad-hene's help. I sent Ferrin and Helene back to guard the princess under the secrecy of a veiling spell, in case my suspicions about the Ad-hene proved correct."

"The Frithemaeg were watching this whole time?" I think of all the times the shadows crowded in, when I'd felt so, so alone. Had Ferrin and Helene seen me crying? All those moments of weakness?

Titania nods. "Ferrin arrived in my court a few hours ago with news that the sorceress had finally unveiled. We'd been preparing for the event, especially after you discovered the runes in the Black Dog's tunnel and under the desk."

"Why didn't you come sooner? Why didn't you stop her?"

"Even we did not know it was Morgaine le Fay behind all this until Ferrin and Helene saw her reveal herself in the garden. I suspected if we intervened too soon that Richard would be lost." Titania's silver eyes slide over to the king. "We failed you once, Your Majesty. I do not intend to do so again."

"My sister," Richard says sharply, "is she safe?"

"Helene is watching the princess. The last sparrow reported she was still at Kensington Palace."

"What about Morgaine?" Richard asks.

"The sorceress left the dinner at the Orangery not long after the Ad-hene took Emrys away. Ferrin and Helene did not deem it safe to follow. She could be anywhere."

The night fills with wailing. Red and blue lights pound against the thick smoke on both sides of the river. Emergency sirens which sound too much like Banshees.

"We have to find her. Put an end to this." Richard's voice is as grim as the scene across the river.

"No," I find myself shouting over the sirens' song. "Not yet."

All eyes turn to me.

"Morgaine might be powerful, but I do not think she is a match for the full brunt of the Frithemaeg," Titania says. "Even with London's technology against us."

"It's not her magic I'm worried about," I say. "It's her other powers. In a few hours the people of Britain are going to wake up. They're going to turn on the news and see the symbol of their kingdom in ruins. Morgaine means to blame this on the Fae, so the vote will sway toward the M.A.F. Once the people see these ashes, once they hear it's the Fae's fault, they won't forget. Even if we defeat Morgaine and expose Julian Forsythe, the damage will be done. The integration, everything we've worked for, every meter of ground we've gained will be lost."

"What are you proposing?" Richard asks.

"The press is a powerful enemy and they can be just as powerful as an ally." I think of Anabelle's original plan. The one set in place before everything fell apart between us, around us. "It's time to bring them back to our side."

"You want me to hold a press conference? Now?" He gestures at the smoke scraping the sky and the days of facial hair foresting his jaw.

"Your kingdom needs you, Richard. Now more than ever," I tell him. "It needs the truth."

"Lady Emrys is correct," Titania says. "The sorceress believes you are dead and she does not know of the Frithe-maeg's presence. There is still time to set things right, to show your people that you are alive and whole."

"Will your strength hold?" I watch the Faery queen with hawk eyes. Scalping her snow-stung features and tinsel hair for signs of sickness. Titania does not waver.

"I have some hours left." Titania nods down to Richard. "His Majesty's blood magic seems unnaturally strong tonight. If I remain close I should be able to sustain my own strength."

I touch Richard's arm. Blood magic buzzes and hums through the meeting of our skin. Leaping between us like an electrical current. Titania and the other Frithemaeg see it. Their eyes grow wide.

"You've found a way to wield it!" For the first time since her arrival, the Faery queen looks shaken. Her fingers curl tight around the mane of her Kelpie. Bone white in their effort to keep the beast still. "How?"

"We share it. Through our soul-tie," I tell her.

Titania watches us, reading our auras. Her fingers loosen, and her lips soften into a smile. "You have found your wholeness. I am glad."

"We should go." Richard nods at the news van wheeling across the bridge and weaves his fingers into mine. "The vultures are already circling."

"I never dreamed there would be a day where we were the ones chasing the paparazzi," I say.

Hand in hand we start to walk toward the smoking carcass.

The news crews have already found a meaty bone to pick.

A rumpled Julian Forsythe stands tall inside a ring of microphones and cameras. He's screaming to be heard over the song of emergency vehicles, the shouts of rescue workers trying to make sense of the smoking, blackened char which was once the Palace of Westminster.

"I was in my office, working late for the good of the British people, when I heard a scuffle outside my window. I saw King Richard being spirited into Westminster by some Fae. I was just on the phone with the authorities when everything exploded!"

Reporter Meryl Munson, looking as fresh and awake as ever, jousts her microphone under the young politician's nose. "So you're saying King Richard was inside the building when it collapsed?"

We've reached the edge of the reporters—holding hands and quite visible. But no one seems to notice us. All eyes are fastened to the politician, the smoldering ruins behind him.

"I hope I'm wrong," the glacial-eyed puppet tells the cameras, "but I fear the worst. My only consolation to the people of Britain is that when I'm elected prime minister I will do all in my power to wipe these creatures from our island. To protect the British people and avenge the death of our king."

Richard stops. "I think this kingdom has seen enough revenge, Julian."

The circle turns outward. The cameraman closest to the king drops his lens. A hybrid hiccup-scream leaves Meryl Munson's open mouth. Julian Forsythe stands— lost in the crowd he just commanded. For once he does not have a silken response.

One by one the cameramen start to recover, focusing their lenses on the king. Richard is a strange and wild sight, still dressed for his coronation, with scarlet and sapphire emergency lights blazing across his jutting hair, his just eyes. His stare cuts straight into Julian.

The young politician tries his best to recover. "Y-your Majesty! Thank God you're alive!"

Richard's jaw grits and his nostrils flare. I feel his anger swell in my own chest and gather it up like stray yarn so it doesn't accidentally set off a curse. It's not rage or wrath, but a righteousness which gilds his words, booms for every microphone to hear. "It was not the Fae who kidnapped me from the coronation carriage. Those were your loyal M.A.F. party members. It was not the Fae who locked me up beneath the Palace of Westminster and destroyed the building. That was your wife."

"He—he's been spelled!" Julian is red and spluttering—as if he has a biscuit lodged in his throat. He points at me with a wild trigger finger. "It's that witch beside him. She's controlling him! Making him say these things!"

Richard lets go of my hand and walks, all calm, into the center of the circle. All of the lenses turn inward, watching as the two men stand face-to-face.

"My words are my own. Unlike yours," the king says. He grabs Julian's wrist and shoves up the sleeve, exposing the bracelet of inked runes.

Richard holds Julian Forsythe's wrist for all the cameras to see. "The woman masquerading as Julian Forsythe's wife is a sorceress named Morgaine le Fay. She has been controlling him with magic runes. She ordered my kidnapping, sabotaged the government, and tried to bury me in the ruins of Westminster."

Julian has the look of a man who just watched a gruesome death. His eyes rally—toxin blue—and he tugs his wrist away. As if he could pull back the truth Richard just laid out for the world.

But the questions have already started—piling like

winter-starved wolves onto a fresh kill. Hungry and tear-ing. Too many to face.

He bursts away from Richard, shoves through the pack of reporters and breaks into a run. The cameraman whose lens smashed to the sidewalk starts a pursuit, but Richard holds up his hand.

"Leave him. We have what we need. I'd like to film a more formal address if I could."

The cameras which just recorded Julian Forsythe's retreat turn inward again. For once the reporters are silent. They offer up their microphones and listen.

A sparrow bursts through the ash—all blackened soot and feather—and lands in Titania's cupped hands. The Faery queen's face withers as she reads its parchment message.

What is it? I send her my thoughts. I can't speak out loud, not while I'm standing by Richard's side. He's fin-ished his speech, but the reporters are still chaos around us: cameras, lights, wires, microphones, rapid-fire ques-tions.

"Princess Anabelle's human security has taken her to a bunker." Titania's voice weaves through the reporters' bobbing heads. They don't hear any of it. Or see the long queue of Frithemaeg and Kelpies standing at attention along the riverside, covered in layers of the Faery queen's veiling spell.

My thoughts sway to Eric, ski masks, and unwavering stun guns. *The Protection Command is compromised. They're the ones who kidnapped Richard in the first place,* I tell the Faery queen.

"It's not the mortals who concern me. Morgaine is with them." Titania says this and the blood in my veins jets colder than the river. My hand becomes a vise over Richard's bicep.

We've lingered here too long. Morgaine is already trying to acquire her second royal puppet. If anything happens to Anabelle . . . If I fail Kieran's final wish . . .

There's a scream and suddenly the cameras jerk away, focus on the river's edge, where the dark shapes of giant Kelpies and their Fae riders have materialized. Queen Titania guides her mount closer. Reporters scatter like nervous colts, legs quivering and eyes wide.

Titania takes no notice of them, as if they're just as invisible as she was moments before. She guides the water-spirit to where we stand, offers her hand to Richard.

"Your Majesty, we must hurry. Your sister is in danger."

Paparazzi shutters click as Richard clasps hands with the Faery queen, pulls himself onto the Kelpie's back. I follow: loop my arms around Richard's waist, bury my face into the back of his neck, and wait to fly.

Twenty-Eight

Richard and I are the first into the bunker—navigating the maze of doors and guards with my clumsy improv spells. It's different from the last safe room Anabelle and I took shelter in, though if I hadn't approached it from the outside I would hardly know. It looks the same, from the brick walls to the tea tray to the fake potted palm in the corner. But this time the television is on, alive with the explosion footage some late-night Londoner caught on their phone's camera. Anabelle watches it from the settee—alive, but far from safe. Morgaine sits beside her, arms bared. Her runes lock together perfectly under the sheen of the fluorescent light.

Anabelle should be running. Fleeing at the sight of those black marks. Instead she's just sitting with her hands folded over the button-down cardigan in her lap. Her eyes focus intently on the television as flames bloom across its screen. Watching destruction play out in slow motion. Stones collapse into themselves, as if the proud breath the building held for centuries has finally leaked out.

"I don't believe it . . . ," Anabelle whispers at the screen, burrows her hands deep into the discarded jumper.

"Don't worry. You're safe here. Underground."

"Why would she do something like this?" The princess's voice is fuzzy and pulled long, like a patient going under for surgery.

I step farther into the room. Richard glides next to me, grim-faced as he watches the sorceress with his sister.

Frithemaeg drift through the walls, take their places along the room's perimeter. Queen Titania plants herself by the television and its looping shots of Parliament's fiery death.

Morgaine doesn't look up. All of her attentions are on Anabelle. "She was a Fae. In my day it was well known never to strike a deal with a Faery. They always have a hidden agenda."

"I've heard that before." Anabelle nods, head bobbing like an ocean buoy. It's a slow movement, adrift. Her eyes stay staring at the screen. There's no ice in them anymore. No fire either. Just blank: a glaze which carves an endless hole in my stomach.

Why isn't she running? Why isn't she bringing the roof down on our heads?

"I shudder to think of what might have happened if I hadn't escaped from that prison. If I hadn't been able to warn you about the Faeries' plan."

"But you came too late," Anabelle says. "It's all broken. They destroyed the Palace of Westminster. They killed my brother."

Too late.

I look back at the princess's hand. A string of runes circles the bones of Anabelle's wrist, thin and silky like a garden snake. Sick starts to rise in my throat.

We're too late. Anabelle is marked. She listened to the sorceress's lies, let the ink under her skin.

"Yes. But I saved you." Morgaine's words are feather soft. "Together we can rebuild our brothers' legacies. Arthur's and Richard's. We can build a new Camelot. With you as queen."

Richard's aura flares beside me. I grab his arm, harness some of his magic before it can lash out on its own accord. Give us away.

"Not yet." I nod at the gaps in the room which the final few Frithemaeg are just now filling. "We can't give Morgaine any chance to escape."

The grainy, shaky shot of the explosion gives way to Meryl Munson's stern face. "My crew and I set out expecting to find only tragedy here on the Thames, but it seems this morning has much more to offer. A phoenix has risen from these ashes—just moments ago King Richard and his companion Lady Emrys appeared to reveal some very startling facts about the source of the explosions."

Richard's face appears on the screen, an exact replica of the unshaved one next to me.

Morgaine hisses on the couch, bristling like a cat held over water. "Impossible!"

"But . . . you told me Richard was dead. You said Emrys killed him." The hazed stupor of Anabelle's face disappears. She's frowning. "You lied to me."

"Silence!" The sorceress snaps at her and stands, prowls closer to the television. She grips the sides, brings herself almost nose-to-nose with the digital king. Only inches from the veiled Titania.

I look to the Faery queen for her signal to drop the veiling spell, but Titania's hand stays still. She's watching the princess.

"Why did you bring me here?" Anabelle's frown carves deeper, canyons her brow and chin. The glaze in her eyes starts to peel. She's looking around the room, down at her wrist. What she sees there douses her expression like a bucket of ice water. "YOU GAVE ME A TATTOO?"

She starts rubbing the fresh marks with frantic fingers, as if they'll come off.

"You asked for it!" Morgaine snarls at the screen. "I said silence!"

Richard's sister stands, cradling her inked wrist like a wounded fledgling. She stares at the sorceress's rune-writ back. Fire and ice resurge, livid in her eyes. "You lied! You said everything would go back to the way it was before! You said I would forget!"

Anabelle's blood magic throbs through the bunker, does what her fingers could not. Tattoo ink starts rolling down the plane of her arm, wreathing against her pointed elbow. Drip, drip, dripping down to the rug. The circlet of symbols around her wrist has watered away, the black replaced by fresh, bright blood.

The sorceress turns, back against the bricks. Stun-eyed at the sight of her ruined runes.

"Sit down!" she tries to command the princess, but her control is gone, washed away by the legacy of her half brother's magic.

"You tried to kill my brother." Anabelle's arms fall to her sides—bloody and clean. She starts walking to Morgaine, step by slow step.

"To give *you* power. To make *you* the queen you were meant to be," the sorceress's words are hasty, tumbled.

"I don't want that." Anabelle keeps walking.

"Then what do you want?" Morgaine shrinks against the wall. "The Ad-hene? Come with me and I'll carve a love spell into Kieran's chest and make him yours."

At the sound of Kieran's name the room shivers and writhes. Anabelle's fists clench—ink black and rage white.

"I want you gone. I want my brother to be safe. I want to forget." Her words are tight with fight, love, and pain. She raises both her hands. They're shaking, but strong. "I can do all of those things myself."

Morgaine stares at the creases of the princess's outstretched palms. "You think you can fight me? I have centuries on you, child. You can't win."

"I don't have to," Anabelle says. Hairline cracks ebb and blaze across the ceiling. Dust starts to fall again, sifting down through the lights. Called from the earth above. And I realize, this time, she's in complete control.

She's making the cracks on purpose.

"Coad!" she shouts the curse, and I shred back our veiling spell.

The roof holds and Richard runs to his sister, dodging

hourglass trickles of dust from above. "Belle! Don't you dare!"

Anabelle freezes at the sight of him. Her hands drop and the magic she was working falls away. Forgotten. Richard reaches her and she curls into his shoulder the way a child hides from midnight thunder. Her fingers are titanium tight around his cape.

The rumble around us ceases; the bunker's framework falls still. Spells shed all around the room and the Fae appear: a beautiful, brilliant noose around Morgaine's brick-walled corner. The sorceress doesn't move. Her crimson lips stay flat. Those black eyes land back on me. Stare and stare and stare. Without a word.

"This kingdom will never be yours," I tell her. "Your circle of revenge is over."

"Is it?" she says slowly.

"We have you surrounded." Titania unveils only inches from the sorceress. Morgaine doesn't even flinch. "Your magic is no match. Surrender."

"And what? You'll let me rot away in a cell for another thousand years?" Morgaine has the nerve to laugh. "The Ad-hene have left the Isle of Man. Your prison is no more, oh Queen."

"I don't need a prison to contain mortals who use

scribbles and trickery," Titania says. "Surrender and I'll allow you to live out whatever days your fading runes have given you in peace."

"A Faery queen gone soft!" Morgaine laughs again. "You're nothing like Mab, are you? You've spent too much time around this lot."

Titania's gaze spears—regal and disgusted—down the length of her nose. "I could unmake you now, if you desire."

"But you see, that's exactly it. I'd rather not die." In one swift motion Morgaine steps away from the wall and snaps her fingers. There's a *crack* so loud it sounds like the room has split in half. Drywall and mortar dust swallow us. White as mist under the brash lights.

I throw an arm over my face, try not to choke in the bunker's chaos. Shadows flicker past, spells are shouted—darts of light web back and forth through the room. By the time the dust clears, the ring of Fae is broken. Half the wall is missing, its bricks crumbled to dust to reveal a long stretch of dark, its edges lined with runes.

Another vanishing act.

Ferrin and Lydia start to run for the opening.

"DON'T!" I scream at the younglings. "Don't go in there!"

Titania looks at me sharply. "We cannot let her escape, Lady Emrys."

"The tunnels with her runes . . . Alistair looped them. He made a new labyrinth beneath London. You can't get out without an Ad-hene." I look straight at Ferrin and Lydia. "If you go in there, you'll be trapped."

"So we just let Morgaine walk away?" Mortar dust has settled in the Faery queen's hair like snow. "Let her escape?"

"All sixteen Ad-hene were under the Palace of Westminster when it exploded. There are none left to guide her out of those tunnels." I can't help but look over at Anabelle as I say this. She's still clutching her brother as tightly as she's gripping her magic. Controlled and undone all at once.

I have no way of knowing if she heard.

"Morgaine just walked straight into her own prison . . . ," Titania says, and looks back at the hole in the wall. We stare at it together, taking in the surreal mixture of gap and brick. Somehow, the television is still working, hanging from the remaining wall as precariously as a child's loose tooth. A pixelated Richard is still speaking into a battalion of microphones.

"Our great kingdom has been attacked, but not by the Fae. What you see behind you is the work of a mortal named Morgaine le Fay, who's been masquerading as Mrs. Elaine Forsythe. She and her husband do not have the interests of the British people at heart. If you doubt this, look behind me."

The television goes dark—and for a moment I think the power finally shut off—but it's just the camera focusing on ash clouds.

"The Fae have been our allies since the time of King Arthur the Pendragon. They have protected us from enemies we did not even know we had. If we want to survive, we must keep this alliance. Apart we are weak. Together we are strong. A perfect union."

The Richard on the screen looks down at the woman beside him. The one whose hair blends with the night. That was the moment he squeezed my hand. The moment our Morse code smiles leapt across at each other. Not so secret.

He goes on, "We will have our moments of doubt. We will have our share of naysayers. But I plan to stand by Queen Titania and her Fae. My vision for the integration is even clearer now than ever before. We cannot live in a world ruled by fear and uncertainty. I will keep my word to the Fae. We will take these ashes and rise. Together we will build a new kingdom."

I look over my shoulder to find the real Richard. Anabelle is slouched against his shoulder like a rag doll. Shadows nest under her eyes—shades of weary and relief. Black and blood slick down her right arm, pool like a dark soul at her feet.

"What did you think you were doing, Belle?" Richard looks down at his sister. "You almost got yourself killed!"

The princess's eyebrows quirk, animated by sibling banter. "You really think I was going to let the roof fall on my head? Don't be daft!"

Richard blinks. "But—"

"I had a plan. I always have a plan," she says. "Kieran taught me how to shield myself. The collapse wouldn't have touched me."

"And the marks?" I nod at her mess of an arm. "Were those part of your plan?"

"The spell Morgaine used to freeze everyone in the Orangery didn't work on me. I pretended to be frozen. I heard everything she said in the garden—about the blood magic being stronger than her runes. About Kieran . . ."

Anabelle swallows. "Anyway, I figured if her freezing spell wouldn't work on me, her other runes wouldn't either. I knew the only way Morgaine would let me close is if she thought she was controlling me."

"You got a tattoo to save my life?" Richard's voice is laugh and serious all at once. Gravity heavy. Suspended in disbelief.

Anabelle nods. "I tried. I had to. After the Ad-hene took Emrys away, Morgaine approached me in the Orangery. She said she knew I was hurting—that she could take the pain away and make me forget everything that happened. I thought my blood magic would protect me. But when she carved the runes in, they ended up working. Everything got hazy. Until just now."

"When you started getting emotional," I say. "When your blood magic kicked in and purged Morgaine's rune-craft."

"Have I ever told you how bloody brilliant you are?" Richard squeezes his sister's shoulder.

A smile slips onto the princess's face—so different from the ones she saved for Kieran. More solid. Made of something stronger than flutters and heartache. "Not nearly enough as you should."

"Belle, you're bloody brilliant," Richard says, and

plants a kiss on his sister's head.

Titania, however, is mercury rage—fury and bright from listening to Anabelle's tale. She turns on the younglings, lashes them with a voice like a whip. "You let Morgaine mark the princess without interfering?"

Helene takes the strike of her question well, without flinching. "I wasn't aware it had happened. It must have been while Ferrin and I were deciding who should return to court and warn you. Her wrist was covered with a sleeve the whole time."

The Faery queen stares: vicious, speechless, sterling. Finally she turns to me. "The Guard needs much reshaping, Lady Emrys. The day will come when I can endure London for more than a few short hours, but I fear it will not be soon. Given your newfound powers I'm wondering if you might be willing to take up some of your old responsibilities."

Her words whisk—airy and light—in my head. It takes me a moment to pull them all together, find their meaning. "You want me to lead the Guard? But I'm still mortal."

"If we are truly to be united, these things should not matter," the Faery queen says. "You're a strong leader, Lady Emrys. They'll need your guidance if they're to piece the Palace of Westminster back together."

Richard blinks, surprised. "You can do that?"

"All things can be made whole with time," Titania tells him. "We will take these ashes and rise. Build a new kingdom. Just as you promised your people we would."

"You mean to fix it with mending spells." I think of the vase Anabelle sprayed to pieces in Windsor's ballroom. How I pulled its few dozen shards back together with a single spell.

But it will take more than a few spells to fix Morgaine's utter destruction: stones shattered into millions of dust particles, ashes spread to all corners of sea and sky. "It'll have to be done stone by stone. That could take months, years to rebuild."

The Faery queen's gaze silvers over the bunker's damage: Ink stains. Blood drops. Dust-covered royals. Daunted Frithemaeg. A hurting heart. A ruined wall.

Titania looks back to me.

"Then we must get to work," she says.

Twenty-Nine

My sleep is dark. Dreamless. It fills my night hours, spills into the days. The five moon scars on my arm stay closed and Guinevere does not return. Her face is lost to the mists. Swallowed by a Labyrinth which can never be unlocked, now that the Ad-hene are dead.

Most mornings I wake up with Richard by my side. Our fingers are usually entwined, as if we're terrified to let each other go even in sleep. So many times we keep holding on, our fingers wrapped like stubborn vines, soaking in the morning light, staving off the day as long as we can. Days of fresh integration laws, rebuilding plans, training ourselves in new magic, whipping the Guard into shape. The responsibilities are as endless as before.

But now we are armed to face them. With our trowels and our swords. Our magic and our love.

This morning Richard stays asleep and I let him lie. My eyes are still half-dazzled when I shuffle into Buckingham Palace's dining room. I don't notice Anabelle until

I've already taken a seat. She sits across the table, sipping a cup of tea. While I'm still wiping unseemly crust from my face, she's already pinned and painted. Hair and makeup ever flawless.

"Morning."

Anabelle has been staying here at Buckingham ever since Phoenix Night (a title the newspapers coined). Yet the princess has made herself scarce, keeping away from us and the press. Appearing only for meals and the blood magic training sessions we've started in the garden.

"Sleep well?" I ask.

"I'm trying." She's looking down at her tea, running a finger around the rim of her cup.

"Well, that's something," I offer.

Silence.

"I could use some help packing for my holiday in the Highlands," I try again.

She nods. But not in the way I'd like.

Lawton brings a tray to the table. Its edges brim with my usual: a full English breakfast, black coffee, and the morning's headlines. I clear my throat and look at the headlines. JULIAN FORSYTHE JAILED FOR ATTEMPTED REGICIDE cozies up next to WINFRED REINSTATED PRIME MINISTER and RESTORATION OF THE PALACE

It's been nice, having the press on our side. It keeps my appetite up as I tuck into the plate of sausage, eggs, tomatoes, beans, and toast. Eggs first this morning, I decide, and stab a fork into the over-easy yolk. Gold pours like feelings all across my plate just as Anabelle speaks.

"Richard told me everything that happened in the tunnels. About what Kieran did."

I watch the egg bleed out, until my plate is swimming in yellow.

"His true self did shine through. In the end. He gave his life to keep you safe. He saved us all." I tell this to my beans and toast. But these next words—these next three words—I cannot say them to the broiled tomato, which suddenly reminds me of a pulped heart.

I look up. The light of a cloudless, morning sky drips down Anabelle's face, as rich as the egg yolk. Bringing out every part of her beauty. Her torn.

For a moment I'm afraid to say. I'm afraid the roof will cave in again.

But I think of how the roof has always held above our heads. The windows stay unshattered. The spells Anabelle performs in our garden sessions are as solid as she is.

She needs to know. She's strong enough to know.

"He loved you." I say this and her face starts slipping. Along with the light. Tears—smoky with mascara ink—creep and well at the ledges of her high cheekbones. Gray as the clouds which have suddenly crowded the window.

"That makes it so much worse," she whispers. Tears keep rolling to the end of her chin. The storm outside breaks open.

Snow. Real snow. Not rain or hail or paint chips. It floats, twirls, spins past the windowpanes—as graceful as dandelion seeds. Death and life and beautiful: a cold crown over Anabelle's bent silhouette.

She sniffs, wipes the wet from her face. But the snow outside keeps falling, new tears and *what if*s dew Anabelle's eyelashes.

"It's silly, really," she says. "I only knew him for a few days."

I reach across the table and grab her hand, where the rune scabs are still healing on her wrist. "It's not silly. It's real. It's okay to let yourself hurt."

Anabelle's eyes meet mine. Her tendons and bones flutter under the cup of my palm. Outside the storm howls: white, white, white. So I can see nothing else.

"He never said good-bye." Her words are ghost thin,

as pale as the world outside the window. "He promised he would."

I hold her hand tight, but it's not enough. So I leave my plate, come to her side of the table, so she doesn't have to be alone.

We sit together. Her tears flow into my shoulder and the snow piles in drifts against the window. Sky's sorrow and winter's heart—covering everything.

A few minutes pass and Richard comes swinging into the dining room like the first child awake on Christmas morning. "Did you see? There's a bloody blizzard outside! In November! Oh—"

He spots his sister—curled in my arms—and stops short.

Anabelle peels her face out of my shoulder. Smeared and wet and raw. *Sniff, sniff,* wipe. The flakes outside grow smaller. Sun starts to peek through lacework clouds, frostwork windows.

Richard comes and sits in the chair beside us. He places a hand on Anabelle's shoulder. "I'm sorry, sis."

"I'm not," she says with a voice of rust and nails, "We wouldn't be here if . . . if it wasn't for him."

Kieran fought his fate so that we could be here to live

through ours. I look across the princess's shaking shoulders, meet Richard's eyes. They're a strange mix of fresh, sad, and serious.

Richard leans in to hug his sister, so she's crammed between us. "Whatever you need, Belle. We're here."

"It will pass. In time." Anabelle straightens up and wipes her face again. The sun burns strong through the clouds—gray wisps away, bursts into a dazzling white—and I know she's right.

Richard squints out the bright, bright windowpanes. "You've just made some schoolchildren rather happy."

Anabelle turns, seeing the snowfall for the first time. The after-storm light gleams on her wet face. A glow which reminds me of the Ad-henes' scars. She takes in the unmarked white with a laugh twisted into a cry. "But— what about our training session in the garden?"

The hours in the garden are just as much for my instruction as for the royals'. Learning how to use Richard's blood magic as my own is a frustrating process. The spells don't always work the same—many times it feels as if I'm trying to mold fine china out of Play-Doh. But slowly I'm getting a handle on it. Anabelle and Richard are too.

"It's just a bit of snow." I look out into that wide stretch of white. "But we could practice inside if you'd like. I think we're safe enough now!"

The princess shakes her head and eyes her brother. "Don't think I've forgotten that Christmas you ambushed me with snowballs at Balmoral Castle."

Richard raises his eyebrows. "Is that a challenge I hear?"

Anabelle stands. Seeds of a smile pocket the corners of her lips. "Little did you know I've been working on my snowball-throwing arm for years! I will have my revenge!"

She says this as she runs, tears for the door. Her hair streams gold behind her, lashing free, the same way it did that dawn on the boat. When her brother was lost and she stayed strong. When Kieran first saw her and fate's course changed.

"Outside it is." Richard looks at me. "Care to join in our epic battle?"

I follow the siblings onto Buckingham's portico. The new cold of the air catches me and I pause on the final step, watching Anabelle and Richard tumble through the snow. Make their marks.

I stand here and think of Kieran. Sitting under the

dawn on that boat, with sorrow in his voice and a spark in his eye.

It is behind us now. We can only look forward. Hope for better things.

And we will. She will.

Ice and cold explode across my neck. Stinging like a spell. A swear slips from my lips as I try to shake off the pain of the snowball—now fluff and dew across my blouse.

Anabelle stands several meters away, dusting her palms off. "You made it too easy, Emrys!"

Across from her Richard is laughing, packing snow into his hands. Ready for a fight.

I jump off the step, into the snow. Into the fray.

Thirty

The Highlands have always been beautiful—hills rolling like songs, fog balleting over black waters, ruddy skies which catch the sun's fierce and spread it over wide wilderness—but now it feels like a dream. Its slopes are unmoored; violet crests of stone rise from the valley's evening shadow. The setting sun flares amber over the hills, lining them so their edges shine like new copper.

It feels like a dream, yet Richard and I are both very, very awake. Hiking from our lochside cabin to where the hills reach their highest note.

I breathe deep. Fill my lungs with the clean, almost-snow silver of the air.

"We could've tried flying up, you know." Richard lets out a huff and leans against a boulder that's twice his size.

"I think we could use a bit more practice before we risk levitating ourselves hundreds of meters off the ground. It's a long fall." I look back down at the valley we've risen from. Our cabin is as small as a biscuit crumb by the spilled-tea loch. "Besides, I've never actually hiked up a mountain before."

"Glad I could give you a new experience." He laughs.

"You've given me plenty of those." I smile at him.

"I hope the majority of them were more pleasant." Richard's skin is glowing in the last efforts of the sun. He wipes his face, looks up the rocky trail. "We're almost there. Trust me, it'll be worth the climb."

Beautiful, hard things always are.

We stand by a bend, where the path wraps around the hill. I can't see what lies ahead, but I know. I can already hear the music.

I reach out and take Richard's hand. His fingers are cool, like the air around us, like the traces of last week's snow which lurk in the boulder's crevices. Autumn—the dying season—is nearly gone. Winter is ready to sweep over in sheets of gray and freeze.

Before I might have been cold. But holding Richard's hand sends a fresh swell of blood magic through my veins. Swirling heat and life.

"We *will* try flying," I promise him. "When we're ready."

"I can't wait." He pulls me forward. We conquer the last few steps together.

It's everything I imagined and more.

We're at the top of the world. Standing on the crest of the tallest peak. Everywhere I turn the land is on fire, painted by the sun's tangerine rays. We stand in the middle of a castle's ruins. Its broken walls rise and fall like a diving Kelpie's back. Faery lights are stuck in the crevices, shining their phosphorescent glow on to the real vision. Dinner for two, still steaming. Strawberries and beef Wellington. On another table sits Richard's turntable. A familiar song is pulling from the speakers, echoing long past us. Into the hills.

Richard pulls me over to the table, reaches out to the candelabra centerpiece. Its candles stand proud, unlit.

"Aile." He summons the fire, like I taught him. In the fashion of the Ad-hene.

I watch the flames dance across his hand, drip from his fingers like lava, all the way to the candles' wicks. Behind me the sun dips low. The shadows of the valleys rise, spread up the hills, and plume into the sky. Far, far off, just above the crest of a hill, the first star peeks through.

Richard walks up beside me, slides his arm around my

waist. His palm is still hot, tingling from the lick of those flames. "I know it's not so much a surprise . . ."

"Surprises are overrated," I tell him, thinking of all the ugly twists of the past month. "I've had quite enough of them to last me a good long while. It's nice to have a bit of stability. Dependability."

"I really thought we were gone. Otherwise I would've kept my mouth shut."

"We *were* gone." I keep staring at first star. It has the same silver glare as Kieran's scar. The same hint of hope.

I don't think I'll ever look at Polaris the same way again.

Richard's thoughts must be straying along the same paths. "Do you think Morgaine will find a way out of the tunnels?"

I find his hand on my waist, hug it tighter against me. It's a question I've asked myself many times over. Every time I see a sewer drain or pass an Underground entrance, a chill washes up my spine. She's down there, somewhere. Looping, plotting, raging. Walking in never-ending circles, calling out for the Ad-hene who no longer exist.

"No. She's trapped." I say this to the valley shadows which are growing, spreading. The stars blooming on the far horizon. "Besides, even if she does find a way out, we'll be more than ready for her. Our magic is getting stronger every day." I think of our training sessions, how every day the spells come more easily, the magic flows and binds us closer together. A magic so strong that the Fae still depend on it for sustenance. Once we master it we'll be able to gather the world at our fingertips.

"We'll be a force to be reckoned with," I add.

"We'll have to be, with all that's ahead. There's a lot to rebuild."

He's right. My thoughts drift to Anabelle and the rubble left by Phoenix Night. Things starting to piece back together, yet still not whole.

From this point I can see it all. The valleys and the mountaintops. The gain and the loss. Some things have been lost altogether: my old magic, Guinevere, Kieran.

Yet so much has been saved.

I turn to Richard. Put my back to the stars and the memory of the price that was paid. The costs which led us to this moment.

He's worth them all.

"I need you, Emrys. I want you by my side for every step of this journey." One hand slides up my waist, the other brushes my cheek. Tucks back all of the half-colored hair behind my ear. "I have a kingdom at my feet and the power of Arthur Pendragon in my veins, but I would lay it all down in a heartbeat for you. Because I'm yours. Always and forever. This is my solemn vow."

His hands pull away. I watch, breathless, as he gets down on one knee.

Here we are, caught up in a halo of candlelight. The brightest light on the highest hill. Richard pulls something from his pocket. Something that catches and crafts the light, sings it alive.

My ring. The one I lost down the sink drain. It's here, between his fingers. Jade and silver filigree shining even brighter than I remember it.

"Emrys Léoflic, will you make me the happiest man alive and be my queen? My wife?"

I think back to the tunnels. How my *yes* rang endlessly through those enchanted walls. How it's probably still echoing, around and around and around. Eternal. I imagine it rising from the depths of the earth, the way I did as a newly formed spirit. Flying up, up, up to this mountaintop moment.

"Yes." I kneel down. We're both on the ground now, knees steady on these worn stones. On the same level. "I thought you'd never ask."

He laughs. The sounds breaks through the music, draws me closer to him.

"How did you find this?" The jade of my ring glows bright as a cat's eye against the candlelight. "I thought it was gone for good."

"Ferrin gave it to me. Apparently she retrieved it from the sink just after you lost it."

So that's why Kieran couldn't summon it. It had already been found.

Richard goes on, "I had her help me put a bonding spell on it, so it won't fall off your finger again. Unless you want it to."

I slide my finger back into the ring, clasp my hand in his.

"You're mine and I'm yours. Always and forever. This ring isn't coming off," I promise. "No matter what."

Wind gusts up from the valley, raking fingers of ice through my hair. Richard's flames stay strong. The turntable's needle keeps grooving into a new song.

Everything changes, yes, but not everything falls apart. Some things come through the fire stronger than before.

We're still on our knees when we kiss.

This kiss. It's rage and heat and flame. It's the shout of

life and fight into an empty space. And it doesn't matter that the song has changed or that the wind is blowing. It doesn't matter that the cold is creeping in, snaking into the cracks between our bodies. It doesn't matter that the sky above us is dark and dizzying and endless.

I'm the spark and he's the tinder. Night has fallen, black and cold over the world. And winter might still be on the horizon, but together we are burning.

Acknowledgments

There's a rumor floating around in the world of YA authors that writing sequels is one of the hardest things a writer has to do. After working on this book, I can tell you this rumor is one-hundred percent true. Sequels are unmanageable beasts. Hard to coax out of the shadows, almost impossible to tame.

Thankfully, I didn't have to wrangle this story alone. My wonderful senior editor, Alyson Day, and assistant editor, Abbe Goldberg, were there to encourage me from the first paragraph to the final period. My tireless critique partner, Kate Armstrong, believed in this story all the times I didn't and that made all the difference. The Lucky 13s cheered me on while wrestling sequel beasts of their own. Trish Ward was my ever-willing Old English proofreader. Adrian Cain of the Manx Heritage Foundation graciously answered my emails and made sure the Ad-hene conjugated their spells properly.

Many thanks to my readers, whose enthusiasm for

these characters make everything worth it. Many thanks to my family and my husband, who believed in me, loved me, and fed me (it's awfully hard to cook dinners *and* tame sequel beasts at the same time).

As always, my highest and final thanks goes to God, who continues to bless me with stories and places to tell them. Soli Deo Gloria.

HOW DID THE FAERY AND MORTAL WORLDS FIRST COLLIDE?